Cooking Up a

Amelia Berry grew up on the North Yorkshire coast and now lives in Worcestershire. She has been writing professionally since 2013, and is also published as Ally Sinclair, Alison May and, in collaboration, as Juliet Bell. She is a former Chair of the Romantic Novelists' Association, and currently works as an associate lecturer for the Open University.

Also by Amelia Berry

The Highland Cookery School

A Recipe for Love
Cooking Up a Christmas Storm

Amelia BERRY

Cooking up a Christmas Storm

hera

Penguin
Random
House

First published in the United Kingdom in 2025 by

Hera Books, an imprint of
Canelo Digital Publishing Limited,
20 Vauxhall Bridge Road,
London SW1V 2SA
United Kingdom

A Penguin Random House Company
The authorised representative in the EEA is Dorling Kindersley Verlag GmbH.
Arnulfstr. 124, 80636 Munich, Germany

Copyright © Amelia Berry 2025

A CIP catalogue record for this book is available from the British Library.

Print ISBN 978 1 83598 054 5
Ebook ISBN 978 1 83598 052 1

Printed and bound in Great Britain by Clays Ltd, Elcograf S.p.A.

Look for more great books at
www.herabooks.com | www.dk.com

For Paul. Still, and indeed, again.

Chapter One

Why had she answered the phone? Jodie never answered unknown numbers. Nobody in their right mind answered unknown numbers. They were always charlatans trying to tell you they were from your bank or that you needed new loft insulation. Either of those would be preferable to this.

'Jodie, love, I'm not unsympathetic, but your girl gave notice three months ago and she's long gone and you're not paying, are you?'

'I'm going to, Alan. I…' Jodie hated herself for this. She put a crack into her voice and sniffed theatrically. 'Since Gemma went I don't know what I'm doing. I just need a bit of time to get myself together.'

'That's what you said last time.' Her landlord's voice was impassive. 'It's gone on too long. I let you stay after Gemma moved out but your name was never on the agreement.'

'I'll sign an agreement,' she offered, more in desperation than hope.

'You've got to the end of the month.'

'That's this week!' Jodie protested.

'Right, so on Monday I'm coming round and changing the locks. And you'll still owe three months' rent.'

'I…' Jodie started to argue again but the line was already dead.

She stared at her phone. It was Wednesday. She had until Monday. How on earth did a person with no money, no car – bloody Gemma had taken that too on the slim grounds that it was registered in her name and she'd paid for it – move house in less than a week? At least she did still have a job. Not a great job, but if she talked nicely to Diane, maybe she'd give her an advance on the next couple of weeks' money and Jodie could offer that to Alan for the rent and then... Her phone pinged in her hand with an incoming message.

From Diane:

> Where TF are you?

What? Jodie swiped and tapped into her calendar. She wasn't working today. She'd swapped with Geraldine so she was doing Tuesday, Thursday, Friday. Today was Wed... she stared at the calendar. Today was Tuesday. On the one hand she had a whole extra day before she was homeless. On the other hand, bollocks.

She typed fast.

> Sorry. Had an emergency.

Her gaze settled on the wet patch where she'd knocked over her water glass an hour before.

> Had a flood at the flat. Thought I'd messaged you but it didn't send. I'll be there in 30.

Jodie whirled around the flat grabbing keys, bag, finding shoes, pausing in front of the mirror by the door to wipe the worst of last night's mascara off onto her sleeve. Her phone pinged again.

> Don't bother. I'm sorry, but I did say – one more screw-up and you're done. I need staff I can rely on.

Jodie hit the call button and waited one ring, two and then three before Diane picked up.

'I'm sorry, pet.'

'But I need this job. I got confused about the day…'

'I thought there was a flood.'

Damn. 'Well, yeah, but then I got confused about the day because I swapped shifts and…'

'I was supposed to be taking Lulu to a university open day this morning, but instead I'm here bollocking you and making Americanos for twats.' She heard Diane move away from the phone to talk to a customer for a second. 'Not you. I meant them other twats.'

'I know. I…'

'No, Jodie. I gave you a trial cos of your mum, but you've only been here a month and you've given me more grief than my own kids. I'm sorry. I'll send you your money up to last week.'

'But—'

'I've got a queue, love. Take care of yourself, won't you?'

Jodie stared at the dead phone in her hand. No job. Fine. That completed the set with no girlfriend, no car and no flat. It was a royal flush of failure. She weighed her phone in her hand and hit 2 on her speed dial.

Calling Gemma

It would go to voicemail. It had gone to voicemail every time Jodie had called since Gemma left. The first few times she'd left messages asking to talk. Then she'd explained how she'd do better in future. Then there'd been the times – regrettable times, late at night after she'd downed one bottle of wine and opened another – when she'd yelled and called Gemma some pretty unforgivable names. In her defence she'd followed all of those up with longer messages full of profuse apologies. And then there'd been the begging phase, imploring Gemma to come back. She wasn't proud of that. Now she was being cool. Friendly, chatty, casual. Not needy at all. Just cheerily trying to catch up with an old mate.

The beep sounded on the end of the line. The recorded voice started. 'The number you have called is not in service.'

She hung up and rang again.

'The number you have called is not in service.'

Gemma had changed her number. Jodie stared at her handset. It was her only link to her ex and it had been severed. No warning. No message to let her know. Nothing.

That meant there were only two choices left. There was the one she'd been mostly making ever since Gemma had gone. That involved staying in bed and ordering Deliveroo she couldn't afford on a dangerously close-to-maxed-out credit card.

The other option was unthinkable. And Jodie was thinking it.

The ringing phone startled her. And then confused her. She stared at her mobile, trying to marry it up with the repetitive trill she could hear. It wasn't her mobile ringing. It was the landline.

Jodie almost smiled, realising Gemma's apparently endless competence hadn't extended to terminating the landline contract she'd insisted on keeping up.

Jodie pulled herself to her feet and grabbed the handset from the breakfast bar that divided the living area in the flat. Nobody rang this number. Nobody she could think of, apart from Gemma's nan, even knew the number. Gemma did. Jodie pressed the answer button on a wave of hope. Maybe this would be her explaining that she'd lost her phone and that the last few weeks had been a horrible mistake and she was desperate to come back.

'Hello?'

'Gemma Bryant?'

'Yes!' What? Wait. No. The person on the other end of the line wasn't saying she was Gemma Bryant. She was asking if Jodie was. Too late.

'Hi. I'm so glad I got hold of you.'

'But...'

The woman on the other end of the line didn't even pause. 'I tried your mobile but I think I must have written the number down wrong.'

'Sorry. Who is this?'

'Oh God. I'm sorry. This is Bella Smith at Lowbridge Castle. The cookery school. I should have said that to start with, shouldn't I?'

Jodie was, obviously, none the wiser. And the last thing she needed today was to waste time talking to someone who thought she was somebody else entirely. She had enough to worry about with the no-home thing.

'I'm sorry. I've never done this before.'

And the no-money thing.

'You're the first person we've officially hired.'

And the no-job thing. Finally, what the voice on the other end of the phone was saying filtered through. 'What?'

'Yeah. So I know it's been a little while but if you're still interested I'm ringing to offer you the job.'

'The job?'

'We were all blown away with your ideas, and we can't wait to get started.' The woman paused. 'I mean if you're still keen. It's like we talked about on the phone. We know the money isn't brilliant but accommodation's included and you're welcome to join us for meals if you want to, or not if you don't, of course. So what do you say?'

A job. Accommodation included. It was like the universe had finally looked down on Jodie and given her a break. It wasn't her break though. It was Gemma's. She couldn't just take it. Could she? 'Just like you said on the phone?'

'Oh, thank you again for doing the interview that way. The downside of living in the back of beyond – there's no way our Wi-Fi will handle a video call!'

Jodie must be dreaming. A job offer with a place to live from someone who had no idea what Gemma Bryant looked like.

'So it is a yes?'

What did she have left to lose? 'Yes.'

'That's brilliant. When can you start?'

Well, given that Jodie was being evicted in six days…
'As soon as you like?'

'Seriously? Like Monday.'

'Monday.'

'Fantastic. Can't wait to welcome you to the High-lands.'

Jodie froze. Welcome her to the where now?

Chapter Two

Pavel Stone grabbed the barbell Anna Flint was unsuccessfully trying to lift from the chest-press stand. 'I think this is maybe a wee bit heavy for you, pet.'

'Nonsense.' The woman lying on the bench was seventy-five if she was a day. 'I'm lugging boxes in that shop morning, noon and night. And Darcy did a talk at Ladies' Group about how important strength training is if you've been through… *the change.*' She mouthed the last two words theatrically as if saying them aloud might summon dark forces.

'Well, strength training is a good idea at any age, but…' He carefully removed the 120 kilos he'd been lifting before Anna arrived. 'You're starting out. Try with just the bar until you've got the movement.' He leaned slightly over the rack and held the bar until Anna had it securely in her grip. 'OK. Hands a little bit further apart, bring that down to your chest and press up, palms to the sky, and repeat.' He watched Anna through five more repetitions. 'How did that feel?'

'Fine.'

'Good. So next time we can pop some more weight on.'

'I should think so. I didn't come here to just twirl that wee stick about.'

Pavel laughed.

'It's very good of you to open this place up,' Anna added as she pulled herself up to standing. 'It's a long way to Lochcarron for them Zumba classes and whatnot. Although…' She dropped her voice. 'You know they've got a gym and pool up at McKenzie's place now.'

Pavel nodded. The McKenzie estate was a forty-minute drive from the village and was, according to their own publicity, the epitome of modern Highland aspirational eco-tourism. He was supposed to go over there with a mate from Strathcarron to bid for the contract to build their all-new spa complex, and from the brief he'd read he didn't think there was anything very eco or aspirational about the way McKenzie did business. But it was a mate asking and he needed Pavel's help, so he'd agreed. It wasn't a decision that sat quite right with him.

He took Anna through the rest of her workout – keeping things suitably simple. 'So what does your mother lift?' she asked.

Between them, Anna and Pavel's mum, Nina, pretty much ran Lowbridge village. They were great friends and also engaged in a long and hard-fought competition for the position of top dog. 'No. She's a Pilates woman.'

Anna frowned. 'Should I be doing Pilates? I'd probably be great at Pilates.'

Pavel knew better than to get into the middle of this argument. 'Maybe focus on one thing at a time. I mean, you're already lifting way more than her.'

Anna nodded, apparently satisfied – for the time being at least – with this conclusion.

He waved her off, pulled the shutter on his garage gym half closed – closed enough that anyone unfamiliar with the set-up wouldn't feel like they could just wander in, but not so closed that his regulars would be discouraged from their workout. It wasn't as though anything was likely to be stolen. His weight set was, by definition, heavy to move, and the last time anything had been nicked in Lowbridge was a cauliflower from the front of the village shop, and after much Miss Marple-ing by Anna and Pavel's mum the conclusion had been that Queen Latifah – Anna's husband's West Highland terrier, not the global music and movie star – had been the culprit.

He strolled along the main road through the village, past the string of houses on one side and the shallow gravel beach that went down to the loch on the other. He paused, as always, to check his granddad's boat, beached on the shallow strip of shingle. There were plenty in the village who called it Pavel's boat now. That didn't quite sit right either.

Pavel stopped outside the Weatheralls' house. Gareth was standing at the bottom of a stepladder eyeing the guttering above him. 'You all right there, mate?' Pavel called.

'Aye. Gutter's overflowing. Probably just leaves, but it needs clearing out.'

Pavel was expected over at the castle but 'a friend in need…' had been one of his granddad's favourite sayings. 'Let me give you a hand with that.' It was no bother and jobs like this were always quicker with two. Afterwards he got cleaned up at the Weatheralls' kitchen sink, refused the offer of a cup of tea for his trouble and went back on his way.

By the time he reached the Low Bridge that connected the village to its namesake castle, he'd also offered to walk Mrs Timberley's dachshund later, run a couple who were staying at the pub over to Skye on his boat the next morning, and reassured Mrs Taggart that he'd be back in plenty of time to open the pub up before lunch.

He paused on the Low Bridge and let the sound of the running water wash over his senses, breathing in deeply, just for a second, before continuing over the bridge, and turning left towards the castle coach house. Adam Lowbridge was standing outside, staring up at the grey stonework in front of them.

Pavel faux bowed to his old friend. 'M'lord.'

'Piss off.'

They did this routine every time. He was never going to stop calling Adam by his official title as Baron Lowbridge and Adam was never going to stop hating it. 'So this is the job?'

Adam nodded. 'Yeah. Well, that's the idea, but money's not on our side.' He shook his head. 'I've probably wasted your time.'

'Come on.' Pavel led the way into the coach house that stood just outside the gate to the main part of Lowbridge Castle. 'Let's take a look at least.'

'I guess I can add it to the list of things we can't afford,' Adam muttered. 'Bella thinks it'll be fine.'

'Of course it will.' Adam's fiancée, Bella Smith, appeared behind them in the doorway to the coach house. 'People pay silly money for shepherd's huts and yurts and stuff, don't they? At least this has walls.'

'Not necessarily watertight walls,' Adam pointed out.

'We're really stuck,' Bella explained. 'We can't do residential cookery courses because there aren't enough accommodation rooms that are up to scratch.'

'And without that we're not bringing enough money in.'

Bella leaned into her fiancé's shoulder. 'Which means Adam is still in Edinburgh half the time for work to keep everything together.'

Pavel's heart went out to his friends. He knew that from the outside everyone assumed that if you were a laird and you lived in a castle you couldn't possibly have any financial worries at all. But he also knew that between a falling-down building and a looming inheritance-tax bill financial worries were a large part of his friends' day. He looked around the coach house. The work wasn't complicated but it also wasn't a small job. Pavel sucked the air through his teeth.

Adam winced. 'Oh, it's never good when builders make that noise.'

'Sorry. I mean it's not massive, but there's quite a bit of plumbing and all the light fittings down here are making me anxious...'

'So, expensive?'

'It'd be mates' rates...' Pavel did some rough maths in his head and named a figure.

Adam's face fell. 'Yeah. That's what I thought.'

'Too much?'

Bella closed her eyes for a second. 'It's fine. Maybe we could put people up in the house.'

'Where?' Adam asked. 'You, me and Darcy are living in the main wing and the rest of the rooms upstairs are worse than out here.'

'I know.'

'What about the Dower House?' Pavel asked. There was a cottage at the far side of the castle.

'Earmarked for our new starter.'

'You've taken someone on?'

'To do marketing and events. And to help with the cookery school a bit. Apparently she's a dab hand in the kitchen.' Bella glanced at her watch. 'Speaking of which...'

'What?' Adam looked blank.

'Isn't it time you went to pick her up? Train gets in at eleven.'

Adam frowned. 'I thought you were picking her up.'

'I've got a class.'

'I've got a Zoom with a client. Ravi'll kill me if I miss it.' He shook his head. 'Can Darcy go?'

'She's out riding,' Bella replied. That wasn't unusual for Adam's stepmother. She'd taken to life in the Highlands after growing up in New York incredibly well, and that was — at least in part — down to the fact that living at Lowbridge meant she had space to keep horses. 'I told her I didn't need her back till the students turned up.'

'Flinty?'

Normally the estate's former housekeeper, Maggie Flint, would be on hand to help out whether she was asked or not. Today Pavel shook his head. 'I took her over to Portree first thing. Sorry.'

'Shit.' Adam closed his eyes for a second. 'Pav... mate...'

Pavel laughed. 'Sure. Who is she and where am I meeting her?'

—

Jodie's first shock after deciding that all her problems would be fixed by moving to the Scottish Highlands was discovering that, in order to arrive at Strathcarron station at a sensible hour, she needed to set off the day before.

Staring at the map hadn't in any way helped her understand this conundrum. The UK was, in her mind, quite a small country. There was London, the south coast, and there were the Home Counties and then there were... she wasn't sure... possibly dragons, but they were quite handy not-too-far-away dragons, weren't they?

It turned out they were not. Making one's way from west London to Strathcarron involved an actual sleeper train – something Jodie thought only existed in Poirot movies – and then another train from Inverness right across the Highlands to bring her to Strathcarron. She'd expected to alight in some sort of cute Highland market town. Diane, her now former boss, had told her about childhood holidays in the Highlands. Jodie had got that it was off the beaten track, but she hadn't imagined so far from the beaten track that there wouldn't be at least a Costa and a Tesco Express.

She hauled her wheelie case off the train, picturing a decaf latte with hazelnut syrup, and followed the one other person who got out at Strathcarron along the platform and out... into what? In front of her was a small patch of grass with a tree and a telegraph pole, surrounded by a tiny cul-de-sac with three houses and the path to the station platform. The other woman strode off towards the house to their left. Jodie stopped. And looked. Beyond the buildings was a road, a field and then mountains. Proper snow-capped mountains from a storybook. A giggle bubbled up from her belly. She was through the looking glass here, a million miles from anyone who knew her and nobody at all knew she was here. She'd actually managed to disappear. Apart from that, somebody was supposed to be coming to pick her up.

No.

Somebody was supposed to pick Gemma up. She took a deep breath in and ran through the same set of thoughts she'd been battling with ever since she'd left Reading. *Hi. I'm Gemma Bryant. Hi. I'm here to start work. Hi. I'm your new events manager. Hi. I'm a total fraud. Please don't send me back.*

Jodie shook her head. Keep it simple. That was the key to any good lie. Don't overembellish. Don't add more detail than you need. Stick as close to the truth as possible. That gave you much less chance of getting tripped up.

At least it would if there was any of Jodie's real-life experience that was going to be useful to her. *Hi. I'm a failed barista, dog walker, student, shop assistant…* she paused… *girlfriend, daughter, and basically human*, she added, *and I'm here to run your business.* That wasn't going to work, was it?

She ran through her mental script one more time as the white Transit pulled up in front of her. The side decal proclaimed *Stone & Son Builders*. Jodie ignored it. She was expecting someone from the Highland Cookery School.

The chap who got out of the van was a tiny bit harder to ignore. Comfortably over six foot and almost as wide across the shoulders. Jodie suppressed a tiny gasp of appreciation. If she was in the market for a distraction he looked like a damn fine one. Jodie would, very happily, climb him like an oak tree.

'Miss Bryant?'

That was her. Miss Gemma Bryant – events manager extraordinaire; serious professional woman; and not one to hook up with random hot builders at all.

'Miss Bryant?'

Miss Gemma Bryant was strictly a relationship woman. And right now Gemma Bryant was wholly focused on her new job.

'Miss Bryant? Gemma!'

Finally the voice cut through her thoughts. 'Sorry?'

'Are you Gemma Bryant?'

Jodie caught the hesitation, she hoped, just in time. Although was there really any length of time – even a fraction of a second – that a person could plausibly pause before recognising their own name? For goodness' sake. She'd been rehearsing this all night. 'Hi! I'm the new Gemma Manager Event.' What?

The muscled god in front of her frowned. 'You're...?'

'Gemma. Just Gemma.'

'I'm Pavel. Pav. Adam and Bella are tied up at the estate so they asked me to come and pick you up.'

Jodie eyed the van warily. *Don't get in vans with strange men* seemed like a fairly basic rule for life. It was definitely one her mother would have expected her to learn by this point, but this was a strange man who knew Gemma's name and was here to collect her at a time and place when a lift service had been promised. Jodie realised she'd been picturing something more in the black-cab – or at least identifiable-Uber – vein than the white-Transit-van category.

'Hop in then.' He grabbed her case and pulled the van's side door open with one hand to lift it in, before stepping in front of Jodie to hold the passenger door for her. 'Your carriage.'

The drive started out along the banks of a lake. It was pretty. It put Jodie in mind of childhood holidays in the Lake District with high hills in the distance and a welcoming tea shop never too far away.

'How far is it?' she asked, as casually as someone who wondered if she was supposed to know that already could manage.

'Less than an hour. The pass is clear, so we can go the fast way,' Pavel said.

The road rose sharply up into the hills, zigzagging away from what Jodie now realised was the coastline rather than just a lakeside. 'It's beautiful.'

Her granite-faced driver's expression softened a little. 'That it is. Sorry it's a bit of a trek. I guess that's one thing Bel and Adam'll be wanting you to think about.'

Jodie's ears pricked. Bel must be Bella, who was the woman who'd phoned. The job was events manager, according to the email to the hastily set-up *GemmaBryant2025* email address she'd given her over the phone with some spluttered explanation about a dead laptop and a hacked email account. And Adam was… almost certainly a name she was supposed to know already.

'Yeah,' Pavel mused as he drove. 'It's going to be tricky to get students over from the station. Maybe a minibus? But you'll probably want a four-by-four?'

Students? Jodie racked her memory back through the phone conversation. *Highland Cookery School* had definitely been mentioned. So students for the cookery school made sense. 'Will they not drive themselves?'

'You didn't.'

No. Obviously.

'And if they all drive you'll need parking.' He shrugged. 'There's some outside the coach house and just over the bridge.'

Jodie's head was reeling. Minibuses, parking, students. All these appeared to be things that she was supposed to have insight into and plans for. She couldn't just turn up in goodness knows where, declare herself an events manager and start managing events. She had no idea what she was doing. Somebody, probably the somebody who was supposed to be paying her wages, would notice that in a heartbeat.

Her own heartbeat was picking up pace. She glanced sideways at her driver. 'So what's your role?'

He shook his head. 'Just a mate doing a favour.'

'So you don't work for Bella and...' Name? Name? 'Adam!'

'No.'

Great. So she had fifty minutes to try to glean as much as she could about what on earth was expected of Gemma Bryant from somebody who wasn't going to be sitting at the next desk from her tomorrow morning. 'So do you think it'll be a good place to work?'

'Yeah. Bel and Adam are great.'

That was a good start. 'And what sorts of events do they do?' Was that a reasonable question for an events manager to ask?

'Anything that'll stick one to McKenzie, I reckon.'

He dropped the name in as though Jodie was expected to know what he was talking about already. Gemma would definitely just smile and nod. Gemma would probably understand, but Jodie only had the rest of the drive to her new workplace to get to the point where she could feign understanding in front of her new boss. 'McKenzie?' she asked.

'Skirting the edge of their estate now,' Pavel muttered. 'John McKenzie's an entrepreneur. Wants to buy up Lowbridge. They're working their arses off to avoid that. I'd say basically you're here to make sure they're profitable enough to be able to afford to say no.'

Jodie laughed – a swell of hysteria pushing its way out of her lips.

Pavel turned his head quickly to look at her, brow slightly furrowed.

'Sorry. It's not funny. It's just…' Just what? 'Just a lot to take in,' she offered.

Her heartbeat thudded harder in her chest. She had stolen Gemma's job offer. Gemma was off enjoying her new life in Cornwall, so she didn't need it, but it sounded like these people did need Gemma. And Jodie wasn't Gemma Bryant. She wasn't an events manager. She was a mess.

'Are you OK?' Pavel Stone's gaze was flicking in her direction.

'Fine.' Her rapidly whitening knuckles told a different story.

'Let me know if you're going to be sick,' Pavel murmured.

'I don't feel sick.'

'OK.'

'I…' She opened one eye and quickly closed it again. 'Can we stop?'

The road was single track and the passing places were few and far between. 'Not here. Hold on. As soon as we're down into the village.'

She nodded mutely. The sweat that was gathering on her top lip and the shiver running down her spine weren't sickness. They were something else, something Jodie knew too well.

The road came down to the shoreline again and flattened out before the first buildings. Jodie fixed her gaze on a pair of small boats tied up on the shingle beach. Pavel pulled the van over to the side of the road, where it sloped down towards the sea edge. 'OK?'

She was already halfway out of the van, jumping to the floor and bending double, sucking air into her lungs.

She was on firm, solid earth. She squatted down and pressed her hands into the pebble beach. Safe. Jodie opened her eyes and looked around, trying to remember the routine they'd taught her to bring the panic down.

Five things you can see.

She focused on a particular round grey pebble streaked with white. That was one. The broken skin by her thumbnail. That was two. The chipping paint on the bough of the upturned boat in front of her. Three. A tuft of yellowed drying grass poking through the shingle. Four. And the toe of Pavel Stone's work boot to her side. Five.

Her breathing began to slow. She just had to keep going and keep her mind in the here and now, not let herself collapse or run as far away from here as she could. Jodie forced herself to continue the exercise.

Four things you can hear.

The water lapping on the shore. One.

A car passing on the road behind them. Two.

Her own heart beating a little too hard. Three.

'Are you OK?' Pavel's voice. Four.

Jodie couldn't reply yet. Her brain was only holding on to the moment because she was using every fibre of energy to keep her thoughts in a nice neat line.

Three things you can touch.

The pebbles under her palms.

Her belt digging into her waist.

Her breath shallowed as she struggled to focus on a third thing. And then a hand touched gently on her shoulder. 'You're all right,' he said.

Two things you can smell.

The ocean.

Pavel Stone.

One thing you can taste.

The image of pressing her lips to his pushed all the other pictures out of Jodie's head. It would, she absolutely knew, be delicious. It would take her out of this state and make her feel something urgent. It would be such a Jodie thing to do. Acting first and worrying about the fallout later. The real Gemma had tried to help her be better than that.

One thing you can taste.

Sea salt on the air.

'Gemma, are you all right?'

She nodded and pulled herself away from his hand and up to her feet. 'I'm absolutely fine.'

'Seriously,' Pavel wasn't letting up, 'anything I can do to help?'

Jodie shook her head. She didn't need help. She'd almost messed everything up already. Pavel was a friend of the people she was going to be working for. She should never have let him see her like this. Gemma glided through life. From now on, Jodie needed to keep her head down and not show the mess that was whirring around inside her. 'I said, I'm fine.' She climbed back into the van. 'Let's go.'

Pavel hesitated for just a second before he made his way back to the driver's seat. 'Whatever you say.'

The final part of the journey took them up along the river to the road bridge and then back down the far side, where Pavel pulled up outside a large stone building.

'Wow,' Jodie murmured. 'Bit of a walk to get back to the village then.'

'There's a footbridge there. I could have dropped you there but I figured with your luggage...' He paused, presumably realising that Jodie's moving-to-Scotland baggage amounted to a single suitcase. 'You travel light?'

'Always.'

'Here we are then,' said Pavel. 'So that's the coach house, and then the main castle is through there.'

The main castle. Jodie climbed down from the van and looked up at the huge stone walls, suppressing a giggle. Take that, Gemma Bryant. You might have left for bigger and better things but who was the one moving into an actual castle? 'Great.'

'Hi!'

Jodie turned towards the voice. The woman jogging through the arch towards them was about Jodie's age, with long dark brown hair pulled back into a ponytail, wearing a white T-shirt and black jeans.

'I'm Bella! I'm literally just finishing off a class – they're wiping down their benches while their cookies cool – so I can't chat, but I wanted to say hi and welcome. Adam's...' She stopped and looked around. 'Adam's somewhere. And Darcy. They'll sort you out. So sorry.' She turned away, paused and turned back. 'Sorry. Welcome. Came to say welcome and then didn't say it. You're Gemma?'

Jodie nodded without pausing. Actually, was that too fast? Had she started nodding before Bella got her name out? 'Yes. Yes. I am. Gemma Bryant. Yes.'

OK. That was definitely too much. Nobody was that excited about their own name.

'So glad you're here.' Bella smiled brightly. However oddly Jodie was acting, it didn't seem to have bothered her new boss. Why would it? Presumably she wasn't meeting her new employee primed for possible identity fraud.

Nobody would steal someone else's job in the back end of nowhere and brazenly turn up pretending to be the legitimate new employee. The very idea of it was insane. Bella turned to Pavel. 'I don't suppose you could hang on until Adam resurfaces?' She looked back at Jodie. 'I don't want to leave you on your own.'

'It's fine,' Pavel reassured her. 'I'm sure we can track him down. Or Darcy.'

'Thank you.' Bella rushed away.

So that was Bella. Bella had been the woman on the phone, so she was guessing she was the boss. It seemed like she ran the cookery school. Unfortunately the fact that there was a cookery school was pretty much the only thing Jodie had already learned about her new workplace, so this deduction didn't particularly help her.

Who else was there? Adam. She was guessing Adam was Bella's partner? Business partner or partner partner? Maybe both? But Darcy? Surely she wasn't expected to know everything at this point. Or was she? 'Darcy?' she enquired tentatively.

'Adam's stepmum. She was married to the old laird.'

Laird? Jodie vaguely thought that was either Scottish for lord or possibly some sort of mythical Highland pixie.

'And kind of their bookkeeping person. She'll probably be in the office if she's not out at the stables. Adam will be off on the land somewhere, so Darcy's probably easier to find. Come on.' He strode through the arch. Jodie pulled her case awkwardly across the cobbles behind him. Pavel stopped, reached over and lifted her case as if it was candyfloss light. 'I can take this.'

'Thanks.' Jodie took the chance to look around. The castle didn't get any less castle-ish for getting closer to it. 'This place is huge!'

'Well, it's a castle.'

'Yeah, but...' Jodie wasn't super familiar with castles. The word brought primary school history lessons to mind. She knew about keeps, and then what? Mottes and baileys? She didn't actually know what those last two were. Was motte a fancy history word for moat?

Anyway, Jodie's mental picture of a castle was a simple, fairly squat tower on top of a mound. Lowbridge Castle was nothing like that. From the coach house you came through the arch into a courtyard with stone buildings on four sides, all extending up to at least two storeys.

'They own all this?'

'Yep.'

Bella had been young though. The owners of a place like this were old, and wore wax jackets and sensible tweed skirts. Or they were Russian oligarchs who'd won it off some poor posh English sap in a gambling club somewhere in Kensington. Normal-looking women with Yorkshire accents didn't live in places like this.

'Come on.'

She followed Pavel through a wooden door, and then down a corridor and into a large kitchen. There were people gathered around an island unit in the middle of the room, apparently hanging on Bella's every word.

'Excuse us,' Pavel called.

Jodie scurried after him, through a hallway decorated with dark wooden panels, gilt-framed oil paintings and an actual suit of armour, and then through a smaller door into an office.

Pavel tapped the door as he entered. 'Darcy?'

'Pavel! Sweetheart, what can I do for you?' The voice that responded was female, enthusiastic and, slightly surprisingly, American.

'Hi. This is Gemma.'

Gemma. Yep. That was her. Jodie squeezed past Pavel's sizeable frame. The woman sat at the desk was tall, slim, and had a face that would have given Audrey Hepburn in *Breakfast at Tiffany's* a run for her money. She jumped up from behind the desk and enveloped Gemma in a heavily perfumed hug. 'Welcome to Lowbridge. I have strict instructions not to put you to work yet. Today is for settling in and finding your way around. All of this,' she waved a vague hand towards the desk and the office as a whole, 'can wait until tomorrow.'

'You OK now then?' Pavel was looking at her sympathetically.

He was pitying her. While Jodie had been fantasising about him kissing her, he'd been assessing her as weak, overemotional and deserving of pity. And he'd been right. Jodie forced down a rising wave of panic. She was not going to lose it again. That was Jodie. This was Gemma. Gemma was strong and calm. 'I'm fine,' she insisted.

'OK. Well, hope you settle in well. See you soon.'

Jodie watched him leave. She'd slipped up already and showed all her Jodie mess on the very first day. She needed to be much more careful from now on.

Chapter Three

Pavel pulled the van onto the gravel outside the house he'd lived in his whole life. Technically he didn't live in the same house now. His flat over the garage had a separate entrance and was officially number 12A on the street, but the place had been his granddad's house, and then his mother's, and it was the only place Pavel had ever called home.

Jill's car was already on the driveway and she was sitting on the bench that overlooked his mother's front garden. 'Where have you been?'

'Sorry.' He'd all but forgotten he was supposed to meet Jill. 'I was picking the new girl at the castle up, and then...' He shook his head. There was something private about seeing someone lose their grip on themselves. 'Got caught up talking to Darcy.'

Jill laughed, shaking her mass of curls. 'And I'm stuck here waiting on the driveway.'

'You could have gone in,' he pointed out as they fell into step together.

'You promised me lunch at the pub. All I'd find in your place would be protein powder and those horrid nut bar things that don't count as sweets.'

'I have other food.' Pavel was still protesting as they reached the pub at the end of the village.

'No. You don't, which is why you are going to Bel's new course next week.'

Pavel pulled a face. 'Last time I did a cookery school day it didn't go so well.'

Jill laughed. 'You were fine. I was the one that ended up in A & E.'

Pavel and Jill had both attended the very first session at Bella's Highland Cookery School. Jill's knife skills had proven problematic when she sliced into her finger, and Pavel's constitution had proven even more difficult when he'd promptly keeled over in a faint at the sight of blood gushing from his friend's hand.

'Don't pretend you couldn't do with improving your cooking skills.'

He did, when his mum wasn't around, tend to live on protein shakes and ready meals. It would be good to be able to do better.

'And then you can cook me dinner rather than have to come to the pub all the time?' Jill slid her arm through his as they walked towards the door to the pub.

'But the pub has the best food for a post-sermon come-down.'

Jill laughed. This was their tradition. On Sunday mornings Jill – the Reverend Jill Douglas, to give her her proper Sunday name – preached at least two sermons, sometimes an hour or more's drive apart across her sprawling rural parish, and then she landed at Pavel's for a late lazy lunch and debrief and a chance to vent, a little bit, not so much that it would upset any angels, about some of her less easy-going parishioners. 'Only cos your mum cooks it,' Jill pointed out. 'Imagine if you could do that yourself.'

As was usual for a Sunday lunchtime, Pavel's mum, Nina, was behind the bar. Officially Mrs Taggart owned and ran the pub, but it was increasingly a community endeavour. Nina pointed them to a table in the back corner of the pub. 'We've got beef and chicken left but I think we're out of pork. The pie's good though. Game pie. Not mine. Bella's, but that girl knows her away around a casserole dish.'

They ordered one chicken – Pavel would never turn down his mum's roast chicken – and one pie and settled back with their drinks to put the world to rights. Pavel enjoyed these Sunday afternoons. He was needed, as a listening ear and a friend. It felt good to be needed.

'Look,' Jill took a deep breath, 'I don't want to make things awkward but there was something I wanted to ask you.'

Pavel put his glass down and gave Jill his full attention.

'Do you want to go out with me?'

The question was a genuine surprise. Jill was brisk and bubbly and friendly to everyone and if Pavel ought to have suspected she thought about him that way he'd definitely missed some signals.

'Like no pressure but we hang out all the time. You never mention seeing anyone else. I wondered if we should try a proper date?' She looked around. 'Somewhere other than the pub your mum helps out at.'

'I…' He paused. Jill was full of confidence, always, and her tone was every bit as bright as ever, but he knew her well enough to have caught the tiny wobble as she spoke. She was putting herself out there by asking. That was brave.

'OK. So I think that was a long enough silence to answer that question.' Jill buried her head in her hands. 'Oh goodness,' she muttered.

'No. Sorry.'

'No?'

'No,' Pavel was messing this up, 'not no. Just no the silence wasn't an answer.' Pavel admired brave. 'Let's do it,' he said.

Jill looked up. 'I do not want a sympathy date.'

'It's not...'

'You're sure?'

He nodded. 'We'll go over to Portree. I'll book somewhere. A proper restaurant.'

'That sounds nice. Only...'

Whatever caveat she'd been about to offer was cut off by his mum arriving with two overladen plates of food.

'This looks great, Nina,' Jill told her.

'Thank you.' Nina glanced around the pub. There was no one at the bar, and nobody obviously waiting for attention. 'Mind if I take the load off my feet and join you for a minute?'

Whatever Jill had been building up to remained unsaid.

–

'So officially this is the Dower House.'

Jodie didn't entirely know what that meant, but the cottage was a squat stone building, set slightly apart from the rest of the castle. The cottage had its own small garden enclosed by a drystone wall and planted with strongly scented roses, still clinging on to their final blooms despite the late October chill. From outside Jodie could see frilled net curtains at the windows. Jodie was not a net curtain person. Net curtains made her think of nice, orderly homes lived in by tidy, well-mannered people.

But it was a free house and it was a house a long way away from anyone who was angry with Jodie. She smiled her best Gemma smile – lips closed, demure and cheerful but not childishly excited. 'It looks lovely.'

Darcy wrinkled her nose. 'It's... well, it's fine.' She paused under the small porch way. 'It's been empty a couple of months now. Veronica – Adam's grandmother – lived in it before and she's, well, she's not the homely sort, so I don't think it's been decorated since her mother-in-law had it so... it might be a little bit dated. I'm sure Adam and Bella won't mind you putting your own stamp on it though.' She led the way inside. 'So like I said, officially the Dower House.'

'And unofficially?'

'Well, your house,' Darcy replied. 'We talked about putting you in the coach house, but the hope is to make as much of that into guest accommodation if we can ever afford it. We didn't think you'd want Pavel banging around you the whole time.'

Jodie bit back a very un-Gemma-like smirk at the thought of Pavel Stone banging around her.

'And you're self-contained out here, so if we do start having guests you'll have a space of your own, you know?'

Jodie followed her into the cottage. It was, by Jodie's standards, huge. The ground floor had two reception rooms, one laid out as a dining room with a round, polished dark wood table, a kitchen, a bathroom, a surprisingly large hallway and two double bedrooms.

'There's two more bedrooms upstairs,' Darcy added. 'In the attic space. Those would have been for the dowager's servants.'

What? 'Servants?'

'Yeah. I know. How the other half live!' Darcy grinned. 'We've never had much more than a housekeeper in the time I've been here, but when this was built the idea of the dowager only having one maid and a cook, or a butler, was quite austere.'

It was a four-bedroomed house. Jodie's work accommodation was a four-bedroomed house, on a country estate where the main house was an actual castle. Less than a week ago she'd been hiding from her landlord and waiting for the electricity to be disconnected. And OK, so nothing here was to her taste – the bed was covered with a 1970s-style shiny polyester counterpane – and however much Jodie might have craved a nearby coffee shop and access to Deliveroo, there was no way she was turning her nose up at a four-bedroomed house. And if Jodie was OK with it, then Gemma would be absolutely delighted. Jodie smiled her Gemma smile. 'It's great. A lot more space than you get in London!'

'Tell me about it. A place like this would be a mansion in New York.'

Would Gemma ask? What was intrusive and what was polite interest? Jodie knew there was a difference and she also knew she quite often got it wrong. 'So what brought you to Scotland?'

'Love. What else?'

She'd smiled as she answered so maybe this was acceptable polite interest. 'So will I get to meet the lucky person?'

'Ah no. Sorry. I think Bella said when she interviewed you? I'm Adam's stepmom. His dad was the baron before him. He passed away.'

31

In the interview? Gemma had been told all that in the interview, so of course she knew. Of course she wouldn't be a weirdo who asked questions about a dead guy. 'I'm so sorry. I did know. Sorry. I…' What? I forgot about your dead husband. Gemma would never say that. She thought. Pavel had said 'the old laird'. The previous laird. If lairds were barons, and not pixies, they were, presumably, a one-at-a-time sort of gig. Even Jodie should have been able to work that out. She had to focus more. Listen more. If she was going to pass as Gemma she needed every clue she could get. 'I'm sorry.'

'It's OK. She did kinda throw information at you. I'm sure you were concentrating on the work stuff.'

'Yeah. But still.'

'Seriously, do not worry about it.'

Jodie would try not to. She would absolutely worry about all the work stuff Darcy was so confident she would have taken in.

'Hi!' A woman's voice called through to them from the front porch. 'Darcy? Gemma? Are you out here?'

'In the bedroom,' Darcy replied.

Bella appeared in the doorway. 'You found someone to show you around then?' Bella asked.

'Yes. Thank you. Darcy's been lovely.' Super lovely. Barely took offence at all when quizzed about her dead husband.

'Great. Well, I wanted to check you had everything you needed. I put some bread – home-made – and milk and teabags in the kitchen, but you'll have dinner with us tonight, yeah?'

All Jodie wanted was to hide away and have time to think about her cover story and how she was going to get through being Gemma for the next few weeks, but the next few weeks had already started and were rapidly running away from her.

'Oh, you should,' Darcy chipped in. 'Bella's cooking is amazing.'

'It's just spag bol tonight. I had to make a literal tonne of ragu for today's cookery school so we're going to be eating it for weeks, I'm afraid.' She frowned. 'I've got Quorn ragu for you though.'

'What?'

Bella grinned. 'I remembered you saying you were vegetarian.'

Jodie shook her head. 'I'm not...' Oh. Gemma, the real Gemma, was veggie – failing to commit to do the same was just one of the ways Jodie had let her ex down. How on earth had that come up in an interview though?

Bella frowned. 'I was sure you said...'

'Yeah. Sorry. I was, but then, well...' Well what? 'To be honest, it was always more my ex's thing. Once we split I kinda slipped back into eating bacon sandwiches.' That was sort of true, apart from the part where she was pretending to be the ex in question, and the fact that real Jodie had quite often eaten surreptitious bacon sandwiches, wafting the smell out of the kitchen window while the real Gemma was out at work.

Bella's frown eased. 'Oh, I get that. I was once teetotal because the guy I was dating was dead anti-alcohol.' She grinned. 'It wasn't really dating. It was one weekend. But it felt like a really long weekend.'

'Anyone out here?' The man leaning through the door was tall, with broad shoulders and sandy light-brown hair. 'I'm Adam. Sorry I wasn't here to meet you. Completely lost track of time.'

'That means he was in the garden,' Bella added.

Adam held out a hand for her to shake and then pulled it back with a grimace. 'Bit muddy still actually. Sorry.'

'It's OK.'

'Had to get the last of the onions up.'

Jodie nodded like she had any idea at all about onions or vegetables in general.

'But I bet you're looking forward to getting stuck in with that?'

What?

'I was so pleased when Bella said you were a gardener.'

What?

He smiled broadly. 'Nobody here is interested at all.'

'That's not true,' Bella objected. 'I'm very interested once you've cleaned the mud off things and I can get cooking with them.'

'Sure. But it'll be nice having someone else around who knows their way around a greenhouse.'

Jodie had been picturing a desk and a computer and probably quite a lot of time spent scrolling Insta while nobody was looking. She'd imagined she'd have a suit and an office and be called Ms Simpson... Ms Bryant by eager-to-please young underlings. 'Events manager' didn't make Jodie think of weeding or... she struggled to come up with a second gardening term. 'I don't want to get in your way,' she ventured.

'Not at all. You're welcome out there any time.'

'But that's not Gemma's job.'

She tried her best not to look too delighted.

Bella turned to her. 'So don't feel you have to. Once he's got you out in the garden you'll be stuck there all day.'

'Not at all. I'm just saying she's very welcome to chip in because we know she loves gardening.'

Jodie's terror at the risk of getting caught out as a garden novice was slowly being replaced by something else. Gemma had told them she loved gardening. They'd never had so much as a window box. Did Gemma love gardening? Another tick on the list of ways Jodie had been a terrible girlfriend. Failure to show interest in your partner's hobbies and interests.

Bella and Adam were still cheerfully bickering about how much of Jodie's life was going to be spent up to her elbows in soil.

'Stop crowding the poor girl,' Darcy interrupted them both. 'Why don't you settle in and you can come over to the main house for dinner when you're ready?'

Adam nodded. 'Good idea. Take some time. And I promise no work talk tonight.'

'What?' Bella sounded anguished. 'But I want to talk about Hogmanay!'

'Tomorrow,' Adam insisted. 'Let her settle in a bit first.'

Time on her own sounded wonderful. A few hours to get her head around what on earth she was supposed to be doing here. Another thought snuck in. A few hours would also be long enough to get herself several miles away from this place.

Chapter Four

Jodie closed the door behind her hosts and leaned back against it. Of course she wasn't going to run. That was ridiculous. The situation she was in was, perhaps, a little unusual, but she was here now and she was going to see it through. She just needed to get her bearings and settle in.

She looked down the hallway of the Dower House. The walls were lined with paintings. Small portraits. There was a name for them, Jodie thought. Minis. Miniatures. That was it. There were miniatures all along the walls. Men with impressive beards. Women with large brooches and tartan sashes. The great and good of Lowbridge in years gone by, she guessed. All looking down at her. All wondering what on earth Jodie imagined she was doing here. The faces morphed slightly in her imagination. You should go, they seemed to be saying to her. Even the décor knew she didn't belong.

The thought had taken hold now. That happened – something would intrude into her consciousness and rather than just fade away it would sit there calling to her. Sometimes it was innocuous enough – the urge to have another chocolate, that turned into the urge to finish the box – but once that thought was in her head the chances of Jodie ignoring or overriding it were always slight.

You could run, the thought reminded her. You could go right now, before Bella or Adam or Darcy suspect anything is amiss. If she left right now it would be as if she'd never come here at all. She could simply disappear.

—

Pavel walked Jill back to her car outside his place, and waved her off. As she rounded the bend he took a deep breath in. Sunday afternoon. He didn't think he had anyone coming to use the gym, although it was open so people from the village often wandered in. He didn't have any work booked. He didn't have to walk Mrs Timberley's dog or take over from his mum at the pub until evening. He checked his phone. No messages. Nothing from his mum asking him to run someone to somewhere. Nothing from Anna at the shop asking him if he could pop over and fix whatever DIY disaster Hugh had caused. Nothing at all. Pavel shuddered slightly. Having nothing to do was novel for him. He tried to remember the last time he was awake and unoccupied. Almost certainly before… he didn't want to settle on that thought, but there was no point shying away from things. His grandfather had always taught him to look problems straight in the eye and get on with doing what was needed to solve them. He probably hadn't had a hunk of free time since before his grandfather got sick. Before then he'd helped out a bit on the boat and done a bit of labouring alongside college, but after that he'd stepped up and filled the gap in Lowbridge life his grandfather had left. It had been the right thing to do. His granddad's failing health had created a problem – jobs that needed finishing, people who were going to be let down – and Pavel could solve that problem. And so he had.

None of which helped fill Pavel's afternoon. What did other people do? His mum baked, or planned village events with the precision and cut-throat attitude of a reigning Mafia don. Jill watched trash TV. She'd attempted to convert him on many occasions, explaining the ins and outs of the relationships on *Vanderpump Rules*, but Pavel never saw the attraction. He could do a workout, but his workouts were tightly scheduled on a four-day upper-lower-body/push-pull split. And today was a rest day.

He could – and Pavel slightly balked at the thought – he could try cardio. Mostly Pavel told himself that having a job where he was moving and carrying all day ticked off his basic cardio needs so there was no requirement to Lycra up and go running about the village. Today though it felt like a choice between doing that or doing nothing. And the thought of doing nothing made him itch to do anything.

He jogged back up the stairs to the flat, pulled on shorts and an old T-shirt, grabbed a water bottle and set out. The thing with running, he figured, was to distract oneself as much as possible from the actual running. It was like eating leeks or taking particularly odious medicine. Clearly nobody enjoyed it but you did it because you knew it was somehow good for you.

With that in mind he pulled up a playlist that claimed to be motivating and energising, popped his earbuds in and set out at what he hoped was a gentle warm-up jog. The received wisdom about running was that you shouldn't set out too fast, so you didn't hit a horrendous wall of pain ten minutes in and stop dead.

Ten minutes later Pavel reached the Low Bridge that linked the village to the castle estate over the river and stopped dead. Biologically he was sure it wasn't physically possible to puke up a lung, but all the sensations in his body were telling him otherwise. He leaned on the railing and tried to gulp in as much air as he could. He was still standing there, wholly occupied with the business of remembering how to breathe, when a noise coming from the castle side of the bridge made him look up.

Gemma Bryant, whom he'd deposited at the castle not more than three hours before, was hauling her wheelie suitcase down the path towards him, dragging it behind her with a fairly impressive determination. Pavel suppressed a smile. She stopped when she saw him.

'Where are you heading?'

'I… I'm…' She hesitated before glancing down at her case and marching resolutely towards him. 'I can't do this.'

'Do what?'

'All this. I made a mistake taking the job. Best all round if I head off now and they can find someone else.'

Pavel's heart went out to Adam and Bel. The last thing they needed was another problem. 'What did they say when you told them?'

'They'll be fine about it.'

'They *will* be fine about it?' That wasn't how you behaved. 'You're leaving without telling them?'

'I don't want a fuss.'

'Like them discovering you've gone, having no clue where and calling the police, for example?' Pavel was incredulous. 'That type of fuss?'

'I left a note,' she muttered.

'Oh, well, fine then.' Bloody English girls coming up here without a clue. Pavel shook his head at the uncharitable thought. Bella was a bloody English girl and she'd settled in fine. Jill was another one. Darcy was from New

39

York, for goodness' sake, and had embraced the Highlands like she'd been born to live here. It wasn't Gemma's southern-ness that was the problem. 'So where are you heading?'

'Back to the station.'

So maybe it was partly her southern-ness. He shook his head. 'The station it took us an hour to drive from? How are you getting there?'

—

Jodie folded her arms across her body at Pavel's tone. *How are you getting there when the drive here made you lose your mind?* was clearly what he was implying.

'I'll get a bus.' She would not be pitied.

He frowned.

Jodie ignored his scepticism, grabbed the handle of her suitcase and made to march past him.

'It's Sunday.'

'So?'

'No buses,' he said.

Jodie glanced back at the castle. Was she actually stuck here?

'If Bella hired you,' his tone softened a little, 'she must have thought you were the best person for the job.'

Not, in the circumstances, as reassuring as Pavel probably imagined.

'Why are you being nice to me?'

He frowned. 'Why wouldn't I be?'

A thousand reasons. Jodie was a stranger. She was a stranger who'd had a meltdown in front of him within an hour of them meeting. But he was being nice to her. Was that her way out? 'You could drive me. I could pay you.' She could not pay him.

'I could but there's no trains after about three on a Sunday.'

'There must be trains somewhere.' She stepped towards him. Pavel was a big, solid hunk of man. Maybe she could damsel-in-distress her way to persuading him to help her out.

'I'd have to take you to Inverness.' He glanced at the smartwatch on his wrist. 'No. Sorry. I've got stuff to do this evening.'

Inverness was Scotland, wasn't it? This was Scotland. 'It can't be that far.'

'Couple of hours. Longer at this time probably.' He glanced upwards. 'It's nearly dark already.'

Two hours across the Highlands in the dark was a lot to ask. 'I'm stuck here then?'

'There are worse places to be stuck.'

Not for Jodie. Another layer of reality had pricked her resolve. She didn't have any money, so even if there was a train she couldn't buy a ticket, and there was no way she could pay for a cab to the station.

Could she hitchhike? Why on earth not? She could get herself to Inverness surely – with its sensible station that actually served a purpose – and then hop on a train and hide from the guard. That was a plan.

Pavel was still leaning on the bridge railing staring back at her. She couldn't carry on past him. He'd make some sort of sensible point about practicalities and her fledgling new 'hitchhike and hope for the best' plan would get scuppered too. 'I guess I'll head back then,' she said.

She made her way a little further back towards the castle, out of sight of her nemesis on the bridge, and stopped. Hitchhiking and fare dodging her way south by train was a perfectly good idea. If her way wasn't blocked she'd be halfway to somewhere new by now.

Jodie's palm itched. She rubbed it absent-mindedly. Once she had an idea, she wanted to crack on with it. Waiting made her feel like there was somehow too much blood in her body and it was running too warm. It made her want to step out of her skin and run away. When she wasn't doing something there was nothing but the thoughts, and the thoughts got in the way. They over-whelmed her with practicalities and minutiae and often a thousand and one other things that didn't even relate to the task at hand, but that somehow had to be dealt with before her mind would let her get on at all.

And right now it was Pavel's disapproving face that was sitting at the front of her attention, pointing out all the flaws in her idea, without the man himself having to say a word. She could try to hitchhike, from this village in the middle of nowhere that probably saw about one car go through per day. And then what? Without this job she had no income, so she'd be in Inverness or Aberdeen or Edinburgh without a place to stay or a job to pay for one. She'd have no choice but to swallow her dignity, press the emergency button on her life and call her parents to bail her out. Again.

She'd avoided that after Gemma left. She wasn't going to give in now. Right. Doing anything was better than standing here thinking about it all. Back to the Dower House. Back to spag bol with the family. Back to trying to be the best, and most convincing, version of Gemma that she could. She started to trundle her way back and then stopped at the sound of footsteps behind her. She turned to see Pavel jogging towards her. She flagged him down. 'Do you mind not telling anyone you saw me here?'

He looked at her for a second before he answered. There was something she couldn't quite fathom about his expression, like he felt let down by her. Jodie shivered and told herself it was just the autumn evening air. 'You're not going to make another bid for freedom tomorrow?' he asked.

'No.' She wanted him to believe her. She wanted to believe it herself. What would Gemma say? Gemma was better than Jodie. Gemma would play it down. 'A first day wobble.'

'All right, but if you change your mind, tell them, for goodness' sake.' His instruction was softened by a smile. 'At least then they'll be able to tell you when the trains run.'

'I won't need to.' She was aware that she was gripping the handle of her case so tightly that her knuckles were turning white. 'It's going to be absolutely fine.'

She managed to find her way back to the Dower House without – she hoped – anyone seeing her, and by the time she'd put her case into the biggest bedroom she'd almost convinced herself that her escape attempt was nothing more than first day nerves. Anyone could feel like that in the midst of such a big change.

This evening was dinner with the family. Another wave of panic hit. Jodie couldn't do dinner with the family. People's families never quite got Jodie. Gemma's parents had hated her. She always felt like she was one step behind the conversation and whatever she said was never quite right.

Jodie's parents, of course, had loved Gemma. Everyone loved Gemma. Gemma was polite and thoughtful and didn't lumber in with whatever thought popped into her head. That was the new plan. Same as the original plan. The only way through was to be more Gemma.

–

Pavel watched Gemma Bryant drag herself and her worldly goods back through the castle archway. It was getting too dark to continue his run along the road. He could absolutely justify strolling back home from here, grabbing a shower and getting on with his evening. A new idea stopped him.

He made his way down the path to the coach house outside the castle gate. As he'd guessed, the door was unlocked. Inside there was a definite smell of damp, but his walk around with Adam earlier had left him relatively confident that was simply from a couple of leaks that could be fixed and a lack of habitation. The rest of the work, while time-consuming, wasn't complex. He'd need to call in a few favours, and work some evenings, but it was doable. Adam and Bella needed the coach house available for guests to make Lowbridge a viable concern. That was a problem.

And where there was a problem Pavel wanted nothing more than to find a solution. What were a few more hours' work and a few quid on materials when balanced against helping out a friend?

–

Jodie went over to the castle just before six. What time did posh people eat dinner? In her mind later seemed smarter. More cosmopolitan and continental, but Lowbridge didn't scream cosmopolitan. Maybe dinner here was served promptly at five p.m. by an elderly cook who had no truck with flighty English lasses breezing in an hour late.

She made her way into the grand hallway and was greeted by a very bouncy chocolate Labrador. Jodie loved dogs. Of all the four-legged waifs and strays her mum had taken in, the dogs were always Jodie's favourite. Dogs were simple. Waggy tail for happy. Downturned tail for sad. She bent down to pet her new friend. 'Hello. Who are you?'

The dog rubbed its face happily against Jodie's calf.

'Dipper!' The voice shouting from the other side of the door past the stairway was recognisably American. 'Dipper!' A second later Darcy appeared and shook her head at the Labrador at Jodie's feet. 'She likes you!' Darcy narrowed her eyes. 'You don't have a pocket full of roast chicken, do you?'

Jodie shook her head. No. Obviously no.

'Then she actually likes you.' She shrugged. 'That's not saying much. Dipper has no discernment at all. She tries to run away with the postman most mornings.' Darcy nodded at the large grandfather clock that was partly obscured by the suit of armour. 'Wine o'clock, I think?'

Jodie glanced at the clock. It appeared to be stopped at ten past two.

'Come on through.' Darcy led the way down a substantially less grand corridor, and into the kitchen Pavel had marched her through earlier when they first arrived. That felt a very long time ago already.

Bella was sitting on a stool at the kitchen island with her laptop open in front of her. Adam was on his phone leaning on the worktop. He hung up the call as they came into the room. 'Hey. Settled in OK?'

Jodie hadn't settled one bit. She hadn't opened her suitcase, let alone unpacked. She'd spent most of the time since they'd left her in the Dower House plotting, and then failing, to escape. What would Gemma say? 'Yeah. It's lovely,' she told him.

He raised an eyebrow. 'It's decorated like the inside of an ageing great-aunt's knicker drawer.'

She couldn't help but laugh.

'Sorry. Budgets don't run to redecorating at the moment, but if you want to have a go, feel free. There's remnants of paint and stuff from other rooms in the small hall. Help yourself.'

She could paint the fireplace wall red in the living room. She'd always wanted a red wall. Had she? Jodie wasn't actually entirely sure, but now she'd thought of it she very much wanted one right now. Gemma would have hated a red wall. She was all Scandi-neutral and minimalist. *Be more Gemma.*

'It's fine, really,' Jodie reassured them. It wouldn't be sensible to decorate, and sensible was her new Gemma watchword. Being here was a stopgap while she sorted herself out and worked out her next move. She'd be here until she got her first pay packet. Second at most. And then it would be time for this version of Gemma Bryant to simply disappear.

Darcy was pulling glasses from a cupboard and opening bottles. 'Red or white?' she asked.

Jodie, honestly, wasn't a drinker. She was an awful drunk – she got loud and embarrassing so it was better all round if she abstained. Gemma had exquisite taste in wine though and also exquisite manners. The Gemma she was creating would be the sort of sophisticated woman who would have one or two drinks and never get lairy at all. 'I don't mind. Whichever you're opening.'

Darcy opened a bottle of red and poured four glasses, topping them up to finish the bottle. She held Bella's glass in front of her. 'Work time over.'

'I need to send this email.'

'Adam!' Darcy called in reinforcements.

'No work after six on a weekend,' he insisted. 'Seriously, laptop closed in five, four, three...'

Darcy joined in with the rest of the countdown. 'Two, one!'

Bella pulled her fingers from the keyboard just as Darcy flipped the lid down. 'Finished.' She picked up her wine glass. 'Actually I might not drink tonight. I'm feeling a little bit off.'

Adam frowned. 'Off how?'

'Little bit queasy. I'm fine. Probably just hungry.' She pushed her stool back from the island and stood up. 'Speaking of which...'

Bella opened the fridge. From where Jodie was perched on her stool at the island she could see that the fridge was rammed full of Tupperware.

Adam frowned. 'Why did you make so much ragu?'

'I wanted it perfect, and Hugh got such a good deal on the beef so it seemed worth buying more.'

'We're going to be eating bolognaise for the rest of our lives,' Darcy murmured.

'No. We won't. I'll freeze some and I'll take a batch to the Strachans, and I've already messaged Jill to ask if she wants some for the pensioners' lunch club. And we can put it on the lunch menu at the pub. We'll get through it in no time.'

It didn't take long for Bella to reheat the ragu and cook pasta on the stove. Adam moved around her, finding bowls and cutlery. Jodie watched mutely. This was what home

47

life was like in adverts. Couples together in the kitchen laughing and exchanging affectionate glances. This was the life that Jodie was supposed to fit into.

'They asked loads of questions today.' Bella started filling them in on the lesson she'd taught that afternoon. 'What's the difference between ragu and bolognaise?'

'Aren't they the same?' Jodie was glad Darcy asked the question.

'Well, technically a bolognaise has more tomato and less big bits of beef. A ragu is meatier. We're in Lowbridge not Bologna though so I think it's fine.' She stirred the pot in front of her. 'So, Gemma, what really made you apply for this job?'

'Erm, well...' What would Gemma say? 'The place looked amazing and I was ready for a change.'

'Something less corporate?' Darcy prompted.

Was that what Gemma had told them? Her previous job had been for a restaurant chain, so maybe that was true. Jodie nodded. 'Exactly.'

'We're so glad you're here,' Bella added. 'Having another pair of hands is going to make everything so much easier. At the moment Darcy is all over our finances, so invoices and bookings for the cookery school, and Adam has a landscape design business so he's in Edinburgh part of the time, but he still looks after the land and the gardens – like the actual physical estate, you know?'

Jodie nodded. She didn't know at all. With hindsight, her time on the train here would perhaps have been better spent googling the Lowbridge Castle Estate than scrolling Instagram.

'And I'm the cook obviously.'

'Bit more than that,' Adam interrupted. 'Bella is the absolute driving force behind all of this.'

'It's a team effort, but I run the cookery school and actually teach the classes.'

So there was an estate and a cookery school. Jodie tried to nod like someone who totally understood what running those things would involve.

'And I've got so many ideas but there are only so many hours in the day. Like we could develop the garden more.' She squeezed her fiancé's arm. 'You're growing so much amazing stuff now but next summer we're going to have a glut so if we could do a pop-up farm shop?'

'We don't want to compete with Anna and Hugh.'

Bella shook her head. 'Of course not.' She turned back to Jodie. 'They run the village shop.'

'And Anna is slightly terrifying,' Adam added.

'She's not that bad, but yeah. It all needs thought. And marketing! We're all over the place with that.' Bella grinned. 'We were so excited when you said you'd designed campaigns for Pizza Now!'

Had Gemma done that? She definitely remembered a phase when they got free takeaways.

'So we know you're going to be so much help with promotion and marketing. We've got Instagram and a Facebook page but I never know what to put on it. And there's a lot more to marketing than that, isn't there? I bet you've got loads of ideas.'

'Well…'

'But Hogmanay first. That's what we're most excited about. That whole plan is incredible.'

Jodie swallowed hard. *That whole plan?* What plan?

'So bold to suggest putting on such a big event so soon. That's what we need though, isn't it?' Bella turned to her fiancé. 'Bit of ambition?'

'Sure.'

'So what do we need to do first?'

Jodie was screwed. Apparently there was a whole plan that she was supposed to know about and she was also supposed to be some sort of digital-marketing guru. They were all waiting for her to speak. What would Gemma say? Business things probably. Important, clever business things. 'So… I think the strategic thing to do would be to really think strategically and focus in on the strategy and make sure we have the right…' Jodie paused. She couldn't say strategy again. What were other words?

Adam held up his hand with a smile. 'No work after six on a Sunday. Come on, Bel. She's been travelling all day. She's barely had time to unpack.'

Hadn't started unpacking, actually.

'Give the woman a minute to get settled.'

'Sorry.'

'It's OK.' Jodie smiled as brightly as she could. It wasn't OK. By her reckoning she had until about tomorrow lunchtime to work out how to do Gemma's job, once she'd worked out what on earth that job was.

Once Bella started dishing out food the conversation moved on, allowing Jodie a few minutes' respite. The rich meaty sauce sent warmth through Jodie's body. She'd always thought of comfort food as nursery food – fish fingers and beans, dippy egg and soldiers – food that was easy and that brought back the safety of childhood. This was something else. This was very grown-up comfort – luxurious and heartening. If this was the rejected practice batch, Jodie could only imagine the final version must be food beyond her puny understanding.

Bella chewed thoughtfully. 'I put a little bit more pork in the finished one. It adds flavour but keeps it moist as well.'

'This is perfect,' Jodie insisted. She would love to be able to cook like this.

Darcy nodded.

'Bella's never entirely happy with a recipe,' Adam explained. 'She's always got an idea for how to make it a little bit better.'

While they ate, Adam and Darcy filled her in on a bit more of the history of Lowbridge Castle. By the time she was pushing her bowl away after her second portion, she thought she had it clear in her head. Adam was Baron Lowbridge, generally known by people who bothered as 'the laird' or, given how recently he'd inherited the title, 'the new laird'. Darcy shrugged at that. 'I was the lady for fifteen years and I was always the new lady.'

'You're still the lady,' Bella pointed out.

'Dowager lady.' Darcy shuddered. 'Sounds ancient though, doesn't it?'

Bella explained that she wasn't the lady because she wasn't married to Adam.

'Yet,' Adam insisted forcefully. 'Soon though.'

Bella nodded. 'We should have done the registry-office thing the first time we talked about it.'

'But then you got all excited about a big, romantic castle wedding,' he replied.

Bella rolled her eyes. 'Who got all excited?'

Adam laughed. 'And you humour me about it beautifully.'

'In the spring is the plan at the moment,' Bella continued. 'We'd like to start doing weddings generally and so why not? I'm thinking we can use the large dining room for...'

Adam shook his head again. 'Is this wedding planning or work?'

'Can't it be both?' she shot back.

'So romantic,' he muttered.

'Anyway,' Darcy swept in to change the subject and head off the argument, 'tell us about you, Gemma.'

For a fraction of a second Jodie almost looked behind her to see who Darcy was talking to before she caught herself. She was Gemma. 'Well, you already know about my work life,' she ventured. They'd have discussed that, presumably? And Gemma must have filled in an application or sent a CV.

Darcy waved a hand dismissively. 'Oh, no more work. What about you? Seriously, what did make you want to come all the way up here? I'm sure there are less corporate jobs nearer home.'

'Er...' The best lies were always grounded in truth. 'Honestly, I just broke up with someone. This is kind of a fresh start.'

'I'm sorry.' Darcy squeezed her hand. 'Were you with him long?'

'Er, her.' Jodie got the correction out of the way fast and braced herself for the second part of the coming-out chore. 'I'm bi. So yeah. It was a her.'

'I'm sorry. Shouldn't have assumed. That's fine. Great. Wonderful,' Darcy floundered beautifully. 'Isn't it?'

Adam nodded. 'Of course.'

Bella looked up. 'Do you think we should do a room somewhere as a proper bridal suite?'

Adam jabbed her in the ribs. 'Gemma was telling us about breaking up with her girlfriend.'

'Sure. Maybe in the main house rather than the coach house? So they're not right next to their guests if they want to... y'know.'

Darcy pursed her lips. 'Ignore her. You were telling us about you.'

Jodie would rather have turned the conversation back to bridal suites and accommodation plans.

Darcy was not having it. 'Go on.'

'She...' She what? 'I don't know. I think things had run their course.'

She hoped her vagueness would come across as understandable reluctance to talk about a painful episode. She was spared further questions by the sound of a door opening and closing and voices coming down the corridor to the kitchen.

'I'm just going to drop these bits off.' The voice was a woman. Local from the sound of her accent and very definite about her intentions.

'I'm quite sure that isn't necessary.' Equally definite but more refined, with a hint of resignation.

Adam jumped up to greet the newcomers. 'Flinty! Grandmother!'

Jodie took a second to take them in. The visuals absolutely matched the voices. The first woman, Flinty, according to Adam's greeting, was shorter, solidly built with greying red hair. Her companion was tall, slim, neat silver hair pulled back into a bun and spectacles suspended on a thin gold chain at her neck.

'I brought you some Brussels. First crop from Hugh's garden. I don't know why he grows them. Anna can't stand the things. I thought "Bella'll be able to do something with 'em", so here you are. I left 'em on the stalk so they'll keep better.' She handed the massive stalk of sprouts over and looked around. 'Well, hello.'

'Grandmother, Flinty, this is Gemma. She's starting work here tomorrow.'

Flinty slapped her cheerfully on the arm. 'Welcome, love. Are they looking after you? Was the Dower House cleaned properly?' Did she cast a sideways look at Adam and Darcy as she asked that?

'It's lovely. Thank you.'

'And you're the girl from London then?' The second woman, Adam's grandmother, said London in a tone that suggested some weakness of character.

'No. Reading.' Wait. Gemma was from London, wasn't she? Originally. Would she have told them that? 'I'm from London, but I was living in Reading is what I mean. Like most recently. Not now. Obviously. But before. Yesterday. Reading. Yeah.' Stop talking, Jodie.

The woman was definitely looking at her more intently now. 'Whereabouts in London are you from?'

Gemma was from Hounslow but she said Richmond when she was trying to sound fancy. 'Richmond?'

The woman tilted her head. 'Are you asking me?'

'No?'

'Don't interrogate the poor girl, Veronica,' Darcy cut in. 'You'll have her doubting her own name.'

Almost everyone laughed.

Veronica was still gazing directly at Jodie, inspecting her, assessing her. Jodie plastered on a smile. She'd almost slipped up there. She couldn't let that happen again.

Chapter Five

Jodie barely slept, and when she did she dreamt fitfully of Gemma rising up from the stream next to the castle, like a troll under the bridge and decrying Jodie for her failure as both a girlfriend and a human. Finally, she dragged herself from bed, through to the tiny bathroom, turned the shower up as hot as it would go, which turned out to be alternately scalding and freezing, and let the cycle of hot and cold shock her back into her body and out of the rolling wave of anxiety.

She was not about to be unmasked. Jodie was far away from anyone who knew her. The only danger was that she would slip up and give herself away. To avoid that she needed to be the best possible person that she could be. And that meant the person least like Jodie. Jodie was – she ran through the bank of quotes from her family, from her exes and from her former employers in her mind – unreliable, easily distracted, prone to making impulsive decisions and deeply disorganised. In short, Jodie was a mess.

As she got dressed, Jodie resolved that Gemma would not be like that at all. Gemma would be punctual. She would listen to instructions. She would think before she acted. She would have all her work perfectly organised in colour-coded binders. Jodie picked up her phone.

What felt like three or four minutes later at most, Jodie checked the time. She'd been looking at pastel-coloured binders on the internet for nearly forty minutes, which meant she was now officially late for work. Late for her first day in the job she desperately needed to not mess up, in a place that was literally four minutes' walk from her front door. Gemma would never have let that happen. Gemma would be over at the castle already, notebook open, pens neatly laid out, bright, professional smile plastered on her face.

And now Jodie had wasted another three minutes thinking about what Gemma would do. She shoved her feet into her trainers, which didn't go at all with the one pair of non-jeans trousers that she owned, grabbed her jacket and set off at a run down the path to the castle. She hurtled into the kitchen. 'Sorry. I…'

She stopped. Her only audience was the dopey-looking chocolate Lab she'd met the previous afternoon. She hauled the gorgeous doggy's name from memory. 'Hello, Dipper.'

Dipper wandered over and sniffed Jodie's hand.

'Where is everybody?'

The dog didn't reply.

Jodie made her way tentatively further into the castle, through the grand hallway Darcy had brought her into the previous day. 'Hello!'

'In here!'

The voice came from somewhere in front of her but beyond that Jodie wasn't sure. She carried on into a corridor lined with doorways. She stared at the row of closed doors, paralysed by indecision. What would Gemma do? Gemma would knock politely on each one and open them until she found where she was supposed

56

to be. Jodie couldn't entirely see that option working out. What if she picked the wrong door and there was someone in there and they weren't the right someone, or it was a bedroom or something and the person was still asleep and then she'd have woken them up and she'd have to explain who she was and…?

'She's in there.' Adam came out of the door three along from where Jodie was standing. 'Sorry. She meant to come over to the Dower House rather than force you to hunt for her, but when she gets her head into work everything else sort of goes out of her brain.'

Jodie knew how that could be. 'It's fine. My fault. I'm late.'

Adam shrugged. 'Barely. Go on through.' He pointed at the door again. 'She's in the yellow room.'

The room Jodie was directed into was painted green against all previous advertising. Bella was sitting on the sofa, laptop on her knee, paperwork spread out around her. 'Jodie!' She looked up and grinned.

'Hi. Sorry I'm a bit late.'

'No. I didn't tell you where I was going to be. You've probably spent the last hour wandering around this place getting stuck in cupboards with ghosts.'

'Do you have ghosts?'

'Only a couple. Only one that really bothers us.' Bella scooped scattered papers from the seat next to her. 'Come in. Sit down. Shall we start off by me telling you a bit more about everything here?'

Jodie tried – she did try – to concentrate on the stream of information Bella supplied about the castle and the estate and the Lowbridge family, followed by an even more rapidly delivered information dump about their plans for the place: the developing cookery school born out of Bella's previous life as a chef; the walled garden that Adam's father had loved and which Adam was currently nurturing back into productivity to supply fruits, vegetables and herbs for the cookery school; the coach house, earmarked for transformation into guest accommodation but currently little more than a badly heated money pit; the ballroom which was intended to be their function room for parties and weddings; and, of course, the land itself.

'So historically that would have been the main thing. We still have sheep. I don't really get involved with them.' She paused. 'Apart from sometimes when they decide to follow me about the place. But they're more Adam's thing. He understands all that rural stuff. And he's responsible for the gardens and the land, but one or two weeks a month he goes back over to Edinburgh because he had a business there before he inherited all of this and honestly that's the main thing keeping us going until we get everything else properly up and running. And Darcy does the accounts and invoices and all that stuff. Veronica, Adam's grandmother, still helps with that.' Bella paused. 'I say helps. I mean more "checks that we're doing it properly".'

Veronica was the woman who'd questioned her about where in London she was from the evening before, wasn't she? Would she be here checking on Jodie's work as well? She shuddered slightly at the thought.

Bella didn't seem to notice. 'So shall we?'

'Sorry?' Jodie had been thinking all the ways Veronica might catch her out and had stopped listening to a single thing her new boss had been saying.

'Shall we take a walk around? I know Darcy showed you some stuff yesterday but I don't think you went in the coach house, and honestly there's bits of the castle I still get lost in.' She grinned. 'Adam and his gran, and even Flinty, act like living somewhere like this is totally normal.'

'I guess it is for them.'

'Yeah. To the manor born and all that.'

Jodie ran through the characters in her head. 'Flinty and Adam's gran are the women who came round last night?'

'That's right.'

'And are they together?'

'Yep.' Bella grinned. 'So from what I can work out they had some sort of thing when they were young but then the baron – Adam's granddad – set his sights on Veronica, and everyone said how lucky she was and her parents were super proud that she was going to be Lady Lowbridge and there didn't seem to be a way out.'

'But they're together now.'

'Just recently. It's adorable.' Bella paused. 'Never let either of them hear you say that though. Flinty would clip your ear, and Veronica would... I don't know. Probably freeze the blood in your veins with one of her looks.'

That definitely fit with the image of Veronica that was forming in Jodie's mind.

Bella was already striding out of the room. 'So what did Darcy already show you?'

'Not much. Only the Dower House really. I think she was trying not to overwhelm me when I'd only just arrived.'

'Right then. The grand tour.'

She followed Bella outside, quickly trying to get her bearings. The castle buildings were arranged around a square courtyard. The Dower House was up the path from the front right-hand corner. Bella was leading her out towards the back left. Through there they discovered the stables.

'Darcy's domain,' Bella explained. 'She's the horse lover. Space for three more horses permanently stabled though so we could rent that out. Un-serviced at the moment. If we were going to hire a stablehand we'd need to charge more, I guess.' She shrugged. 'No idea what the going rate for stabling is though.'

Jodie shook her head. Surely even the real Gemma wasn't an expert on stabling fees as well.

The tour continued around the outside of the castle and back into the corridor on the right side of the building. 'We don't really use these rooms at the moment.' Bella swung open a door. 'This could be incredible though.'

Jodie followed her boss into a decidedly faded but still impressive hall. The ceilings were double height, and although they'd come in a side door she could see that there were grand double doors at both ends of the room and on the far wall leading outside. 'This is the ballroom?'

'Yeah. Seen better days obviously, but it's pretty much watertight for the time being at least. Thanks to Pavel.'

The room was past its heyday but Jodie could see the potential. 'So if you did weddings would you do the ceremony in here?'

'Could do. There's the large dining room as well or the small hall, and the courtyard, and the church if people want that.'

'In the village?'

Bella shook her head. 'No. We have a chapel here.'

Jodie's eyes widened.

'I know. It's insane.' Bella looked around. 'Come on.' She led the way down the corridor and into the hallway

Jodie had been through before – she recognised it from the suit of armour. 'Don't mind Colin.'

'You named the suit of armour?'

'Adam's dad did, I think. I like it though. He sort of looks like a Colin.' Bella stopped. 'I was going to go to the kitchens but once we're in there we might as well get settled with a cuppa so shall we do the rest of outdoors first?'

'Sure.' The idea of sitting down was far more attractive, but Gemma, Jodie had decided, was naturally amenable. And the longer she followed Bella around nodding politely while features of the castle were pointed out to her, then the longer it would be before she was expected to actually do any of Gemma's job.

They made their way out of the opposite side of the castle, and along the side of the building. Bella pointed out a pathway that they passed at the end of the castle wall. 'So that takes you down to the Dower House. Well, your house now.'

Well, obviously it did. The castle and its immediate grounds were a bit ragged at the edges but the shape of the thing made sense. There was an order that appealed to Jodie. The castle was wrapped around that central courtyard. At the corner Jodie thought of as bottom left was the coach house and the gates from the road. At the top left was the pathway through to the paddock, presumably also reachable around the outside past the coach house, so that ye olde coachmen didn't have to lead their horses right through the middle of the castle complex. The top right was closed off, so far as she could tell, and the bottom right brought you out near the Dower House and then up along a high wall she could see in front of her towards whatever Bella was about to show her.

'This place does my head in,' Bella muttered. 'I still get lost looking for the under-butler's second pantry.'

'You have a butler?'

Bella shook her head. 'No. We have Flinty but she says she's retired. Although I don't think it would go down well if we said we were hiring a new housekeeper. And the stables get mucked out somehow and I'm bloody certain Darcy isn't doing that herself. Hey. Maybe we do have a stablehand.' She shrugged. 'It gets done though so I'm not going to worry about it.' She shrugged again. 'It's all a bit hand to mouth, I'm afraid. Which is why your starting salary is a little bit basic.' She continued towards the corner of the wall in front of them. 'I'm sorry about that. We know it's not what you'd expect to be earning.'

Jodie's last job had been minimum wage with a boss who she suspected of being a little less than meticulous about dividing up their tips, so technically Bella was right – any sort of regular salary was not what she'd been expecting a week ago at all.

'Hopefully with the cottage you won't need to spend too much though day-to-day. And you can eat with us whenever you want to.'

If Jodie was smart she could probably live at Lowbridge without spending anything at all. That would mean no shopping in the small hours of the morning when she found herself wide awake with only her thoughts. She could do that. She could take the apps off her phone. Or she could get one of those blocker apps that don't let you spend more than five minutes on a particular app and then give you electric shocks or something if you try to log back in. She was hazy on the details of how these things worked.

And somewhere like Lowbridge must offer lots of low-cost activities she could take up. She could start hiking. Jodie took a deep breath in. Good seaside air. It was probably doing her the world of good already. She would go for long walks up the hills and along the clifftops and get fit and full of inner calm. Which was all very Gemma. 'The salary's fine,' Jodie reassured her, despite not actually knowing what the salary was.

'No, it's not, but it's all we can afford.' Bella grinned. 'At least until you transform our marketing and we're overrun with customers.'

Jodie forced a laugh. 'I'll get right on that then.'

They'd come to the corner of the walled area they'd been walking towards. Bella pushed open a small wooden door in the wall and made her way through. Jodie followed and found herself in an expansive walled garden. Deep into autumn, most of the soil was bare and there were a few sections still covered in green, apparently waiting for harvest. 'A vegetable garden?' Jodie hoped her tone sounded more confident in that guess than she felt.

'Yeah. Adam's pride and joy. And the first place to check if you're ever looking for him.'

On cue, the very bouncy chocolate Labrador bounded towards them from the greenhouse that seemed to run most of the length of the far wall.

'Hello, gorgeous.' Jodie bent and rubbed the back of the dog's neck.

'Dipper!' Adam's voice carried from across the garden as he followed the dog over to them. Dipper, over-whelmed by excitement, dashed back over to her master and then back to Bella and Jodie and then back again, until Adam finally closed the space between them, and Dipper could run happily in small circles around the group, ensuring her flock were properly herded together. Adam looked back over the garden. 'So what do you think?'

'It's great.' The looks on her employers' faces suggested she was expected to say more. 'Very green and also brown.'

'Yep. It is that.' Adam grinned. 'At the moment it's mostly what my father planted before… Yeah, but I'm already thinking about next year. And we're still harvesting carrots obviously.' He gestured towards the nearest set of beds, which were covered in a sea of thin vibrant green leaves. Jodie tried to nod like someone who wasn't expecting to see orange cylinders hanging off a carrot tree. 'And I've barely started bringing the sprouts in yet.'

'Ugh,' Bella sighed. 'I've got a mass of them from Hugh already.'

'I thought you liked sprouts.'

'I do, but not everyone else does. I don't know how I'm going to use them all. I can't imagine a sprout-themed cookery school day being a massive draw.'

Adam shrugged. 'I'm sure our new business and marketing guru could sell it. You did say you could sell anything.'

Gemma had said that? Jodie fought to keep the surprise off her face. She couldn't imagine Gemma coming off that cocky. Gemma was the sweet and kind one who always said the right thing. Jodie was the screw-up. She smiled as brightly as she could manage. 'Sprout Day might test my abilities a bit.'

'Is there anything else we can do with them?' Adam asked.

Bella and Adam were both looking at Jodie. What did she know about sprouts? They were horrible. That wasn't helpful. They appeared in Christmas dinner like evil little bitterness bombs. 'Massive Christmas dinner?' she asked.

Adam glanced at the beds behind him. 'It'll have to be really massive.'

Bella half smiled. 'Maybe you need to stick "Imaginative uses for sprouts" on the to-do list, Gemma.' She gave her fiancé a quick peck on the lips. 'We'll leave you to it. Gemma's probably chomping to actually get to work rather than tag along after me all day.'

'I don't mind.' Did that sound like she was putting off getting to work? 'I mean it's useful finding out where everything is. Efficient really to do all this first.'

Bella chattered all the way back to the castle about plans and ideas for making the estate profitable for the long-term. The cookery school was clearly her baby and where her heart lay but her brain was going at a thousand miles a minute with thoughts about the stables and the walled garden and converting the coach house and opening a tea shop or a pop-up restaurant and offering regular guided tours. 'That's tricky with all the community groups though,' she added.

'With what?'

Bella sighed. 'We haven't even talked about that, have we? The castle also runs as a kind of makeshift community centre. So we have parents and toddlers here on Tuesday and Thursday – in fact I think Nina's coming over to talk about that this afternoon. Then there's book club once a month. They bring a little bit in for the room hire and teas and coffees, but mostly we just do it for the community. Make sure the locals know we're not just another big estate who don't give a crap.'

Something Pavel had said on the way over rang a bell. 'Like the Mc... McKenzie, is it?'

'Exactly. If you tried to hold your meeting there they'd charge you an extra fee for breathing the air.' Bella pulled a face. 'Not that any of our groups would stand for that anyway. I'd sort of love to see what the Ladies' Group would do if we tried.'

'Who?'

'Ladies' Group. They meet here most weeks. AKA the people who actually run the village. You should probably come to that.'

Jodie was instantly picturing a room full of Hyacinth Buckets, pearls clutched, lips pursed, disapproval ready to deploy at the slightest provocation.

'Seriously, worth starting on the right foot with them. Next meeting is…' Bella frowned for a second. 'Not the first week of the month, not a green bin week, not a fish delivery day or the mobile library, but Anna's sister is visiting at the weekend so… Thursday. At Nina's house. You'd be very welcome.'

Jodie reminded herself that the Gemma she was trying to be was endlessly amenable. 'Sounds great.' She beamed.

'Good. Tea?'

'Great.' Jodie was not a tea drinker. Or a coffee drinker. It was a great social faux pas on her part, she knew, and probably evidence of the extent to which she wasn't a proper grown-up. Gemma, she thought, loved tea. The Gemma she was creating would be the warm, capable type who was forever popping the kettle on and sorting out other people's woes over a nice hot brew.

This resolve was weakened slightly by the first sip of sad brown water.

'Do you take sugar?'

Sugar had to help, surely. Jodie chucked two heaped teaspoons of sweetness into her mug and stirred. It did help. It didn't help enough to make the ubiquitous-ness of tea drinking in anyway explicable. 'Mmmm,' she murmured. 'Lovely.'

'So I guess your job is to take all our mad ideas and impose some order on them.'

Not exactly a formal job description but it was the best Jodie had had so far.

'And then to work out how we're actually going to persuade anyone to come and spend money on them,' Bella added. 'So organisation, and marketing.' She paused. 'And social media.'

'Right.'

'And special events.' Bella grinned. 'I should have said that first, shouldn't I? I mean, that's the actual job title.'

Jodie suddenly felt she ought to be writing things down. She opened her notebook and wrote *events* and *social media*. She knew there'd been more in Bella's list than that but the other things had already danced out of her head. Things did that. Catching hold of her thoughts was like chasing butterflies across a meadow. Her mother loved butterflies and hated those displays in museums where some mad Victorian had pinned pages and pages of the poor things into a scrapbook. How on earth did they get the butterflies to stay still? They probably gassed them, didn't they? That sounded awful. Did they make them fly into a box and then fill it with gas, or did they put tiny masks on them like a creepy insect doctor? Jodie had only been under anaesthetic once. She remembered the anaesthetist though. He had blond hair and kind eyes.

'So what you do you think?'

Bella had been talking to her the whole time, hadn't she? Jodie had been chasing butterflies and counting back-wards from ten and Bella had been talking to her about the actual job she was supposed to be doing. Jodie nodded hopefully. 'I agree.'

'Great. I've been telling Adam we need to go for it and do something big but he's nervous about the money. He's always nervous about money, but I think you have to grasp the nettle.'

'Right.' What on earth had she agreed to?

'That's why I was so excited about your Hogmanay proposal. Everyone else's plans were all for small, sustainable growth and I get that, but yours was bold. And you were so confident you could pull it off.'

'Absolutely.' *What proposal?* thought Jodie.

'Great. So where do you want to start?'

No idea.

'What do you need from me?'

Absolutely everything.

'Well…' Jodie had nothing.

Bella pulled up an email up on her phone and scrolled through. 'I love it. The balance of community and visitors coming in. Properly Scottish but not cheesy.'

Jodie nodded. 'Yeah. That's what I was going for.'

'Brilliant. Where do we start?' Bella was staring at her, eyes full of faith and hope.

There was no choice, was there? Jodie had no clue what they were supposed to be talking about. 'OK. Well, the thing is…' The thing was what? Jodie was back in school, standing in front of a teacher desperately trying to explain why, despite her genuinely good intentions, she hadn't done the coursework or finished the project or remembered her reading book. 'It's just that…' The dog ate her homework? She left her folder on the bus? Her mum put the permission slip in the washing machine?

'Oh my goodness!' Bella gasped.

'What?'

'You lost your email, didn't you?'

What?

'Your laptop blew up.' Had it? Of course. She'd had to explain why Gemma suddenly had a new email address. Had Jodie actually said her computer blew up? In her head she'd been vaguer and, she thought, more plausible than that. 'You've probably lost all your notes.'

Jodie could have kissed her new boss. She didn't. Spontaneous snogging was not Gemma's style at all. 'Yeah. Sorry.'

'I'll forward all this back to you to your new address.'

Thank goodness.

'Morning.' The voice behind them was deep and already familiar.

Bella jumped up. 'Pavel! When did you get here?'

'Just bringing the toddler group outdoor play stuff back for Mum. Adam said we could stick it in the south wing.'

'Course you can.'

'Mum said to give you a few quid for the storage.'

Bella shook her head. 'Don't be daft.'

Pavel folded his arms. 'You know she'll insist.'

'And I'll refuse. It's space we're not using anyway.'

'I thought we needed the money.' Jodie blurted her thought out loud before her embryonic inner Gemma had the chance to censor her. 'I mean, it's not up to me. Sorry.'

Pavel nodded. 'She's right.' He pulled a small wodge of notes out of his pocket and pushed them into Bella's hand.

'Fine.' Bella half smiled at Jodie. 'See. You're already paying for yourself.' She turned back to Pavel. 'I'm guessing this won't get enough building work done for it

69

to be worth handing it straight back to you for the coach house, will it?'

He shrugged. 'I'm sorry. I know the quote was higher than you were hoping.'

'It's OK. Stuff's expensive.'

It certainly sounded as though everything at Lowbridge was expensive.

'But that's why Jodie's here.' Bella looked up as Adam came into the kitchen. 'We're totally doing the Hogmanay thing.'

Adam rolled his eyes. 'Are we?'

'Yes. And don't be a killjoy about it. One big event to put Lowbridge on the map.'

'With no accommodation?'

Bella's face fell. 'Right. No.' She leaned forward, burying her face into her fingers for a moment.

Jodie's brain raced to catch up with the conversation. 'So what exactly is the problem?'

'The problem,' Bella's voice was flat, 'is that we're planning a late-night party in a village miles from anywhere and we have no overnight accommodation for people to go back to afterwards.'

That did sound like a problem. Late-night parties meant drinking and that meant no driving back to hotels which meant people needed to either stay close by or be driven to wherever they were sleeping. 'The castle's massive though. We must have loads of room.'

Adam shook his head. 'Loads of damp, unheated, unlit room with no working hot water. Your cottage is fine. The wing of the castle where we actually live is ok. Bit dated but liveable. There's maybe one room in the coach house that's not too bad?'

He glanced at Pavel, who nodded. 'Yeah. The one where you and Bella stayed when you first came back is OK so long as you're not too set on the hot water working all the time.'

'The coach house is watertight?' Bella offered.

'So why can't we put people in there?' Jodie asked. She could see it in her head. 'Call it high-end glamping or something. Historic living? I don't know. Make it a feature somehow?'

Bella was staring at her. 'That's what I said.'

'So why can't we?'

The two women looked at each other. Bella turned to Adam. 'Why can't we?'

'Is it safe?'

Pavel didn't quite meet anyone's gaze. 'It's not going to fall down. If you sold it as camping I could disconnect the electric so it'd be safe. You could have battery lamps or something?'

Jodie could see it. Twinkly lanterns lighting the way from the castle to the coach house. Rustic accommodation but rustic accommodation in a solid stone castle outbuilding. 'I think it would be lovely.'

'Can we?' Bella asked Adam.

'We wouldn't be able to charge much.' He was smiling though. 'Honestly, it'd be easier to sell to McKenzie than try to distract you when you've got an idea.'

'Don't even joke about that!' She turned back to Jodie. 'The McKenzie estate is further up the coast.'

'Yeah. We drove past it?' She looked to Pavel, who nodded his confirmation.

'The guy who owns it offers to buy this place about twice a week, but it is not for sale.'

'Why not?' From the hard set of Bella's face that was absolutely the wrong thing to say. Gemma wouldn't have asked. She'd have politely accepted Bella at her word.

'Because it's everything that's wrong with tourism in a place like this. No soul. No authenticity. No sense of community.' Bella was adamant. 'And the brownies in the cafe are awful.'

Adam nodded. 'All true. She's mostly mad about the brownie thing though.'

'There's no excuse for bad cake,' Bella hissed.

'Pavel hasn't told you he's working for the enemy then?' Adam asked.

Jodie turned around quickly enough to see Pavel wince. 'I'm not working for the enemy. I'm helping a mate out with a quote for some work there. He probably won't even get the job, and he might not need my help if he does.'

'Hmm.' Bella turned back to Jodie. 'Anyway, once we've planned our grand Hogmanay extravaganza we'll leave them in our dust.'

Jodie nodded. So she was planning a grand extravaganza of some kind. Excellent.

–

Pavel left Lowbridge and headed back over the footbridge to the village. Bella had been frosty about him possibly working for the McKenzies. He understood it. McKenzie would see the Lowbridge estate broken up and subsumed in a heartbeat, but the building work they were doing there had the potential to keep a full crew of labourers in work for months, and it would be better if those workers were local. At least that way the money McKenzie was paying out would find its way back to the shop and pub, rather than disappearing from the Highlands altogether.

Which didn't mean he wasn't still planning to make it up to Bella. He glanced behind him before heading into the coach house. The electrics were the trickiest part, but he knew a couple of sparks who owed him favours. The rest he could do himself. The coach house was a slightly beaten-up little Cinderella but, to help his friends, Pavel could fix up the downstairs and a couple of first floor rooms at least. Gemma's rustic glamping idea was all very well but there was no way they'd be able to charge as much as if the space was properly renovated, and Adam and Bella needed some proper income.

Happy that he understood the scale of the work he needed to do, Pavel wandered back over the bridge and along the shoreline towards home, where he jumped straight in the shower. He was going on a date. With Jill. Jill was probably his best mate these days. They got on well. They always had a laugh. She was pretty, kind, funny – there was no reason not to be excited about this date.

He closed his eyes under the flow of the hot water and told himself that again. Going out with Jill was a good thing. He was very happy about it.

'Knock, knock!' His mother's voice rang through from the living room.

Pavel flicked the shower off, and grabbed a towel. 'I'll be through in a minute.' By the time he was half dry and had the towel properly secured around his waist his mother was in his bedroom pulling clothes out of the neatly organised wardrobe and throwing them on the bed.

'Where's your purple shirt?'

'What?'

'Your purple shirt. For tonight?'

'I don't own a purple shirt.'

His mother pursed her lips. 'Don't get smart with me, young man.'

Pavel rolled his eyes. 'I'm not being smart. I can't magic clothes that don't exist into being.'

His mum pulled a hanger from the rail. 'This one.'

'That's red.'

She barely paused. 'That's what I said.'

Another set of footsteps came up the stairs and knocked at the front door.

'We're in here, Netty.'

'I'm not dressed, Mum.'

Another sigh. 'It's only Netty.'

His mum's friend popped her head around the bedroom door, glanced at the shirt and nodded. 'Good choice. Purple suits you, love.'

'It's red,' Pavel muttered.

'What trousers is he wearing?'

'I'll wear jeans.' The question wasn't directed at him but Pavel answered anyway.

His mother shook her head. 'Jeans? For a first date?'

'We're only going for a drink and a pizza in Portree. I've been for pizza with Jill a million times.'

'Those were friend pizzas. This is date pizza. It's a whole different thing.'

Netty nodded. 'She's right. Date pizzas are fancier.'

Pavel took a deep breath. 'It's just pizza and I think I'm capable of dressing myself. Thank you very much for your input.'

The two women shook their heads. 'We're just excited,' his mum muttered.

'The whole village is excited,' added Netty.

Wasn't that the truth? Anna in the shop had spent a good twenty minutes trying to persuade him he needed twelve red roses when he'd popped in earlier to get bread, milk and dog food for Mrs Timberley. The shop didn't normally have flowers. He had a strong suspicion they'd got them in specifically for him.

'It's such a good match.'

Netty nodded.

'And we've not had a wedding in the village for years.'

'Not since Darcy and the old baron.'

'God rest him,' his mother added.

'Adam and Bella are getting married,' Pavel pointed out.

'Well, they say so, but they've not set a date yet, have they?'

Netty clapped her hands together. 'You could beat them to it.'

'It's just pizza.' Pavel felt like he was stuck on repeat.

'Such a good match though,' his mother murmured. 'And you like her, don't you?'

For the first time there was a hint of disquiet in his mum's voice that stabbed at Pavel's gut. She wanted him to be happy. Of course she did, and she was excited about the idea of him finding someone and falling in love. There was nothing wrong with that. Pavel was the one overcomplicating things here. Jill was great. He and Jill together were great. Everyone agreed that they'd make a great couple. The only people not besides themselves at this apparent blooming of new romance were the ones who'd thought they were already going out.

Pavel's phone buzzed on the floor next to the bed.

He tapped to answer.

'Hi. I'm really sorry. Mr Oakley from the post office in Lochcarron had a heart attack.'

'Is he OK?'

'I'm not sure, but his wife's on her own cos Millie's on bed rest until the baby comes, so I need to go and be with her.'

'That's fine.' Pavel felt the knot in his chest ease a little. 'I understand.'

'Thank you.' She paused. 'I'm really sorry though. We can reschedule?' Her voice was hopeful.

'Yeah. Yeah. Of course we can.' Pavel nodded. 'Looking forward to it.'

His mother folded her arms. 'She's dumped you already?'

'Something came up with work.'

Netty nodded. 'That'll happen if you're married to a minister.'

'I'm not married to...'

The women had already moved on though. His mum took Netty's arm. She cast a glance back towards Pavel. 'These are your choices, pet. Reverend's wife or lonely old cat woman.'

'I don't even have a cat.'

'See,' his mum stage-whispered to Netty. 'Can't even hold down a pet.'

'I thought you were going over to see Bella this afternoon.'

His mum grinned. 'We are. Plenty of time to torment you first, love.'

76

Chapter Six

'Something with ragu or something with sprouts?' Bella asked. 'Or there's bread and cheese and salad and stuff.' She was standing in front of the fridge, having suggested that they take a working lunch break. Jodie had been unable to find a reason to object.

'Whatever's easiest.'

'Bread and cheese is easiest but that doesn't get any sprouts eaten up.' Bella pulled a face. 'What am I going to do with a pantry full of sprouts? Do you like sprouts?'

For the first time since she arrived Jodie decided honesty was the only way forward. She was already stuck dutifully drinking gallons of tea. Never-ending sprout soup would be too much. 'Not really,' she admitted apologetically.

'No. Lots of people don't.' She frowned. 'I can't just give you a cheese sandwich. I'm a professional.'

'You don't have to cook fancy lunches for me,' Jodie insisted.

Bella shook her head. 'Not fancy. Just something with a bit more to it than cheese between two slices of bread. How about a sort of Italian-inspired cheese on toast?'

'OK.'

'Great. I'll sort that out. You work out what we're doing with a massive glut of sprouts.'

Jodie nodded. Sprouts. Right. She could do things with sprouts. She pulled her notebook in front of her and wrote *Things To Do With Sprouts* at the top of the page. Number 1 was easy. Number 1 they'd already discussed.

1. Massive Christmas dinner

What else could you do with sprouts?

2. Fun With Sprouts TikTok series
3. Sprout-based sports and games. Sprout tennis???
4. Sproutapalooza
5. ...

Five was a challenge. She glanced back over her list. Five was blank. Four didn't technically mean anything. Sprout tennis was insane. So she had two ideas. Two.

Bella put down a plate laden with ciabatta rubbed with garlic and then gently toasted before being topped with pesto, slices of tomato, chicken and cheese and heated under the grill in front of her. 'This looks incredible.' Jodie took her first bite. The flavours danced around her mouth. She hadn't had food like this since... well, ever. Her mum had loved to cook but her ingredients were frugal and her time was short. Gemma, the real Gemma, was a great cook. Of course she was, but she'd never served anything that tasted half as good as this. Even though they'd broken up the thought felt disloyal. Gemma had always tried to encourage Jodie to eat better. She took a second bite of the happiness sandwich. 'This is better than Pret,' she murmured.

'I should bloody well hope so.' Bella was smiling. 'Do I take it you're not a big cook?'

She'd applied for a job as events manager for a cookery school. And Gemma cooked. Gemma cooking had been the only way any sort of vegetable had got into Jodie in the last couple of years. 'I mean, I do like to cook...' She needed to make this a little more convincing. She looked around the kitchen for inspiration. 'Boiling things, you know, frying them.' What else did you do? 'Putting them in the oven...'

Bella laughed. 'It's fine. Everyone exaggerates a bit at job interviews.'

What had Gemma said? 'Sorry if I talked myself up a bit.'

'Only a touch. It's fine. We didn't hire you to cook, did we?' Bella chewed her very fancy sandwich thoughtfully. 'Although, you will still have to help with the cookery school. Maybe you could film some stuff for socials?' She looked up at Jodie. 'If you think that's worth doing. I mean you're the expert.'

'Yep. I've got that on my list!' Jodie felt a little surge of pride. 'We could make an online series of things to do with sprouts. You know, like people think they don't like them but here are some fun alternative ways to cook them?' Doubt crept in. 'Are there fun ways to cook them?'

'There are fun ways to cook anything.' Bella paused. 'I mean you can do them with bacon and chestnuts, or with chilli, or pancetta.'

Jodie wasn't a food expert but still. 'Isn't pancetta just posh bacon?'

Bella pursed her lips. 'Basically yeah. So I can't count that as a different thing?'

'Maybe not.'

'OK then. Cheesy creamy sprouts. Like cauliflower cheese.'

'But sprouts?'

'Exactly.'

'So that's three fun things to do with sprouts,' Jodie confirmed.

'What else is on your list?'

'Massive Christmas dinner.'

'Obviously.'

'And then...' She scanned down. 'It gets a bit thin, to be honest.'

Bella leaned over to read Jodie's pad. 'What's Sproutap-alooza?'

'I have no idea.' This was her first work task and she had nothing. Gemma would probably have built some sort of sprout empire by now.

But Bella was laughing, not frowning. 'It's OK. We didn't hire you to work for the sprout marketing board. Filming some recipes for socials is a good idea though. We could release them in the run-up to Christmas?'

Jodie nodded. 'And we can do other clips and stuff before then. Like from the cookery lessons, like you said?'

She could film Bella's demos. She could even film herself and make a thing of it. 'We could make a virtue of me not being a great cook,' she suggested. 'Sort of compare and contrast what I make with yours, and show the progress over time?'

Bella was nodding.

'Like if I can learn,' Jodie continued, 'then you can too?'

'Sounds great. You don't mind being online though?' Bella asked. 'I did look at your socials. You're pretty private.'

Jodie froze. Of course she'd have looked Gemma up online. That was what everyone did these days, wasn't it?

Jodie could picture her ex's profiles. Her privacy was tight, and her profile pics were all cartoony images rather than actual photos – the result, she'd said, of some ex before Jodie's time who'd got weird when they broke up.

Jodie's socials, on the other hand, were a catalogue of drunken nights out and hot takes she probably should never have posted. 'It's fine,' Jodie reassured her.

'Excellent. You can be the public face of the Highland Cookery School then.'

Jodie was an idiot. Her socials might be an open book but that wasn't her book any more. She couldn't be the public face of anything. 'OK.' She nodded.

Maybe the next session wouldn't be for ages anyway. Maybe by then this problem would somehow have gone away.

'OK. Well, tomorrow's class…' Bella started.

Tomorrow was not ages away.

'…is technically supposed to be specifically for blokes. Cooking for useless lads and hopeless dads, sort of thing.'

'Is that the official name?' Jodie tried to sound relaxed.

'I don't think it ever got an official name. We sort of talked about it at Ladies' Group and then Jill told some of the women in her congregation and now it's full. Anyway, we can squeeze you in and we'll tell them you're there for work. It'll be fine. Two until five tomorrow.'

Jodie nodded. On the one hand that was another afternoon that she could pass off as work time without her having to do any of the things Gemma was apparently expert in. On the other, she had twenty-four hours to work out how she was going to be a social media star without actually appearing on social media.

'Shall we get on then? Let's talk Hogmanay.'

Jodie dutifully turned to a new page in her notepad. Making notes was a good worker sort of thing to do, wasn't it?

'So from your plan I think the key thing to remember is nothing cheesy. Like Scottish obviously, but authentic. So we can have a piper. It's traditional and people expect it, but we don't want pipe music playing in the elevators the whole time, you know?'

'Do we have elevators?'

'No.'

'I don't think that'll be a problem then.'

Bella laughed. 'You know what I mean.'

Jodie neatly wrote *Hogmanay Plans* at the top of her paper and added *No Cheese* on the next line. She underlined it twice for good measure.

—

'You didn't have to give us a lift over, darling.' That wasn't what Pavel's mother had said when she'd been setting out for Lowbridge Castle. At that point she'd been quite adamant that, since Pavel's date was cancelled, he really had nothing better to do.

'No problem,' he laughed.

'Are you coming in?'

He followed Netty and Nina towards the kitchen door, turning at the sound of another vehicle pulling up beside them. Flinty, the castle's allegedly retired housekeeper, and Anna from the village shop jumped out. 'Just bringing Bella's order for tomorrow over,' Flinty announced.

Pavel helped unload boxes of ingredients from the back of Flinty's antique Land Rover, and carried them into the castle kitchen. Bella and the new girl were sitting together, heads bent over a notebook. The new girl looked up as they came in. Pavel caught her eye. Something tugged at him. He'd felt it when she'd jumped out of the van in a panic. He'd even felt it, pricking at his irritation, when he'd caught her trying to do a runner. He wanted to wrap himself around her and tell her everything was all right.

He helped Bella and Flinty unpack the delivery into the castle pantry, and followed them back into the kitchen. Gemma was still sitting at the kitchen island. Now she looked considerably less guarded and significantly more flustered with Pavel's mum, Netty and Anna opposite her. He hoped for a fruitless second that they weren't giving the poor woman the third degree.

'Where's Richmond?' Anna asked.

'West London,' Gemma spluttered.

'North Yorkshire,' his mum replied at the same time. 'It's where that Rishi feller was MP for.'

Anna narrowed her eyes. 'She can't be from London and North Yorkshire.'

'I'm not,' Gemma offered. 'I think there's two places called Richmond.'

Nina shook her head. 'Well, that's going to cause confusion.'

Anna nodded. 'Shouldn't be allowed.'

'I was living in Reading though.'

The three women exchanged a look. 'I went to Reading once,' Netty offered. 'For a wedding. Gareth's cousin married a girl from there. It didn't last.'

The older women nodded.

'And what were you doing in Reading?' Anna was still asking the questions.

'I was working in a…' Gemma seemed to start and then stop herself. 'I was in marketing for a restaurant chain.'

83

Anna nodded. 'Marketing. That's what this place needs. Get some more people in.'

'That's the idea.'

'Good. Lots of people coming to see the Christmas lights.' Anna nodded approvingly.

Gemma's face was blank.

Anna's expression was pointed. She shot a look at Pavel's mum. 'Even if they won't be a patch on last year's.'

'The whole committee agreed on white lights,' Nina huffed.

'Not the whole committee,' Anna muttered.

Pavel thought it might be time to step in. 'I don't think Gemma's here to talk about the Christmas lights.'

Netty turned the conversation back to the newcomer. 'So what are you planning?'

'Erm… well…'

Bella jumped in. 'We were talking about Hogmanay.'

'What about it?'

'Gemma is helping us plan a big event for New Year. Hopefully put this place on the map for functions and overnight stays.'

Flinty moved around the kitchen island to join the other three women of Lowbridge village. 'What sort of event? All Americans wanting to tell you about their heritage?'

Bella sighed. 'If they're Americans who can pay then absolutely. And I'm sure you'll all be delighted to share that great sense of Highland community with them. Right?'

'Course we will, pet,' Pavel's mum agreed.

Anna shrugged. 'I suppose I can get some shaggy-cow postcards and tins of shortbread in at the shop.'

'Have you told Veronica about this?' Flinty asked.

'She knows we want to do events.'

'Aye, but Hogmanay. I mean, it was before your time but Hogmanay at the castle used to be a big thing.'

Pavel didn't remember that. 'Was it?'

'It used to be a big party for the great and good but the village as well. When did it stop?' Flinty frowned. 'It was long before Covid, wasn't it?'

'After Adam's mother went,' Anna muttered. 'The old laird lost himself for a bit, I think.'

Flinty nodded. 'Aye. It would have fallen back on Veronica to host and she…' She paused. 'I think she always struggled with that a bit.' She looked up at Bella and Gemma. 'She's still the dowager lady though. She ought to be involved.'

Pavel caught Gemma's frown. *Don't say it. Don't say it.*

'I thought Darcy was the dowager lady?'

Too late. She'd said it.

'It's complicated. The dowager is the laird's mother,' Bella explained.

'Or the old laird's widow,' Anna added.

'So Veronica was the dowager when the old laird was alive, but now he's died everyone moves up a step. So two dowagers.' Bella nudged Gemma on the arm. 'And part of your job is very much keeping them both on side. Darcy's easy.'

'And Veronica?' Gemma asked.

A short silence fell over the group.

'Well, Darcy's easy,' Bella repeated.

'So tell us about this Hogmanay thing?' Pavel's mum dragged them back to the previous topic.

'I thought you wanted to talk about the parents and toddlers?' Bella asked.

Nina patted a hand to her forehead. 'Completely slipped my mind. Yes. I hope Pav paid you for storing the play stuff, but we still need to talk about parking and…'

'Shall we go in the yellow room?' Bella led Nina away. 'I'll let Gemma bring the rest of you up to date.'

—

Fantastic. Jodie watched her boss disappear into the heart of the castle and lifted her head to meet the three pairs of eyes opposite her. To her side, Pavel was leaning on a cupboard. He didn't seem so keen to pepper her with questions but his presence was still front and centre of her mind. There was something about the way he looked at her, something far more unnerving than the constant questions about Richmond and Reading and her past career.

She smiled as brightly as she could manage. Gemma would be great at this. Gemma was charming. Gemma didn't fluster. What would Gemma do?

'Would you like a cup of tea?'

'Oh, don't bother yourself. I can do that.'

Jodie was pushed back onto her stool as Flinty started filling the kettle.

'You tell us about your big plans.'

'OK. Well, New Year's Eve.'

'Hogmanay.' All four of them corrected her.

'Quite. Yeah. Well then, anyway.' She peered at her notes. She'd tried to write down all the things Bella was saying but her only plan at the moment was to try to read the plan she was claiming to have written to get the job and somehow hope the real Gemma had made it sufficiently detailed that fake Gemma could learn how to stage a gala event from one read-through. That obviously hadn't happened quite yet though. 'The plan is for an event, which will be here, at the castle, on Hogmanay, for...' For what? 'For people to come to and to be at and...'

'What people?'

'People who buy tickets?' Jodie tried.

'So long as they're not a hundred quid a pop like that McKenzie place,' Flinty muttered.

'Do they have a Hogmanay party there?'

'Not like this,' Flinty conceded. 'Theirs is more the great and the good for McKenzie to schmooze up to. MPs and MSPs and all that. But if they did sell tickets you can bet they'd cost a pretty penny.'

Jodie wrote *price?* on her notepad.

'Give us the chapter and verse then, love.' Flinty, still the only one of the three women in front of her she actually knew, folded her arms.

'Give her a break.' That was Pavel. He was looking straight at her. Jodie looked back and caught his gaze. She found she was smiling.

Three other heads also swivelled towards Pavel, all offering much harder stares.

'It's only her first day.'

Flinty stepped back from the table and started pouring boiling water into the teapot.

'Have you even introduced yourselves?' Pavel added.

'We met last night,' Flinty replied.

'And I'm Anna. I run the village shop.' The older of the two strangers nodded a greeting. 'And this is Netty. Nina's through with Bella.' She shot a look at Pavel. 'All friends now.'

Flinty was pouring the tea. Anna was talking again. Netty was joining in too. From the hallway she could hear Dipper barking.

'So how many people at this thing?'

Jodie barely registered the question.

'And food? You'll be doing food?'

'Aye. Neeps and tatties.'

The voices were starting to swirl around her.

'And haggis.'

'No. That's Burns Night.'

'Well, obviously, but Hogmanay as well. My dad always did haggis at midnight.'

'You can't just give them haggis. They'll need something before that.'

'Especially if they're going to be dancing.'

'And drinks. Do you need a licence to do drinks?'

'Only if you're selling them, I think. Not if it's in the ticket price.'

The voices kept talking. Talking, talking, talking. So many ideas and suggestions and questions. And it was all noise. Too much noise sometimes made Jodie feel like she was being pressed on from every side.

'There's your tea, pet.' Flinty put the mug down at Jodie's side, brushing her arm.

The brief touch jolted her into life. 'Sorry. I have to go and...'

And she ran. Out of the kitchen and across the courtyard to escape towards the Dower House. As she got nearer though she changed her mind. She didn't want to be back inside those walls with the images of Lowbridge's history looking down at her. She needed to be away somewhere she could breathe. She carried on past the door to Adam's walled garden and along the wall, and then up a small winding path that climbed up the hillside. She didn't stop until her lungs were burning and the breath was rushing from her body.

She squatted down. Her heart was drumming too fast still and her breath remained jagged. She breathed as deep as she could, like her mum used to tell her to, and counted in her head. Breathe in for four, three, two, one and hold. And now breathe out for six, five, four, three, two, one. And in… Forcing herself to slow and control her exhale was supposed to bring the feeling of pressure down. She could see the grass, and her hand, and the knees of her trousers and… she looked up.

Oh.

She was on the top of the headland above the castle. The water in front of her was deep blue-grey, and vast clouds rolled across the sky above her. Across the water was a lush green island rising from the sea. It was astonishing. So much beauty it was almost overwhelming, but the sense of overwhelm was spectacular rather than horrifying. She inhaled the new feeling of comfort. Jodie was tiny. That felt good. Whatever was freaking her out didn't matter. Next to the vast sky and the deep water everything in her head was too small to matter. Jodie breathed in, long and slow and deep, without having to count.

-

Pavel started towards the door to check if Gemma was all right, just as his mother reappeared in the kitchen. 'All sorted for parents and tots.' She looked around. 'Did you scare the new girl off?'

'No!'

'No.' Anna and Flinty were in agreement.

'Maybe,' Netty conceded.

'If we did she scares very easily. We were simply trying to help,' Anna insisted. She reached across the kitchen island and pulled Gemma's pad towards her. 'Let's see what she's got down then.' She frowned as she read the first line. '"No cheese". Well, you've got to have cheese if you're doing a dinner.'

Netty nodded. 'Gotta have a cheeseboard.'

'Even on a buffet,' Nina added. 'Everyone loves a bit of cheese. Except vegans.'

'That's true.' Flinty sipped her tea thoughtfully.

'Well, they won't all be vegans.'

'Some might,' Pavel suggested. What was he doing? How did they manage to suck him in like this?

Anna turned to Netty. 'Didn't your lad go out with a vegan for a while?'

'Tanya,' Netty confirmed. 'It was fine though. You can get special cheese.'

Anna neatly crossed out *No* on Jodie's pad and wrote *Vegan* in its place. 'See. They don't know what they're about without us keeping an eye.'

'I'm going to go and make sure she's all right,' Pavel told them.

His mother looked up. 'Who?'

'Gemma. She ran out a bit suddenly.'

'She did,' Anna confirmed. 'I wondered if it was her bowels.'

'She won't want anyone coming after her if it was her bowels.'

'I don't think…' The women were back to poring over Gemma's notebook. He left them to it.

Gemma Bryant wasn't in the courtyard. She was staying, Pavel remembered, in the Dower House. She'd probably have headed back there, and his mother was right – it was entirely possible that she'd rather be on her own, but she'd been upset. He'd felt it when she'd spun out during the drive over on that very first day. Pavel couldn't put his finger on why, but he really didn't like seeing Gemma upset. There were no lights on at the Dower House. He knocked once, and then twice, but there was no answer and no sign of movement inside. He carried on up the hill instead.

Gemma was sitting on her heels at the top of the cliff, fingers twisting into the grass, staring out across the loch towards Raasay and Skye. For a second he thought he might be intruding and wondered about turning back, but he'd set out to check if she was all right. And the need to make sure pulled at him. 'Gemma,' he called softly.

She didn't turn.

'Gemma!' He raised his voice slightly. No response. He took a step closer. 'Gemma!'

Finally she jolted alert and turned towards him. 'Oh. Sorry. I didn't realise…' She shook her head. 'I didn't hear you.'

'Are you OK?'

She pulled herself up to her feet, wiping the knees of her trousers with her palms. 'Yes. Absolutely fine. I just needed…'

'It's OK. They can be a bit overwhelming if you're not used to them.' He grinned. 'Or if you are.'

'It's not them.' Gemma was still staring out across the sea. 'I get a bit…' She shook her head. 'It doesn't matter.'

'A bit what?' If he knew what it was, maybe he could help.

'Nothing.' She nodded towards the view before them. 'It's beautiful here.'

'It's my favourite place.'

'I can see why. I'd forgotten how much better I always feel by the sea. I grew up on the coast.'

'I thought you were from Richmond?'

–

Of course she was. 'Yeah. My grandparents were on the coast. I spent a lot of time there.' The best lies started from the truth. Her grandparents had lived on the coast. In the same house as her and her parents. So Jodie had, indeed, spent a lot of time there. 'Near Hastings. I don't go back much now.'

'Are they still…' He winced slightly. 'I mean, are your grandparents still with us?'

'My nan's in a home. My grandpa died a while ago.' That was true.

Pavel took a step towards her and turned to look out at the view. 'My granddad died a few years back. My dad wasn't around when I was little so Granddad was more like a dad. I miss him.'

It was easier to talk like this, both staring out to sea, not looking directly at each other. 'I miss mine too. He was fun.' She knew that was true, but it was hard now to grab hold of a specific memory. The images that ran through her head were jumbled. She could remember the house full of people and noise and animals. She could remember walking on the pebbled beach with her granddad and him pointing out the waders and the seabirds, and he never got cross when Jodie got excited and shouted too loud and made the birds scatter. 'He was kind when I found things hard.' What was she saying? Gemma wouldn't be the type to stand on clifftops and get all melancholy staring out to sea. Gemma was calm and sensible. Gemma wouldn't drag all the attention on to herself. 'I'm sorry about your granddad,' she offered.

'Thanks. He was a hard act to follow.'

'What do you mean?'

'Just that he did a lot for people.'

'Like you.' She'd only been here five minutes but it was already crystal clear that Pavel was the guy the village came to if they needed something sorted out.

'No.' Pavel frowned. 'I mean I try, but…'

Jodie told herself not to get dragged in. She wasn't part of this. She was only passing through Lowbridge. 'But what?'

'It's not enough. I just never quite live up to him, you know?'

Jodie couldn't reply. She did know. She knew exactly what it was like to know you were letting everyone around you down, and she also knew that someone like Pavel Stone who was so clearly adored and fit right into this village couldn't possibly feel that way at all.

Chapter Seven

The following morning Jodie hid at the Dower House, scouring over the Hogmanay plan real Gemma had written for her job interview. A month ago Gemma had put a bomb under Jodie's life when she'd announced she was leaving for a new job in Cornwall. She'd got her fresh start all sorted before she'd told Jodie anything was amiss, so Jodie already knew, on some level, that this had been a well-planned break-up. But now she knew Gemma had applied to Lowbridge as well. That meant it wasn't an impulsive application to the hotel in Cornwall. It wasn't an opportunity that had fallen in her lap. She'd been planning to go. She might have applied for hundreds of jobs. And Jodie had had no idea.

The realisation sat heavy in Jodie's gut. Her partner had been disengaged enough to spend weeks, or longer, preparing to make a break and hadn't given Jodie any sort of warning. Jodie could imagine why. Jodie would have made a scene, wouldn't she? The conversation would have ended with Gemma having to calm her down and pointing out that *this* was why it was so hard to talk to Jodie about things. She'd created an atmosphere where the person who loved her didn't dare talk to her about how she was feeling.

She dragged her attention back to the plan. She could see why Bella was so impressed by it. Gemma's imagined

Hogmanay Gala sounded incredible. There was a ceilidh, a full three-course meal, whisky, champagne, and options for residential guests to take part in cookery classes and wildlife walks and even a New Year's Day cold-water wild swim. It all sounded fabulous. And like it would require a lot of organisation.

Jodie started with all good intentions. She got out her notebook with a definite resolution to start a proper to-do list from which she would then tick off tasks one by one until Hogmanay was upon them and the gala was complete. What she actually did was stare at the item *Vegan Cheese* in her, now heavily annotated, notes from yesterday, spend nearly an hour googling vegan-friendly cheese alternatives, and then look at wellingtons online. She was in the Highlands. Buying wellies on her credit card wouldn't be wasteful. It would be sensible.

She reminded herself that she wasn't spending. Instead she added thirteen options for wellingtons to the hundred open tabs in her phone's browser. And she hadn't spent a penny. Jodie congratulated herself. She was definitely growing as a person now she was working on being more Gemma. She probably deserved a little reward.

Ten minutes later she had ordered a luxury pamper kit of bath products and two boxes of chocolates. But that wasn't shopping. That was a little treat because she'd done so well with the wellingtons. Thinking about it though, she probably did need the wellingtons.

She was saved from further expenditure by a knock at the door. She answered to find Veronica Lowbridge, the more frightening of the two dowager ladies of the estate, standing on her doorstep.

Veronica smiled tightly. 'Miss Bryant, may I come in?'

'OK.'

Veronica walked straight into the Dower House dining room. Jodie flitted past her and flicked her notebook closed. 'How are you settling in, dear?'

'Fine. Thank you.' Jodie was on edge. 'Of course, you used to live here, didn't you? It must be strange seeing someone else in your house. I mean, not your house, not any more. But, well, still the estate's house so sort of. And I hope you don't think I'm taking over, well, I suppose I am a bit, but not in a bad way I hope and…' Her guest made no move to interrupt or respond. Jodie could not have silence. Silence in company was almost as bad as too much noise. And it was never really silent, was it? There was always something. A hum from an overhead light or a whistle from a radiator. 'I just meant that you're always welcome. Well, of course you are. It's your estate. Well, Adam's estate, but yours too I suppose and, well… *mi casa, su casa…*'

Finally Veronica nodded. 'I see. I just came to check your National Insurance number. I'm helping Darcy set up your PAYE.'

'Right. Yeah. It's NP…' Wait. No. National Insurance numbers identified you, didn't they? How had she not thought of that? She knew her own backwards and forwards. She'd had to sign on enough times to have that down, but what would happen when Veronica put that in the computer to sort out Gemma's pay? Would lights flash and Jodie's real name appear instantly on the screen? Then what? Jodie was picturing police helicopters and a cage dropping from above to capture the villain. 'Actually hold on… Not NP… Oh. Silly. I thought I knew it.'

'It will be on your payslips from your last job,' Veronica pointed out. 'If you've got those.'

'Yeah. Of course.' Jodie gestured vaguely towards the rest of the house. 'Haven't unpacked those yet.'

'That's fine. Why don't you find it and bring it over to the office?' Veronica nodded curtly. 'As soon as possible.'

Jodie saw her visitor out, hoping her heart wasn't thumping so hard that Veronica could hear it. Could she find out the real Gemma's number somehow? Could she make one up? What would happen if she used Jodie's NI number and Gemma's name?

'Gemma!' Bella was walking towards the Dower House, passing Veronica on her way back to the castle, waving enthusiastically, jacket pulled tight around her against the Highland chill. 'I'm doing some lunch. Bit early cos students'll start turning up in an hour or so. Do you want to come over?'

Jodie nodded. What choice did she have? She couldn't refuse on the ground that she was busy trying to sort out the finer points of the fraud she was currently committing.

'So how did you get on this morning?'

'Good,' she lied. 'Mostly reviewing the plans and starting to put together a fuller to-do list.'

'Brilliant. You'll have to let me see that later.'

Jodie nodded vaguely. Later. She would definitely be able to show Bella her list at some point later.

'So this afternoon you're going to start your social media stuff?'

Right. The thing she'd hoped wouldn't come up for weeks, and then accepted was going to come up soon but not until after she'd had a sleep, was now an hour away. And she hadn't made a plan. That was fine. It was still a whole hour away. She nodded brightly. 'Yeah. Lots of ideas.'

'Brilliant. What have you got in mind?'

97

'Erm...' It was the obvious next question when you thought about it. 'We could do little mini interviews with some of the real students, I thought? Just super short. Like what they learned. And...' And what? Jodie was not a social media guru. She mostly mindlessly scrolled through reposted Reddit threads and Instagram reels of what people's toddlers ate in a day. 'And sprouts! Obviously. Loads of stuff with sprouts.'

Bella laughed. 'You really think you can make sprouts happen.'

Jodie did not think that at all. She nodded anyway. 'Why not?' There were a million reasons why not. It wasn't even clear to Jodie how talking about sprouts online would help them get through the incoming glut anyway. 'I'll film some normal stuff as well. Just bits of the class we can use for promotion.' Was that right?

'We'll have to ask their permission, but if anyone objects we can work around them. And you can film me doing demos.' Bella paused. 'Probably don't put full demos online? I guess we don't want to be giving it away free?'

Jodie followed her boss back into the castle kitchen.

'Unless that's like a loss leader sort of thing,' Bella continued. 'And you think it's worth it to give people a proper taste of what they'd get if they came on a course?'

Loss leaders? They were a thing, weren't they? That was what Diane had called it when they gave away yesterday's croissants free with large drinks at the coffee shop. 'I think on social media people always want more content, so we could probably put some demos up.' That was how Jodie scrolled anyway. Like how she never tired of watching buttered toast being cut down into toddler-appropriate triangles. Logically she should, but actually every video just made her want to watch more.

'Whatever you think. Our marketing and promotion are in your hands.'

Jodie tried not to look actively terrified at the idea.

'Lunch is just soup and bread rolls. They're not quite the right shape. I'm keeping the nicer-looking ones for them to make steak sandwiches this afternoon.'

'I'm sure it'll be great.' She watched Bella ladle soup into bowls. 'It's not sprout, is it?'

Bella grinned. 'I did think about it. Chicken and vegetable so you're safe. Using up the veggies from the garden that were about to go over, and roast chicken in the fridge from the weekend. Waste not, want not.'

Jodie shuddered at the familiar phrase from childhood. Everything in Jodie's home had been handed down, repurposed and mended a thousand times. She could picture her mother scooping leftovers into a big pan on the stove. 'Waste not, want not,' she would say, just like Bella.

'What's up?'

'Nothing. It smells great.' She started on the soup, which, like everything Bella had served her so far, was absolutely delicious. 'This is wonderful.'

'We're not paying you very much. The least I can do is feed you.'

They ate quickly and then Jodie was happy to help Bella set up for the cookery school session. She had a very clear idea of where she wanted everything and Jodie was very happy to be able to look helpful without having to demonstrate any aptitude for events planning or marketing.

Adam appeared as they were finishing up, grabbed a bowl and heated the rest of the soup in the microwave. 'You don't need me for anything this afternoon?'

Bella shook her head. 'Gemma's here if I need another pair of hands.'

'Great. I'll be in the office if anything kicks off.'

Bella laughed. 'If anything kicks off?'

'You never know. Room full of men with whisks – anything could happen.'

'Yeah. Someone could over-beat their meringue. The horror!' She kissed her fiancé quickly on the lips.

Jodie looked away. Had she and Gemma shared that sort of casual intimacy? Not recently, she thought. Gemma hadn't liked big public displays of affection anyway.

'And Pavel's coming. I think he'd be way more help than you if someone got fighty.'

Adam shook his head. 'Charming.'

The first students appeared at the kitchen door as Adam disappeared. Bella was all smiles. Jodie tried to think how Gemma would behave. Friendly but professional – a perfectly competent middle ground between Jodie's own twin tendencies to withdraw into herself or be entirely too much. Bella thrust a sheet of paper into her hand. 'Can you tick people off? It'll give you a chance to meet everyone.'

'OK.' The first two students were older men – one in his seventies at least and the other maybe fifty or sixty.

The older man nodded at her. 'They call me Strachan.'

'And me,' the younger one added.

Jodie checked her list. There they were halfway down. *Old Man Strachan* and *Young Strachan*. 'Right. I can't call you both Strachan.'

The faces she was looking into were blank. 'Everyone else does.'

'Aye. And my boy's parking up. He's Strachan too.'

Jodie rechecked the list. There he was in neatly typed letters: *Also Strachan????* The row of question marks reassured her. Even Bella had recognised the Strachan thing was getting silly at this point. A younger man came in – maybe nineteen or twenty, closely followed by Pavel Stone.

'Pav's got some labouring work for me next week, Dad, if you don't need us on the farm.'

'Vet's coming on Monday but apart from that you're fine.'

The boy looked back at Pavel. 'Tuesday to Friday OK?'

'Great. Thanks, Strach. You've helped me out there.'

The young lad disappeared into the castle to use the toilet and the older man shook Pavel's hand. 'Thanks for that. It does him the world of good to get out and off the farm for a day. And the money he brings in makes all the difference.' He turned to Bella. 'Your lad's been great holding the rent level but it's getting harder and harder, and we'll need to start adding to the flock's feed soon.'

'I know. Anything we can do to help, let us know. And take a lasagne with you when you go. For you. Not for the herd.' She turned to Pavel. 'You too.'

'And some sprouts,' Jodie added.

The men stared at her. Pavel shook his head. 'Already got a load from Hugh.'

Old Man Strachan smiled at Bella. 'We'll take the lasagne though. And there's all the lamb you can use for you next year, lass.'

'Which we will pay you a fair price for.'

The old man shook his head. 'Better than that other lot offer anyway.'

'What other lot?' Jodie asked.

Oldest Strachan frowned. 'You can tell you're new round here.'

Young Strachan clarified. 'The McKenzies. Offered to buy our lamb for their shop, paying less than the supermarkets. And he's all shouting about locally sourced everything and charging his customers a premium for it.'

Bella shook her head. 'The more he runs the price down, the more chance you'll pack it in and we'll lose the rent. One more step towards Adam having to sell.'

Old Man Strachan patted her hand. 'You won't let it come to that though, will you?'

'Not if I can help it. And especially not now Gemma's here to help.' She turned to Jodie. 'If we had a proper shop here we could sell produce from across the estate, not just our own herd. We should talk about that.'

'OK.' Great. She was starting a retail empire as well, and saving a whole community, not just one business. She felt her heart rate jump up. Breathe. Concentrate on the here and now. The final two students arrived. Two younger men. Jodie ticked them off her list, thankful for a simple, solid task.

The first of the pair told them he'd been sent by his mum because she didn't think any woman would look twice at, in her words, such a useless domestic waste of space, and the second was here after an ultimatum from his girlfriend who sounded like she was regretting her foolishness for having looked twice. They both seemed harmless enough, but were very clear that their culinary skills peaked at pouring milk over cereal.

'What about the rest of you? Does anyone cook very much already?' Bella asked brightly.

The general staring at the floor suggested that no, the group were not regulars in the kitchen. Old Man Strachan piped up first. 'My Betsy did everything in the kitchen.'

The younger Strachans both nodded. 'Nana was a great cook,' the youngest agreed.

'Since she went, we've been a bit stuck in our ways, haven't we, lads?'

'Toast and ready meals,' Middle Strachan confirmed.

'And oven chips. And sausages. Granddad fries a mean sausage.'

'What about you, Pavel?'

'It's lack of time really.'

Bella raised an eyebrow.

'And my mum still cooks for me.'

Jodie suppressed a giggle at the six-foot hunk of man's slight sheepishness about his mother still popping round with a shepherd's pie.

'And what about you, Gemma?'

Jodie realised all eyes were on her.

'I'm here to help out,' she offered.

Bella grinned. 'Sure, but you're going to do the lesson while you're here, aren't you?'

'Yes.' Bella already knew she wasn't much of a cook but Jodie also knew that the real Gemma was and had mentioned that in her phone interview. She needed to keep this pitched at the level where her interview talk could be viewed as harmless exaggeration rather than wholescale deception. 'I used to cook with my family when I was little, but I've got out of the habit, I guess.'

'Great. Well, apparently nobody's vegetarian, and I know you three love your chips, so we're going to start with a classic today. Steak sandwich and chips. And then either pavlova or Eton mess for dessert depending how neatly things turn out. How's that sound?'

'Ambitious,' Youngest Strachan joked.

'I mean, a nice piece of steak isn't a cheap thing so it'll be a shame if we ruin them, but also it's one of the most basic bits of cooking there is. Simply applying oil, heat and a bit of seasoning to a good ingredient and letting the magic happen. If you can master that it'll stand you in good stead. And it's a crowd-pleaser, isn't it? And great for a date night if you want to invite someone over. Dessert first though. Meringues take a while to cook and then they'll need to cool.'

Bella started off trying to divide the group into pairs so Jodie could float a little bit, but the three Strachans so clearly came as a set and, as they pointed out, wanted to learn together so they could cook for the whole family. 'How many Strachans are there?' Jodie whispered to Bella.

'Honestly not sure anyone knows.'

That meant that after the two latecomers had paired up, Jodie was left with Pavel. She sidled over to his station at the side of the kitchen. 'Hi again.'

'Hi.' He looked sideways at her and Jodie looked away. She felt shy around him. That wasn't like Jodie. Normally when she liked someone she was a bull in a china shop. She charged in, no thought to the consequences. That's how she'd been with Gemma – it had been lucky Gemma was open-minded enough to see past Jodie's chaos. For a while at least. The thought played itself through Jodie's head again. *Normally when she liked someone...* She liked Pavel Stone. Not just fancied or desired or lusted after. Liked.

Pavel broke the silence. 'I should probably tell you that last time I did one of these sessions I ended up keeled over on the floor.'

'What?'

'My… er… friend I was with cut herself.' He shrugged. 'Not great with blood, it turns out.'

'OK. Well, I'll try not to bleed then.'

'That's kind of a goal for everyone,' Bella called. 'Right. Let's get started.'

Meringues, it turned out, were mostly an exercise in whisking. Egg whites were whipped up into what Bella referred to as stiff peaks. She lifted her beaters out of the mix and tilted the bowl to show how the egg white held its shape. She set the group separating eggs and beating the whites. The other groups got electric beaters, but Bella approached Pavel and Jodie apologetically.

'I'm really sorry but my other electric whisk conked out when I was checking the equipment this morning.' She smiled hopefully at Pavel. 'And I thought Pavel's strong. You can totally count it as arm day.'

Pavel rolled his eyes, but set about their egg whites with an impressive gusto. Jodie satisfied herself with watching the display, as the muscles tensed slightly under his warm, tanned skin. 'I've always had a thing about forearms.'

'Sorry?'

Jodie bit her lip. She'd said that out loud, which was, unfortunately, the sort of thing she did. Her unfiltered mouth had got her into a lot of trouble over the years. It was definitely not the sort of thing Gemma would do. 'Nothing. You're doing really well.'

'Aren't you going to have a turn?' He held the whisk and bowl towards her.

'Fine.' Jodie started to mix as quickly as she could, spinning her wrist until her muscles seized up.

Bella appeared at her elbow. 'If you alternate turning from the wrist for a bit and then from the elbow you'll fatigue a lot slower.'

Jodie tried the change of technique and quickly concluded that Bella was a big fat liar. She handed the egg whites back to Pavel, barely any more beaten than when she'd started. 'Can I film you?'

'You what?'

'Can I film you? Just your arms? I mean... I don't...'

Pavel paused his whisking to stare at her for a second. 'So you really do have a thing about forearms?'

He had definitely heard that then. 'It's to put online.' That sounded worse. 'Instagram. I'm going to film the stages of the recipe and make a reel.'

Pavel was biting back a smile. 'Whatever you say.'

She recorded fifteen seconds of whisking, and put her phone down. 'See. It's for the 'gram. It's work.'

Pavel didn't reply.

'It's not for...' There were no possible other uses for a video of Pavel's forearms that didn't make her embarrassment much, much worse.

'How are you getting on?' Bella asked. Never had an interruption been so welcome.

'Fine,' Jodie answered quickly. 'We're fine.'

'She's been filming me,' Pavel added, his face entirely straight. 'She wouldn't tell me why.'

'It's for Insta...'

Finally he broke into a grin.

'You know what it's for!'

'I know you're probably not a meringue porn weirdo? Yeah.'

Eventually Pavel's clearly superior upper-body workout routine got their egg whites to the much-lauded 'stiff peak' stage and Jodie was able to tip spoons of caster sugar in, one at a time, phone carefully angled over the bowl with her free hand, while Pavel continued to mix.

Bella explained that, as they were pushing the limits time-wise, they were going to make small individual-portion meringues today, but that the recipe would work as well to make a big showstopping pavlova. They spooned their mixture into the neat circles Bella had marked up on greaseproof paper in advance.

'Low heat for a long time is key for meringues,' Bella told them. 'Don't be tempted to whack the heat up and cook them quicker. Low and slow, and then time to cool. That's why we're getting these in first and then we'll let them cool until right at the very end of the session. The good news is that in real life you can make these days before. They'll keep for a couple of weeks in a sealed tub.'

They moved on to slicing potatoes for twice-cooked chips.

'I thought three-times cooked was all the rage?' Middle-aged Strachan asked. 'All that Heston Bloomin' Thing business.'

Bella laughed. 'You don't want me getting all cheffy at you though, do you? This is proper home cooking. And parboiling and then frying is more than enough.'

Jodie made her excuses and left Pavel chopping away, and approached the Strachans' bench. 'Is it OK if I take some pictures of you? For our social media?'

Old Man Strachan grinned at her. 'For your OnlyFans is it, pet? Like Pav's big arms.'

So everyone had heard that? Brilliant.

His son and grandson almost dropped their paring knives. 'How do you know about OnlyFans, Granddad?' His face paled. 'Actually don't answer that.'

'I keep up to date. Hugh was talking about it in the shop. His nephew's lass works in forestry.'

The group were silent for a second, waiting to see how this story was going to work out.

'Has fellers paying through the nose for videos of her taking her wellies off at the end of the day. They like it if she describes how things smell.'

Youngest Strachan recovered first. 'OK. So Granddad does know what OnlyFans is.'

'One chap offered her a diamond bracelet if she'd send him her dirty socks.'

Gemma would definitely step in and get things back on track now. 'OK. Well no. This is for the cookery school social media. To promote the classes.'

Old Man Strachan nodded. 'Makes sense. There's probably not much call for old guys and potatoes.' He looked up and grinned. 'You take your pictures though, pet. Make sure you get my good side.'

The oldest Strachan was great fun. 'Actually, can I ask a few questions? Like a student testimonial sort of thing.'

'You can do what you like, love.'

'Great.' Jodie started by asking why he was taking the class.

He paused for a second. 'Well, since my wife went, I've been at a bit of a loss. In my day lads weren't expected to know their way around the kitchen. It's not right though, is it? We've all got to eat.'

Jodie agreed, followed up with some questions about what they were making and then finished with, 'And what would be your favourite thing to do with a sprout?'

Old Man Strachan winced. 'Just stick it in the bin, love. Stick 'em all in the bin. Don't even give 'em house space.'

Not exactly the ringing endorsement for sprouts she'd been searching for, but at least she had something. Jodie repositioned herself to video the next part of Bella's demonstration. After parboiling the potatoes the plan was to deep-fat-fry them. 'You can do oven chips though. For that you'd toss them in oil and spread them out on a baking tray with some salt. Or you can do other seasonings if you want fancy seasoned chips.'

The Strachans frowned as one. 'Nobody wants fancy chips,' Middle Strachan commented.

'Aye,' his son concurred. 'Chips is chips.'

Jodie moved back over to Pavel's station.

'You never know.' Bella smiled. 'You might be entertaining someone with more adventurous tastes. Like I said, this is a great menu for a date night.'

A date night? *Hey, Pavel, why don't we try this together sometime?* The thought popped unbidden into her head. No. No china-shop bull. Getting together with Pavel might be lots of fun, but she'd mess it up, and he was Bella and Adam's friend so messing up with him would mean messing everything up. Classic Jodie, when she was supposed to be being more Gemma. It would just be one dinner though, her brain pointed out. One little dinner…

'Gonna make this for the minister, ay, Pav?'

Pavel's cheeks had turned slightly pink.

'Maybe,' he muttered.

'So what's going on there, lad? Gonna make an honest woman of her?'

'What?' Pavel's face was static. Jodie scrutinised him for clues. He wasn't giving her anything. 'That's jumping the gun a bit.'

The other men laughed. 'Ah, you can't be casual with a Reverend, lad,' Oldest Strachan pointed out. 'They operate on different rules.'

'We're just good friends.'

'That's not what your mam is saying.'

'OK, everyone.' Bella clapped her hands together for attention. 'Shall we concentrate on the cookery and give Pavel a break?'

—

Oh, please, can we? Pavel sent up a silent prayer, and then caught himself. Should he be praying for the teasing about Jill to stop? She was the Big Guy's representative around here after all. He might have His own thoughts on Pavel's attitude to their relationship. Strachan was right about one thing. You couldn't be casual with a minister of the church.

They ended the session by sharing a meal of the food they'd prepared, sitting together around the table in what Adam referred to as the small dining room.

'We won't do this every week,' Bella explained. 'Mostly we'll make things for you to take home, but for this first session I thought it would be fun to eat together, because part of the joy of cooking is sharing the food with others. Food is a communal, a social experience.'

'Oh sorry!'

Pavel started slightly as Gemma's wine glass knocked against his shoulder and splashed a puddle of red wine onto his arm. She grabbed her napkin and started dabbing at the spreading red stain on his sleeve, pressing her hand against his arm.

'Sorry. I'm so clumsy,' she spluttered, and then seemed to pause. 'I mean sometimes. It was an accident. Sorry.'

'It's fine. It's just a spot.' Most of Pavel's clothes were covered in a layer of dust and grime from time on building sites. A spot of wine on his sleeve wasn't going to trouble him.

Gemma moved away, placing her glass down next to her unfinished dessert. 'I should go and see if Bella needs me to do anything.'

He watched her retreat. And it was a retreat, wasn't it? She'd left like a person who'd stood too close to something dangerous, not like a dutiful employee who had places to be. Pavel took a sip of his water, and told himself he was imagining it. Like he was imagining that his arm still tingled where she'd touched him.

Across the table, Strach stood up and swayed slightly.

'How many have you had?' Old Man Strachan asked.

'Three or four.'

'Oh.' Old Man Strachan looked from his son to his grandson and then to his own empty glass. 'We never said who was driving home, did we? Guess it's a long walk back for us then.'

Pavel checked his watch. He'd promised his mum he'd be down at the pub in time to help with closing, but that would be fine. He could make it back to the village before chucking-out time. 'Come on then,' he said. 'I'll drive you.'

Three tipsy Strachans was a problem he could fix.

–

Jodie, Bella and Adam saw the students out, all full of steak and chips and pavlovas of varying degrees of messiness. As they came back into the kitchen she retrieved her pudding from where she'd abandoned it in her haste to get away from the pure temptation of Pavel Stone's ridiculously chiselled body. That was all it was, right? The body. This feeling was pure ¬ and entirely understandable – lust.

Which was very Jodie and, in the olden days, would have been very likely to lead to some very unwise life choices. Fortunately, Gemma would never act on such a base instinct, especially not towards a man who was a) apparently not single, and b) not single WITH A VICAR. Which was the most morally superior form of not single a person could be.

'Thanks for your help today.' Bella squeezed Jodie's shoulder as she sat down next to her. 'You were great.'

Jodie shook her head. She was not, and never had been, great at any job. Sometimes she managed to fake it well enough to get by for a few weeks, but ultimately she always messed up. 'I didn't do anything.'

'No. You took loads of pictures, and you charmed the pants off the Strachans.'

Adam looked impressed. 'Wow. Old Man Strachan's a tough nut to crack.'

'He was sweet.' In her red-wine-fuelled fug, Jodie thought all the students had been lovely. 'And he recorded a great little interview for our socials.' As soon as it popped into her head, Jodie pulled out her phone and started uploading. Instagram and Facebook. 'Are we on TikTok?'

Adam shook his head. 'Feel free to set it up though.'

'Seriously, this is great. You are great.' Bella beamed. 'I'm so glad you're here.'

Jodie swallowed an unexpected lump in her throat. 'I'm glad to be here.'

After the afternoon in the kitchen and the hour spent after dinner cleaning up and clearing away, Jodie hoped that sleep would come easy when she returned to the Dower House. She felt tired in her bones and her eyelids were heavy long before she climbed into bed.

But Bella's voice was stuck in her head. They were grateful to Jodie, glad she was here, and, more than that, there were pinning their hopes for the development of Lowbridge Castle on Jodie. All their grand ideas for events, and accommodation and residential cookery schools rested on Gemma's grand plan for a Hogmanay extravaganza. Which Jodie couldn't deliver.

She lay under the weird shiny counterpane and found she had no more ways of distracting her brain from the reality of what she was doing here. Bella and Adam and Darcy weren't just her ticket out of a crisis any more. They were real people, real people who'd welcomed her into their business, and into their home. And asking herself what Gemma would do wasn't going to help her out of this mess, because Gemma would never have got herself into this position to start with.

And the vultures were already swirling. She'd got through the day without anyone else asking about her NI number, but that was a temporary reprieve. Veronica wouldn't let it go, and if she did then Jodie wouldn't be getting paid so the whole plan of earning some money to get herself back on track would be useless anyway. She was going to get found out, and all that faith that Bella had in her was going to evaporate. She'd be just another person Jodie had let down. This was an absolutely gold-standard Jodie Simpson cock-up.

By morning she was resolved. There was no choice. She couldn't do what they thought she'd promised them.

And every time she thought about running away, she saw stupid Pavel's stupid face in her mind making her promise to tell them before she tried to do a bunk. For the first time in her life she was down to breakfast early, pent up with nervous energy for what she knew she had to do next.

Bella appeared in the kitchen a few minutes after Jodie. 'You're up early. Tea?'

'Thanks.' What was she saying? She didn't like tea. 'No. Sorry. No thank you. Actually, I need to talk to you about something.'

Bella turned, frowning. 'What's up?'

'Right. Well.' She'd rehearsed a hundred forms of words for this in her head while she lay in bed staring at the ceiling through the night. None of them were good enough. 'It's a bit complicated, and I need to say first that I'm really, really...'

'Babe!' Adam's voice cut through her build-up from the hallway.

'In the kitchen!' Bella shouted back.

Adam barrelled in, laptop balanced on his arm in front of him. 'Have you seen this?' He turned the laptop towards them. It was open on Facebook. 'It's shown me this about four times already this morning.' Old Man Strachan stared out at them. Adam scrolled through the comments. 'Basically the internet is in love with him. *He's so sweet. He must have loved his wife so much. Love seeing older people still learning...* He's a megastar.'

Jodie pulled her phone out of her pocket. She'd switched it to silent while trying, and failing, to sleep, but now she saw her notifications were going crazy. It wasn't just comments on the original post. It was duets and stitches on Instagram and TikTok. She tapped to see more. Old Man Strachan declaring, 'Stick it in the bin, love. Stick 'em all in the bin,' had been repurposed for discussion of bad boyfriends, toxic bosses and multiple governments. 'Strachan's going viral,' she giggled.

Adam nodded. 'And look at this too.' He flicked to the Messenger screen from the cookery school's Facebook page. 'So many new enquiries about the cookery school off the back of it too. People want to learn to cook at the place the sprout guy goes to.'

Bella's jaw fell open. 'Oh my God.' She jumped up out of her seat and wrapped Jodie in a hug. 'Thank you.'

'I don't… I didn't…' This hadn't been planned. It was one stupid clip. It was luck. Not skill. Jodie shook her head. 'I didn't know it would do that.'

'But it did. And you did it!' Bella squealed.

She had done this, hadn't she? Jodie exhaled. None of this changed anything. She couldn't stay. She was still going to slip up at some point. National Insurance. Forgetting where she grew up. Failing entirely to know how to plan a big event. Something was going to catch her out.

'And that's not all.' Adam opened a different screen on his computer and placed it down on the island unit between them. It was open on the castle's official website. 'I know we'd only talked about it but Bel was so excited. She woke me up at about half-five and I figured once we were both awake we might as well get stuff done, so the website is officially updated.'

Finally Jodie focused properly on the screen in front of her.

Lowbridge Castle Hogmanay Gala! Book tickets

No. No. 'You're selling tickets?'

'Well, we're not exactly flush for time,' Adam pointed out. 'Only two months to go, and imagine if you did all the work and nobody came.'

'That would be awful,' Bella replied.

'And it would probably pretty much bankrupt us,' Adam added. 'I'm sure that won't happen though. In fact we already have our first two bookings.'

'What?' Jodie whispered.

'I mean, it's Nina and Anna, who must be cyberstalking us to get in that fast, but still. They bought four tickets each, so they can stalk away. Darcy's putting the basic info up on our socials right now, and sending something for the parish newsletter and Visit Highlands and Lowbridge Online. I'm sure you'll be able to make some cool videos and stuff as well though?'

The metaphorical stable door was open. Jodie's horse was miles away skipping across the mountains beyond her control.

Bella was beaming. 'It's so exciting. Seriously, this is a whole new phase for us, and I feel like it's the proper beginning of everything Lowbridge could be. Still with the cookery and the garden and all the produce at its heart but more than that. Bringing people here and...' She grinned. 'Sorry. I know how I get. I fell in love with this whole place as soon as I got here. There's this spot up past the walled garden, right up on the cliff where you can see right out to Skye and there's the sea and the clouds and everything feels possible.'

'I know where you mean.' Jodie had stood there herself. She'd felt the calm and the vastness of possibility and, for once, it hadn't terrified her.

'More enquiries for the cookery school, and a good Hogmanay would make a real difference?' Bella was looking at Adam for confirmation.

'It could.'

'So we could really stay here?'

Adam nodded. 'And keep the estate together.'

'Is it really that desperate?' Jodie asked.

'Yeah. We're still waiting for the final inheritance-tax bill from my dad, but even with a payment plan I can't see how we'll manage without selling a massive piece of land at least. And the most likely person to want to buy around here is McKenzie.'

'And he'll squeeze and squeeze and make it harder and harder for anyone else to survive.' Bella shook her head. 'Sorry. We didn't want to put all this on you.'

But it was all on Jodie.

'I know you're going to do everything you can anyway.' Jodie nodded.

'What was it you were trying to tell me?' Bella asked.

'What?'

'Before we got distracted, you were saying something?'

This was it. She could still tell them. She should still tell them. For a split second it felt as though her brain was flashing forward. She could see Adam's anger. She could see how Bella's face would fall. She could see all the hope and the trust they had splintering and shattering in a single moment. And she could feel, deep in her gut, how completely they would blame her and how entirely she would know that they were right.

Jodie shook her head. 'Nothing.'

Bella frowned. 'It was something.'

'No.' There was something else holding her back as well. Not just the fear of how they would react, something else. Something quieter, but it was there. There was another voice that said, why not try? It was mad. It was the voice that got her into trouble again and again. It was the voice Gemma had helped her to realise wasn't helping her. But maybe? Maybe she could try.

'I offered you tea and you looked like I'd offered you rat poison,' Bella continued.

There it was. There was always an exit ramp if you looked hard enough. 'Yeah. OK. It's stupid. I feel stupid, but I don't like tea.'

'What?'

'I accepted on the first day to be polite, and then I realised I'm going to be stuck politely drinking tea forever if I don't say something.'

Bella's face erupted into a loud, open laugh. 'That's priceless. Oh, mate, I'm so glad you said. Imagine you sitting here in ten years' time with us still forcing endless cuppas on you.'

Imagine you sitting here in ten years' time. Maybe she could. Maybe her name didn't matter. It was just a label after all. Maybe she could do this. Gemma had written a really good plan. Maybe if she followed it to the letter, everything would work out OK.

Chapter Eight

Pavel left his van outside the McKenzie estate visitor experience hub and looked out for Tom Barclay. Tom was a decent builder, based in Lochcarron, but the spa at McKenzie's place would be the biggest job he'd bid for, and Pavel was well aware that most of the McKenzies' building work had been done by big national outfits. Tom was going to be a minnow in amongst some big fish.

'Pav!'

Pavel waved to his friend across the car park and jogged over to join him.

'Thanks for coming.'

'No bother.'

'Now I know they're probably going to go with someone bigger, but they've got all this guff on their website about supporting the local economy so I'm going to be leaning heavily on that.'

Pavel nodded. 'Sounds good.'

'Did you take a look at the plans?'

'Aye.' Tom had sent over the architect's spec for the new spa the week before. 'Looks fancy.'

'And they say they want all top-end materials and finish.'

'Sounds pricey.'

Tom grinned. 'You get what you pay for.'

'True enough.'

Pavel had done a lot of site visits to deliver a lot of quotes in his time, and corporate jobs were often the easiest. The person you were talking to was in the same boat as you. You both had a job to do. So long as it got done, nobody was going to burst into tears about dust on the flock wallpaper.

This meeting wasn't like that. They were barely through the doors to the McKenzie estate's vigorously tartaned foyer before a purple-clad woman descended on them. 'Pavel Stone!' she squealed. 'I didn't have you on my list.'

'Fiona?' Fiona MacCellan. Of course it was. With hindsight, Pavel should have anticipated that. Despite steering clear of Facebook and muting the old school WhatsApp group, he knew that Fiona had taken a job with John McKenzie when her father had been forced to sell the family estate. 'It's Tom's meeting. I'm just the hired help.'

She glanced at Tom and then down at her tablet. 'Tom Barclay.' She held out a perfectly manicured hand. 'So how about I give you guys the grand tour and then we have a talk about the spa itself? Mr McKenzie is absolutely set on it providing the best relaxation and wellness experience in the Highlands.'

Was he now? Over the course of the next hour Pavel discovered a lot of things that Mr McKenzie was set on making the best in the Highlands. Not only the spa, but the hotel, the retail space, the four gourmet eateries.

'We're very lucky to have Mr McKenzie leading on all of this,' Fiona gushed.

'No doubt.' Pavel had lots of doubts, but with Adam unable to pay him for the coach house refurbishment he couldn't turn down potential work.

Finally they arrived at the proposed spa site. Pavel let Tom lead on the questions. The plans were ambitious. 'Nothing but the best,' was Fiona's instruction on materials and finishes.

'Does he have a budget in mind?'

'He does but he's not sharing that at the moment.' The voice that cut across Tom's question was smooth and confident. He held a hand out. 'Mr Stone.'

Pavel shook John McKenzie's hand.

'And Mr Barclay, I presume.' He turned quickly back to Pavel. 'Surprised to see you here. Thought you were well and truly Team Lowbridge.'

Pavel stumbled to find a response.

'Don't worry. I'm joking. We know there's no real competition there.'

Did he mean there was no need for the two estates to be in competition or that he didn't see Lowbridge as competition? Pavel bristled silently.

McKenzie turned his attention away. 'Could I borrow you for a moment, Miss MacCellan?'

'Excuse us.'

'New Year? I don't think so.' Fiona's voice drifted towards him. She was still deep in conversation with McKenzie.

'I'm not having them out...'

Pavel's eavesdropping was interrupted by his phone.

'Pavel!'

'Hi, Jill.'

'Look, I wanted to say sorry properly for the other night. It was a real emergency.'

'I know.' He'd never doubted it.

'I just didn't want you to think I'd got cold feet, you know? About us… going out. Cos I haven't.' She paused. Pavel didn't answer. 'Unless you have?'

Why would he have? The memory of Gemma brushing his arm at the cookery school flashed into his mind. He shut it down. That was nothing. He'd told Jill he'd take her out. Of course he would do what he'd promised. 'Course not.'

'Great. Do you want to try again then?'

They fixed a date for Saturday lunchtime. 'I'll see you then.'

Fiona was standing unobtrusively at his side when he hung up the phone. 'That must have been your nice clergy lady?'

'What?'

'Sorry. You know what gossip's like round here. My dad was in the Lowbridge shop last week. Apparently Anna told him all about it. I think she's pretty much bought a hat.'

Pavel sighed. 'We're mates. It's one date.'

Fiona's face was blank for a moment. 'It's nice that everyone approves though. That must be…' She stopped. 'Anyway, did you have any more questions about the site?'

—

If the Hogmanay Gala was definitely happening, and Gemma was definitely planning it, and Jodie was stuck being Gemma, then there was no option but to crack on. The key, she decided, was not to look at the whole seven-page event plan. The key was to tackle one thing at a time.

First up, booking musicians for the ceilidh. Actually, that was second up. First up was googling precisely what a ceilidh was and what sort of band she would need to engage to play at one. That was a simple task though – a quick check and then on to actually looking for a band.

Two hours later the thing that always seemed to happen had happened again. She'd watched parts of seventeen different ceilidh videos on YouTube, and was now, for some reason that she couldn't entirely explain, reading the Facebook page of an American bluegrass band who were available for private parties in Nashville, Chattanooga and all points in between.

Lowbridge was probably a touch too far away.

Why did Jodie always do this? That wasn't fair. She didn't always do this. When she'd been at school she'd struggled, always struggled, with coursework and deadlines but she'd done her schoolwork at the kitchen table while her mum made dinner. Somehow having someone else there, knowing they were expecting her to concentrate, quietened the distractions in Jodie's mind.

She picked up her laptop from the dining table in the Dower House and made her way into the castle. She'd intended to work in the kitchen, like she had done as a child. Bella was nearly always there, bustling around. Today the kitchen was empty. She made her way across the hallway and knocked on the door of the estate office.

'Yeah!' Darcy called out. 'Come on in.'

Jodie pushed the door open.

'You don't have to knock.'

'I wondered if I could work in here for a bit.' There was a fairly moth-eaten armchair in one corner. 'I can just perch here.'

Darcy frowned. 'You've got a whole house and we have about a hundred and eight rooms and you want to camp in my corner?'

What could she say? *I can't concentrate if there isn't a proper adult around to keep an eye on me* wasn't really an explanation. 'Sorry. Don't worry about it.' She started to back out.

'It's fine. I'm joking.' Darcy called her back in. 'I get it. When I first came here I found all of this a bit overwhelming. I was used to never being more than three feet away from another human and then I come here and you can spend half a day looking for the people who live in your house. It's unnerving. You make yourself comfortable, sweetie.'

'Thank you.'

Jodie settled into the squishy armchair and opened her laptop. Darcy's fingers were tapping away on her keyboard on the edge of Jodie's hearing. And so she got to work and quickly found three ceilidh bands within a couple of hours' drive, and sent an email through the website of the one that had the best testimonials and reviews online.

She braved another look at the real Gemma's plan. Music, people, venue and refreshment were the four headings under which she'd organised everything. And Jodie had done something about music.

People next. That meant selling tickets. That meant letting people know about the thing. A wave of overwhelm hit her. Where was she supposed to start? Jodie closed her eyes for a second. Darcy was still tap-tap-tapping away. Facebook. She could start on Facebook. She could search for groups about life in the Highlands and visiting the Highlands and share word of the event there. That would mean she would need a graphic. Suddenly she was on fire. The sounds of Darcy working a few feet away drifted into white noise and Jodie was wholly occupied creating images to share far and wide advertising the upcoming Hogmanay Gala.

She was putting the finishing touches to her image when an email pinged in.

> Thanks for getting in touch. Normally we'd be booked up for Hogmanay by now, but you're in luck. We weren't planning to play this year for family reasons but it turns out we are available so we would love to come over to Lowbridge.
> Cen 'The Ceilidh Guy'

Jodie scanned the rest of the email confirming the price and the timings she'd suggested were acceptable and replied straight away.

> That's fantastic. You're booked. Is it OK to take pictures and info from your website for our promotions?

Cen was clearly still online because his reply popped up less than a minute later.

> No problem.

She added the band's details to her graphics and set about posting them everywhere she could think of – Facebook groups, Instagram, Bluesky and Threads – and then she edited together a series of images for TikTok. Next up, the tourism websites. Over the next hour she sent details of the Lowbridge Hogmanay Gala to listing sites, travel bloggers and vloggers, the local tourist board and every Scottish community or visitor guide she could find.

Her flow was only broken by Darcy pointedly clearing her throat. 'Are you coming for dinner, sweetie?'

Jodie laughed. It was barely past lunchtime. She'd only just sat down. All she'd done was send a few emails while Darcy was at her desk. Only Darcy was standing by the door. Jodie rubbed her eyes. 'Sorry. I didn't hear you get up.'

'I got up an hour ago, honey. I've been in the kitchen with Bella.'

Jodie finally checked the time on her screen. Twenty past six.

'You were engrossed.'

'Yeah. That happens sometimes.' It used to drive Gemma up the wall – those moments when Jodie disappeared into a task and was oblivious to the world around her. 'Sorry.'

'Don't be. I saw the Instagram post. It looks like you got lots done.' She smiled. 'Come on. You can tell us about it over dinner.'

'Ragu or sprout-based?' Jodie asked, warily.

'Fingers crossed for ragu,' was the reply.

Chapter Nine

Jodie woke up full of the fervour and good intentions that had carried her through the previous afternoon. And she had a system now. She just had to find Darcy and sit at her feet until she got into the swing of things. Who was to say she wasn't an event planner? She was definitely planning an event.

She took her laptop back to the estate office after breakfast but it was empty. A Post-it note stuck to the monitor simply said *Gone riding.*

Right. Plan B. She made her way to the kitchen, where Bella was sitting at the island, head bent over a notebook. 'I've been thinking about food for the gala,' she announced almost before Jodie was through the door.

'Great.' Food and venue were the next things on Gemma's plan. 'So we'll need a caterer?'

Bella's face was instantly set like thunder.

Not a caterer then. 'Sorry. I didn't know if you'd want to...'

'I'm not having someone else cook for our first big event, and food's our, what do you call it, USP, isn't it? That's what you said in the interview.'

Jodie added USP to her mental list of Gemma words she needed to google.

'I'm thinking canapés and then a buffet. We'll need to hire in heat lamps, or find some second-hand maybe. But it'll be less serving staff than a sit-down meal, and staff costs on New Year's Eve are a biggie.'

That all made perfect sense and Jodie wouldn't have thought of any of it. 'You're the food expert,' she managed.

Bella grinned. 'I thought we might have a practice run at some of the canapé ideas this morning? So we're a well-oiled machine for the big night.'

'You know I'm not much use in the kitchen.'

'And I told you, you might have to help anyway.' Bella's tone was gentle. 'You'll be fine. I'll talk you through it.' She pushed her notebook towards Jodie. 'These are my ideas.'

'What are tattie scones?'

'They're sort of…' She stopped. 'They're a Scottish thing. Actually I asked Flinty to come and talk us both through those.'

'But what are they?'

'Sort of potatoey scones.' Bella raised her eyebrow. 'You know what tatties are. You've got neeps and tatties on your plan for the night.'

That was true. Neeps and tatties were absolutely on the plan under food. Jodie just hadn't got to googling those yet.

'I guess I didn't know you could make scones out of them.'

'Apparently you can.' Bella started towards the door. 'Come on. Flinty said if we walked over to the shop, she'd drive us back.' She paused, her face dropping slightly. 'I need to say goodbye to Adam.'

Adam was heading to Edinburgh for the rest of the week to focus on his real business – landscape gardening for wealthy city clients – which was the main thing keeping the castle afloat until Jodie worked her highly anticipated magic and transformed Lowbridge into a sought-after events destination.

Bella reappeared a minute later, rubbing her eyes with the sleeve of her jumper. 'Ridiculous. He's back on Saturday and it's not like I even see him that often when he is here. I spent half of yesterday morning wandering the grounds looking for him.' She took a deep breath in. 'Stupid. Come on then.'

They walked across the Low Bridge and along the shoreline the length of the village.

'You probably haven't had much chance to explore over here?'

Jodie shook her head. 'I drove through with Pavel when I arrived but I haven't really left the estate since.'

Along one side of them was the village, but along the other was the sea, and beyond that an island.

'So that's Raasay?' she asked. 'And Loch Aber Cross?' She'd got her phone out and pored over the map after her walk up to the top of the headland. Jodie loved maps. She loved the way the world translated down into lines and colours. It made sense of things that weren't always sensible.

'Yeah. It's not a lake loch though. It's a sea loch. Like an inlet.'

Jodie understood. 'I love being by the coast.'

'Me too.' Bella turned towards the village, pointing out the pub as they walked by. 'And then up there is the community hall. It's pretty run-down though. We keep talking about fundraising to reopen it, but so much goes on at the castle now. I think it feels less urgent than it did.' The pub nestled next to a row of tiny stone cottages. As they continued along the seashore, the row of older houses thinned out and were replaced by a small estate of newer builds. Behind the houses the hill rose up into the mountains. It was spectacular.

At the end of the estate Bella stopped and crossed the road towards the buildings. 'Village shop.'

Jodie stopped. 'Where?'

Bella laughed. 'Oh. Yeah. I've been here too long. I've sort of forgotten what regular shops look like. Come on. You'll get used to it.'

Jodie remembered very well what normal shops looked like. They had aisles and shopping trolleys and car parks. They weren't what seemed like the entire contents of a big Tesco crammed into a domestic garage. There was fresh fruit and veg at the front, and then shelves on shelves on shelves of tins and packets. 'They've got everything in here.'

'Oh, don't be silly, love.' Anna popped up from behind a display cabinet. 'We couldn't fit everything in here. Non-food stuff's out the back.'

'Out the back' didn't mean in some unseen storeroom. Following Bella through Anna's back garden they found tinfoil, bin bags, toiletries and stationery stacked up in the garden shed.

'This is bonkers.'

'Needs must, love,' Anna explained. 'There used to be a post office and a greengrocer and everything up by the pub but one by one they all went.' She shrugged. 'And then the community hall had to close so we couldn't even have the tea room there any more.'

'So you opened this?'

'Well, someone had to. Otherwise the whole place was going to die a death. People can't drive to Lochcarron every time they need milk.' She smiled. 'It wasn't my retirement plan.'

'Like you were ever going to retire.' Flinty's deadpan voice carried across the garden. 'Is Bella back there?'

'Aye.'

'Came to give her and her shopping a ride back over.'

Jodie followed the other women back into the garage shop.

'While you're here, Margaret,' Anna addressed Flinty. Logically, Flinty couldn't be her actual name, but she definitely gave off stronger *Flinty* energy than *Margaret*. 'We need to talk about Christmas decorations.'

'We've already had our instructions from Nina. White, gold and silver.'

'White.' Anna shook her head.

Flinty shrugged. 'It'll be a change.'

'Exactly.' Anna offered this single word with the same intonation as a witness in the final scene of a courtroom drama declaring that *that* was the man who killed their father.

'White is pretty,' Jodie suggested. 'Classy?'

'White is all very well,' Anna muttered. 'But we've done red and green for Christmas for the last ten years. People already have the lights.'

Flinty pursed her lips. 'And at the last meeting we agreed on something different.'

'We didn't all agree,' muttered Anna. 'And she wants to switch on on twenty-second November.'

'Yes.'

'It's too soon. We're not some big shopping mall that plays Christmas tunes from the middle of September. Decorations go up at the start of December. They always have done.' Anna folded her arms.

'I think the earlier switch-on sounds good.' Bella beamed. 'We can be festive for longer.'

'First December is quite long enough.'

'I think we thought earlier might be better. Make a bit of an event of it.' Jodie was only half listening, but she caught a change in Flinty's tone. 'And we have our own Lowbridge events expert now.'

That sounded good. She wondered who that was.

–

Jodie was still reeling slightly from that particular penny dropping as Flinty drove them back over to the castle, flinging the Land Rover round the bends with barely a glance at the road. 'It's grand that you're sorting out the Christmas light switch-on. Hopefully having someone else involved will stop Anna and Nina turning it into World War Three.'

'I thought they were friends?' Bella asked.

'They are,' Flinty confirmed. 'Very good friends. Who also both want to be Queen Bee, and you can't have two queens in a hive, can you? Don't worry, Gemma. I'm sure you'll be able to keep the peace.'

Keeping the peace sounded like a very Gemma thing to do. Her stories from work had always been about how everything was in a mess but she'd managed to sort it out. Her team bickered like schoolkids, she said, but Gemma always saved the day.

Back in the castle kitchen Jodie tried to help put the shopping away, but every time she put something on a shelf either Flinty or Bella – or, on a couple of occasions, both – slid in behind her and moved it. Eventually she gave up and perched herself on a stool at the kitchen island to wait.

Flinty's tattie-scone lesson started with the basics. 'So you start off by making your mash.'

'Great.' Bella was opening and closing cupboards, grabbing pans and utensils. She dumped a bag of potatoes in front of Jodie. 'How many do we need?'

'Couple of decent-sized ones? It's just a practice batch.'

Jodie looked at the potatoes. She wasn't sure what they were doing in front of her. Bella handed her a chopping board, knife and peeler. Oh. Right. OK then. Peeling and chopping potatoes. Jodie clapped her hands. 'I can do this. We did this on Tuesday.'

Flinty stared. 'You hadn't chopped a potato before Tuesday?'

'Of course I had.' Had she? Chips came from the chip shop and roast potatoes came out of a bag in the freezer or on the plate already on her roast dinner in the pub. Before that… 'With my mum,' she murmured.

'Good. Well, you need to chop them up and pop them to boil with a good bit of salt.'

'Parboil?' Jodie asked hopefully, testing out one of Bella's cooking words from the lesson.

The two other women exchanged a look. Flinty shook her head. 'No pet. Just boil-boil.' She turned back to Bella while Jodie did her best not to peel the skin off her knuckles. 'You need a good floury potato. Nothing too waxy.'

Bella nodded as if that was obvious. Jodie didn't even know what the difference might be. Waxy sounded like a bad thing for food.

While the potatoes bubbled they weighed out the flour. Flinty nodded approvingly at Bella. 'I mostly do it by eye, and you'll be all right doing the same once you know what you're aiming for.'

That was the part of cooking that was a mystery to Jodie. She understood recipes. She couldn't necessarily follow one, but she understood the idea. All the quantities and instructions were laid out and if you followed it to the letter you'd end up with the result you were supposed to get. That wasn't what happened when Jodie tried to follow a recipe, but that was, she'd always assumed, because Jodie was doing it wrong. The idea that there was a world beyond recipes where you could look at a potato and know how long to cook it and whether it was floury or waxy was a whole new mystery.

Flinty prodded the potatoes with the tip of a knife. 'They're going to need a good fifteen minutes. Why don't you fill me in on the big Hogmanay plans while we're waiting?'

'Yes. Why don't you?' Jodie turned towards the new voice. Veronica was standing in the doorway to the rest of the castle. 'I asked Darcy but she said you had everything in hand.'

Veronica's presence put Jodie further on edge.

'She absolutely does,' Bella grinned. 'She's a godsend.'

'I don't know about that. I'm not much help in the kitchen,' Jodie muttered.

'It's not the kitchen where we need the help.'

'So…' Veronica pulled up a seat at the island. 'I am all ears.'

Jodie could have handled this if she'd had a chance to prepare. If she'd had a chance to rehearse and get her thoughts and her words all into a neat line she could have made it sound like she knew what she was doing. She was almost nearly sure that she could. She had not had that time. 'I don't want to go on.'

Veronica didn't reply straight away. Did Jodie catch her brow creasing ever so slightly? 'Oh while I'm here, did you remember to give Darcy your National Insurance details?'

Out of the frying pan. 'I...' She what? 'Actually, I think my old payslips were electronic. On my old laptop.'

'It blew up,' Bella helpfully reminded them.

'So I heard,' Veronica murmured. 'You'll have to ask them to send a paper P45 then. If you don't have one already.'

'Right. Yeah. I didn't think of that.'

Veronica was still staring at her. If she said anything else about her NI number she was going to slip up even further, but she couldn't talk about the grand plans for Hogmanay either. Not without sounding like the fraud she was. There must be something. 'Actually, while the potatoes are boiling I thought I might try to film some more social media stuff.' Jodie glanced round the room for a safer port than the elder Dowager Lady. 'With Flinty. And Bella. And maybe...' She turned back towards Veronica and her voice tailed away. 'Well, with whoever wants to.'

'I'm tired.' Bella slumped onto a stool. 'Do Flinty first.'

'What are we doing?'

'I'm filming people's food tips for social media. To promote the cookery school.'

'And Flinty helps out sometimes with classes. She has brilliant tips.'

Great. Jodie pulled out her phone. 'Can I ask you some questions then? About cooking and food?'

'And sprouts,' Bella chipped in.

Flinty sat up a little straighter. 'I don't know.'

'You'll be great,' Jodie reassured her.

'Where do you want me? Should I get my hair done first?'

Veronica's lips pursed even further than normal.

'You look perfect,' Jodie insisted. 'And you can sit right there.' She asked Flinty about her favourite foods and her cooking tips, and closed with, 'And how do you feel about sprouts?'

'Love them,' Flinty declared. 'And I have a tip. I bet you've been told you have to cut a little cross in the bottom. Utter nonsense. Just makes them soggy. Save yourself the time.'

Jodie stopped filming. 'That's great. Maybe we could do a whole love-em-or-hate-em thing with sprouts.'

'I still don't see how that actually uses any up?' Bella questioned.

It was a fair point.

Veronica cleared her throat. 'So if you've finished with that little distraction, maybe we could get back to the Hogmanay plans?'

Of course. She wasn't going to be diverted entirely, was she? Maybe Jodie should be grateful. At least she wasn't asking about National Insurance numbers any more. 'Basically for Hogmanay there's four main things. The music, getting people to come, the venue, and the food.'

'Yes, dear. I have read the plan.'

Of course she had. 'So for music I've booked the ceilidh band. Tickets are on sale and I've shared that all over the place. And today is food. Bella's in charge of that, though.'

'And the venue?'

Jodie frowned. 'Well, here.'

'Again, you don't need to state the obvious.'

'Veronica!' Flinty's tone was exasperated but affectionate.

'Oh, don't mollycoddle the girl. She's here to do a job.'

'The ballroom,' Jodie continued.

'And what needs doing in there before however many people arrive expecting the party of the year?'

She'd put her finger on the thing Jodie had been trying her hardest to ignore. The ballroom was a mess. At best it needed the full Marie Kondo. At worst it would probably turn out the supersized cobwebs were holding the roof up and the whole thing would collapse around her ears.

The scale of the job wasn't the thing holding her back though. Well, it was, but not the scale of the whole job, more the scale of walking to the ballroom, opening the door and looking at what needed doing.

'That's next on the list,' was the best she could come up with.

Veronica nodded curtly. 'Very well. I'm sure you'll let us know if any assistance is required.' She glanced at the bubbling pot on the stove. 'Those must be nearly done.'

The group jumped to attention. Flinty prodded a potato with the tip of a knife. 'Yes. Good for mashing now.'

Bella nodded. Jodie shrugged. There was no recipe, so how on earth were you supposed to know?

Flinty strained the potatoes into a bowl, and grabbed a bottle of milk and butter from the fridge. 'You can mash them, pet.'

Jodie picked up the masher.

'Not yet. Give them a minute or two to dry out a touch. You can't do scones with a soggy mash.'

Once the potato was mashed, initially by Jodie, but very quickly by Flinty who took over with an exasperated,

'Don't just tickle it, girl,' they added flour and mixed the whole lot into a dough, which Flinty then rolled out and fried in neat triangles in a hot pan. 'Try that.'

Jodie, Bella and Veronica all took small nibbles of a finished scone. Bella nodded. 'These'll be great for canapés.'

Veronica nodded. 'They need a pinch more pepper.'

Flinty glowered at her partner. 'I don't think they…' She took a bite and sniffed. 'Maybe a touch.'

Any crowing Veronica might have allowed herself over this small victory was curtailed by Pavel's appearance at the door. 'Oh. Sorry. I didn't realise you had a crowd in.'

'We always have a crowd in,' Bella laughed.

'True. I was just checking…' Jodie caught something in his tone. Pavel was floundering. 'Oh, it doesn't matter.'

Bella frowned. 'Really?'

'Yeah. It's nothing.'

He was definitely masking something. But what?

Bella stopped him as he turned to leave. 'Are you free tomorrow?'

'I was going to…' Again Pavel hesitated. 'I can be.'

'Any chance you could spare an hour to give Gemma a hand in the ballroom?'

'What sort of hand?'

Any sort of hand you want to offer, Jodie thought.

'Just clearing it out. Bit of muscle with the bigger stuff.'

Pavel frowned. 'Not like you to need a big strong guy to help with the heavy lifting.'

'I'm doing cake decorating with a baby shower but, yeah, actually I'm not feeling a hundred per cent.'

Jodie hadn't noticed that her boss was under the weather. That was typical. Jodie didn't notice things. She didn't take care. She didn't think. 'What's wrong?'

'Nothing. Just keep having these mad waves of nausea. I threw up yesterday morning, but I was fine after.'

Veronica and Flinty exchanged a look.

'Nausea?' Veronica asked.

'In the mornings you say?' Flinty added.

'What do you…' Bella's face froze. 'Morning sickness? No. I mean, it can't. I mean…' She pulled her phone from her pocket and opened the calendar app. 'Oh.'

–

'Hello!' Forty minutes later a voice carried through the castle to the yellow room, where Jodie was squashed onto the sofa between Flinty and Darcy, while Veronica was sitting neatly on the wing-backed chair near the fire and Bella paced up and down along the full length of the room.

Pavel was standing quietly by the door, having tried to make his excuses several times and been instructed to stay right where he was by everyone from Veronica down.

Finally a body associated with the voice appeared in the doorway. The woman was in her thirties, wrapped in a bright pink coat over jeans, cherry-red Doc Martens, a head of hair that looked entirely uncontrollable and, Jodie noted, a dog collar. This must be Pavel's famous vicar. She stopped in the doorway when she saw him. 'Oh. Pav.'

And then she looked up.

'Oh. And everyone. I didn't realise this was a group activity.'

'Did you get it?'

Jill nodded, and pulled a small carrier bag from the capacious pocket of her coat.

'And not from the village shop?' Bella asked.

'Straight out of the vestry.'

Jodie was as confused as she'd ever been. 'You keep pregnancy tests in your vestry?'

'Yep. Imagine being a young lass round here who's worried. Buy one of these in the village shop, or even in Lochcarron, your dad'll know before you've even got it home. And there's not a chemist until...' She frowned.

'Portree,' Veronica offered.

'And you don't want a trip in Pav's boat if you've got morning sickness.' She grinned. 'No offence, Pav.' She looked around the room. 'Although in this case, Bel, I think most of the village might already know.'

Veronica shook her head. 'Not at all. Only family here.' She glanced across the room. 'And Miss Bryant.'

'And me and Pav,' Jill pointed out.

Veronica waved a hand to suggest that either they were family or they didn't count as being here. 'The point is, nobody here will say a word. Will they?'

A room full of adults stared at the floor and shook their heads as one.

'Very good.'

Jill looked up first and the whirlwind of brightness and big hair finally stopped with her beam of attention on Jodie. 'You must be Gemma.'

'Yes. I must.'

'Are you a hugger? I'm a hugger.'

There wasn't room to be hugged or hugger on the cramped settee but it didn't seem to deter Jill one bit, and Jodie found herself enveloped in warmth and perfume and goodwill.

'So great to have you here. Have you settled in all right? Do you need anything?'

'I'm fine.'

Veronica cleared her throat. 'Reverend, are we perhaps getting a little distracted from the main point?' She nodded towards Bella, who had managed to stop pacing but was now rooted to the spot, turning increasingly pale.

'Right. Yes. Of course.' She held the pregnancy test out to Bella. 'You just pee and wait.'

'Right.'

'Shall we wait here?' Jill asked.

Bella nodded. 'Yes. I'm not telling you though. If it's positive, I have to tell Adam first.'

'That's fine,' Jill reassured her.

Jodie glanced around the room. Flinty and Veronica looked decidedly like the idea of anyone knowing anything before them was an anathema.

Bella made it as far as the door. 'I don't think I can...' She looked around the room. 'Gemma, I know this is really outside of your job description, but can you?' She nodded towards the door. 'Moral support.'

'Oh!' Jodie pulled herself out of the sagging sofa and followed Bella into the hallway. 'Are you sure? I mean, Veronica's family and Darcy and Jill's...'

'That's why. I can't... I mean, I do not have time to be pregnant. I need someone who isn't going to gush.'

'I don't think Veronica would gush,' Jodie pointed out.

Bella's tense face cracked a smile. 'No. But... you're not a gusher, are you?'

Jodie thought she might well be a gusher, but that was Jodie. Gemma was much more contained.

They'd reached the door to what turned out to be a bathroom. 'Now stand there and don't let Poppy come in.'

'What?'

'I mean, not that you can stop her.'

'What are you talking about?'

Realisation crept over Bella's face. 'You haven't had taps randomly turn themselves on, or stuff turn up somewhere completely different from where you put it?'

Well, yes, actually she had. Just yesterday the pen Jodie had been using had completely vanished from the arm of her chair and reappeared an hour later on the floor next to the main hall coat stand. Not knowing where she'd left things was an entirely normal part of Jodie's day though. 'Maybe.'

'That's Poppy. Castle ghost.'

'Ghost?'

'She's harmless. I think she gets bored and...' She stopped talking and stared at the pregnancy test in her hand. 'I'm putting this off, aren't I?'

'Yeah.'

'Do you want to take it for me?'

Jodie shook her head.

'Right.' She ripped the cellophane off the box and read the instructions. 'One minute then.'

'Good luck. You know, for whichever you're hoping for.'

Bella took a deep breath in. 'Right.'

Jodie waited in the hallway. It couldn't have been more than fifteen seconds before Darcy joined her. 'I'm sorry. I couldn't wait.'

Jill was only a second after her. And then Flinty. Finally Veronica. 'Well, if everyone else is out here.'

Only Pavel had stayed in his place on the other side of the door. Jodie made her way back to where he was waiting. 'Everyone's on tenterhooks.'

He shrugged. 'Bella said to wait here.'

'Do you always do what you're told?'

He considered for a second, more seriously than Jodie's tone deserved. 'I try to do what's right,' he finally responded.

'That's...' What was that? 'How do you know what's right?'

'What's best for the people around you.'

'What about what's best for you?'

He didn't get the chance to answer, before Darcy yelled from the hallway. 'She's coming out.'

Jodie ran back into the corridor. 'I'm sorry. They all just appeared.'

Bella's eyes were red but she was smiling. Jodie found she was holding her breath.

'And?' Veronica asked.

Bella smiled even wider. 'I'm afraid I need to talk to Adam first.'

Jodie let out an un-Gemma like squeal of glee, that was hidden by Darcy's much louder shriek. Within seconds, Bella was enveloped in hugs and shouts and congratulations. Jodie hung back, composed herself. Gemma was here for work. It wasn't for her to get excited. This wasn't her family. This wasn't her home.

Sooner or later she would mess things up. She would do something wrong, or they would find out about the massive, great, definitely wrong thing she was already doing and everything would fall apart. She wasn't going to be here when Bella had her baby. She wasn't a part of this. She never would be. Being part of a place like this was more than Jodie would ever deserve.

Chapter Ten

Pavel offered Bella his congratulations, promised faithfully not to say anything to Adam until she'd spoken to him, and headed back out towards the coach house. He stopped by the door to check nobody was watching before going inside. Youngest Strachan, Strach, would be joining him tomorrow for a few days so they'd get into the bigger jobs and try to speed through the most urgent decorating then. Pavel figured that if Tom got the job at McKenzie's he'd be able to use the money from that to pay Strach for his time. That plan pleased him – if he was going to take money from John McKenzie he might as well redirect some of it to Lowbridge to level the playing field a touch.

He was collecting a new tap for the second bathroom from his van when Jill came out. 'Hi.'

'Hi.' He leaned against the van, holding the tap awkwardly behind him.

'What are you doing?'

'Nothing.' He angled the tap back into the van. 'Just checking I've got everything for my next job.'

'Right. So Saturday still OK?'

'Yep. Yep. That's what we said.'

'It is, isn't it?'

'Yep.'

She took a step towards him. Jill always hugged goodbye. And hello. And often several more times mid-conversation. Today she stopped, patted him tent-atively on the arm, and stepped away. 'I'll see you then then.'

He was still by the van when he heard a new set of footsteps behind him.

'Oh. Sorry.' Gemma Bryant was walking towards him, phone in one hand, Post-it note stuck to the other. 'Bella's on the phone to Adam, and Darcy and Flinty are halfway to redecorating the nursery already.'

'So you're hiding?'

She shook her head and then stopped. 'Not hiding. Just, it's a lot of noise, you know? So I thought I'd look round out here.' She nodded towards the coach house. 'See if I could get some pictures for the website. For the whole indoor fancy glamping thing.'

Pavel shook his head. 'I could do that for you.'

Gemma frowned. 'It's fine. I can do it.'

Obviously she could. 'It's just, it's a mess in there at the moment.'

'Right. Then I can see what needs clearing.'

'No.' He moved to stand in front of the coach house door. 'It's not safe.'

'I promise not to turn any lights on.'

She was right in front of him now. He was physically blocking her path. If she took another step forward they'd be touching. That thought sat in his head for a moment. Pavel stood aside, and let her squeeze past.

She made her way straight through the first door on the ground floor, and into a half-painted bathroom. She stopped. 'I didn't think they were doing any work out here.'

Pavel ran through his options. He could lie, pretend that there was some sort of stealth decorator working on the coach house that none of them knew anything about. That sounded ridiculous, and also, he realised, wasn't even a lie. Honesty then. 'They don't know I am.'

'What do you mean?'

'Adam and Bel can't afford the work, so I'm doing what I can myself. As a surprise for them.'

Jodie didn't know how to respond. 'That's... that's so kind.'

'It's fine. I like being useful.'

'That must be a good feeling.'

'What do you mean?'

'I just tend to cause problems.'

Pavel looked at her for a moment, long enough that she had to pull her gaze away. 'I don't think that's true.'

'I...' What was she thinking? She wasn't. That was the problem. She wasn't thinking like Gemma. She needed to keep her guard up, especially, it seemed, around Pavel Stone. 'I just meant you're useful with practical stuff, aren't you? What I do's more...' What was the word? Probably if she had a clearer idea of what it was Gemma supposedly did, she'd be able to describe it more clearly. 'Anyway. I should get back.'

'Don't tell them, will you?' Pavel asked. 'About the work. I don't want a big fuss, especially now they've got a baby to think about as well.'

'Won't they notice your van's still here at some point?'

Pavel nodded in acknowledgement. 'Yeah. I guess I'll get what I need out, drive it home and walk back over. I hadn't thought of that.'

She grinned. 'Clearly subterfuge is not in your blood.'

'But it is in yours?'

'What? No. I'm not... I didn't... Straight as a die, me. Is that the phrase?' It didn't sound right. A die was cubed, not a straight line. 'Dead honest and everything.' Finally she caught his expression, the little half-smile that pulled at his lips and broke the tough-guy exterior. 'Fine,' she muttered. 'I won't say anything. If there's anything I can do to help though?'

'If I need any more advice on the cloak-and-dagger stuff you're the first person I'll call.'

She headed out of the coach house and back to the castle. She definitely had an ongoing urge to lick one of his forearms, but it was getting harder to pretend that was all it was. The beautiful beefcake had the audacity to be amazingly kind as well.

But he was dating the friendly vicar, and Jodie couldn't tangle the web she was weaving any further than she already had. The only approach to Pavel Stone was to keep a distance. And the best way to do that was to fill her racing brain with something else. Instead of heading back to the yellow room, or into the kitchen – where she guessed everyone would be gathered – she made her way down the side corridor and towards the door to the ballroom.

This was the job she'd been putting off. This was her white whale. This was the broken shower curtain in her flat in Reading that she'd ignored for a year but on a grand, grand scale. The mistake she was making was to think about sorting out the ballroom like a Jodie rather than like a Gemma. Gemma would not be freaked out by the scale of the task. Gemma would power in there, get everyone on side and have the place shipshape in no time. She'd probably even sing a cheerful song while she was doing it. Jodie's imaginary Gemma was morphing day by day into a Julie Andrews character. Maybe she could skip the cheerful song.

Jodie pushed open the door. The key, her mother used to say, was to break things down into little jobs. Rather than try to eat the whole elephant you focused on just the trunk. Like with a roast dinner – carrots first, then half a Yorkshire pudding, then peas, then meat and stuffing, and then the rest of the Yorkshire pudding. One thing at a time so you knew where you were.

She looked around the ballroom. She could picture what it could be. You'd put the band at the end nearest where she was standing, and open up the double doors at the other end that led to where exactly? Although she understood the basic shape of the courtyard and the outbuildings, the precise geography of the interior of the castle still eluded Jodie.

She collected her notebook from the kitchen and drew a square to represent the basic layout of the main building around the courtyard, and marked the kitchen where she was standing, and the hallway that led to the small dining room, the main stairwell and then on towards the yellow and blue rooms and the estate office. By that point she could already see the problem. There was no way on earth her plan was going to be big enough.

That was OK. She knew exactly where to look for a suitably massive piece of paper. There was decorating stuff in the small hall. Now where on earth was the small hall? Flinty bustled into the kitchen at the right moment. 'Cup of tea, love?'

'No thank you. Erm, do you know where the small hall is?'

'Past the ballroom, same side of the corridor.'

The room, which judging from the stack of paint cans and folded ladder in the corner was the small hall, would have challenged anybody's understanding of the word small. It was smaller than the ballroom, but it was like describing the Earth as 'just a small planet'. Possibly true by comparison with the rest of the universe, but only really a useful description for people who'd grown up on Jupiter.

Alongside the discarded paint cans she did find what she was looking for – a stack of half-rolls of old wallpaper. She grabbed the cleanest-looking one and headed to the Dower House to collect her pride and joy.

Jodie was well aware that adult colouring was thoroughly 2017 as an activity but, in her defence, she'd loved a colouring book before it was trendy and she had never wavered in her affections since. Her most adored possession, the first thing she'd packed when she ran away from Reading, before clothes or toiletries or the very swishy noise-cancelling headphones Gemma had bought her for Christmas two years ago, was her colouring pencils. She stroked the tin almost reverentially and hugged it to her body to carry back to the ballroom, where she rolled the wallpaper out on the floor, secured the corners with whatever came to hand and set about to draw some more.

She started with the parts of the castle she knew, and had already sketched in miniature on her notebook. On the wallpaper there was space for the land around them. She added in Adam's garden and the Dower House to one side, the stables and pasture to the other, and the coach house and road leading up to the vehicle bridge. Then it struck her she could only draw in the ground floor of the actual buildings, so she created a box off to the side and redrew the outline of the castle to allow her to fill in the first floor.

And then she set out exploring the blank spaces on her hand-drawn map, a few rooms at a time, before coming back to her drawing and adding details, colouring in spaces to a key she created – yellow for bedrooms, blue for bathrooms, and then shades of red, pink and purple for the more 'public' parts of the castle where visitors and cookery school students came in. Then she added greenery to the outside space, before rolling up her paper, packing up her pencils and walking the short path to the walled garden. There she unfurled her work on a dry bench and filled in the locations of the greenhouses and individual beds, allowing herself to add in splashes of colour for the planting and even a slightly fanciful bumblebee hovering over the scene.

She didn't stop until it started to get dark. Bella found her as she was making her way back to the Dower House. 'Where have you been? I thought you were going to start on the ballroom.'

Damn. That was what she'd been going to do and then she'd needed to find out where the big double doors went, and then she'd thought that half an hour familiarising herself with the layout of the castle would be a good idea and then… and then she was in the walled garden adding shading to the neat little pencil outlines of countless worn red bricks. The real Gemma would have had a team of eight strong men clearing out the ballroom by now. 'I'm sorry. I got a bit distracted.'

Bella grinned. 'You weren't the only one today.'

'Oh sorry. How are you feeling?'

'Weird. Good. Weird. Having a baby right now wasn't the plan.'

'But it's good weird? What did Adam say?'

Bella pulled a face. 'I think he was a bit in shock. Him and me both though.' She finally noticed the roll of wallpaper under Jodie's arm. 'What have you been doing?'

'It's silly. I thought, you know, it can be a bit confusing learning your way around this place so I thought I'd draw myself a little map, and it sort of got out of hand.'

'Show me?'

The sun was dipping behind the islands so Jodie carried her makeshift site map into the kitchen and unfurled it in front of Darcy, Flinty and Veronica, who were already ensconced in the kitchen. 'Oh I say.' Veronica placed the glasses that hung on a slim silver chain around her neck neatly onto the bridge of her nose. 'You drew this?'

Jodie nodded. 'I know I've got a million other things to do. I'm sorry.'

Veronica inspected the drawing. 'It's excellent.'

'Oh look,' Darcy squealed. 'You've drawn Dipper in.' She pointed at the brown Labrador padding happily across the courtyard.

Jodie couldn't help but smile at the reaction. 'And you're on it.' She pointed at the stables, where Darcy was leading her horse out to the paddock.

'It's brilliant.' Darcy grinned.

'It really is.' Bella clapped her hands together. 'Could you make something like this for visitors? Like a site map. We wouldn't need the upstairs cos that's private, right?'

The other women nodded.

'I think that's a marvellous idea,' Veronica nodded.

'Don't be stupid.' Jodie slammed her mouth closed too late. She'd just called Veronica – Lady Veronica, the Dowager Baroness Lowbridge – stupid.

'I'm sorry, dear?'

'I didn't mean you're stupid. You're not stupid, but I'm not an artist. You have to get a proper designer for stuff like that.'

'I think, dear, that if Bella is in agreement and we pay you to create a drawing for us then you are very much a proper artist.'

'Oh.' Jodie dropped down onto a stool. 'I guess so.'

'It's so good.' Darcy was still in delight at the drawing of Lowbridge in front of her. 'You never said you liked art.'

Jodie brightened up. 'It was my favourite subject at school. I wanted to do it at university, but then…' Then, exams and coursework had built up and organising it all had got on top of her, and Granddad had got ill around the same time, and…

'Then you changed to business management?' Veronica suggested.

What? Of course she had. Or rather Gemma had. Gemma who would have laughed at the idea of studying something as frivolous as art. 'Yes. That's right. Seemed more sensible for careers and things.'

'You will draw a visitor map for us though, won't you?' Bella was beaming. 'It would be so great, for the cookery school packs, and if we're going to open to the public for castle tours at some point.'

'If you think I'm good enough.'

'Seriously,' Bella tapped the roll of discarded wallpaper in front of them, 'anything half as good as this would be incredible.'

'Another thing to pay you for,' Veronica added. 'Did you ever find your National Insurance number?'

Jodie shook her head. 'Slipped my mind. Sorry.'

Chapter Eleven

Pavel's mother was on her hands and knees cutting back dying growth in the front beds when he set out for the castle. 'I can do that.'

'I'm sure you can.' She narrowed her eyes. 'Are you implying I can't?'

'Not at all.' Pavel knew better than to risk suggesting any such thing.

'Is it cooking today?'

Pavel nodded.

'Good. Important skill if you're going to pin down a busy working woman like the minister.'

'Pin down?'

'Tie up.' She hesitated, suppressing a giggle. 'If you know what I mean.'

'Mum!'

'I meant, it's not like when I was growing up now, is it? You can't expect your wife to do all the cooking.'

'You didn't do all the cooking.' Pavel's dad hadn't been part of his life, but they'd lived with his grandfather who was a force of nature in the kitchen.

'Your granddad did the three things his mother taught him and nothing else. And a right performance he made of it too.'

That was fair. Granddad's days in the kitchen were marked by using every single pan and utensil in the place and then declaring that it wasn't the chef's job to wash up. 'I miss his makowiec though.'

His mum smiled at the memories of poppyseed roll at Christmas. 'Me too.'

Pavel almost swallowed back the thing he wanted to say next. 'I'm sorry I never went to Poland with him now.'

His mum sighed. 'Why didn't you?'

Honestly, Pavel wasn't sure. 'It never seemed the right time. Things needed doing here.'

That was true enough, but his granddad had talked more and more about visiting Warsaw again after he got ill, and Pavel hadn't fixed that for him. He planned to. He'd got as far as looking at flights and thinking about how and when he might fit in a break from working, but it had never felt like the right time, and, in the end, he'd left it far too late.

Pavel fell into step with the two lads from Lochcarron as he crossed the Low Bridge. 'I did chips for Becky and the bairn at the weekend,' one of them enthused. 'She said it was better than the chippy.'

Inside, the Strachans were already gathered, and Gemma was perched on a stool to one side of the room. She raised a hand in greeting and quickly dropped it again.

Today's recipe, Bella announced, was lasagne, and they were going to end up with two things to take home. A fully cooked lasagne ready to pop in the oven to reheat and a whole additional family portion of ragu that they could freeze and use at home for lasagne or bolognaise. 'And for dessert,' she continued, 'sticky toffee pudding.'

As with all Bella's meal plans this one seemed to be designed to drill a whole range of basic kitchen skills into them. Béchamel sauce for the lasagne involved making a roux. 'We did that on the practice day,' Pavel remembered.

'Was that before or after you passed out?'

'Before? I think.'

Sticky toffee pudding involved a cake batter, enhanced and enriched with dates, but, before that, they started on the lasagne by browning their mince, and then building up the flavour base for their ragus.

'Onions. Garlic. Seasoning.' Bella beamed. 'These three things are the beginning of so many wonderful things in the kitchen. Sometimes a carrot and a stick of celery. Sometimes peppers. Sometimes tomato. These are the basics. An onion is such a simple, cheap ingredient, but don't let that trick you into thinking you don't need to take care of it.'

As Pavel kept a hawklike eye on their slowly softening onion, Gemma crushed the garlic alongside him, and slid it into the pan.

'How do we know when it's done enough?' she asked.

'I have no idea.'

Bella leaned past him and peered into the pan. 'You're looking for a change of colour. Golden not blackened and a change of texture. You'll feel the onions soften as well as you see it. Like I said, it needs a bit of care and attention.'

Pavel felt Gemma's body tense alongside him as Bella moved away. 'What's up?'

'Nothing.'

'Seriously you were all happy a minute ago and now you're all black cloudy.'

'I'm not great with things that need care and attention.'

'I'm sure that's not true.'

She shook her head. 'You're very kind but you barely know me.'

A good ragu was, according to Bella, a long-term endeavour, so they layered up their lasagnes with her pre-made version, and their own béchamel sauce, before moving on to the sticky toffee pudding. Jodie had closed down the chat with her cooking partner before. Gemma would never have done that. Gemma was cool, relaxed, easy company. What would Gemma say?

'So do you like sticky toffee pudding?'

Pavel laughed. 'Who doesn't like sticky toffee pudding?'

Fair point. 'What's your favourite dessert then?'

Now he sighed. 'Actually I was thinking about that earlier. Makowiec.'

'What?'

'It's Polish. Like a poppyseed cake. My granddad used to make it at Christmas and Easter.'

'Wait!' Jodie stopped him. 'Can I film this for social media?'

Pavel shrugged.

'You should let her. It'll make you famous, lad,' Old Man Strachan called across the kitchen.

'Did you see his clip?' Jodie asked.

Pavel nodded. 'My mum showed me it. I didn't even know she knew about Instagram.'

'It went crazy on TikTok. Still is,' Jodie added.

'I'm not sure my mum's ready for TikTok. Go on then. Turn me into a food influencer.'

Jodie watched Pavel through her phone. 'So tell me about your favourite sweet?'

'Well, it's a cake really. Makowiec. Sort of a poppyseed roll that's traditional in Poland. My granddad used to make

156

it every Christmas and Easter and it always makes me think of him, and of where his family came from.'

She kept videoing just for a second at the end, focused in on Pavel's face. Then she tapped to stop. The moment he was remembering felt private somehow. 'Thanks. That's great. I didn't realise you were Polish.' Jodie almost bit her own tongue off. Was that rude or just stupid? 'I only meant, I mean I realised Pavel – it's not a Scottish name, is it? Not that you can't be Scottish and called Pavel. I just didn't think about it. I mean, I'm sorry.'

Pavel was barely suppressing a laugh. 'My family's Polish, but I was born here. So was Mum actually. My great-granddad was a pilot in World War Two and afterwards he brought his wife over and they stayed. She got pregnant in Poland so my granddad always said he was a proper Pole cos he started off over there. And he used to go back to visit grandparents and cousins and stuff. Near Warsaw.'

'What about you?'

Pavel shook his head. 'Never been.'

'Aren't you interested? It's part of your,' she shrugged, 'heritage?'

Did Pavel's jaw tense a little before he answered? 'I think I've got enough to concentrate on right here.'

Jodie waved her cooking buddy off at the end of the class and was instantly thinking about all the things she still needed to do. The ballroom remained uncleared. Tickets were selling but they needed to sell more. The Hogmanay menu still changed every time Bella thought about it. She had a band, she reminded herself. One thing was done.

Darcy was already pouring the wine when Jodie came back into the kitchen. She handed Jodie a glass. 'Come on. Enough work for today.'

She ought to refuse. She ought to insist that she still had things to do. She gratefully accepted the wine.

'I saw Anna and Nina in the village today,' Darcy told her. 'They want a meeting with you about the Christmas light switch-on.'

Jodie tried to keep the panic off her face. 'When is it?'

'Depends which of them you ask.'

Bella filled her own glass with apple juice and pulled a face. 'This is not going to be fun for nine months.'

'Sorry, hon.' Darcy sipped her own drink. 'Do you want us to hold off in solidarity?'

'Don't be silly. Just try to pretend you're not enjoying it too much.'

Darcy turned her attention back to Jodie. 'I should warn you. I think expectations are quite high for the lights switch-on. They're very excited about having a professional events planner.'

'How high?' Jodie's panic level was rapidly rising.

'They were talking about getting a special guest.'

'Like someone to dress as Santa and give out sweets?' Jodie asked.

'Erm…' Darcy didn't meet her gaze. 'Anna mentioned Elton John.'

Bella spluttered out her apple juice.

'They think Elton John is going to come to Lowbridge to turn on the Christmas lights?'

'It might be my fault,' Darcy whispered down towards the floor.

'How?'

'Anna was being a bit, you know, how she can be about some professional coming in and taking over, so I might have talked you up a bit. Just to get her onside. And while doing that I might have said that you have lots of great

158

contacts.' She looked up. 'I'm so sorry. I never said Elton John. I promise.'

'OK.'

'You don't know Elton John, do you?'

'No.'

'I'm so sorry.'

Jodie knew she ought to be furious but actually she let out a tiny giggle, and then another, and then it grew into a full, deep belly chuckle.

'You're not mad with me?'

Jodie shook her head. Obviously she was going to be a huge disappointment to Anna but in this specific instance it was, at least, not her fault. Of course she didn't know Elton John. But that was OK, because the real Gemma didn't know Elton John either. This wasn't her screw-up.

'So, putting Elton John to one side...' she started.

'Anna did say they'd be happy with Kylie,' Darcy added.

'Putting Elton and Kylie to one side, what's the deal with the lights switch-on?'

Bella shrugged. 'Don't ask me. I've only been here since the summer.'

'What?' It was only November now, and yet Bella was so entirely at home here. 'You seem like you've been here forever.'

'Really?' Bella smiled. 'I don't know. I never thought I was one for settling in one place but then I came here and...' She checked on the lasagne in the oven. 'Five more minutes. And, well I don't know, it felt like home.'

A little bit of Bella's glow seemed to be transferring to Jodie. Maybe she could pull off the same thing. If Hogmanay went OK, then who was to say she couldn't cut it as Lowbridge's events manager? The little community here seemed to be big enough, in its own weird way, to envelop anyone who washed in. Maybe she could forget the idea of moving on after a couple of months.

'Oh, while I remember,' said Darcy, 'Veronica's still on at me about sorting out your payroll. We do need your NI number ASAP.'

And that was why she couldn't just be Gemma forever. Jodie fought the rising need to crumble into a panic. 'I'm so sorry. I don't have any payslips. It was all digital at my last place.' Was that plausible?

Darcy nodded. 'And your laptop died?'

Jodie almost laughed. That one lie about the broken laptop saved her again. 'Yeah. I know it's a bit irregular but I don't suppose you could just give me cash for the first month, could you?'

Darcy glanced at Bella who nodded. 'So long as we've got a record so we can get it all right and legal as soon as.'

'Thank you. Thank you so much.' Bullet dodged, for the moment at least.

Bella opened up her laptop while they ate. 'We're up to twenty-five bookings for New Year, and three emails enquiring when accommodation booking will open.' She grinned at Jodie. 'Are we ready to go with that?'

'I just need to sort out some pictures. In the next few days though.' Pavel had told her that if she could stall the accommodation bookings just a little bit, he'd have at least one room finished in time for her to take photos for the booking page, with the rest ready for Hogmanay itself, which would allow them to charge indoor-accommodation prices rather than glorified camping. By which time, Bella and Adam's inevitable objections that he shouldn't and mustn't complete any more work without payment – payment they couldn't afford – would be too late to make a difference.

Jodie wandered back to the Dower House after dinner full of good food with a pleasing red-wine glow. For the first time since she arrived she felt strong enough to pull her own personal tablet, not the laptop Bella had lent her, from the bottom of her bag and open her email. She wasn't sure what she was expecting to see. For weeks she'd refreshed her email obsessively, waiting for Gemma to reply or make contact somehow. It was almost a shock to realise that she'd barely thought of doing that since she arrived in Lowbridge.

She swiped away sales emails and promotions and then stopped. Finally, halfway down the second page, there was a name she recognised. Not Gemma. She opened the email.

> Hello Tiger,
> I hope you're all right. I tried to phone the flat and your mobile and then I even emailed your Gemma, but I didn't get anything back there either. I hope you're all right. We know how highly you thought of her. I don't want to worry your mum but if she knew you'd gone AWOL she'd have the police round in a heartbeat.
> Let us know you're OK. And know that your mum would love it if you could make it home for Christmas.
> Lots of love
> Dad x

Jodie's parents had always been lovely to Gemma, but somehow over the time they were together, things between Jodie and her mum and dad had got a little distant. Nothing had happened, nothing she could put her finger on at least. It was as though Jodie could sense her mum and dad's nervousness about the relationship. And worse than that, she shared it. Gemma was the best thing that had ever come into Jodie's life. They all knew she could only mess it up.

She clicked reply.

> Hi,
> Sorry – I'm fine. Been very busy with new job in Scotland! I'm fine. No drama. No need to worry. Definitely no need to worry Mum.
> Work is so full-on though, I don't think I'll make Christmas but I'm well.
> Don't worry,
> Jodie xx

She read the message back and deleted the final *Don't worry*. Of course they would worry. Caring about Jodie was nothing but worry. No need to make it worse by giving them any sort of idea of the mess she was actually in right now. She could channel Gemma on that front as well. Stay calm. Don't be a cause of stress.

She blanked the tablet screen and buried it back in the depth of her suitcase. Then she turned on her work laptop instead, and opened her Lowbridge email. The first message was from the ceilidh band leader. She tapped to open and scanned the first line.

> I'm really sorry...

What? She read on.

> Double-booked... impossible to turn down... huge apologies

162

The list had gone: music, people, venue, refreshments. Music had been ticked off. Music was sorted. Whatever else was going on, Jodie knew she had one thing covered. Her mental tally of one thing done, two things in progress, and one thing that had become her great white whale tipped back to two in progress and a pair of massive angry sea mammals.

She was about to reply – possibly not a very professional Gemma-styled reply – when someone banged loudly and insistently on her front door. She opened it to find Darcy and Bella both talking at once. 'Have you heard?'

'About the band…'

'What about the band?'

Chapter Twelve

Darcy thrust her phone into Jodie's hand. It was open on Facebook, on a very prominent ad for Hogmanay at the McKenzie estate. A wonderful evening of Scottish tradition and local food, the text promised.

'Isn't that what we said?'

'It's exactly what we said,' Bella hissed.

Jodie scrolled down. Something else caught her eye. *Double-booked* indeed. She pointed at the details of the musicians. 'That's our band. Was our band. They cancelled us.'

'They stole our band?' Bella asked.

'Yeah.' Jodie scanned the advert again. It was basically the evening they had been planning but glossier and more expensive. 'You said they didn't usually do a big Hogmanay thing?'

Darcy shook her head. 'They didn't. It was just an invitation party for McKenzie's rich mates. They invited me and Alexander.' She glanced up at Jodie. 'My husband,' Darcy explained. 'McKenzie invited us for Hogmanay back when he was trying to persuade Alexander to sell.'

'So what?' Jodie read the advert again. 'Are they just doing this because we are?'

'You bet they are.' Bella spat the words out.

'But why?'

164

'Cos they want us to fail so Adam has no choice but to sell up.'

Darcy nodded. 'More than that though. It's personal because you turned him down. John McKenzie won't have liked that.'

The Hogmanay Gala was their idea – well, Gemma's idea – and they'd been doing it first. Competing was one thing, but competition was fair. There were rules to competition. This wasn't competition. It was sabotage.

'What are we going to do?' Bella looked uncharacteristically defeated.

What would Gemma do? Sensible, capable Gemma would take some time and make a new plan and think things through. Sometimes being Gemma didn't quite cut it. 'We're going to carry on regardless,' Jodie announced. 'We're not giving up because someone offered the band more money. We'll find another band. A better band. And we'll have your incredible food, and we'll make the ballroom look amazing. We won't just put on a Hogmanay party. We'll put on a party that puts theirs to absolute shame.'

'Really?' Bella didn't look sure.

Jodie didn't feel sure, but that wasn't the point. 'Really,' she insisted.

—

After Bella and Darcy had headed back to the castle, still bitching about the evils of the McKenzie dragon on their doorsteps, Jodie paced up and down the hallway of the Dower House. An hour ago everything had been going all right. She'd been starting to feel at ease at Lowbridge. She'd been starting to think she might be able to make

Hogmanay happen. She'd even wondered about sending a cheeky email to Elton John's people.

Now that was all going to be taken away from her. She had no idea how she was going to turn their Hogmanay plans around. The risk of being exposed was still there at every turn. She could only put off the payroll question for so long, and then what?

Without even realising she'd made a decision, Jodie was in the bedroom stuffing clothes and possessions back into her case. It was the best thing to do – accept her failure and move on before she let everyone down even further. She picked up her laptop. She would leave that, of course. It wasn't hers to take. And realistically she couldn't go anywhere right now. Setting off at midnight would be worse than trying to find public transport on a Sunday afternoon.

She opened the computer and started to type, not that it mattered anyway.

Hogmanay To-Dos

1. Find a new band
2. Finalise menu – with Bella
3. Make ballroom look incredible
4. Sell all the tickets

She wasn't going to do any of this, obviously. Cutting her losses was the best choice, but while she was still here, there was no harm in doodling a little.

She opened a web browser and started searching again for ceilidh bands, sending the same plea to all of them. Was anyone at all still available for Hogmanay? Or could they recommend someone who was? Lowbridge, she emphasised, had been badly let down. She threw herself on the mercy of band leaders across the West Coast, Highlands and Islands.

On to number 2 on this list. Bella had already talked her through the canapés, and the rest of the food would be incredible as well. Jodie knew that. They just had to give it to people to eat. She stopped. A hundred and fifty tickets. You couldn't simply hand food to 150 people around the kitchen island, could you? They'd need a bar, wouldn't they? And someone to staff the bar. Were you even allowed to run a paid bar or did you need a licence of some kind? Bella had talked about hiring serving platters and heat lamps, hadn't she? And they'd need crockery and glasses and servers. Jodie quickly added 2b, c, d, e, f and g to her list.

The fog in her head was starting to descend. *One thing at a time.* That was what her mother had always said. She reminded herself that it didn't even matter. She wasn't going to have to do any of this anyway. It was just a list. No danger in just making a list.

Jodie checked the time. Coming up to two a.m. Gemma would definitely go to bed now. Jodie was still too twitchy. Instead she searched for glassware hire, and catering supplies, and agencies that offered waiting staff. On the latter she quickly established that getting staff in the Highlands on New Year's Eve would cost them an arm and a leg, which she was pretty sure they did not have to spare. She checked Gemma's extensive plan for Hogmanay once again. No staffing costs listed.

Stupid Jodie. Staffing was so self-evident that the real Gemma hadn't even needed to write it down. Of course they were going to need staff. But who? And how would they pay for them?

By three a.m. the practicalities of serving food to so many people had officially defeated her. She told herself she was tired. She told herself she should definitely go to bed and in the morning she could slip away. But the itch in her brain wouldn't stop. And it was almost morning already. Maybe the problem wasn't that she needed to sleep. Maybe the problem was that she'd been cooped up in the Dower House all night. What she needed to do was move around.

The side door to the castle was open, as it always was, so far as Jodie could tell. She stepped in and along the corridor to the ballroom. She pulled the door closed behind her and switched the light on. She could see in her mind how the party itself would flow. People would arrive through the main castle doors into the hallway. For anyone who came from the village that would mark the event out as special, given how used everyone seemed to be to wandering in and out through the kitchen like they owned the place.

They'd serve welcome drinks in the hallway and then shepherd people through to the dining hall, which Jodie now knew was different to the small dining room, the dining room or the small hall. They'd have tables in the dining hall and at one end of the ballroom, all to the sides to allow the smooth flow of people through the doors, and the band and space for dancing at the other end of the ballroom. At midnight they'd open the side doors to the outside so people could watch the fireworks shooting into the night over Raasay and Skye.

The only things standing between her and this vision were several decades of accumulated grime and junk. Sod making lists. Sod breaking things down into bite-sized chunks. Sometimes it was a question of getting the bit between your teeth and powering through the big horrible job so quickly that your brain didn't get a chance to notice how overwhelming and impossible it all was.

She started at the corner nearest to the doors to the dining hall, not for any other reason than that that was where she found herself standing. There was no system to what she picked up first. There was no plan to sort things for storage, versus rubbish, versus things she would use in the ballroom. She picked up the first thing and started.

And the first thing was a chair. Or at least she thought it was a chair. When she picked it up she discovered that it was a chair back and seat, rather precariously balanced on a set of legs which, on closer inspection, didn't actually match the rest of the chair at all. She moved it to one side.

Next up was a heap of dust-covered fabric that turned out to be curtains. She hit as much of the grime away as she could to find a rather nice deep green colour. She unrolled one curtain. It was big, presumably big enough to hang at the grand, and currently undressed, windows to the ballroom. She gathered all the curtains she could find together and created a new pile.

And on she went.

–

Pavel checked his watch. Having foregone his morning workout he should make it to the castle in time to get the last few little jobs he needed to finish done before Tiny Strachan turned up to take over. Strach was delighted with the whole idea of working on the coach house in secret, out of view of the main castle.

Pavel headed into the main building before making his way over to the coach house. It was barely seven in the morning so the household would most likely still be in bed, but he wanted to check before he started bringing kit in and out. The sound of banging from the side corridor surprised him.

Burglars were all but unheard of in Lowbridge, but sheep wandering in through open patio doors were a much more present danger. Pavel readied himself to shoo a confused ewe away from the building, but opened the door instead to find a slightly wild-eyed, distinctly cobweb-covered Gemma Bryant, standing in the middle of the castle's ballroom surrounded by what looked like varying sizes of mountains of junk. 'What are you doing?'

'Tidying.'

Pavel looked around the mounds of stuff. 'Are you though?'

She stopped and slowly turned around. 'Yeah. I'm organising.'

'Right.' He moved to the middle of the room. 'What's this pile then?'

'Furniture – not broken.'

'And this one?'

'Furniture – broken but fixable.'

'OK.' He scanned the room. If you really tried to get into Gemma's mindset there was a sort of system. The mounds were broken down into furniture, textiles, smaller household items. He moved to the biggest pile of all. This one didn't seem to have an obvious theme. 'What about this lot?'

The determined expression on Gemma's face faltered slightly. 'That's things that didn't fit into any other category.'

'Right.' Despite the surface chaos, she'd clearly done loads. 'What time did you start on this?'

She shrugged. 'Couldn't sleep. What time is it now?'

'Seven-ish.'

'Shit.'

'Have you been up all night?'

She ran a slightly grimy hand through her hair. 'Maybe.'

'Maybe?'

'Definitely.' She folded her arms. 'I… sometimes I get something in my head and it like itches away at me and I can't sleep until I've dealt with it, so…'

'And the messy ballroom was itching away at you?'

She nodded. 'You don't get that?'

Pavel shook his head. 'I sleep like a baby.'

'That's a stupid phrase. Babies are terrible sleepers.' She laughed. 'You don't have any younger brothers or sisters?'

'No. How many have you got?'

'One… two.' She stopped and shook her head. 'About two.'

'About two?'

–

About two? The incredulity in Pavel's face was entirely understandable. Who didn't know how many brothers and sisters they had? Well, someone who had one and who had remembered halfway through the word that Gemma had a sister and a brother, and panicked that that might somehow have come up in her job interview. So now Pavel thought she had an uncertain number of brothers and sisters. She shook her head. 'Exactly two. I have been up all night.'

He flipped one of the non-broken chairs over and sat down. 'So I told Bella I'd help in here. What do you want doing?'

She shook her head. 'It's fine. You're busy with the coach house.'

'It's fine. Strach's over later.' He looked around. 'Do you think we need a skip?'

Jodie had no idea. She'd never cleared out a ballroom before. 'I guess. It's not my stuff though. Shouldn't we check with Bella before we get rid of things?'

Pavel nodded. 'Should check with Adam probably. Some of this could be stupidly valuable.'

'Really?' Jodie hadn't even thought of that. She'd just been chucking stuff around. 'I broke a side table.'

She clambered over the pile in front of her and pulled the tabletop from the 'broken furniture – probably not fixable' area. Pavel took it from her hand. 'I think you're all right. Not a lot of chipboard in a genuine Chippendale, I don't think.'

Doubt was rushing through Jodie's head now though. This was what she did. She waded in, didn't think and messed things up. 'We need to put it all back.'

'What?'

'Put it all back.' It was the only option. Put everything back exactly where she'd found it and resume her previous plan of just slipping away. She grabbed the broken tabletop back off Pavel.

'Gemma!'

She could feel the panic rising. She had to get ahead of it before the bright fizziness turned black and started to close around her. 'It'll be fine. We'll put it all back and then Bella or Darcy or Adam, or whoever, can come and look at it and they won't know I did all this and…'

'Gemma.' Pavel's hands were on her shoulders, softly, not gripping her, holding her gently on the spot. 'Gemma, you don't need to put it all back. This place was a mess.'

'Yeah but...' She could feel the room around her contracting, squashing her in.

'But nothing. What you are suggesting is moving a whole lot of crap into one disorganised mound out of multiple actually relatively organised mounds.' Pavel's face filled her vision. 'Breathe.'

Jodie did as she was told.

'Breathe.'

'I'm breathing.' In and out and the panic was receding. 'I'm OK.'

'OK.'

She realised he was crouching at the knees to bring his face down to her level, his face that was inches away from hers, and the hands that had been anchoring her gently back into herself were now creating pools of heat on her skin. Pavel's face and Pavel's touch were all there was.

And his lips, close. She could almost feel the taste of them, the warmth, the way that she would melt into him. She leaned towards him, just a little and...

He jumped backwards like she'd slapped him. Oh. No.

'I'd better get back to the coach house.' He was already in the doorway, holding it open as he spoke to her. 'I'll send Strach over maybe to help you later.'

'Right. Thank you.' What had she been thinking? Pavel was just being kind. He was dating a fucking vicar. This was why she had to learn to think before she acted. This was the whole thing that trying to be more Gemma was supposed to avoid. Jodie wanted the floor beneath her to open up and eat her whole.

At least that was what most of her brain wanted. But there was another part, the bad part, the incorrigible part that could no more be Gemma Bryant than it could fly to the moon, that was whispering something else. He didn't pull back straight away, it whispered. There was a moment, not even a moment, a fraction of a hint of a moment, before he'd remembered himself, where she was absolutely sure Pavel Stone was going to kiss her.

–

'You all right, Pav?' Adam Lowbridge was grabbing a bag out of the boot of his four-wheel drive outside the coach house.

Pavel nodded. 'I'm fine.' He was fine. Why wouldn't he be fine? He'd had a chat with Gemma in the ballroom and nothing else had happened at all.

'What are you doing here at this time?'

'Just checking what needs doing in the…' Not in the coach house because that wasn't officially happening. 'The ballroom. With Gemma. She's fine.'

'OK.' Adam grinned. 'I'm guessing you heard Bella's news.'

A change of subject. Pavel silently thanked the universe. 'Congratulations.' He pulled his old friend into a hug. 'Darcy knows so I think you can assume everyone knows.'

'Yeah. I wasn't supposed to be back until tonight, but I squashed all my meetings into yesterday and then drove through the night.' He shook his head a little sheepishly. 'And then I realised that was a crazy idea and ended up having to pull over somewhere off the A9 for a rest. I wanted to see her, you know?'

Pavel nodded. He didn't know though, did he? Not really. He had people he loved. So many people. He was lucky, but he didn't have that one person that he'd drive through the night just to see, to the point of exhaustion, beyond the point of good sense or sanity. A shiver ran down his spine.

'She's probably still in bed.' Adam looked up towards the first floor of the castle.

'Adam!' Bella's scream echoed across the courtyard.

'Or not.' Adam grinned as he turned to pull the woman running towards them into his arms.

Pavel stepped back. He was intruding on a private moment now. Adam and Bella had forgotten he was there the second they clapped eyes on one another.

He went back to the castle and into the kitchen. Darcy was sitting at the island, still in her dressing gown, swiping through headlines on a tablet and sipping on a mug of coffee almost the size of her head.

'Oh, I'm sorry.' He turned to leave.

'Don't be. Come in. Coffee?'

He let her fill a mug for him, and took a stool at the island. 'Everyone's up early today.'

She frowned. 'You're the first soul I've seen.'

'Bella's outside, and Adam's back.'

Darcy beamed. 'Oh, I'm so glad. I felt so bad for him with us all being here and him hearing about his baby over the phone. I haven't seen Gemma yet.'

'No,' Pavel answered quickly. Too quickly? 'I haven't either. Not this morning, I mean. Obviously I have seen her at other times.'

'Course you have, sweetie.' She looked up. 'Speak of the devil.'

Gemma stopped dead in the doorway to the kitchen. 'Hi.'

He nodded. 'Hi.'

'Thanks for before,' she added.

'Before?' Darcy asked.

'Oh, I was sorting out the ballroom and I got a bit...' She shook her head. 'Pavel was very helpful.'

'This morning?'

Pavel stared at his shoes.

'Yes,' Gemma confirmed.

He could feel Darcy's eyes boring into him without needing to look up.

'You will not believe this!' Bella marched into the kitchen, with Adam trailing behind her. The romantic reunion seemed to be firmly on hold.

'What?' Gemma asked.

'Two different sets of people just cancelled for Hogmanay.' She was waving her phone at them, as though the communication device itself was to blame. She tapped on the screen. 'Listen to this. *As we have now heard that the Lowbridge celebrations no longer offer a ceilidh or...*' She seethed out the next words: '*Professional catering, we have decided to cancel our booking.*'

'What?' This time Gemma's question was a yell. 'Who told them that?'

'Who do you think?'

Gemma's face was blank but the penny in Pavel's head dropped quicker. 'McKenzie?'

'So they stole our band and now they're taking our customers?'

'And bad-mouthing the food,' Bella added. 'They're doing a whole Hogmanay party just to spoil ours,' she added.

A bell rang in Pavel's mind. 'I heard them talking about New Year when I was over there.'

Bella's eyes narrowed. 'I can't believe you're working for them.'

'It's not even definite yet.'

'Even so...'

Pavel stared down at his feet.

'He has to earn a living.' That was Gemma. He glanced up. She didn't meet his eye.

Bella folded her arms. 'What were they saying?'

'Just something about New Year and not having someone outdo them, or outshine them. Sorry. I didn't hear much.'

Adam sighed. 'Sounds pre-planned then.'

'So what are we actually going to do?' Darcy asked.

Pavel hated to be the voice of reality but someone had to. 'What can you do?'

'I'll tell you what we can do,' Gemma answered. 'We can fucking destroy them.'

-

She looked across the room at the four faces staring back at her. 'I mean destroy might be quite a strong word. Sorry.'

'No.' Bella folded her arms. 'Destroying them sounds good to me.'

'Bel, I mean...' Adam's tone was more placatory.

His fiancée caught him in her eyeline. 'I am going to have to push an actual human out of my vagina because of you.'

He nodded. 'Destroy away, sweetheart.'

'That's what I thought.'

'So what's the plan?' Darcy asked.

Jodie and Bella stared at each other for a second. Jodie had a number of initial ideas but they all required tanks and flamethrowers. Gemma would think of something smarter than that.

Finally Bella broke the silence. 'Council of war,' she announced.

A council of war turned out to involve Jodie, squashed into the big sofa in the yellow room once again, this time between Anna and Nina, while Flinty and Jill followed Bella out towards the office, fussing over whether she was doing too much 'in her condition', and Adam and Darcy went to make tea. Veronica sat, silent and apparently serene, in front of the fireplace.

'While we've got you,' Nina started.

'Elton John,' Anna interjected before Nina could get going. 'Do you think he'll be all right with a room at the pub or will he have an entourage?'

'I don't know Elton John.'

Anna pursed her lips. 'Darcy said…'

'Sorry.'

'What about Kylie Minogue?' Anna asked.

Jodie shook her head.

'Well,' Anna frowned, 'any of the Nolan sisters?'

'Like off *Loose Women*?' Jodie could feel herself getting sucked in. 'Coleen?'

'Yes.' Anna's voice was hopeful.

'Sorry. No.'

Nina folded her arms. 'Do you think we're getting hung up on the celebrity idea?'

'Maybe a bit,' Jodie muttered.

'What if we let Miss Bryant tell us her vision for the switch-on?'

Anna harrumphed slightly. 'Go on then.'

Across the room, Veronica, who had not been joining in the conversation at all, very slightly tilted her head towards them. Gemma had no plan for a Lowbridge Christmas lights turn-on. Jodie was fully on her own now.

Both Nina and Anna were staring at her expectantly. Jodie had never been to a Christmas lights switch-on. In her mind they involved a member of Steps pressing a big red button. She added 'all of Steps' to the list of celebrities she did not know.

'Perhaps you could tell Miss Bryant a little more about the lights themselves?' Veronica spoke quietly but definitely. 'I imagine it's hard for her to come up with a plan when she's never seen the thing.'

Why hadn't Jodie thought of that?

'Well, they start at the pub, and they go right through the village to Anna's shop at the far end. Lights up outside as many houses as possible.'

'And the boats,' Anna added.

Nina nodded. 'Some of the small boats put lights round the cabins or up the masts.' She smiled. 'That's my favourite part. My father started that years ago. My Pavel organises that now. You'll have to *liaise* with him.' She turned to Anna. 'Liaise is what they call it in business, you know.'

Jodie's body and brain flashed back to a moment in the ballroom a few hours before. She could liaise vigorously with Pavel Stone.

'And this year, the lights are going to be all white,' Nina added.

'Yours might be,' Anna muttered.

'They all will be.'

'It's been red and green for years. Red and green was good enough last year. I don't see why it's not good enough now.'

'It wasn't all red and green. It was white and red at the pub, and then blue at the community hall. It looked like we'd all come out for different football teams.'

There was a noise from the seat by the fireplace that almost sounded like someone suppressing a giggle.

'Are you all right, Veronica?' Jodie asked innocently.

She was biting her lips together as she nodded. 'Absolutely fine.'

'OK. So predominantly white lights,' Jodie continued. 'Right through the village?'

'Exactly.'

'Does the castle get involved?'

Nina shook her head silently, shooting a very definite sort of look in Veronica's direction. 'I think the previous laird thought it was a bit frivolous, perhaps.'

Veronica wasn't laughing any more. 'I'm sure my son had his reasoning. However, the Lowbridge family did used to get involved.' She turned to Anna. 'Don't you remember coming to carols by candlelight here when we were children?'

'Even after you were the lady,' Anna confirmed.

'Yes.' Veronica nodded sharply.

'Why don't we do that then?' All of a sudden Jodie had a vision of the Lowbridge Christmas lights switch-on in her mind. And it didn't require a single pop star or loose woman to be lured to the middle of nowhere with the promise of a night in a room above the pub and one of Nina's pies for dinner.

'Do what?' Nina asked. 'I mean, anyone can get some random celebrity to come and press a big red button.'

'Not anyone apparently,' Anna snipped.

Jodie ignored her. 'What's special about Lowbridge is that the lights are done by the whole community, so what if we gave the whole community the chance to shine and then finished up here for carols to kick off the festive season?'

'What do you mean?' Nina asked.

Jodie could see it all. 'We make it a rolling light switch-on, so we start at the shop at the far end of the village and then it's a slow walk along the coast road and people put their lights on as we go past and then join the walk, until everyone's together and we come to the pub and then over the Low Bridge to the castle, which is lit up last, and then Jill could lead a...'

'Jill could do what?' The woman herself appeared in the doorway – Reverend Jill, who was, apparently, perfect for Pavel.

Jodie couldn't quite meet her eye. 'I was wondering if we could end the Christmas lights switch-on with carols in the chapel here.'

'Oh, that would be wonderful. The chapel hasn't been used for years, apart from...' She stopped and glanced at Veronica.

'Apart from my son's funeral. It's all right, dear. Say what you mean.'

'It would be nice to use it for something joyful?' She directed the question at Veronica, who simply nodded silently.

'So?' Jodie looked from Nina to Anna.

Nina nodded. 'I think that sounds charming. A real community event.'

Anna was less convinced. 'If the shop's first not many people will see us switch on. If they're all joining along the way. Last year we did the whole thing in front of the shop. That's where the big tree goes.'

'I thought this year we might put the big tree up by the pub,' Nina shot back.

'The big tree has been in front of the shop ever since we opened.'

'Which was only four years ago.'

'Four years is a tradition.'

'It is not. Tell her, Gemma.'

'I… er…' She glanced up and caught Veronica's gaze. The older woman gave a tiny shake of the head. 'I mean, I think that could go either way.'

'I believe many people set their lights on a timer,' Veronica cut in. 'So if the timings were worked out, it wouldn't necessarily have to stop them joining the parade from the beginning.'

Jodie noted her slow walk had been upgraded to a parade, but she did appreciate Veronica's attempt to defuse the situation. Was that twice in one conversation that she'd helped Jodie out now?

'It won't be the same without the tree.'

Jodie felt Nina's shoulders slump slightly next to her. 'I suppose if we're starting at the shop, having the main tree there would make for a nice start to the big parade.'

It was a big parade now? Great.

'We'd be the grand opening then?' Anna asked.

'Yes.' Nina clearly knew when she was beaten. 'Fine. But white lights on the tree.'

'Of course.' Anna smiled. 'Never let it be said I'm not a team player.'

If Nina was going to take issue with that claim she was robbed of the opportunity by the rest of Bella's council of war arriving. Darcy, Adam, Flinty and Bella squashed themselves into the available space.

Nina glanced at Adam. 'The laird's joining us?'

'Yep.' He nodded.

Jodie could feel the look Nina and Anna were trying to exchange around her. 'We've never had a gentleman at one of these before,' Anna noted.

'Well, it's his house and he wants to come,' Bella pointed out. 'And it's his estate we're trying to save.'

'Yes, but…' Nina shook her head. 'Normally we get on with things and tell *them* what they're supposed to be doing later.'

Flinty nodded in agreement. 'You don't want them getting ideas that they're actually in charge.' She glanced at Adam. 'Sorry, lad.'

'What if I promise to just sit quietly? You can treat me like Bella's assistant,' Adam suggested.

The women nodded as if to acknowledge that that was exactly how they viewed the laird of the manor whether he was in the room or not.

'So why have you got us all here?' Anna asked. 'It's not Ladies' Group until…' She paused, and muttered to herself, 'Meat delivery yesterday, book club last week, Netty's nail appointment tomorrow… Thursday.'

'This couldn't wait. I think the McKenzie estate are trying to sabotage us.'

'What?'

'I wouldn't put it past them.' Anna sucked the air in. 'That boy was a terror even as a child. Once shot his catapult right at Edward Woofwoof.' She turned to Jodie. 'My Hugh's previous dog.'

'OK. Well, he's moved past catapults now,' Jodie explained.

'Of course. You can't sabotage a castle with a catapult.' Anna explained this as if to a particularly slow child.

'You can if it's a big enough catapult,' Nina pointed out.

'If it's that big it's not a catapult any more, is it? It's a trebuchet.'

Jill's eyes widened. 'The McKenzie estate have bought a trebuchet?'

'No.' Jodie glanced at her employer for moral support but Bella was busy stifling giggles into her sleeve.

'Perhaps Miss Bryant would like to tell us what is going on.' Veronica once again brought things back to the point.

'So we're trying to put on this Hogmanay event, as a sort of unveiling of our event space and big publicity boost for the whole estate.'

'Oh, I love Hogmanay,' Nina murmured.

'I can't be doing with it. Me and my Hugh like to be in bed by nine thirty.'

'Oh, I bet you do,' Darcy smirked.

'I beg your pardon, young lady.'

Darcy's face was all innocence. 'I thought you'd already bought tickets though?'

'I don't want to miss anything, do I?'

Jodie's brain was reeling. How did anyone follow a conversation here? Things jumped from one place to another with nothing to grab hold of. She tried again to anchor them back in the issue with the McKenzie estate. 'They've definitely stolen our band, and we've had two different sets of people cancel their bookings.'

'That could be coincidence,' Jill suggested.

Jodie shook her head. 'The people who cancelled said they'd heard about problems at Lowbridge. Someone must have told them that.'

'Someone who'd got access to our bookings list,' Bella added.

'So like maybe they hacked into it, or...' Jodie looked at Darcy and Bella. 'I don't know. I don't think any of us has left their laptop on a train or anything?'

The other women both shook their heads.

'We'd announced the band online so it would be easy to find out who we'd booked for the ceilidh,' Darcy pointed out.

The scale of the task of getting everything ready for Hogmanay had already been too much for Jodie. Starting again whilst also trying to uncover a mole was impossible. 'I don't know. Maybe we should cancel the whole thing. Cut our losses?' She looked at Bella, who had been so kind to her and so welcoming and given her not only a job but a home and a sense that this was a place she might find some sort of peace. 'I'm sorry. I've let you down.'

'You didn't tell McKenzie our plans. You haven't let anyone down.'

The rest of the eyes of the group were suddenly all turned towards her. 'Why are you so sure she didn't?' Anna asked.

What? 'I didn't...' Jodie started to protest. 'I wouldn't. I...' What could she say? She was pulled back into a million different childhood moments, all the times her exuberance had got the better of her, all the times she'd tried to do something nice but forgotten some tiny detail and messed the whole thing up. Sometimes it felt like her whole life was explaining and apologising and pleading innocence. Maybe it didn't matter any more whether it was her fault or not. Things fell apart around Jodie Simpson. 'I didn't,' she spluttered. She stared at Bella. 'I promise.'

'Of course you didn't.' Bella gave Anna a hard look. 'I would never even have imagined that you might. You're part of Lowbridge.'

Jodie already had a mouth open to defend herself before she'd registered Bella's reply. 'You believe me?'

'Of course.'

'Oh. OK.' Jodie leaned back into the sofa, her body tingling with fight-or-flight energy with nowhere to go.

'It's a good idea though,' suggested Veronica. 'To get a person on the inside.'

'What do you mean, Grandmother?' Adam asked.

Anna and Nina both glared at him.

'Sorry. Sorry. I'll be quiet.'

'Quite right too, lad,' Flinty muttered. 'What do you mean, Veronica?'

'Obviously nobody here is a mole, but if the McKenzie estate are trying to sabotage things, we're not going to find out what they're planning next, sitting here. We need somebody over there.'

'Pavel might be working over there?' Bella suggested.

Nina shook her head. 'Most of that's not until the new year and it'll be out at the new spa site, not in the office where he can see what's going on.'

'I'm not sure Pavel is built for espionage,' Jill added.

'That's true. He gets all flustered if he has to tell a fib,' Nina conceded. 'Always has.'

Jodie could picture Pavel's honest face, him leaning towards her, just inches away from…

'Oooh.' Darcy clapped her hands together and pulled her phone from the pocket of her dark indigo jeans. 'I saw something. Wait.' She tapped and scrolled. 'Here we are. *Executive Assistant required. Major Highland Hospitality Business. Duties include…* blah, blah, blah. *Enquiries by email to Fiona MacCellan.* That's them, isn't it?'

Bella nodded and shot a look at her fiancé. 'That's Fiona that wants in your pants, isn't it?'

'She doesn't want in my pants.' He caught the look from the group. 'Sorry. Sorry. Silent observer. She doesn't though.'

'She works at the McKenzie place?' Jill asked.

'She does,' Flinty confirmed. 'It's sad. The whole place ought to be hers.' She turned to Jodie. 'It was her pa that John McKenzie bought most of the land from.'

'And now she's their visitor experience manager or some such bollocks,' Bella added.

Jodie felt, as she so frequently did, that she wasn't keeping up. 'OK, but how does her hiring an assistant help us?'

'I believe that what Darcy is suggesting is that one of us applies for the job,' Veronica explained.

Bella nodded. 'And she knows me.'

'And me, obviously,' Adam added. 'Sorry. Silent.'

'And me,' Darcy continued. 'Presumably you too, Jill?'

'Yep. And also, in case you forget, I do have a full-time gig that isn't just this place. Reporting to a higher power?' Jill tapped her dog collar.

The group nodded indulgently. 'It's nice for you to have something to do, love.' Flinty smiled.

'She knows me as well,' Nina explained. 'I taught her and her sisters in primary school.'

'Well, if I'm the only one,' Anna sighed dramatically. 'I suppose I could be persuaded to go undercover.'

For a second even Nina was reduced to silence. Flinty and Veronica exchanged a look. Eventually Bella cracked. 'I wondered if someone younger might...'

'Oh. Well, that's age discrimination straight away.' Anna folded her arms. 'I thought you were better than that.'

'Yes. Well, of course. No. It's not that. It's more...' Bella floundered and gave up.

'I mean, are you sure she doesn't know you?' Jill tried. 'A lot of people come into the shop.'

'That's not a problem, is it? I can say I've worked in a shop before. It doesn't tie me to this place.'

'No. Right.' Jill nodded. 'I don't suppose it does.'

'You don't have any experience in tourism though, do you?' Nina took a more direct approach. 'Or being an executive whatever it was?'

'How do you know I don't?'

'Because I've known you all my life and you were the receptionist at the doctors before that closed, and then you did the post office and then you retired and now you do the shop.'

'Those were all perfectly good jobs.' Anna pouted.

'They were. Not saying they weren't. But these'll be looking for tourism and hospitality and that, won't they? And, I don't know, designing the internet and things.'

'I have never designed the internet,' Anna conceded.

'And, although we appreciate the offer, you are really needed in the village, aren't you?'

The group jumped on Bella's words. 'You are,' Flinty agreed. 'That shop would fall apart without you.'

'It would,' Nina confirmed. 'And your Hugh. He wouldn't know which way was up if you were off all day.'

Everyone nodded.

'That's true,' Anna agreed. 'You know what men are like. Sorry, lad. Laird. Laird lad. It seems like I'm needed here.'

'That's OK. We understand.' Bella left a beat before she continued. 'And I think we have someone who'd be even better…' Anna shot her a look. 'I mean, just as good. And nobody at McKenzie knows her and she already has her CV all polished and up to date.'

All the eyes in the room turned to Jodie. What was happening?

'So what do you think?' Bella asked. 'Could you be our woman on the inside?'

'I...' Could she?

'It would mean you'd have to trust us to handle most of the gala planning here,' Bella added.

'And you'd have to pick a pretend name, I guess,' Darcy said. 'I mean, Gemma Bryant is on our website now. No picture yet. But you'd have to pick a name and be a whole other person. That would freak me right out.'

'So what do you say? Do you think you could handle that?' Bella asked.

Everyone was staring at her. So the suggestion was that Jodie wouldn't be here pretending to be Gemma Bryant and pretending to be an experienced events planner. She'd be somewhere else, pretending to be a brand-new executive assistant. And she'd be pretending to be a whole third person. No. Wait. It didn't have to be that complicated. 'Jodie,' she announced.

'What?'

She smiled as broad and confident as she could manage. 'Hi,' she said. 'I'm Jodie Simpson and I'd love to be your new assistant.'

'Did you get the email?'

Jodie was sitting at the kitchen island in the main castle after the rest of Bella's council of war had left and Adam had retreated to his garden.

Jodie nodded. They'd been entirely unsuspicious about her request that they email her CV over to her because of her unfortunately spontaneously exploding laptop. And now Bella and Darcy were gathered to help her tweak and amend her CV to make sure Jodie, pretending to be Gemma, pretending to be Jodie, was perfect executive assistant material.

First she had to get through reading the real Gemma's CV without looking like she had no idea what it was going to say.

She scanned through the personal details, changing Gemma's name to her own. 'I can't say I live in Reading, can I?' She glanced again at the job ad open on her phone. 'They're not offering accommodation, so they'll be expecting local candidates.'

'You can't put here though.' Bella frowned. 'We'll have to use someone's address from the village.'

'Nina's?' Darcy suggested. 'She takes in lodgers sometimes since her dad died.'

'OK. I'll text her and check it's OK, but put it for now.'

Jodie typed in the address Darcy dictated to her. 'Why would I be staying there?'

'I dunno.' Bella shrugged. 'Maybe you're shagging Pav.'

Darcy giggled. 'Someone ought to. It's a damn waste.'

'I thought he was with Jill,' Jodie asked as casually as she could.

Bella and Darcy exchanged a look. 'I don't think he's with *with* her.'

'Not yet anyway.'

Noted.

'I think we should keep your work experience as close to the truth as possible,' Bella suggested. 'Less chance of you slipping up that way.'

That was sensible. Only an idiot or a sociopath would get a job based on a CV they weren't familiar with.

Gemma's first listed job was as *Visitor Host* at Reading Abbey during her degree. Jodie paused. Gemma had never mentioned that. She'd mentioned volunteering to pick up litter there a couple of weekends.

Jodie read on. *Retail Supervision Associate*. She'd been a shop assistant, hadn't she? She scanned down to the most recent employment. *Marketing Executive* for Pizza Now. Jodie cursed herself again for not paying more attention to Gemma's work, but Jodie could have sworn that Gemma's boss – a slightly too flash chap called Evan – had been the executive.

The penny that was dangling in the air of her brain started to drop. Had Gemma padded her CV a little? Jodie looked through the employment history again. Not a little. Quite a lot. That was Gemma though, wasn't it? And it wasn't a lie, not in the way Jodie had lied. It was confidence. It was Gemma giving herself credit for the work she'd actually done. She'd always said her boss was useless and she carried him. Surely she deserved the rewards.

'I'm wondering if we should change marketing exec in your last job to assistant?' Bella asked. 'So it looks less weird that you're applying to be an assistant now? If that's OK. I mean I don't want to do you down.'

'I agree.' Always better, like Darcy said, to keep your lies as close to the truth as possible.

-

She got an interview. Or rather Gemma pretending to be Jodie got an interview. Of course she did. Gemma was the perfect candidate, just made slightly less high-flying by Jodie's interventions. Which created a new problem. Jodie's lack of corporate executive clothes had gone unnoticed so far in the laid-back atmosphere at Lowbridge

Castle. Now she had to explain having nothing to wear that was interview appropriate.

'I lost a lot of weight, you see,' she offered. 'So I didn't bring any of my old work suits cos they didn't really fit any more, and I haven't really needed anything like that here.'

'That's fine, sweetie. I have all the clothes.' Darcy beamed. 'We'll find something perfect.' She looked down at Jodie from her impressively model-esque height. 'And then we'll ask Flinty to take it up.'

Darcy really did have all the clothes. Jodie pulled a black suit from the wardrobe. 'What about this?'

Darcy's usually irrepressible smile faltered for a second. 'What's wrong?'

'Nothing. It's a nice suit. I wore it for Alexander – my husband's – memorial. I haven't…' She shook her head. 'I haven't since.'

Jodie cursed herself in her head, and slid the suit awkwardly back into the wardrobe. 'I'm sorry.'

'It's all right.'

'What was he like?' Was it rude to ask that? Darcy hadn't seemed to mind before. Maybe it was ruder not to ask and look like you didn't care.

'Oh. Gosh. Nobody ever asks me that any more. He was just the laird to people here. They all knew what he was.'

'But *who* was he?'

'Oh, bless you.' Darcy sat down on the end of the bed. 'He was my Alexander. We were something of an odd couple to most people. He was very studious. Quiet. A little bit obsessive even. Always said he got on better with nature than people. Sometimes I think I was as much his interpreter as his wife.'

'You make him sound difficult?' Jodie wished she could swallow the comment back. 'I'm sorry. I didn't mean…'

'No. You're right. I think lots of people did find him difficult. Even Adam sometimes. But not me. For me he was the easiest person in the world.' She dabbed her eye delicately with a fingertip. 'I wonder if that's what love does. Makes the most complicated things in the world utterly simple.' She took a deep breath in. 'Thank you for asking, Gemma. Normally people don't. I get it. They're embarrassed and they don't want to upset me, but it means I never get to talk about him. And I loved him so much. I think it's good to remember him with someone.'

–

Pavel was preparing for his date with Jill for the second time. He'd put two different shirts on and taken them off again. And then put a T-shirt on because it was lunch with Jill. And then changed back to a shirt because it wasn't just lunch with Jill. It was a date with Jill, and that made everything feel so much more complicated.

Finally time made the decision for him. If he didn't leave soon, he'd miss the tide to take the boat over and driving down to the bridge would make him even later. Black T-shirt under open denim shirt won the day by default. He slung his trainers into a backpack, pulled his wellies on and hurried down to the shoreline. Taking the boat was always his favourite way to get to Raasay or Skye. The drive over the bridge was still beautiful, but going over the water was something else. Even close in to shore the sense of scale and being alone in nature instantly gave Pavel a frisson of excitement and possibility, as though life was suddenly big and uncertain and could be anything at all he chose it to be.

As he drew nearer to Portree itself he radioed ahead for permission to moor and was directed to a spot on the old berth. Then it was a short walk up into town. He saw Jill standing outside the pub they'd arranged to meet at. She was looking from side to side, her big blonde curls swinging as she moved her head. He held up a hand in greeting as he approached.

'Hi.'

'Hi.' She laughed slightly and then stopped too abruptly. 'I didn't know whether to go in. I don't know why. I'd normally go in, and then I thought maybe this was different and I should… I don't know.'

He wasn't sure if her nerves were making his better or worse. 'Shall we go in now then? Or, you know, we could go somewhere else if you prefer? There's a seafood place down…'

'This is fine.'

'Right. Good.'

They went into the pub, which was unexpectedly quiet for a weekend.

'Drink? What do you want? You can have wine. Or a beer. Or whatever you want.' Pavel willed his mouth to stop talking. He'd bought Jill hundreds of drinks and he'd never turned into a wreck doing it before.

'Wine. White. Just a small one. I drove over.'

'OK.'

'I mean, I know you would have given me a ride back, but I didn't want to assume. Or for it to look like I was assuming I'd come back with you. I don't mean back with you, like back with you. But…' She took a huge breath in. 'A small wine.'

Pavel headed to the bar. It was possible that he was actually in hell.

It was possible Jodie was actually in hell. The reception area for the McKenzie estate's corporate office was so covered in tartan that Jodie could still see the lines and squares when she closed her eyes. She feared she might never stop seeing them. That garish purple, blue and brown pattern was going to haunt her dreams.

Adam had dropped her at the end of the access road, not wanting to drive further into enemy territory and risk being spotted, which meant she'd walked a good kilometre in the very stylish, but also massively too big, boots she'd borrowed from Darcy. Skirts could be taken up. Shoes were somewhat harder to shrink.

'Miss Simpson?' The woman calling her name was perfectly made-up, perfectly manicured and perfectly dressed in corporate purple. She held out a hand to shake. 'Come on through.'

The décor inside the office was slightly more neutral but still leaned heavily on the purples.

'Have a seat.' The woman gestured towards two low chairs set around a tinted glass coffee table. 'I'm Fiona MacCellan. So today is just a few informal questions to find out about you. I'm going to be asking everyone the same questions so it's fair. You don't mind if I take a few notes, do you?'

Jodie nodded. 'That's fine.'

'So what attracted you to this position, Jodie?'

She'd rehearsed this answer with Bella at some length and agreed that honesty was absolutely not the best policy so rejected 'I want to spy on you on behalf of your main rival with the bonus of you paying my salary while I do that.' Instead she arranged her hands neatly on her lap and smiled in a way she hoped was approachable and warm. 'I love this part of the world, so being part of an organisation so committed to the Highlands and building a modern business without losing the traditional charm appeals.' She also remembered Adam's sole contribution to the interview prep. Fiona was lovely, he said – despite the raised eyebrow from his fiancée – but also a little insecure. She'd respond well to flattery, he thought. 'And also,' Jodie continued, 'it would be so exciting to work for such a well-respected female executive. I'm so impressed with everything you've achieved here. I'm sure I could learn so much from you.'

Was that too much? Fiona's instant smile suggested not. 'Oh, you're very kind. Of course, John, Mr McKenzie, is really the power behind all this. I just help out where I can.'

Jodie's hackles rose slightly. Another of her mother's regular snippets of life advice rang in her head. Men who liked to be seen as the source of power while the women around them ran around and did the work were not to be trusted. You were much better off with a laird who was happy to be told to butt out and shut up.

'We are in quite a remote area here. So I'm asking everyone as well, how they feel about that? It can be a bit hard if you're not used to it.'

Jodie smoothly trotted out her practised soliloquy in praise of the Highlands and the wildlife and the undiscovered beauty. 'Honestly, I don't know why anyone who came here would ever leave.'

'Can I ask,' Fiona put down her pen, 'not officially, but what brought you up here?'

'Honestly,' partly honestly, 'I had a relationship end and I needed to get away so I took a break from work and set off travelling. My plan was to head overseas when my passport came through, but then I landed here and I don't know.' Jodie could feel the beginning of a tear stinging the corner of her eye. 'I felt at home.' The tears were still threatening to fall and something about what she'd said wasn't quite right. 'Not at home exactly. Maybe I felt more myself.'

She blinked hard against the tears.

Fiona seemed oblivious. 'I know exactly what you mean. That's why I didn't leave when...' She shook her head. 'I just couldn't be anywhere else.'

The door Jodie had come in through swung open and a tall, slightly older man in a tweed jacket over blue jeans came into the room.

Fiona jumped to her feet. 'John! This is Jodie Simpson. She's here about the assistant job.'

Jodie stood and accepted his proffered hand. She couldn't shake the feeling that she was being assessed, and not for her professional attributes. This guy was checking her out. She pulled her hand away from his fractionally too tight grip.

'Lovely to meet you, Jodie. I hope we meet again.' He nodded at Fiona and marched out of the room.

The rest of the interview was unlike any interview Jodie had ever had before. Fiona barely made a note and chatted apparently randomly, rather than asking her the bland questions from the printed list Jodie could clearly see on the table. 'Is there anything you wanted to ask me?' Fiona asked.

Jodie had prepared her question for this part. 'I guess what would I be working on? Are there any big projects coming up?'

Fiona nodded. 'Keen to hit the ground running? That's the attitude John loves. Well, assuming you could start quite soon…'

'Straight away,' Jodie assured her.

'We're busy getting ready for Christmas in the retail areas and event spaces and then it's Hogmanay. We're doing a huge multi-layered event experience.'

A what now?

'It's the first event of its kind in the area. I have no idea why nobody else had thought of doing something.' She beamed. 'John is such a visionary.'

You say visionary, I say lying, stealing bastard. Tom-ay-to, tom-ah-to.

Fiona stood and smoothed down her heather-purple skirt. 'Thank you for coming in…'

Jodie texted her lift as soon as she was out of sight of the building and waddled as briskly as she could in ill-fitting shoes back to the road. Adam was already waiting.

'How did it go?'

Jodie thought back over John McKenzie's blatant look over her body and shuddered. 'I don't know. I'm not sure they were deciding based on suitability for the job.'

–

Pavel stared at the menu in front of him. Usually he and Jill chatted easily about anything and everything. Crazy stories from across Jill's parish. Moans and quibbles from whatever job Pavel was working at the moment. TV they'd seen. Books Jill would press on him and he'd forget to read. Normally it was easy.

Today it was anything but. He stared at the menu some more. One of them had to say something. 'So, they do pies…' he tried.

'Yeah. Yeah. And burgers.'

'Sure. Burgers are good. I think there's a specials board. I could go and look. Maybe take a picture.'

'I looked already. When you were at the bar.'

'Right.'

'Pork belly. Something with fish. Maybe risotto?'

'OK. I might try the pork belly.' Silence threatened to descend once more. 'Pork belly. Poooork belly. Belly. Belly.'

'Pavel?'

'Yeah?'

'This is horrible.'

It was. But that was OK. He could fix it. When things weren't right he made them right. 'I'm sure we can...'

Jill shook her head. 'Pavel, it's horrible.'

It was. It made no sense, but it was. 'Why?'

'I don't know. We've had lunch before.'

They had. 'And we've talked like normal humans.'

'And it was fun. That's why I thought this might be...' She rested her face into her hands for a second. 'I'm sorry. I pushed this, didn't I?'

'No.'

'You can admit it.'

'Maybe a bit. But not just you, to be fair.'

She raised her head. 'Who else?'

'Who didn't? Basically all of Lowbridge agrees that this should work.'

Jill took an enthusiastic glug of wine. 'I wasn't aware it was up to them.'

'No.' Obviously it wasn't. 'But...'

'What? I hope you didn't go out with me because the Ladies' Group thought you should?'

'No.' Not just that at least.

Jill sighed. 'I see their point though. This should work. We get on. You're hot.'

Pavel shook his head.

'Your muscles have muscles. Don't pretend you don't know. And I'm, I mean, I'm not supermodel pretty but I scrub up all right.' She paused. 'You could say something nice about me there, you know?'

'Sorry.' Pavel wasn't even managing to make anything better. 'You're gorgeous.'

'Thank you. So what's wrong?'

'I don't know.'

'Bollocks.'

Pavel raised an eyebrow in mock shock. 'Reverend, really?'

'Come on. We both know what's wrong. It's OK to say it.'

To say what?

'I need you to say it. Please. I need you to let me off your hook here. Say it. For me.' She folded her arms and stared him down.

'I can't…' He couldn't hurt her. He didn't want to be cruel.

'Please. This isn't a broken pipe you can replace and make good.'

'I'm sorry.' Pavel took a deep breath and forced the words out. 'I don't think of you that way. I mean I love you.' That was true. 'You're my best friend but just a friend, you know.'

'Thank you.' She took a sip of her wine. 'That's fine. Genuinely fine. I don't want to go out with someone who's only there because he knows everyone else thinks it's a good idea, or because – bless your little heart – he doesn't want to disappoint me. I want to be adored. I deserve to be adored.'

'Too right. So just friends?' He didn't want to lose her. He wouldn't have been here at all if he was blasé about that.

'Friends.' She nodded. 'Don't say just friends. Friends is something. Don't make it sound less than. Friends is brilliant.' Her usual smile was already starting to reassert itself.

'You're sure you're OK?'

'Of course. I mean, I might eat a whole tub of ice cream and watch *When Harry Met Sally* on repeat tonight but this is fine. I promise.'

'So we can have lunch like normal?'

'Oh please.' She grinned. 'When it was a date I was going to insist on going Dutch to set the right boundaries and all that. If we're here as mates you are so paying.'

'Deal.'

'And you're telling your mam it didn't work out?'

Pavel winced. 'Maybe I could email her?'

'Or tell Anna?'

'You could put it in the parish newsletter?'

Jill laughed. 'Same difference. One thing though…'

'What?'

'You don't want this.' She gestured from him to her and back again. 'That's fine. But what do you want, Pavel?'

'What do you mean?'

'Well, you do everything for everyone, but what do you want? For you?'

Pavel didn't want for anything. He'd grown up with love. He was part of a community. He was needed. 'I'm fine.'

'So you don't want anything just for you?'

For a second Pavel's nerve endings tingled and he was somewhere else entirely, standing in a ballroom full of junk, leaning towards a girl he barely knew – and sometimes felt he didn't know at all – and then he was back in the pub in the moment. He shook his head. 'I want a burger and maybe extra chips.'

'Nothing else?'

'Course not. I'm fine.'

–

Two days later Adam dropped Jodie off at the same spot at the end of the lane up to the McKenzie estate main office, wearing a different borrowed outfit. 'Good luck. Don't forget your name's Jodie.'

Jodie had told herself the double deceit would somehow be easier, but the layers upon layers were already blowing her mind. 'I'll try not to.'

She arrived at reception at precisely five minutes to nine – as discussed at length over dinner the previous night. Eight forty-five looked too keen according to Darcy but Veronica was very clear that on time was already late.

'Hi. I'm here for Fiona MacCellan. It's my first day.' Jodie smiled brightly. Even though she was being Jodie, she wasn't being actually Jodie. She was New Jodie, Better Jodie – the sort of Jodie who paid attention and didn't screw up. She read the name badge pinned to the receptionist's jacket. 'Saira. Nice to meet you.'

Saira looked her up and down. 'Good luck.'

'What do you mean?'

Saira shrugged.

'Come on.' Jodie tried her best to sound girly and matey and conspiratorial. 'You can't leave me hanging.'

'Just her. Mr McKenzie's great, but she's all over him like...'

Before she could finish, the door to Fiona's office swung open and Fiona and John McKenzie strode out. 'Jodie.' He strode towards her, hand extended, holding on again for slightly too long. 'Good to see you. I said to Fiona, she's the one. You've got what we need.'

The urge to 'accidentally' stamp down hard on John's booted foot rose strongly through Jodie's body. He exuded sleaze, but it wasn't just her mess if she lost this job the moment she'd got it. She was doing this for everyone who'd welcomed her in and put their faith in her. 'I hope so.'

'I know you do. I can always spot it, can't I, Fi?'

Fiona nodded wordlessly beside him.

'I saw the potential in her. See the same thing in you. A mind we can mould to the McKenzie way.'

Jodie's smile didn't budge an inch. Was this a job or cult? 'Can't wait to get started.'

Out of the corner of her eye she could see that not only was Fiona fixated on John's every move, but Saira was as well. Another piece slotted into place in the jigsaw in her head. I see you, John McKenzie, she thought. I see you.

Once John had disappeared to do whatever terribly important things he didn't involve Fiona in, they got down to work. Fiona showed her round the key elements of the estate. The visitor experience hub. The three retail spaces. The multiple convenience kiosks offering refreshments around the estate. The four different gastronomic experience venues. And finally the main events space, adjacent to what Fiona referred to as the central administration and management hub. 'Over there is the hotel, and we've got lodges all over the site. Four star officially but obviously deserve a fifth. The health club is down there too, and the spa site.'

That building was the job Pavel was hoping to be working on.

'That spa will help us get that fifth star,' Fiona added. 'I mean, we should have had it from the start. John was...' She paused for a second. 'He was very cross about that.' She shook her head and, within a second, the corporate happy face was back. 'I mean, none of us were happy. We're all really invested in this place.'

'It seems like a wonderful place to work.' Jodie reminded herself that she had a whole other job to do. 'Why don't you show me the event space? I'm excited to hear what you've got planned for Hogmanay.'

What they had planned for Hogmanay, it turned out, was everything plus the kitchen sink. Jodie had thought Gemma's plan for a gala evening, with accommodation, a nature walk and a low-key breakfast on the first of January for the survivors was a lot to organise. McKenzie's plans took things to a whole other level. The guests arrived on the thirtieth of December and stayed until the second. As well as the ceilidh – advertised, Jodie noted, as being hosted by the Highlands' most in-demand ceilidh band – on Hogmanay itself there was also a murder mystery evening the night before – which actually sounded fun, and something they could definitely put on at Lowbridge – and live music and a quiz on the evening of New Year's Day. And that was before you got to the menu of additional activities guests could pay extra for during daylight hours. Quad biking, wildlife jeep tours, spa treatments.

'I thought you didn't have a spa yet?'

'There are treatment rooms in the health club, obviously,' Fiona explained, as if the absence of treatment rooms was a horror no McKenzie estate guest should ever have to contemplate.

Jodie read on. 'Cinema afternoons?'

Fiona nodded towards the door off the small event room they were sitting in. 'We have a screening room that seats up to sixty.'

Of course they did.

There was also archery, field and target, shooting and fishing, art sessions and dance lessons.

'We've got someone from *Strictly* coming to do those,' Fiona explained. 'Not one of the good ones. One of them that only lasted a couple of series. We wanted Anton Du Beke, but his people have got him doing panto.'

'Maybe next year?' Jodie muttered.

'Maybe. And we have Jay from Redd Level turning on our Christmas tree lights next week.'

Jodie's incomprehension must have reached her face, because Fiona explained.

'Redd Level. With two Ds. You know, the song where they're on the bus and they're trying to get to the Christmas party.'

'No.'

'You do know.' Fiona popped her tablet down on the floor next to her and held her hands out as if turning a massive steering wheel and sang uncertainly, 'It's Christmas, in my heart. It's Christmas, and I'm gonna dart right back to you. On a train! On a plane! On a bus! There's no fuss. I'll be there for Christmas babe with you...'

By the time Fiona was recreating the plane wings with her arms, the dance routine and the whole damn song was back in Jodie's head. 'I remember. Wow. Was Jay the one that turned out to be gay?'

Fiona shook her head. 'That was Pete, with the white-boy dreadlocks. Jay was the blond one.'

Jodie just about managed to swallow her laughter. Anna and Nina would be apoplectic when they heard the McKenzies had a celebrity for their lights turn-on.

'That's next Saturday. Jay and Santa, of course.'

'Of course.'

'Actually,' Fiona pulled a face, 'I know it's not really your job, but John does like everyone to muck in.'

'OK?' Jodie suspected John McKenzie liked an atmosphere where everyone *else* mucked in.

'Santa will need some elves, and we quite often ask a few of the team to take part. Saira will be donning the tights as well.'

Dressing as an elf was not Jodie's idea of a good time but she was a very long way away from anyone who knew her – given that the Lowbridge locals were very unlikely to put in much of an appearance at the McKenzie place – and she was supposed to be getting the inside track on the set up here. Appearing to be a committed team player was exactly what she needed to do. 'Of course I will.' She beamed. 'Can't wait.'

'Great stuff. John was right. You are turning out to be precisely our sort of person.'

–

Pavel had arrived home from lunch with Jill to find his mother sitting in her garden. He had started to tell her that the grand romance was off. She'd stopped him with a wave of her phone. 'Save your breath. Jill already texted me.'

'Sorry, Mum.'

'Don't be sorry. If there's no spark, there's no spark.' She'd left him with one thought. 'I just hope you don't miss it when there is one.'

A week ago Pavel would have said he didn't believe in sparks. He believed in being a good person and doing what you could and had assumed, he supposed in so much as he'd ever thought about it at all, that at some point he'd do those things alongside someone else who thought the same. He'd have thought that anyone he might fall for would be easy and would fit into the life he had. He'd have imagined someone open and relaxed. He'd never have imagined he could experience a moment where actually nothing happened at all, with a woman he sometimes felt he barely knew at all stuck in his head like a scratched record.

He told himself that the fact that she was the only one who knew what he was doing at the coach house wasn't the real reason he was spending so much time here at all. He was spending every spare minute after, and even before, his regular work at the coach house. The job was bigger than he'd acknowledged and he was exhausted. But it needed doing. Having proper guest accommodation would give his friends the best chance of holding on to the estate. He was determined to continue. And some evenings, if Bella was teaching a class, or was too tired to talk about work, Gemma would sneak over to see how he was doing.

She would sit cross-legged in the corner of the room he was working on, notepad open in front of her, phone in her hand, scribbling down details for Hogmanay and making notes on her day at the McKenzie estate. Most evenings they didn't even chat, but, he was constantly aware that she was there.

This evening he was alone. He could see the light from the castle kitchen, telling him that the household was awake. Bella and Gemma would be at the kitchen island deep in conversation.

Pavel's phone vibrated on the floor alongside him. He checked the message – Tom confirming they'd got the McKenzie job and asking if he could start in a couple of days. Pavel fired off a reply. The idea of working for the McKenzie estate had made him uneasy from the start but now there was a fizz of excitement too. Gemma was at the McKenzie estate, wasn't she?

He'd probably done enough for tonight. He picked up his stuff, and opened the door to the outside world a crack to check nobody was around.

Adam was standing right in front of him. 'What are you doing here?'

'I erm… I thought I'd left something here last time I was over, but no. Can't find it.'

'What? I'll help you look.' He started towards the door.

'No. It's fine. Just some tools, but they're not here. I probably left them at the pub.' He pulled the door closed behind him and strolled as casually as he could out into the dark. 'How's everything with you?'

Adam shrugged. 'Apart from adding a baby to the list of things we can't afford right now? Well, it's full steam ahead with the Hogmanay Gala. I figure we might as well just commit at this point.'

Pavel shook his head. 'How do you do that?'

'Do what?'

'Dive into stuff.'

Adam leaned against the coach house wall. 'Not got much choice. People are coming whether there's a party or not at this point.'

Pavel didn't reply.

'Why do I think this talk might not be about a party?' Adam asked.

What was it about? Pavel had never questioned his life. He was needed in Lowbridge. He fit into a Pavel-shaped hole. It had never felt like a cage before. 'Why did you move to Edinburgh?' Adam had left at eighteen and only returned earlier in the year when he'd inherited the barony, rather earlier than anyone had anticipated.

'What?'

'I mean, you were the heir to the manor and you upped and left.'

'For university.'

Pavel shook his head. 'You didn't go for three years and then come home. You *went* went. I didn't think you'd stay even... even after your dad died.'

'I didn't plan to.'

'So what happened?'

Adam leaned back and stared up at the ceiling for a moment. 'I fell in love.'

'With Bel?'

'Well, yeah, but then she fell in love with here and I sort of started seeing it through her eyes and I don't know. I fell in love with Lowbridge again as well, I guess.' He let the silence sit for a moment, but Pavel knew they'd known each other too long for Adam to let him off entirely. 'Why do you ask?'

'I don't know.'

'Are you thinking of leaving?'

'No.' No. Of course he wasn't. 'I've always been happy here.'

'Then what?'

He wasn't sure he could put it into words. He was good at doing things, and fixing stuff, and helping out. He wasn't always so good at saying the things that needed to be said. 'How do you cope with the shocks?'

'Like my dad dying?'

Of course that was what Adam would think of. It wasn't what Pavel had meant.

'I don't think I did. I tried to power through. It didn't work.'

'What about the rest? Bella?' Pavel did smile now. 'A baby?'

Adam splayed his hands out from the side of his head to show his mind was blown at this point. 'Those are happy shocks though. I didn't go off on some stag do intending to come home engaged. We were not planning a baby. But those are brilliant shocks, aren't they? What could be better?'

'When you got together with Bella, didn't it feel risky? Jumping in so fast.'

'Course it did. But the risk of not seeing her again was worse. That wasn't just scary. It was unimaginable.'

Chapter Thirteen

On day two of her new job, Jodie's alarm insisted that she had to pull herself out of bed at six forty-five, shower, dress, and be ready to depart by seven thirty, to arrive promptly at half eight, to click the coffee machine on ready for John and Fiona's daily morning meeting. The morning meeting, Fiona had told her, was the key to how the whole place operated. So far as Jodie could make out this was when John descended, briefly, from his cloud, to issue instructions to his assistant before vanishing off as soon as any real work needed doing. Jodie had already decided she was going to hate the morning meeting.

She was not disappointed. It wasn't even simply that she hated John McKenzie. She hated the person her otherwise perfectly competent new boss became in his presence. Today she was talking him through the schedule for the spa project.

'So the main contractor is setting up on-site today, and work starts properly tomorrow. The foundations should be done and building started before Christmas but obviously everything's very weather-dependent at this time of year.'

John sucked the air in. 'We know whose fault that was, don't we?'

Fiona's gaze dropped to the floor. 'I'm so sorry about that. I still really don't know what happened.'

Now John turned to Jodie, bringing her in on his joke. 'Such a feather-brain this one. You're going to have to help me whip her into shape.'

Something clenched in Jodie's gut. 'I'm sure she doesn't need that,' she murmured.

John bellowed out a laugh. 'Loyal, are you? I like that.'

After the big boss had swanned off, Jodie pitched her tone as casual as she could manage and asked, 'What was that about the time of year being someone's fault?'

Fiona flushed slightly. 'Oh, it was silly. We went out to tender for the building work much later than we should have, because some papers for the planning committee were lost. I mean I lost them. I don't know how. I had everything filed.' She shook her head. 'I thought I did. So now we're building in winter which is potentially going to be much slower and more expensive.'

'I'm sure it was just a mistake.'

Fiona nodded. 'And John's been very good about it. This is why I need an assistant though. I'm not always the most organised.'

That wasn't what Jodie had seen so far. Fiona appeared entirely on the ball so long as John McKenzie wasn't in the room.

By the next day's morning meeting Jodie had managed to finely hone a daydream about ramming her biro into John McKenzie's windpipe and was enjoying the thought of twisting it right the way into his throat when he finally said something that made Jodie's ears perk up. 'Money's no object.'

'Really?'

'To finally get that obstinate little posh boy off that land, absolutely not.'

Was the obstinate little posh boy actually Lowbridge's very lovely, rather self-effacing, little posh boy?

'He needs to understand that whatever he tries to get that place back afloat we will blow out of the water. We will do it better and louder and he will not stand a chance.'

Fiona nodded mutely.

'Do I make myself clear?'

Another nod.

'For goodness' sake woman, use your voice.'

'I understand.'

'Good.' John McKenzie's expression broke into a smile and he reached a hand over to gently stroke Fiona's face. 'I'm sorry. You know how emotional I get.'

'I know. You're passionate.'

He smiled indulgently, and glanced over at Jodie. 'Hit the jackpot with this one, didn't I?'

Jodie shuddered. She'd seen Fiona's crush on John from the interview onwards, but she hadn't been sure, until now, that anything was actually going on between them. 'Fiona's great.'

He nodded and curled a tendril of hair behind Fiona's ear. 'Especially when she makes an effort.'

As soon as he left the room, Fiona pulled the make-up kit she kept in her top drawer out and checked her mascara, and reapplied her lipstick. 'A professional appearance is so important to perceptions of the estate,' she murmured, like a mantra she'd learned by heart.

Jodie's dislike of John McKenzie hardened a little more. 'You OK?' she asked.

'Absolutely fine.' Fiona's professional smile was back in place. 'Shall we go over our bookings procedures?'

'Sure.' Jodie listened – she really tried to listen – as Fiona talked to her about margins on activities booked on their own versus activities as part of a break package with accommodation, and then about direct bookings, and bookings sites, and tour operator bookings, and a thousand and one other ways Fiona worked to maximise what she called the estate's 'visibility footprint' and encouraged 'user upspending'. This was just the sort of thing that real Gemma would probably have put in place at Lowbridge. Jodie might as well have been listening to the whole speech underwater in a foreign language. 'That all sounds great,' she told Fiona.

Her new boss shrugged. 'All very standard stuff. Anyone could set this up. It's Mr McKenzie who has the real vision.'

At the end of the day she hurried down the estate access road to her pickup point, out of sight of the main office and visitor centre. Flinty's Land Rover was sitting at the end of the lane, pulled in close to the trees. Jodie jumped in. 'Hi!'

'Good evening, Miss Bryant.'

It wasn't Flinty behind the wheel. It was Veronica Lowbridge. Jodie fought to stop her smile faltering.

'Margaret is helping with the cookery school today in your stead, so I said I could come over.' She turned on the engine and eased the Land Rover onto the road, moving smoothly away and up through the gears.

Jodie frowned. 'It's a lot crunchier than that when Flinty drives.'

Veronica's pursed lips didn't quite crack into a smile. 'I wouldn't let her hear you say that.'

Jodie was happy to let the drive back over the hill and around the headland pass in silence, and for the first part of the journey Veronica seemed to feel the same. As they came into Lowbridge village she broke the silence.

'So is your investigation bearing fruit?'

Honestly, Jodie was struggling to do very much investigating in amongst trying to keep up with the work Fiona was passing her way. 'I know that John McKenzie is a dick.'

Veronica's eyebrow shifted infinitesimally higher. 'I think we all knew that already.'

'Yeah. Sorry. I guess I'm still finding my feet. Trying to make sure they trust me.'

'That's important in any deception, I imagine,' Veronica replied.

Jodie's nerves jangled. Which deception was Veronica talking about?

'I did wonder what you'd done about your National Insurance number over there.'

'What?'

'I mean, it's one thing not to be able to find your own, but what on earth would one do if in need of an entirely fake one?' Veronica's gaze didn't shift from the road as she coaxed the ageing four-by-four up the hill out of the village.

'I don't know.'

'I suppose one could pretend to have lost it. And buy oneself some time?'

Jodie's heart thudded rapidly. *Breathe. Breathe*, she told herself. *She doesn't know*. If Veronica knew Jodie would have been out on her ear weeks ago. What Veronica definitely did do, though, was suspect. 'Can't do that forever though.' Jodie tried to keep her voice light.

'No. Sooner or later an employer will request your National Insurance details from HMRC. I dare say Darcy will get around to it at some point. Let's hope the McKenzie HR people aren't any more efficient.'

Jodie froze. She forced herself not to react. Darcy could get her details from HMRC. And then everything would fall apart. No more Gemma. No more chats planning and plotting with Bella. No more Lowbridge. No more Pavel. Nothing.

Something else crept into her mind through the chaos. Why had Veronica told her this? Was it a threat? It didn't feel like she was being threatened. It felt like Veronica was trying to give Jodie a warning.

–

Pavel cleared his pots and pans to the washing-up station in the small kitchen at the end of the cookery session, and came back to find Flinty standing determinedly in front of the youngest Strachan holding Bella's smartphone aloft. 'Gemma says I have to film things for the internet. So go on, lad.'

Strach shook his head. 'Nah. It's bad enough Granddad being all over TikTok. I'm not having him saying I copied.'

Flinty harrumphed lightly. 'Right. Well, you then, Pavel lad.'

'Gemma did me last week.'

Flinty shook her head at the lack of willing influencers to hand. 'Somebody needs to be in my ticky tock,' she insisted.

'In your what?' Veronica Lowbridge asked from the entryway.

'My ticky tock,' Flinty explained. 'It's on the internet to make young people come and learn about sprouts.'

'Not just sprouts.' Gemma followed Veronica into the kitchen. 'It's to promote the cookery school. People's food memories and cooking tips.'

Veronica nodded. 'Have you filmed one?' she asked Gemma.

She shook her head. 'I'm more behind the scenes.'

'And what if McKenzie sees it?' Pavel pointed out.

'He's right.' Flinty nodded. 'It'll have to be you, V.'

Pavel watched as Flinty positioned her, somewhat reluctant, partner on a stool at the kitchen island.

'Right, so I'm going to ask you about food, and you have to keep it short, so as them young ones'll watch it in between their sexting and that.'

Pavel saw Gemma suppress a giggle.

Veronica nodded. 'I shall attempt to be suitably engaging.'

Flinty stopped and looked at Gemma. 'I don't know what to ask her now.'

'Why don't you tell us what your favourite food is and why?'

Flinty nodded. 'But nothing all fancy. You have to be relatable on the ticky tock.' She looked to Gemma. 'That's right, isn't it?'

Gemma nodded wordlessly, suppressing – Pavel could see – another giggle.

'I have had a lot of what you would call fancy dinners, but I think my favourite food would be a buttered crumpet.' Veronica nodded. Job done.

'You have to say more than that. Why's it your favourite?'

'It's what my...' There was a fraction of a hesitation, but only a fraction. 'My partner brings me in bed if I'm

217

ill. Food made with love, that's the best thing, I think.' She turned to Gemma. 'Is that enough?'

Flinty nodded. 'Even better than Old Man Strachan's bin bit.'

'That was perfect. Thank you.' Gemma took the phone from Flinty. 'I should go and…' She rushed back out of the kitchen towards the courtyard.

Pavel followed. 'Gemma!'

She'd stopped in the courtyard. He jogged over to her. 'Are you OK?'

She nodded. 'I'm fine. Just, I don't know… I made Ge… my girlfriend breakfast in bed not very long before she moved out. I'd really made an effort, you know. Scrambled eggs, and I knew they weren't quite right cos they were runnier than I thought they were supposed to be, and our toaster was weird so one side of the bread was a bit darker than it should have been, but I really tried.'

She was talking too quickly, words tumbling over each other.

'It wasn't good enough though.' Gemma was tapping her hand against her leg.

Pavel's heart went out to her. 'Why did you break up?' he asked.

'She got a job in Cornwall. She worked in hospitality for a restaurant and then she got another job…'

'Is that where you met?'

'What?'

'Working for restaurants?'

For a second Gemma's face was blank and then it was like someone had hit reboot. 'Yeah. Yeah. I worked for Pizza Now. That's how we met. And then she moved. And now I'm here.' She folded her arms across her body.

Pavel felt like he'd done something wrong. She'd been upset before but she'd been open. Now she'd closed down. He couldn't piece her together. He'd seen her panic the first day she'd arrived. He'd seen her desperate to run away. He'd seen her charming everyone at Lowbridge with her impulsiveness and sense of fun. He'd seen her covered in dust in the ballroom, just on the brink, he thought, of kissing him.

But then there was another Gemma. A Gemma who watched every word she said, a Gemma he caught in the corner of his eye watching and thinking, a Gemma who seemed terrified of making a wrong move.

He couldn't place the two Gemmas together. The second Gemma was here now. 'I'd best get back,' she said.

–

By the next morning's meeting with John, Jodie's murderous fantasies were becoming more elaborate. Maybe she could feed his tie into the shredder and just watch as it slowly pulled his whole body after it. Maybe it was possible to suffocate someone by laminating them. He was, she was sure, only saved by the brevity of the meeting.

As soon as he was out of the door Jodie set about finding an excuse to get out of Fiona's immediate eyeline for a while. Her interrogation from Veronica on the way home the previous day had really pressed home that she needed to get on with some actual spying as soon as possible. 'So you've got checking on the spa team on the list for today? I could do that?'

Despite Fiona being adamant that John took the lead on the physical maintenance and development of the estate, overseeing the builders still seemed to be on Fiona's to-do list.

'Would you mind?'

'Not at all.'

'Great. If you could make sure they've got everything they need that would be so helpful. I'm overrun with things for New Year.'

'I can help with that too?' Jodie offered.

Fiona nodded. 'It's fine. It's in hand.'

'Whatever needs doing when I'm back.' Damn. She'd engineered a pass out from the office right when she needed to be here looking over Fiona's shoulder. 'Whatever you need.'

The short walk over to the spa site took Jodie past the whisky experience area and beyond the bird feeders, which were sadly devoid of birds. Actually the whole estate was eerily quiet. At Lowbridge there was the constant sound of the sea, and the gulls overhead, and of people coming and going, kids playing in the courtyard on parents and toddlers days, students arriving for the cookery school, pots bubbling on the stove. And birdsong. When you stepped outside and walked up the path towards Adam's garden and the top of the headland there was birdsong.

The building site was fully up and running. She scoured around for Tom, the lead contractor, and tried not to look disappointed when she saw him. 'Jodie.' He waved in greeting.

'Just checking in. Fiona wanted to make sure you've got everything you need.' She gestured to the roadway behind them. 'Access is OK?'

'Aye. If you could guarantee the weather for us we'd be golden.'

'In Scotland? In November?'

He grinned. 'Worth asking at least.'

A van pulled up alongside them. Jodie recognised that van. Stone and Son. Pavel jumped out. 'All right, Tom.' And then he stopped. 'Ge—'

'Pavel, hi.' Jodie spoke quickly to cover his mistake. She was getting too adept at this.

'You guys know each other?'

Pavel nodded. 'Er, Jodie is…'

'I'm his mum's lodger.'

'Yeah. That's right. Lodger. So we know each other. Really well. Well, not really well.'

Jodie tried to shoot him a look that said 'shut up, Pavel'. It didn't work.

'As well as you'd expect. She's in the house with my mum. I've got the flat so we see each other but, I mean, we're not seeing each other. We don't. We haven't. I…'

Jodie turned back to Tom. 'So you're fine here?'

He glanced at Pavel. 'I'm fine. I'm not sure about him.'

'What can I say? I send men loopy.'

'I'm not. I didn't…'

'If you're working here, you should car share,' Tom suggested. 'Isn't the McKenzie way all about minimising environmental impact?'

That was what their website said, certainly. 'That would be, I mean, depending what time you finish, that would be…'

'He'll finish about half five. We got the lights up yesterday and the generator running so we can keep going a bit after it gets dark,' Tom explained. 'You'll give Jodie a ride, won't you? In your big old van?'

Pavel was glaring at Tom now. 'You can have a lift back. Of course you can.'

'Thanks.' Forty minutes in the van with Pavel twice a day for however long this took. They'd have to talk in the van, wouldn't they? She'd been fine seeing him in the coach house while they both got on with their own work. That was sort of comforting. In the van it would just be him and her and the silence, and in the silence next to Pavel she already knew there would only be one thing she could think about.

Back in the office Saira was leaning over the printer muttering under her breath.

'What's up?'

'It reckons it's got a paper jam. It lies.' She shook her head. 'If Miss Thing in there could send things to the right printer I wouldn't have to deal with this anyway. She's got one in her office.'

Jodie smiled her brightest Gemma-pretending-to-be-Jodie smile. 'I can sort it.'

'Fine.' No 'thank you'. Just 'fine'.

Jodie had no relevant special skills with printers, so she did what she always did with any and all recalcitrant technology and turned it off and back on again. The printer offered her a hopeful whirring noise in response and a moment later a single half-printed sheet of A4 slid out of the machine. It was a printout from a spreadsheet, but it looked as though there were supposed to be more lines that the printer had refused to share. Jodie read through what she could see. *Hogmanay Ticket Sales*. Interesting. And then just a list of names. Only eight rows before the technology let them down, but of those eight, two had been highlighted in yellow. Jodie read along the rows. The only thing that seemed to set those two apart was the entry under 'How did you hear about the event?' *Direct Sales Call*.

Jodie folded the sheet of paper and slid it into her pocket, before she headed back to the office. Fiona was at her desk. 'The printer out there's playing up. Saira said to tell you your file didn't print.'

Fiona nodded curtly. 'That's fine. It wasn't anything important.'

By half past five Pavel had thought of a hundred and one topics of casual conversation for the drive back to Lowbridge. Gemma or Jodie or whatever he was supposed to call her now shut them all down. She agreed that the weather wasn't bad for the time of year, that the McKenzie estate was a bit too corporate for her tastes and that Lowbridge was beautiful. Pavel gave up. If she wanted to chat, let her think of something to say.

'So were you going to kiss me in the ballroom?'

Pavel kept his eyes on the road and tried not to grip the steering wheel so tight it came away in his hands. 'What?'

'Just that it seemed like we were going to kiss and then we didn't and you ran away.'

'I didn't run away.'

'OK. Then you walked very briskly away.'

Pavel couldn't stop himself laughing at that.

'So, did you?'

'Did I run away?'

'Did you want to kiss me?'

'Maybe.'

'Maybe?'

Maybe was pathetic. Maybe was dishonest. Maybe wasn't recognising a spark when one was in front of him. 'Yes.'

'Yes?'

'Yes. I wanted to kiss you.'

'Why didn't you?'

'It's complicated.'

'Not usually. Birds do it. Bees do it. I'm pretty sure beefy handymen have done it before.' She opened her mouth in mock horror. 'You have done it before? I mean no judgement but...'

'Yes. I have done it before.'

'So why not with me?'

'I was sort of with Jill. I mean, not with Jill. But also not not with Jill.'

'And you didn't want to mess her around?'

'I didn't want to mess either of you around.' That was true. Not the whole truth but a genuine part of it at least.

'And are you with Jill now?'

'No.'

'OK.'

He pulled the van in in front of the Lowbridge coach house, and turned his head towards her. This was it. They'd acknowledged the nearly kiss. They'd established that the barrier was out of the way. She leaned towards him. She was an inch away from him, and now half an inch. Her lips broke into a smile. 'Well, that was a sad missed opportunity then, wasn't it?'

She grinned as she hopped out of the van and waved as she walked away. What was that? Was that a brush-off or was that flirting? And how on earth was Pavel expected to know?

–

Why hadn't she kissed him? She'd wanted to. She'd raised it. She hadn't intended to when she'd got in the van. She'd intended to sit silently, or at most make polite chit-chat about the weather. She hadn't intended to pick at a healing wound. But as soon as the question was in her head there was no version of Jodie who could have resisted asking it.

And now the moment in the ballroom was something real. They'd shone a light on it and there was no more pretending that nothing was going on. And yet, technically, nothing was going on. He'd definitely leaned in that time, and she'd pulled away. Why had she done that? Jodie wasn't a backing-down-and-walking-away person. Maybe she really didn't know who she was any more.

Bella was waiting for her in the kitchen. They started with an update on Lowbridge's own plans – some positive, some not so good. Adam had opened up accommodation bookings for New Year on the estate website, apparently after a nudge from Pavel to up the price a notch. Jodie bit back her explanation for that. Three new groups had booked for the party. And one more had cancelled because they now had 'other plans'. 'I wish we knew for certain that they were going to McKenzie.'

Jodie hesitated. So far everything she'd done at the McKenzie estate had been ethically dubious but not actually illegal. She had, she reminded herself, saved that honour for Lowbridge. Was taking a job on false pretences a form of fraud? She was telling herself not really. Data protection breaches were definitely against the law though. This was new territory. 'I've got something I can't give you.'

'What do you mean?'

'Like if I'd found a partial list of their ticket holders on the printer it would be really dodgy to show that to you.' Jodie pulled the folded sheet of A4 out of her bag and dropped it on the kitchen island. 'I'm going to the loo.'

When she came back the paper was neatly folded at the other end of the table. Bella smiled innocently. 'Oh, I think you left something over there.'

'So do you think McKenzie really is stealing our customers?'

'I'm bloody sure he is. Those two highlighted lines – they were both booked with us.'

'But how?'

Bella shook her head. 'I don't know. There's only you, me, Darcy and Adam who have access to the bookings here. And I know none of us would tell them.'

Jodie bit her lip. This was another scab she couldn't stop herself picking at. 'Why don't you think it's me?'

'What do you mean?'

'I mean you've only known me a month. Why do you trust me?'

Bella stared at her. 'Heart or head?'

'What?'

'Do you want the heart answer or the rational head answer?'

Jodie wasn't sure she wanted either, but she needed something true. 'Heart?'

'Then I trust you because I do trust you. You've really mucked in since you got here. You're part of the team. Part of Lowbridge. I don't believe you'd lie to us.'

Jodie felt like she'd been given a huge hug and a massive punch in the guts all at the same time. 'What about the head reason?'

'I can see who's logged into the ticket system. Your login hadn't been used between the first customers who cancelled booking with us and then pulling out, or since this last lot booked.'

Jodie nodded. 'I really wouldn't do that.'

'Good.' Bella rubbed the small of her back. 'I went to the GP today. I've got booklets to read about NCT classes and midwife visits and goodness knows what. I feel like I'm officially pregnant.'

'The three tests you did didn't tell you that?'

Bella laughed. 'I guess I'm going to have to take some time off soon then.' Her brow furrowed. 'So you better bloody be part of the team. We're going to need you more than ever.' She rubbed her eyes. 'Oh, Hogmanay. I think this is our last chance to cut our losses and cancel now. We haven't spent for the food and drink yet or staff for the night. If we cancel now it'd be a horrific loss rather than an absolutely catastrophic one.'

'Do you want to cancel?'

'No. Honestly, I don't think it's enough for us to just not lose money at this point anyway. But mostly, I don't want him to beat us.'

Neither did Jodie. Cancelling would be giving up. It would be admitting that she didn't have what it took to hold down a proper job. It would be accepting that no matter how hard she tried – no matter how Gemma she tried to be – Jodie Simpson always messed things up. And it would be letting John McKenzie get away with one more thing. 'He's really horrible. Have you met him?'

Bella nodded. 'He came to Adam's dad's memorial service.'

Jodie shuddered. Nobody deserved John McKenzie coming to see them off.

'Made Adam an offer to buy this place at the actual wake.'

That didn't even surprise her. 'We can't let him win.'

'So what do we do? He's stolen our band and half our customers.'

Jodie thought it through. What Gemma would do was no help to her here. And being Gemma was feeling more and more like a straitjacket rather than an escape. That was why she'd prodded at Pavel in the van. She was who she was. Maybe it was all she could be. And she did have an idea. It was crazy but it was all she had. 'I think we should steal them back.'

Chapter Fourteen

Before Jodie could put any flesh on that plan there was the small matter of not one, but two separate sets of Christmas light switch-ons to deal with. Both of which she seemed to be responsible for organising, and both of which were rapidly merging in her increasingly confused Gemma/Jodie brain.

She checked the notes in her phone.

> McKenzie – Saturday afternoon, Jay from Redd Level, elf costume, overpriced mulled wine.

> Lowbridge – Sunday. White lights – unless Anna goes rogue. Carols. Candles and lanterns for walkers? No celeb – Anna is definitely still expecting Elton John.

Today was Saturday. Her elf suit was hanging on the back of her bedroom door. Darcy had threatened to pour black paint over it, but Jodie had pointed out that that was most likely to get her fired and then they'd have no access to what the McKenzie lot were up to. Looking at the corporate McKenzie purple tartan monstrosity, Jodie wished she'd let Darcy do her worst.

She folded the costume neatly into a bag and headed outside to meet her lift. Since the first night Pavel'd driven her home Jodie hadn't mentioned the kiss that wasn't in the ballroom, or the second kiss that wasn't in the van.

She'd thought about both of them. A lot. When she was alone. When she was supposed to be talking about work with Fiona. When she was supposed to be talking about work with Bella. And every day for the forty minutes in the morning and the forty minutes at night she spent sitting next to Pavel Stone watching the way his forearms tensed slightly when she leaned closer to him.

'Are you working today? It's Saturday.' Jodie would have expected the building work to be suspended for the weekend.

'Wasn't planning to, but Fiona marched over at five o'clock yesterday and announced that the building site needed to be tidy before the lights switch-on.'

'Tidy?'

Pavel nodded.

'But it's a building site?'

'Apparently today it needs to be a pristine and festive building site. She kept saying that Mr McKenzie wanted things just so.'

Jodie almost growled at the mention of the big boss's name.

'You're not a fan?'

'I am not.' She squeezed her thumbnail into her palm and breathed deeply for a second. 'He's a bully. I know men like that. There's only one way to treat them.'

'Knee to the balls?'

Pavel's deadpan suggestion relieved some of the tension in her body. 'It'd be a start.'

Saira was absent from reception when Jodie signed in and made her way past Fiona's office and on to the open-plan area where she had a desk. Saira was standing at the printer, eyebrows knitted together. 'You OK there?'

Saira jumped slightly at the sound of her voice. 'Sorry. Didn't hear you come in.'

'Printer playing up again?'

'Yeah. No. It's fine. I better get back.' Saira scurried away.

Something in the back of Jodie's brain tingled. Was Saira acting strangely? Jodie went over to the printer. The lights were on but the screen was blank. She powered it off and on again and waited for it to sputter back into life. The screen finally lit up. *No pending jobs.* Damn.

'Morning, Jodie.'

Jodie turned back to greet her boss. 'Hi, Fi. How are you?' She asked the question before she'd seen Fiona's face. She looked pale, her usual glossy make-up absent and her hair was scraped into a messy ponytail rather than twisted and pinned into its usual perfect chignon.

'I'm fine.' Fiona smiled glassily. 'Absolutely fine. Very excited for this afternoon.'

'Are you sure you're OK?' Jodie moved forward and touched Fiona's arm. 'You can tell me if there's something you need to talk about.'

There was a pause before Fiona answered. 'What would I need to talk about? Everything's great.'

'OK. Well, I'm here if you need anything.'

'What I need is for the lights switch-on to go without a hitch.' Fiona nodded sharply. 'John has very high standards, you know. It's very motivating, isn't it?'

Motivating wasn't the word Jodie would have chosen.

–

The schedule for the afternoon was packed. Father Christmas – a top Father Christmas, according to Fiona, who used to do Jenners in Edinburgh, before it closed – would be in his grotto supported by his faithful elves from noon, and then the grotto would close at four p.m. and everyone would gather around the Christmas tree to see Jay from Redd Level sing a festive medley and then press the button to start the lights. Then there would be fireworks to close the event.

Jodie changed into her elf suit in Fiona's office, turning in front of the window to try to check her reflection in the outfit. She half-laughed to herself as she realised it was yet another costume. Jodie pretending to be Gemma was now Jodie pretending to be Gemma pretending to be Jodie pretending to be an elf. It sounded every bit as ridiculous as she looked.

Once she was dressed, Fiona ran through the schedule with Jodie for the seventieth time. 'And don't let Saira bother Jay from Redd Level. She's got a tour T-shirt from about nineteen ninety-eight under her desk. I know she's going to ask him to sign it.'

Jodie frowned. 'Saira's only about twenty.'

Fiona shook her head gloomily. 'I think it's for her mum.' She clapped her hands together. 'Right, you two better go and get ready. Father Christmas is already down there. And remember only one present per child, and match the colour of the wrapping to the token the parent gives you. That tells you whether they've paid for the gold or platinum packages.'

'Not whether the kid's been naughty or nice?' Jodie joked.

'If Daddy paid for platinum the kid can be a total shit. They still get the good present.'

Wow. Capitalism had really taken hold at the North Pole.

The grotto had been set up in the small conference room, which had been vigorously transformed by Fiona's team of interior visualisation experts. Jodie couldn't help but wonder what the Lowbridge equivalent would be. Probably her and Flinty balancing on a ladder enthusiastically stapling bits of ivy to anything that stayed still long enough. The McKenzie approach was different. The conference centre, right from the entrance, had been transformed. Visitors were enveloped in a snow-covered wonderland. There were miniature village scenes set up along the walls, with figures skiing, drinking glühwein and roasting chestnuts.

In the grotto itself, Santa was seated on a red-and-gold throne, next to a perfectly trimmed and lit Christmas tree, surrounded by sacks of beautifully wrapped gifts. And then children and their families left via a larger room where there was a full train set displayed as the train to the Pole, and stalls where parents could be pressured into spending more money on sweets and treats for their little darlings.

Christmas at the McKenzie estate was a well-oiled money-making machine. The first few kids were exactly as Jodie would have imagined. Variously adorable, enthusiastic, shy and overtired. Santa, showing his fancy big-city experience, was charming and avuncular with them all. Saira showed the children in, and Jodie handed Santa the appropriate gift and showed the little darlings and their mummies and daddies out again, with a clear direction to the stall where they could purchase their souvenir image of their little prince or princess sitting on Santa's knee.

After an hour or so, the routine changed and the next group was shown in by Fiona herself. She smiled at the little girl and pointed her towards Santa before grasping

Jodie by the elbow and pulling her out of mum's earshot. 'Local competition winners,' she hissed. 'John will expect them to get the cheapest present.' Fiona looked down at her shoes. 'I did ask if… never mind.'

Jodie nodded and waited until Fiona had stepped out. The little girl was regaling Santa with a long story about how she had been going to ask for a pony but a lady from Americaland who lived in a princess castle had said she could have rides on her pony so now she didn't need to ask for one of her own. Jodie bit back a smile of recognition. Darcy would have all the village children riding at Lowbridge if she could.

Santa nodded gravely and agreed that ponies were a lot of work to look after and that probably staying at the princess castle would be the best option for them. 'I'm sure we do have a present for you today though. Shall we see what my lovely elf has got for you?'

The presents for those children whose parents – horror of horrors – had only paid the basic entry fee were in red wrapping. Then there was a gold level and a platinum level. They'd only had one platinum customer so far, and there was a platinum gift right on the top of the pile. Who was to say Jodie hadn't made a little mistake?

She picked up the silver-and-blue-wrapped gift and handed it to Santa. She was sure she saw him smile slightly. 'Here you go, Betty.' He looked up at mum. 'And I hope you both have a very Happy Christmas. Before you go, why don't you take a quick pic of Betty with Santa on your phone?'

Jodie saw mum glance at the *No Photography* sign above Santa's head. 'It's fine. It's his grotto, his rules,' she said.

'Thank you.'

Jodie caught Father Christmas' eye again as she closed the door behind Betty and her mum. 'Do you know how much those platinum tickets cost?'

Jodie shook her head.

'Eight hundred quid.'

'What?'

'I think we just gave Betty an Xbox.'

Jodie shook her head. 'I thought it would be like thirty quid or something. Who pays that much to take their kid to see Santa?'

He shrugged. 'Mostly people who already have an Xbox I should think. She'll appreciate it more.'

'I am going to get fired.'

'Blame me if they try. I only still do this for the fun of seeing the little ones happy.'

Jodie paused. 'Are you doing anything tomorrow, Father Christmas?'

–

The second part of the lights switch-on was outside around the Christmas tree. Saira showed the last child in to see Santa and whispered that she was going out to get ready for the lights. Jodie nodded, smiled politely at the last family: another set of platinum customers whose child already had the wrapping paper off the gift before they were out of the door. 'Ugh. It's not even the newest one.'

By the time Jodie made it outside, she could see that the five minutes out of Jodie's sight had been enough time for Saira to corner their celebrity guest, who despite Fiona's insistence that he was to be treated with VIP kid gloves was signing Saira's T-shirt quite happily and asking if she knew which date on the tour her mum had gone to. He also happily let people take photos doing the Christmas bus song dance, and generally seemed like a good egg.

Fiona appeared at Jodie's shoulder. 'Is it going all right?'

Jodie nodded. People were mingling, drinking mulled wine, playing on the fairground games, which even as a staunch enemy of the whole McKenzie enterprise she had to accept was a good idea. 'I think it's going great.'

'I…' Fiona was skittish, more so than usual. 'I'm trying to see it through John's eyes.'

'Why?'

'He's so much cleverer about things like this. He sees things I don't see. Details I miss. I just want to get it all right.'

'Everything is great,' she insisted. 'And you can see that. You need to trust your own judgement.'

Fiona looked around. 'It does seem to be all right.' Her shoulders relaxed for a fraction of a second. 'Oh. Here he is.'

And right away she was rushing to John's side as he surveyed the crowd from a safe distance at the edge of the clearing. Jodie couldn't hear the conversation but she could see the body language. Fiona submissive and imploring. John imperious. He said a few words to his partner and then left. Jodie made her way over to her boss. 'Everything OK?'

'Yes. Perfect. Just need to keep an eye on time. I'm such an airhead. I lose track of things.'

Fiona, so far as Jodie could tell, had an organisational brain that processed plans more efficiently than any spreadsheet. What she didn't have was one remaining iota of self-belief.

Before Jodie could say anything else another figure on the edge of the crowd took up her attention. Pavel Stone, a good three inches taller than anyone else around, and drawing her across the space like a magnet.

'Hi.'

'Hi.' He looked down at her. 'You look…'

Jodie was suddenly painfully aware of the freckles painted on her cheeks, her purple tights and jaunty pigtails. 'I look what?'

'You look happy.'

Oh. Jodie paused. 'The grotto was fun actually.' She waved her hand at the stalls and the expensively decorated tree. 'This is all a bit much, but it's made me look forward to…' She lowered her voice. 'Our switch-on tomorrow.'

'I wasn't sure if you'd need a lift back so I thought I'd come over.'

'I have to stay until after the fireworks.'

He nodded.

'You can stay too.'

'Oh, I'm not sure I can afford a ticket.'

'You can be my guest.'

He nodded silently.

She stood quietly next to him. There was a small stage set up at the far end of the recreation area. That was where, in about five minutes, John McKenzie would introduce Jay, and Jay would sing his festive medley and press the big red button. Jodie had seen the run-through and knew exactly how it would go. She could picture it in her head. John would be charming and play the host with the most and Jodie would vomit a little bit in her mouth.

Maybe she didn't have to stay right here for the whole event. There were other jobs on her list. She had to get the grotto ready for Monday, when fortunately her elf role would be taken over by some cash-strapped teenager from Lochcarron.

On the other hand, abandoning Fiona when she was strung as tight as a guitar string felt unfair. Surely she could stick out John McKenzie's smug, arrogant face a little while longer.

'What are you thinking?'

'What?'

'You were miles away.'

'Just trying to decide whether...' The end of the sentence died in her throat as she saw a figure at the coconut shy. It couldn't be. She'd talked about family holidays in the Highlands, but what would she be doing here? Jodie moved to put Pavel's pleasingly large frame between her and the woman she was desperately trying to keep an eye on.

Pavel twisted round. 'What are you looking at?'

'Nothing.' But not nothing.

'Who is it?'

'No one.' But not no one. Diane. Jodie's former boss at the coffee shop. Her mum's old friend. Here. Now. What was she doing here? Jodie scanned around. At any moment Diane could turn around and see her and come over and talk to her and say any of a million things that would prove that she wasn't Gemma Bryant pretending to be Jodie Simpson, but just Jodie Simpson messing up life in a new and original way. 'I need to get out of here.'

'What?'

'You want to come with me?'

'Where?'

'Anywhere.'

She saw the hesitation.

'To check something in the office. Everyone's out here. Prime time for some spying. For Adam and Bella?'

'OK.'

She hurried away from the mini stage and the massive Christmas tree and along the track to the admin hub. Now she'd thought of it this was actually a brilliant opportunity. 'Keep watch. Shout if anyone comes by.'

Jodie slid behind Saira's reception desk and wiggled the mouse to light up the screen. Locked. Right. In movies this was straightforward. You just had to remember the name of the one childhood pet the user truly loved. Jodie, unfortunately, had not bonded that well with Saira. The password for the tablet Jodie had been given on her first day was JODIE123. She'd had strict instructions to change it immediately. She tapped in SAIRA123 in the hope that her colleague was less diligent. *Incorrect password.*

Jodie rolled her chair back and a flash of orange caught her eye. There was a Post-it note stuck to the underside of Saira's desk. She unpeeled it and read. *JohnMcKHOT123.* Well, there was a lot to unpack there. She typed it in and Saira's computer sparked into life.

'What are you looking for?' Pavel asked from his vantage point by the window.

'I'm not sure. I probably need to be on Fiona's computer but she mostly uses her tablet and that's with her. And I don't know. There's something about Saira.' Jodie couldn't put her finger on it, but her attitude to Fiona was off.

Most of the folders on Saira's desktop were standard. The same general business files that Jodie had access to. She hovered her mouse over the one that looked unfamiliar. *Special Projects.* Inside there was one folder. *Lowbridge.*

Jodie clicked to open and scanned the file list. Most of the things here had been created a few weeks ago. Did that coincide with the McKenzie estate stealing the band and announcing their own event? One file had been updated more recently. *Ticket List*. And the date was today.

'Someone's coming.'

'I just need to—'

Pavel shook his head. 'No time.'

Jodie switched the screen off and jumped out from behind the desk, just as Fiona came through the door.

'Pavel? Jodie, what are you doing?'

'That's my fault.' Pavel bailed her out. 'I needed some insurance details for my records, just to show everything's in order. Didn't want to disturb you. And I just thought I'd forget by Monday.'

Jodie nodded. 'Yeah. So yeah. That's all sorted. We'll just…' She grabbed Pavel's hand and led the way back towards the Christmas tree, and then paused. 'In here.' She dragged him through the now empty grotto waiting area and into the main grotto. 'Nobody'll be in here now. I was supposed to clean up.'

'It looks pretty clean.'

'Yeah.' It did.

'Did you find anything back there?'

'I think so.'

'Something that'll help?'

Maybe. Honestly, Jodie couldn't quite process what she'd found now. Was Saira working on her special project alone? Or for John? Or was Fiona involved as well? 'I can't think straight.'

'Me neither.' Pavel was standing right in front of her. Close to her. Now Jodie couldn't think at all. They were alone together in a room nobody else was likely to come into in the next hour or more.

'We should go back…' she started, but neither of them moved.

'Do you want to go back?'

'No.' She couldn't face looking into his eyes when she asked, 'Do you?'

'No.'

Now she looked up. 'Good.'

She'd spent weeks since the ballroom imagining his lips on hers. She'd imagined it hard and full of desire. She'd imagined it slow and brimming over with promise. What happened next was better than anything she'd imagined. What happened next was real.

The taste of him, the touch of his lips on hers, and his hands on her waist, the firmness of his body against hers, the stretch as she pulled herself onto tiptoes to reach more of him and the feeling like flying when his arms encircled her and lifted her off the ground altogether. All of it was so very, very real.

Without thinking she wrapped her legs around his body and pulled her lips back just a fraction. 'I'm not too heavy?'

He laughed for a moment. 'I'd bench-press you as a warm-up, darling.'

'Darling?'

'Too much?'

She shook her head. 'Call me that again.'

'My darling.'

'My darling.'

The endearment touched something in Jodie's soul. This wasn't going to be just sex, because there was no doubt in her body right now that they were going to have sex, but this was something more than that. She wasn't just a shag. She was somebody's darling. She touched a finger to the side of his face, and pressed her lips back to his.

And then the tempo shifted, incrementally harder and faster and more desperate. He lowered her to the floor, only to free up his hands to pull at her elf tunic, and help her wriggle out of her tights. She grinned slightly. 'Sorry. This isn't my sexiest look.'

'I'm not complaining.'

She caught his eye. 'Good.' She stepped back towards him and pulled his sweater and T-shirt up from the waist, revealing a taut, slightly tanned torso.

Pavel pulled one of the fur rugs that had been acting as North Pole set dressing onto the floor, before sweeping Jodie's legs from under her to lift her up and lower her down onto the rug. He kneeled in front of her. 'Oh, I don't know if I have any...'

'I'm on the pill.'

'Are you sure?'

She raised an eyebrow. 'Sure I'm on the pill?'

'You're making jokes now?'

'Sorry.'

'Why?'

'What?'

'Why are you making jokes?'

'To hide how scared I am.'

'Of what?'

Almost every instinct was to make another joke, or to grab her clothes and run the hell away. Jodie fought to keep hold of the other instinct. 'I'm scared of how right this feels.' That wasn't quite it. 'How real.'

—

Pavel bit his lip. That was exactly it. That was exactly what had held him back in the ballroom. There was a feeling with Gemma Bryant that something wasn't quite right, something was being held back. And now nothing was. She was naked in front of him, in every possible sense. He took a deep breath in. 'Me too,' he whispered.

'I want this though. I do.'

'Me too,' he whispered again.

Afterwards, after the passion and the heat and the feeling of her all around him had passed, he pulled more rugs and blankets from the grotto and wrapped her snug and close to him.

'That was…' He didn't have the words.

'Yeah.' She nestled her head into his shoulder. 'Were there fireworks going off as we… finished?'

'In here or out there?'

'Both. Either?'

'I think both.'

'Cool.'

'I can't promise the fireworks every time.'

'So there's going to be more times?' she asked, her voice muffled by his chest.

'I… I hope so.'

'OK.'

The silence sat between them for a moment. There was something strangely peaceful about being able to feel her against his body but also staring up at the grotto ceiling, talking only into space. It made him feel like he could say the things he usually left inside. 'I don't really do things like this,' Pavel admitted.

'Have sex in a Christmas grotto? No. Me neither.' She paused. 'Actually… well, I don't do it loads. Hardly ever in summer.'

'So many questions,' he replied. 'I meant I don't really believe in sparks.'

'You think we have a spark?'

'You don't?'

'I didn't say that. But you failed to kiss me twice so we hardly rushed into anything.'

That was true. It wasn't how it felt to Pavel though. Doing something for no other reason than that he wanted to was a rarity. 'It felt impulsive to me.'

'I know your name. Surname and everything. This is practically waiting until marriage for me.' She buried her head deeper. 'That doesn't sound great, does it?'

'Sounds better than being a total coward.'

'I don't believe you're a coward.'

'I think I am. I don't take risks. I don't grab what I want.'

'I have fingermarks on my arse that would beg to differ.'

Pavel laughed. 'I mean I don't jump in. It's scary.'

'I jump into the wrong things.'

'Am I a wrong thing?'

She shook her head. 'No. I'm scared cos I think you might be a very, very right thing.'

And then not looking into her eyes stopped feeling all right at all. He shifted onto his side, cupping her face in his hands. 'I think this could be everything. Let's agree not to screw it up.'

–

That sounded so straightforward. It was a wonderful idea – that you could create something good and pure and precious and then not break it. 'Screwing things up is sort of my speciality,' she whispered.

'But not this,' he replied. 'And I never screw up. I'm so sodding reliable. So if you feel like you're going to screw up, just bring it to Pavel and he'll fix it?'

'Really? You're going to fix me?'

'I don't think you need fixing.'

If only he knew. And that was the niggle at the back of Jodie's head. Pavel Stone was good and kind and honest and reliable and, if she could believe what he said – which by her own logic she must be able to – he was falling in love, right now, right in front of her eyes. With Jodie? With Gemma? With Jodie pretending to be Gemma pretending to be Jodie? It was the tangliest of webs and now she'd tied up someone who deserved a million times better than her. Than any of the versions of her she could ever hope to be.

'I need to...' Needed to what? If she told him the truth everything would fall apart. Could you turn a lie into a truth if you told it hard enough? Gemma's life was going way better than Jodie's. Gemma had a job, which it turned out Jodie wasn't awful at. She had friends. She had, if she accepted what she felt and let it happen, an incredible boyfriend. She had everything she knew she didn't deserve. 'I need to kiss you again.'

He grinned as he bent his head to hers. His lips were soft and warm and the kiss was more confident and more sure. Jodie let herself relax into it. Everything was going to be...

Bang.

She started at the knock on the door, and pulled the rug over her body as quickly as she could, slightly hampered by Pavel instinctively trying to do the same.

'Is that door locked?' he whispered urgently.

Another knock.

'I don't think so...'

The door swung open. Jay from Redd Level was silhouetted in the doorway. 'Right well, not the room

I'm looking for then.' He glanced back at Pavel and caught Jodie's eye. 'Nice.'

'I'm so sorry,' Jodie started.

The door was already swinging closed. 'Wow. Grottos have really changed since I was a kid. Merry Christmas!'

'Merry Christmas, Jay from Redd Level!' Jodie called back.

—

Pavel dropped Gemma off at the castle gates. 'Do you want to come in? You can. I mean, everyone will see you and we'll be the talk of the village before breakfast.'

'Would that bother you?' he asked. 'People knowing.'

Gemma shook her head. 'Not at all. I want to parade you down the high street shouting "look what I pulled".'

He laughed. 'Yeah. Don't do that. You want to tell people though?'

For a second the bravado she wore like a shield faltered. 'If you want to…'

'I want to, but let me go home tonight and tell my mum first. I'll get hell if she thinks Anna knew before her.'

Gemma nodded. 'So long as Anna's not secretly in the Redd Level WhatsApp group I think we're safe for now.'

'I'll see you tomorrow though?' he asked.

'You're coming to the lights parade?'

'I am. After a full morning of fixing all the lights for the villagers who only got them out yesterday and then discovered half the bulbs were blown or the plug was faulty.'

'Oh, Pavel, my hero.' She kissed him, full and hard, on the lips until his resolve about not coming in with her wavered. 'See you tomorrow.' She grinned.

He left the van parked outside the coach house on the grounds that that was where he'd be on Monday, and jogged back over the Low Bridge to the village. His mum was in the kitchen. 'What are you making?'

'Yule log. For after the service tomorrow.' She batted his finger away from the bowl of icing in front of her. 'Bella's doing mince pies and Christmas cake slices. I said I'd bring something chocolate for the kids.' She glanced up at him. 'And the big kids.'

Pavel took a seat at the breakfast bar his grandfather had built. Granddad always referred to it as Pavel's first job, but Pavel wasn't sure that wearing a toy tool belt that was two sizes too big and holding a screwdriver really counted as helping. His Granddad had been adamant though. Pavel had been born handy – good at building things, fixing things and making things right. That, his granddad had always said, was what made a man. Taking care of things, mending them, protecting things that needed protecting. He stroked the grain of the wood, softened and warmed with age.

'What are you looking so pleased about?'

'Yule log?' he suggested.

His mother shook her head. 'That's not yule-log happy. That's… I don't know. Something else.'

'I'm sort of…' What was he doing? His brain lingered over the details he had no intention of sharing with his mum. 'I'm seeing someone.'

He expected her to ask if it was back on with Jill. She nodded. 'That Gemma lassie from the castle?'

'How did you know?'

'I'm your mother and you are not the closed book you think you are. Not to me anyway.' She lifted the board with the rolled chocolate sponge into the space in front of her, and arranged an offcut to look like a smaller side branch. 'Does she make you happy?'

'So happy.'

'Not like that.' She pulled face. 'Really happy? Does she make you feel more like you?'

He shook his head. 'No. She makes me feel much braver than that.'

–

Back at the Dower House Jodie wandered from room to room, trying to quiet the itch in her brain that said she ought to be doing something. Pavel's presence quieted that voice. He filled her senses and kept her in the moment. She felt his absence in every room. There was no way she was going to sleep now.

She made her way over to the castle in the hope that someone would be around to talk to but the usually bustling kitchen was empty. On the island was a square wooden crate full to the brim with Brussels sprouts. That had been her very first task. Work out what to do with a glut of sprouts, and despite making Old Man Strachan a global sensation and getting a few nice comments on Bella's reels about fun ways to cook them, she hadn't actually used up any of the estate's own crop.

An idea hit, one of those ideas that, now it was in her head, Jodie knew wasn't going to go anywhere. She'd need more than just the sprouts, but there was all sorts still in the ballroom and there were art supplies for the toddler group somewhere. Jodie set to work through the night, and then in the early hours, before the rest of Lowbridge was up and awake, she loaded her creations back into the crate and carried them across the Low Bridge to the village.

Chapter Fifteen

After far too little sleep, the Lowbridge lights switch-on day dawned bright and crisp and cold, and Jodie's weather app promised her things were going to stay that way. That ticked one potential problem that was beyond her control off her list.

At half past one, she headed out, over the Low Bridge and into the village. Nina and Anna were waiting for her outside the pub, the last stop on the planned walk on the village side of the bridge. The lights on the pub were all in place, so they strolled back through the village checking everything was in order.

'We have to check,' Anna explained. 'In twenty nineteen there was an incident.'

Nina nodded gravely.

'What sort of incident?'

'One of the old houses had teenagers then.'

'Both off in Glasgow now,' Anna added.

'They'd... how can I put this?' Nina hesitated.

'They'd put tinsel and fairy lights round an inflatable cock and balls,' Anna explained.

'Yes. That's exactly what they did.'

Jodie couldn't suppress the giggle. 'Not really the tone you were going for?'

'Not at all.' Anna was puce. 'Mrs Timberley refused to chair the committee when we started up again. She got some terrible letters of complaint.'

'Mostly from Anna,' Nina whispered.

'What was that?'

'Nothing.'

They came to the final cottage in the first row after the bridge. Anna shook her head dramatically. 'Oh, that won't do at all. Barry! Barry Morgan, you come out here right now and straighten up these snowflakes.'

Jodie and Nina left Anna to her troubleshooting and walked on.

'So my Pavel came home all full of beans last night.'

'Did he?' Jodie kept her gaze straight ahead, determined to play it cool.

'Oh yes. The cat that got the cream. Happier than I've seen him in years.'

Sod cool. 'Really?' Jodie's heart leapt a little bit. The nugget of terror in her gut that maybe yesterday had been some sort of mirage, or that Pavel Stone would get home and instantly regret the whole sordid episode, eased a little.

'Really.'

'Oh. Good. And he told you…' Jodie couldn't end the sentence with anything that sounded even vaguely like Pavel Stone might have said it out loud to his mother.

'He told me you two were seeing one another.'

'Right. Yeah. Is that OK?'

'With me?' Nina laughed. 'Is this you coming to ask his parents' permission?'

'No. Yeah.' This was ridiculous. 'I know you're close.'

'He values what other people think far too much, that lad, but for what it's worth I do like you.' She paused. 'Of course, if you hurt him I will destroy you anyway.'

Jodie laughed.

Nina did not join in.

Jodie stopped. 'OK. Understood.'

'Shall we go and see the tree? You know Anna's done it in red and green, don't you?'

'Actually I might have added to some of the green.'

Nina frowned as they walked in silence to the front of the village shop. The tree stood proud, not yet lit, and covered in small green baubles. 'Are they...?' she laughed.

Jodie shrugged. 'We had so many sprouts. There was no way they were all going to get eaten.'

Nina plucked a makeshift sprout bauble off the nearest branch and turned it around in her hand. Jodie had stuck red ribbon to each one so they'd hang from the tree. 'That's a brilliant idea, love.'

'Really?'

'Really,' Nina confirmed. 'Absolute genius.'

—

Pavel arrived outside the shop about half an hour before the official switch-on was scheduled. Villagers were gathering. Hugh was doling out mulled wine and hot chocolate from a table in front of the shop. Everyone was bundled up against the early evening chill in the air. Cheeks were pink and smiles were wide. He scanned the gathering crowd for the face he wanted to see, only for her to appear right next to him.

'Hi.'

'I was looking for you.'

'I'm five foot nothing. Tricky to spot in a crowd. I saw you coming half a mile away though.'

They both hesitated. 'I'm not sure if I'm supposed to kiss you.'

'For future reference, if you ever wonder that, the answer is probably yes.'

'All right then.' He bent his head to meet her and pressed her lips to his. As they came apart he looked up to find half the village staring at them, including Jill. He watched as Anna, Flinty and his mother all looked from him and Gemma to Jill and back again. 'I…' He didn't have an end for the sentence.

Jill was a better person than him though. 'This is new.' She smiled brightly. 'Happy days.' She walked determinedly over to Pavel and wrapped him in a hug. 'You could have told me,' she hissed in his ear.

'Sorry.'

She pulled back from the hug. 'It's fine.' She moved to include Gemma in their circle. 'Seriously, this is great. When did this happen?'

'Yesterday,' Pavel confirmed.

'It's great. Great. Really great.' She squeezed his shoulder. 'I'm going to get a hot chocolate. Have fun.'

The moment of relief was short-lived.

'What happened between you and her?'

Fair question. 'Nothing. We went on one date. It was awkward. We agreed we're better as friends.'

Gemma nodded. 'So why is half the village looking at me like I'm Yoko Ono and Jill's the rest of The Beatles?'

'Because this village is lightly insane. I think people had made more of it than it was, to the point where we almost got sucked in too.' He could see the doubt on her face. He searched for the right thing to say. 'Jill's a friend. A really good friend, but there's nothing else there. It was a story people told each other and we ended up telling ourselves.' That was it. 'It wasn't real.'

'And this is?'

He reached down and took her hand in his. 'It is for me.'

He felt her fingers squeeze his in response and allowed himself to exhale.

––

'Gemma, we need you.' Nina called her away from Pavel, and over to the tiny platform Hugh had built in front of the shop.

'What's wrong?'

'Nothing, but someone needs to introduce your special guests to turn the first set of lights on.'

'You should do that. You're in charge of all this.'

Nina waved a hand. 'Pish. You put this together. You should have your moment. Just remember to speak right into the microphone. If you have it more than about half an inch away it picks nothing up.'

Jodie felt herself being pushed towards the microphone balanced on the platform. 'Wait. Guests?'

'Yes.'

'Plural? I only invited Santa.'

Nina laughed out loud. 'He brought a friend.' She leaned in and whispered. Jodie's cheeks coloured at the very mention of the name.

'Right. OK.' She picked up the microphone and cleared her throat. 'Hello, everyone…' Nobody turned round.

She glanced at Nina, who gestured to hold the microphone closer to her lips.

'Hello?'

Still no reaction. Nina frowned. A second later she saw Pavel pushing the cable properly into its power supply and the microphone in her hand crackled into life.

'Hello, everyone,' she tried again. 'Hello.'

This time people towards the front paid attention and a ripple of shushes extended back through the small crowd.

'Hello, everyone. Welcome to our Lowbridge village lights switch-on. Erm… thank you all for coming. I hope you will join us on our walk through the village to see the rest of the community's decorations, and then we'll be finishing up at Lowbridge Castle where the Reverend Jill is going to lead carols and I think there are mince pies and yule log and you're welcome to stay and mingle and catch up.' She glanced at Nina for confirmation that she'd remembered everything important and was met with a cheerful thumbs-up. 'Great. OK then. All I need to do now is introduce our two very special guests to turn on our first set of lights. Please, everyone, put your hands together and whoop and cheer and generally go a bit crazy for Father Christmas and Jay from Redd Level!'

There was a second of quiet while people wondered, very obviously, whether Jodie was joking before the man in the big red suit was escorted onto the platform by a very cheerful, if slightly bemused-looking, Nineties pop icon. And then the cheers started. Jodie smiled.

Jay took up a position alongside her. 'Hello again.'

'Hi. Sorry about yesterday.' It was a very brief acknowledgement of the mother of all awkward situations.

'Most fun I've had since…' He shook his head. 'Actually my publicist doesn't like me telling that story.'

'OK. So, I guess now we switch the lights on.' Jodie realised absolutely too late that she had no plan for this. The plan had been not to have a celeb switch-on. And now she had two celebs and nothing for them to do. The lights came on when Hugh pressed the switch on the extension lead behind the counter in the shop. She could hardly ask Jay from Redd Level to hop off the stage and rummage under the carrier bags and veg scales to turn the lights on.

Something was thrust in front of her. Jodie took a second to process what it was. And what it was was a shoe box covered in wrapping paper with half an Edam stuck on top of it. She looked down. Anna smiled brightly. 'Big red button.'

'Right. OK.' Jodie took the box from Anna. 'Is Hugh ready?' she whispered.

'Standing by.'

'All right then. Shall we do a countdown? Ten, nine...'

The crowd joined in. 'Eight, seven...'

'Is that cheese?' Santa whispered.

'Six, five...'

'Yep,' Jodie confirmed.

Jay raised an eyebrow. 'Do we get to keep the cheese?'

'Four, three...'

'Sure.'

Jay nodded his approval.

'Fair enough,' Father Christmas agreed.

'Two, one.'

Two hands came down together onto the cheese button and a second later the lights on the tree flickered into life.

'Aw,' Jay grinned, 'that's really pretty.'

'Yeah. It is,' Jodie agreed. She stepped off the stage, looking for Pavel out in the crowd and seeing him surrounded by kids from the village who were taking turns to get lifted up onto his shoulders for a closer look at the angel sitting on the top of the tree.

A hand on her arm made her turn. Jill. Was she another person Jodie had screwed over in her wake?

'Look. I'm sorry...'

Jill held up her hand. 'Nothing to be sorry about. I wanted to reassure you. I'm sure, the way people talk around here, that you're going to hear that me and Pav were some great romance, but we're friends. Good friends. Romantically it's just not there.'

'That's what he said.'

Jill nodded. 'And he's a terrible liar.' Her voice dropped. 'At least to other people. Anyway, I'm his friend. I'm not competition. You haven't done me dirty or anything like that. Of course, cos he is my friend, if you hurt him I'll have to...'

'Kill me? I know. You're the second person who's told me that.'

Jill laughed. 'His mum?'

'Yeah.'

'And she's way scarier than me. Anyway, I was going to say I'd have to forgive you. Goes with the job, I'm afraid.'

'That is less scary,' Jodie agreed.

'It would be a very aggressive forgiving.'

Jill moved away to mingle with the rest of the villagers. Jodie could see Nina and Anna starting to distribute lanterns for the walk along to the castle. It was turning out to be a really lovely event. Despite herself, Jodie had done something right.

She turned to find Pavel and liberate him from the huddle of kids and found herself staring directly into a distinctly less friendly face. Fiona MacCellan. 'Fi.'

When had she got here? Had she seen Jodie introducing the whole event? That might still be something she could style out. Fiona knew she was living in Lowbridge. But if she'd seen that she'd also have seen...

'You stole my pop star.'

Right. So she had definitely seen that part.

'I didn't even invite him.'

'And Father Christmas. I paid his travel all the way from Edinburgh.'

'It was his day off,' Jodie spluttered.

'Gemma!'

No. No. Not now.

'Gemma!' Anna bore down on them both. 'We're nearly ready to start the walk.'

Jodie nodded mutely. 'I'll be there in a minute.'

'Why are they calling you Gemma?'

'It's a nickname.'

'Gemma short for Jodie?' Fiona wasn't an idiot. Jodie really, really wished she was.

'No. It's like…' What could she say? 'I… when I first came here I'd just broken up with someone and things were really hard and maybe I wanted to be someone else for a while. It was a misunderstanding really. That I didn't correct.'

Fiona shook her head. 'Right. So you moved to the other end of a country and adopted a fake name cos you were having a difficult time.'

Put like that it did sound ridiculous.

'Jodie?' Another voice cut across Fiona's reply. 'Jodie Simpson? Oh my goodness, it is you. I thought I saw you yesterday up where we're staying, but I thought don't be ridiculous. What would she be doing all the way up here?'

Jodie could have kissed the woman hurtling towards them. 'Diane.' Yesterday she'd run and hid away for fear of exposure. Today Diane was a life raft and Jodie jumped gratefully aboard. She turned to Fiona. 'This is Diane. We knew each other before I moved up here. This is Fiona. She's my boss at the McKenzie estate.' She arranged her face into what she hoped was an expression of realisation. 'Oh my goodness. Is that where you're staying?'

Diane nodded. 'Lovely to meet you, Fiona.'

Fiona looked utterly confused. Jodie tried to remember what her CV said her last job had been. Pizza Now, of course. So how to use Diane to get her out of one mess, without getting her into a bigger one? 'I used to do a few shifts for Diane in her coffee shop back in Reading when I was free. She's a friend of my mum.'

Please let her pick up on the family-friend angle and not the terrible-barista element.

'That's right,' Diane confirmed. 'I've known this one's family since she was tiny.'

Fiona still looked bemused. 'Jodie's family?'

'That's right. I lived near them when I was younger. When Jodie moved to Reading her mum asked me to keep an eye out, you know?'

'Right.' Fiona rallied. 'What a coincidence.'

'Isn't it?' Diane squeezed Jodie's arm. 'Are you doing this lantern-walk thing? It sounds absolutely lovely. Are visitors allowed to join in?'

'Of course. If you go over there' – Jodie gestured towards the shop, expecting to see Nina and Anna handing out lights. They seemed to have found a new minion – 'Jay from Redd Level will give you a lantern.'

Fiona stayed quiet until Diane was out of earshot. 'I am so sorry. I don't know what I was thinking. I do this. I don't think and I jump to the wrong conclusions and...'

Jodie shook her head. Now she had to add gaslighting Fiona to her list of crimes. 'No. It's fine. I mean, I did sort of borrow your Santa. I'm sorry about that.'

Fiona pursed his lips. 'His contract does say he can't take any other jobs while he's with us.'

'We're not paying him.'

'That's probably technically allowed then.' She sighed. 'John will be…'

'What if we didn't tell Mr McKenzie?'

Fiona's face froze as if she was struggling to process this radical idea.

'I mean, what we all do on our days off isn't really up to him, is it?'

'I am his…' Fiona lowered his voice. 'We don't make a show of it in front of people. He's very private, you know. But I am *with* John.'

'He's not with you today though?'

'He had to be somewhere else today.'

At home with his wife probably, Jodie thought. And with a flash of certainty she knew she was right. Maybe not a wife, but another Fiona somewhere out there picking up scraps and desperately trying to piece them together into something that made her feel special. She had another question though. 'Fiona, why did you come to this?'

'No reason. I was passing through.'

Lowbridge wasn't a place people passed through. It was barely a place people came to. 'OK.' Jodie didn't bother to hide the scepticism in her voice.

'Ge…' Pavel's voice stopped abruptly. 'Fiona.' He smiled. 'Lovely to see you. And Jodie, hi.'

The recovery was fast enough and Pavel's big, honest face was trustworthy enough for the slip-up to go unchallenged.

'We're starting the walk through the village,' he told them.

'Are you going to come?' Jodie asked.

Fiona shook her head. 'I should get back. I don't want to intrude.'

'You wouldn't be.'

'I might. There are plenty of people here who think my family sold out.' She nodded quickly. 'Lots to do anyway. And John said he might be around this evening so I should go.'

Jodie watched her leave, heading back to a car parked across from the shop in front of the small pebble beach. 'I feel sorry for her.'

'Me too, and she's wrong.'

'What about?'

'People don't blame her family. They definitely don't blame her. You've seen what it takes to hold on to an estate these days. Adam's barely managing and he's got his own business somewhere else.'

'I blame John McKenzie,' Jodie added. 'For pretty much everything at the moment.'

'He's not here.' Pavel wrapped her hand up in his. 'You've got cold hands.'

'I'm sure you can find somewhere warm to put them.'

He shot her a look that managed to combine 'stop now' with 'you bet I can'. Something inside Jodie went a little bit wibbly.

The walk through the village was magical. Houses flicked their lights on as the group approached and finally the pub was lit up in sparkling cascades of white and gold, before they continued over the bridge and into the castle's chapel, lit with candles and the walkers' lanterns.

Jill led them singing 'O Little Town of Bethlehem', 'Silent Night' and 'The First Nowell', before she invited Nina and the children and parents from toddler group up to sing 'Away in a Manger', which involved very little singing and a lot of waving at nanas in the congregation.

'I think we have time for one more. And I hope you'll indulge me with one of my favourites. Let's close with "In the Bleak Midwinter".'

As the first chords played Jodie felt something pricking at her eyes. She wasn't going to cry. No. Jodie was always overemotional. Gemma had said it was adorable, but even she'd pointed out, very sensibly, that most people would find it a bit much. Jodie had to be better at keeping it together.

The congregation around her flowed into song. *In the bleak midwinter, frosty wind made moan.* The words were gentle and plaintive and the voices of the village, raised together, washed over her.

She wasn't upset. The tears that were pricking at her eyes weren't born out of sadness or anger or even joy. They were more like an over-spilling from a soul simply too full of emotion – every emotion. And she let the tears fall, and the words and the music wrapped around her. It was ridiculous. It was pure Jodie behaviour. Gemma would have play-punched her on the arm and told her to pull herself together.

Next to her she felt a hand brush against hers and then wrap her fingers in its grasp. She squeezed Pavel's hand and leaned her head gently against his arm as the tears continued to flow.

–

Pavel didn't crowd Gemma for the rest of the evening, but he did keep an eye on her. The last few days seemed to have unlocked an openness in her that he'd only glimpsed before, but that had brought a vulnerability with it. All her emotions were on the surface, raw and unguarded. Pavel had to find a way to protect her.

Before he could go back over to her he was accosted, or perhaps more accurately ambushed, by Anna, his mother's friend Netty, and Flinty. 'So what's this with you and our Gemma?' Flinty asked.

'We're going out.'

'From what your mother said it sounds more like staying in,' Anna suggested.

'What did my mother say?'

'She said you were *seeing* one another.'

Pavel nodded. 'Yeah. Well, we are.'

'Did you break the Reverend's heart?' Flinty asked.

Jill was currently deep into her third mince pie chatting to Bella by the food table. 'I think she's fine. You can go and ask her though?'

'We're asking you.'

'Right. Well, I think she's fine.'

'Can I keep the same hat?' That was Netty.

'What?'

'Can I wear the wedding hat I bought for you and Jill for you and this Gemma?'

'You bought a hat for me and Jill? We barely went on one date.' Pavel looked to the other two women for moral support but none was forthcoming.

'You don't want Netty to waste a good hat, do you?' Flinty asked.

Pavel shook his head.

'It's in poor taste though. How would you feel if you were the bride and you knew people had bought their outfits for his previous paramour?' Anna folded her arms.

'That's my worry,' Netty replied. 'It's like wearing his ex's wedding dress.'

'I don't think it is,' Pavel tried.

'So you'll get her her own dress?'

'I don't think the groom gets a say in the dress,' Anna pointed out.

'Well good, if he's going to make her wear some other woman's frock.'

'I'm not going to make her...' Pavel desperately floundered for a way out of this conversation. There didn't seem to be one. 'She can choose her own...'

Suddenly he felt a small hand slip into his. 'Ladies.' Gemma smiled brightly. 'I hope you're not haranguing my fella?'

'Not at all. Just making sure he's being a gentleman,' Flinty explained.

'Fair enough. Shall I leave you to it then?'

Pavel tightened his grip on her hand.

'Or maybe I should remind you that this,' she pointed from herself to Pavel, 'is very new. And we're very happy but nobody is going to be buying anyone a wedding dress any time soon. OK?'

Anna shook her head. 'Young people. They don't think ahead.'

'I only wondered about my hat,' Netty added.

Eventually the three of them trundled off, presumably to interrogate another innocent villager about their personal life. He kissed the top of Gemma's head. 'Thank you.'

'You're welcome...' She hesitated. 'My darling.'

'Is that our thing now?'

She shrugged. 'I love it. I don't like babe and sweetie and things like that. Sounds like a fourteen-year-old on TikTok.'

'I wouldn't know.'

'"My darling" is classy. A bit more Mr Darcy. If Mr Darcy claimed he could bench-press Lizzie Bennet.'

Nina came over. 'You two having a good day?'

Pavel nodded. 'The yule log was great.'

'Would have been even better if someone hadn't eaten half the icing before I'd finished making it.'

'Jodie.' There was a stranger bearing down on them.

'I'm called Jodie,' Gemma whispered urgently.

'What?' His mum looked utterly confused.

'Jodie, I didn't think I was going to catch you again.'

'Diane.' Gemma let go of Pavel's hand and kissed the woman on each cheek. 'This is Pavel. He's my...' Pavel caught the gulp she gave. 'My boyfriend. And this is Nina, his mum.'

His mum was still frowning.

'Diane's staying at the McKenzie estate,' Gemma explained. 'Where I work.'

He glanced at his mum. The penny hadn't quite dropped yet. 'The estate over the way. Where Jodie got a job,' he added as casually as he could manage.

He saw understanding dawn. 'Of course, *Jodie*.' She all but winked.

Pavel winced. Play it cool, Mum. Play it cool.

Diane didn't seem to have noticed any weirdness. But why would she? Why would you think that two people you'd only just met were conspiring with an admin assistant from your holiday destination to convince you she had a fake name? 'This whole day was lovely. And I was talking to the chap who runs this place. Apparently they're having a whole big do for Hogmanay.' She sighed. 'It's so far to travel but honestly I'm tempted. I love this part of the world. Always have.'

'Oh, you should come. It's going to be so much fun.' Gemma beamed. 'And staying in an actual castle. Can you imagine?'

Diane laughed. 'You need to be careful. Aren't you supposed to work for the opposition?'

Gemma froze.

'Oh, we're all one big happy family around here,' Nina reassured her.

Diane made her farewells. 'It was so good to run into you,' she told Gemma. 'You look well. I'm pleased.' She smiled. 'I shall tell your mother I saw you.'

Gemma nodded. 'OK.'

'She misses you.'

'Are you going to see your parents for Christmas?' Nina asked.

Gemma shook her head. 'I think we'll be too busy here.'

'Hopefully you'll make it back in the new year?'

'Yeah. Maybe.'

Nina turned away. 'I'd best go make myself useful.'

'There's a lot of making yourself useful around here,' Gemma laughed.

'Tell me about it. Mum and Anna were born to run the world, I think, but the universe landed them with a tiny Scottish village instead.' Pavel paused. He didn't want to ask any more about her family. Not right now. She'd tell him when she was ready. He wasn't going to push. 'Today was really nice.'

'I don't know. I thought yesterday had a certain something.' She looked up at him to catch his eye.

'I meant this was a nice event for the whole community.' He looked around to where Flinty was now roping anyone she passed into helping out. Absolutely anyone. 'The whole community and Jay from Redd Level.'

-

Jodie leaned into Pavel's body. He was right. Apart from the scare with Diane and Fiona the day had gone well. Really well. 'So do you want to stay tonight?' she asked. 'You don't have to. I mean, if you feel like we're rushing into things a bit. We could take it slow, or…'

'Do you want me to?'

More than she could put into words. She didn't really want to let him out of her sight. He was a solid point of reality in this web of confusion she was creating around her. 'Yeah.'

'OK then.'

'The Dower House is quite…' She searched for the word. 'Feminine. And chintzy.' She tried to picture Pavel's tall, broad frame in amongst the florals and the doilies.

'I'm not really coming for the décor.'

'They did say I could redecorate, but I never got around to it.'

'I can help if you want to decorate the place.'

'Oooh,' she sighed. 'And you'll do it all properly, won't you? With straight edges and no splashes of wall colour on the woodwork.'

'Absolutely.'

Now she could picture Pavel very easily in the great-aunt's-knicker-drawer aesthetic of the Dower House – paintbrush in hand, pencil behind his ear, and, for reasons that had nothing at all to do with his decorating skills, stripped to the waist.

'Are you all right there?' he asked.

'What?'

'You were in a world of your own for a moment.'

'Thinking about what we might do tonight.' Which suddenly didn't involve a can of summer-white emulsion at all.

'Miss Bryant.' Veronica interrupted what was about to be a very detailed and quite explicit explanation of how little sleep Pavel Stone was going to get that night. 'Could I have a word?'

'OK.' Jodie dropped Pavel's hand. 'I'll see you back at the Dower House? It's not locked if you're there before me.'

She followed Veronica out of the courtyard and into the lane outside the coach house. Veronica looked to each side as if to confirm that they were alone.

'My dear.' There was something in Veronica's tone that set Jodie's nerves on edge already. 'I'll come straight to the point. I overheard your conversation with Miss MacCellan and the lady who was visiting from Reading earlier.'

'Right.' Jodie didn't respond straight away. What had Veronica heard? Maybe she hadn't got the whole story.

'Just when I feared you were exposed and Miss MacCellan was going to realise that you were, literally, working for the enemy, you were saved.'

'Yes.'

'By someone who knew you long before you came here.'

So she'd heard enough. More than enough. 'Yes.'

'Who thought you really were Jodie Simpson.'

'Yes.'

'Which should make no sense at all.'

Should?

'But actually a lot of things slipped into place.'

Now Jodie was confused. 'What do you mean?'

'The lack of National Insurance number.'

'I just couldn't find…' she started.

Veronica held up a hand. 'Don't. When we interviewed you… sorry. When we interviewed Gemma Bryant, I wasn't convinced she was the right fit for Lowbridge.'

That was ridiculous. Gemma was the perfect fit everywhere she went.

'But, even if it pains me, this is not my estate any more. I must let my grandson and his fiancée have their heads. And they were quite taken with her…' Veronica paused. 'Shall we say her poise? So imagine my confusion when you turned up.'

'Are you saying I'm not poised?'

'You, young lady, are a walking chaos engine.' Veronica's face cracked ever so slightly into a hint of a smile. 'Much more our sort of person, I would say.'

Was that another lifeline being thrown her way? 'You're not cross.'

The smile vanished. 'I am furious. With myself for not nipping this in the bud much earlier. I knew something was wrong, but I don't know. Maybe I'm getting old but I couldn't quite put my finger on what it was.' She looked Jodie squarely in the eye. 'You are, I take it, not Gemma Bryant?'

She could try to lie her way out of things. She could probably buy herself a little more time, but a little more time was all it would be. Veronica was clever and she knew, in her gut, that she was right. She'd squirrel out the evidence whether Jodie came clean or not. 'I'm not.'

It was almost a relief.

'Presumably there is a real Gemma somewhere?'

'My ex. That's who you interviewed. She deserved all this.'

Veronica tilted her head a little sadly. 'We don't always get what we deserve. I'm sure you had your reasons and I don't discredit your commitment since you arrived, but that doesn't take away from the fact that you have lied to my grandson and to Bella, both of whom I care for very deeply, since the moment you got here. You understand that that cannot continue?'

Of course it couldn't. 'I'm really sorry.'

'So am I.' The older woman nodded. 'You have done good work here. I don't know why you did this but everything you've done here, even today, was down to you. Not this Gemma woman. You.'

'What are you going to do now?'

'I'm going to come with you.' Veronica rubbed her hands together. 'People are starting to head off. I imagine Bella's back in the kitchen already. Shall we?'

'Right now?'

'I think so, don't you?'

—

As Veronica had anticipated, Bella and Adam were both in the kitchen, heads bent over her laptop. Bella grinned as they came in. 'What do you think about cranachan for dessert on Hogmanay? When does tradition tip into cliché?'

'I think it sounds great.' Jodie nodded. 'What's cranachan?'

Bella shook her head. 'I don't know why I even ask you food questions.'

Jodie tried to smile. 'Everything you make tastes amazing.'

'And that's why we like you.'

Adam looked up for the first time. 'Grandmother?' He looked from Veronica to Jodie. 'What's wrong? Has something else happened with McKenzie?'

'No.' Veronica took a seat at the island. 'This is something else. Go on.'

Jodie took a deep breath in. There was nothing she could say that would make this all right. There was no reasonable explanation. 'I'm Jodie Simpson.'

Bella laughed. 'You're not undercover now, Gem.'

'Good commitment to the part though,' Adam added.

She looked to Veronica for help. None was forthcoming. 'No. I really am Jodie Simpson. When you rang to offer Gemma the job – well, she was my ex, and she'd already moved out and I answered the phone and…' There was more she could say but she suspected they could fill in the details from here.

'What?' Bella shook her head. 'But I rang and you said… and you're Gemma.'

Jodie shook her head.

'So who are you?' Adam asked.

'I am Jodie. Gemma was my girlfriend and we split up, and I lost my job and I couldn't make my rent and I was wishing for a miracle and then, I know it's not an excuse, but then the phone rang and it was you and I realised you'd never actually seen Gemma and… I'm really sorry.' Jodie could have hit herself around the head. She should have said that first. 'So sorry. And you've been so good to me and I hated lying but I didn't know what to do and I really have tried to do a good job but I'm not Gemma. All that experience isn't me.'

Bella shook her head. 'But you wrote the plan. The whole Hogmanay thing was your idea?'

'Gemma's idea.'

Adam stared at her. 'I don't know what to say.' He turned to his grandmother. 'You knew this?'

Jodie jumped in. 'She found out tonight. She said I had to tell you straight away.'

He nodded. 'And if she hadn't found out? Would you have told us at all?'

Bella looked up too, waiting for the answer. They wanted her to say yes. Of course she'd have told them. She couldn't feed them another lie. 'I don't know. I think I wanted all of this to be true so much. Like if I tried hard enough I could be Gemma. It wouldn't be a lie any more.'

She saw the look Adam and Bella exchanged. Adam turned back to her. 'Does Pavel know?'

'No.'

Adam closed his eyes. 'You need to go and tell him.'

Of course she did.

'Right now,' he added.

'Right. I'll pack as well. I understand you want me out.'

Bella held a hand up. 'Go and talk to Pavel.' She nodded to Adam. 'We need to talk about this as well. We'll see you in the morning.'

'I really am sorry.'

Bella nodded. 'In the morning.'

—

The walk back to the Dower House was about two minutes. That didn't matter. Twenty years wouldn't be long enough to find the words to undo all the damage she was about to cause. The thought of breaking Pavel's heart was the heaviest thing she could imagine. And she was about to do it and she was going to have to look him in the eye when she did.

And whatever she said to make it better wouldn't be enough. She'd tried to take something that wasn't for her. A job. A life. A love.

She opened the door to the Dower House and was greeted by Pavel almost before she was inside. She let him pull her into his arms and kick the door shut behind them. She let him pick her up from the ground and press his lips to hers. 'You took your time,' he murmured.

'Sorry.'

'You're here now.' That was true. She was. Why couldn't they have that one more night? His heart was going to be trampled either way. Why not let them both have one more night before everything fell apart?

'Did you find the bedroom?'

'I found four. You'll have to show me to your favourite.' He lowered her to the floor and she took him by the hand.

'In here.'

He looked around. 'I see what you mean about the décor.'

'We can turn the lights out.'

He shook his head. 'I want to be able to see you.'

Jodie nodded her assent. She wanted that too. She wanted to store every detail of this night in her memory – every touch, every taste, every inch of his face, the creases around his eyes, the stubble on his chin, the way his brow furrowed ever so slightly when she teased him. She wanted to drink it all in and hold on to it all. Whatever came next she'd always have this night.

Later, when they'd finished and rested and begun again, she sat astride him, legs wrapped tight around his hips, torso pressed to torso, staring into his eyes. 'This is perfect,' she whispered.

'Completely.'

'I wish we never had to stop.'

'We don't.'

Jodie bent her head and buried her face into his neck. If only that was true.

Pavel slept beside her, solid and easy and calm. Jodie lay awake, not even trying to sleep. Sleep would simply hasten the arrival of the morning and the morning was when everything would come to an end.

At half past five she rose, quietly, pulling her clothes from yesterday on, and then as silently as she could, stuffing the rest of her stuff back into her case. Her sleep-deprived brain knew two things. Right now she had two different futures ahead of her. Both of them broke Pavel's heart, but she only had to see it happen in one of them. She'd been right. She was far more of a coward than he was.

She stopped in the doorway for one last look, desperately trying to imprint the image of him in her mind so she could hold him there in the long, awful nights she knew were ahead. 'I'm so sorry,' she whispered, picked up her case and set out into the dark of the early morning.

Jodie carried her case through the courtyard so the scrape of the wheels on the cobbles didn't wake anyone in the castle. She stopped by the kitchen door, hurried inside, dropped an envelope on the kitchen island and left.

She was more prepared this time. It was Monday. That meant the school minibus that took the kids to Loch-carron for the week would be picking up in the village at quarter past six, and out here the drivers were used to waifs and strays hopping aboard as the only way of getting anywhere useful. She'd be in Lochcarron in time to get the bus to Strathcarron to pick up a train. And thanks to the wondrous benevolence of the McKenzie estate she had enough money in her bank account to get her far enough away to regroup and work out what she could do next that would leave less pain in her wake.

She took one last look back towards the castle as she hopped on the bus. This was the best thing. It saved Bella and Adam, who were good and kind and generous, from the pain of having to look her in the eye and tell her she had to go. And there was nothing she could have said to Pavel that would make this better. There was only one thing she could say to him and she'd put that in her letter. Adam and Bella would explain it better than she ever could.

—

Sunlight was already streaming through the thin curtains when Pavel woke up. For a second he wasn't sure why he was waking up under a floral counterpane rather than his own simple blue duvet, and then of course he knew. He'd stayed with Gemma. He smiled. He'd slept better than he had for years and woken without the niggling sense in the back of his head that he had to get up, had to push on, had to make himself useful. He felt quite at ease lying back and waiting for his girlfriend to return.

He listened out for the sounds of her in the kitchen or the shower, but the cottage was quiet. Pavel reached for his phone on the floor and checked the time. Already half past eight. She was most likely up and off to work already. She could have woken him for a lift. He smiled at the idea of Gemma deciding to let him sleep.

Pavel pulled his clothes on and picked up his phone. He tapped out a text.

Morning. Are you still at Lowbridge?

Her phone buzzed on the bedside table at the other side of the bed. Great. Pavel headed over to the castle kitchen in search of life, wondering if she was already on her way over to the McKenzie estate. He should probably pick her phone up and take it over with him.

He arrived in the kitchen feeling slightly sheepish. Everyone at the castle was a friend and he knew he'd always be welcome at their table but they weren't used to him turning up for breakfast wearing yesterday's clothes. He braced for the inevitable teasing.

Instead he was met with silence. Adam, Bella and Darcy were all sitting at the kitchen island, but the room wasn't full of the sort of chatter he was used to. 'What's up with you lot?'

'Pav.' Adam tilted his head. 'How are you doing?'

'I'm fine.' He looked around for a mug. 'Do you mind if I get some coffee?'

'Course not.' Adam nodded. 'Get whatever you need.'

'Coffee's fine.' He turned back to the group at the table. 'Seriously, what's up?'

Adam closed his eyes for a second. 'She didn't tell you, did she?'

'Who didn't tell me what?' This really was starting to feel strange.

Adam looked at his fiancée. She was holding an envelope between her fingers. She passed it to Adam. 'Why don't we leave you to it for a minute?'

Adam nodded. Darcy followed Bella out of the room, pausing in the doorway. 'I'm so sorry.'

'Sit down, mate.'

Pavel did as he was told. 'OK. You're freaking me out a bit now. What's happened?'

'So Gemma.' He rubbed his eyes. 'Jodie. There is no Gemma. She was Jodie all along. She was pretending to be Gemma cos she needed a job and yeah...'

'What?' Adam wasn't making any sense. 'She's pretending to be Jodie at the McKenzie place.'

'Yeah. She is, but that's her real name.' Adam spoke quickly. 'She's Jodie Simpson. Gemma, the real Gemma, was her ex and that was who we offered the job to. Jodie pretended to be her.'

'No.' Why would Adam be saying something like this? 'I'm not joking.'

Pavel looked at his friend's face. He really wasn't joking. People didn't do that though. They didn't pretend to be someone else to get a job in a run-down castle in the middle of nowhere. They didn't travel across the country based on a lie and a prayer.

And then Pavel remembered her on the very first day, trying to run away before she'd begun, convinced that she'd made a terrible mistake. He remembered the way she shut down every time anyone asked about her home or her life before Lowbridge. He remembered Bella teasing her for lying about how much she knew about cookery before they offered her the job. He remembered every time he thought he'd seen her, and every time she'd closed down again. He hadn't known what was wrong, but he'd known that something was. He'd known that she wasn't showing him all of herself.

But he had seen her. He'd seen the way her face changed when he called her darling. He'd seen her fighting for breath when panic was overtaking her. He'd seen her weeping at the strains of a carol. He'd laughed with her. He'd made love to her, and that had been real. She'd promised him it was real.

Adam was still holding the envelope Bella had handed him. 'She left this.' He pulled out two sheets of paper and held one out. 'This one's for you. Well, it's for us to tell you but you might as well read it for yourself.'

Pavel unfolded the paper.

> *Please tell Pavel I'm sorry. And tell him it wasn't all a lie. Tell my darling Pavel that all of that was real. I'm so so sorry if I hurt him.*

'If she hurt me?' He looked at his friend.

'I know, mate.' He shook his head. 'She told us last night. I told her she had to tell you. I thought she would.'

Pavel thought back to last night at the cottage. Had she started trying to tell him something? And then what? Fear, he guessed. Fear of how he'd react. 'I wish she had.'

'What would you have done if she had?'

'I don't know.' Was that true? 'Asked her to stay.'

Adam nodded. 'That's what I was going to do too.'

'What?'

'Me and Bel talked about it. I mean we're furious obviously, but she's done good stuff since she got here, and Bel's fond of her. And Darcy's incapable of turning away a lost soul, so yeah. I was going to check if you were OK with it and then ask her to stay. And then Bella was going to make her wash up after every cookery school session for the next six months.'

Too late for that. Gemma – no, Jodie – had made the decision for all of them. And that wasn't OK. Suddenly Pavel wasn't sad any more. He was angry. 'How dare she?'

'What?'

'Run away. Decide for us. Did she tell you where she'd gone?'

Adam shook his head. 'Six o'clock on a Monday morning? And none of us drove her anywhere.'

'School bus to Lochcarron?'

Adam nodded. 'That'd be my guess.'

Pavel was out of the door and jumping into his van before Adam had finished the sentence. School bus to Lochcarron probably meant regular bus from there to the station. He could go straight there without going round the houses to all the tiny hamlets and farmsteads like the bus did. He could still catch her. He could still make things right.

–

And so Jodie's Highland adventure was going to end where it started, at the tiny station in Strathcarron, looking forward to hours and hours of travelling. Twelve hours ago she'd been happy, or at least as close to happy as she ever managed to come. Twelve hours ago before Veronica had called her to one side and blown up the gossamer web of lies she'd constructed. And she'd been kind about it.

That was the thing Jodie's brain kept coming back to. Veronica hadn't called her names or shouted or humiliated her. She'd been kind. Jodie didn't deserve kind.

She checked the information board again. Her first train would take her to Inverness and from there she could change for Edinburgh, Newcastle, even London. She could be far away from here by lunchtime. But then what? She was starting again. Again. The money she had in the bank wouldn't last more than a few weeks and she had nowhere to stay and no job to go to.

At least the station was quiet. There was nobody around to witness her failure. It also meant that as soon as another person stepped onto the platform she was aware of their presence, as if she wouldn't have been aware of his presence in any place on any day. She didn't turn her head as he got closer. 'What are you doing here?' she asked.

'That's what I was going to ask you.'

She slid along the bench to make room for him to sit down next to her. Pavel remained standing. He pulled her phone out of his pocket and handed it to her. 'You left this.'

'Thanks.'

'You're running away?'

So he hadn't come all this way just to bring her phone back. 'I'm leaving.'

'Why?'

Wasn't it obvious why? Bella and Adam must have told him. For him to turn up here he must have known she was leaving, and if they'd told him that they must have told him why. Surely? She finally looked up to face him. And then she knew. His face was blank, cold and, worse than that, closed. Pavel Stone was an open book. Easy, kind, generous. Now he was guarded and she'd done that. She'd taken something beautiful and she'd broken it all over again. 'I lied.'

'I know.' He blew out a long breath. 'I didn't ask about that. I asked why you're running away.'

'You don't want to ask about the lies?'

He looked up at the display board. 'You're getting the Inverness train?'

She nodded.

'Then we've only got ten minutes. I thought if we dealt with the running away first then we might have time for the proper conversation.'

'A row, you mean?'

'What do you think?'

Honestly, Jodie wasn't sure. Pavel didn't seem angry. She wasn't even sure she could imagine him angry. She knew she'd seen parts of him he kept close – the passion and the tenderness – but anger was something else. 'You don't seem that cross.'

Pavel shook his head in clear and utter disbelief. 'I'm furious. And confused. And I don't know what else, but right now none of that matters if you go.'

'It would be worse if I stayed.' It was true. If she stayed he'd make her tell him the truth about everything. All the lies. All the deceit. And everything before that as well. That she was a deadbeat who turned everything she touched to ash, and seeing her as she really was would eventually do the same to him.

'No.' Finally Pavel sat down next to her and took her hand into his. 'No. Nothing would be worse than you leaving. I'm so angry with you. For lying, but even more so for not telling me, even when everyone else knew. But you going now and me not seeing you again is still worse. If you stay I can fix this. I can make it better.'

He was wrong. 'I'll ruin things again if I stay. You're better off...'

He shook his head. 'I'm not going to let you do that. It's a get-out-of-jail-free card, isn't it? You're leaving for my benefit? You are not. You're leaving for yours. Cos you're too scared to stay and face the music.'

She didn't reply. She couldn't. She couldn't admit he was right because if he was right then the next thing would be to stay and try to make things better. Jodie couldn't face failing at that.

'You said you didn't think I was a coward,' he continued. 'But I am. I'm only here now because I found something that scares me even more than admitting how I feel. I'm terrified of loving you. But I'm more terrified of losing you.' He squeezed her hand a little tighter. 'So I'm here. I love you. Stay.' He pressed her hands to his lips. 'Let me find a way to make all of this better.'

Maybe she could. Maybe, even if she messed up, Pavel could be a good enough man for the both of them. Maybe he could love her enough to make her better. She could hear the problem in her head without even saying it out loud. Pavel Stone couldn't fix her. Nobody could.

'I want to stay,' she admitted.

'Then do.'

The station announcement cut through the moment. *The train now approaching platform one…*

'That's me.' She started to stand up.

Pavel shook his head, hand still tightly wrapped around hers. 'Don't.'

'It's…' She looked into his big, kind face. She owed him the truth. Even if it was just this once. 'I think I could love you.' That was only a half-truth. 'I could love you, but I daren't.'

'Coward.'

'Yeah.' It was true. 'But I daren't love you because I don't think I can without hurting you even more. I don't know when or how yet, but I would mess this up and I didn't run because I was scared of how angry you'd be. I ran because I couldn't face being there when you found out. I didn't want to see the damage I'd done.'

Pavel finally released her hand. 'The damage is there whether you see it or not. Maybe you need to face it?'

The train was rumbling on to the station.

'Stay,' he whispered again.

'I can't.' She really couldn't. 'You're right. I should face the damage, but...' There was so much damage. Everywhere Jodie went, she left pain in her wake. It had to stop. Pavel Stone couldn't fix her. She had to stop herself. 'I'm sorry.'

Chapter Sixteen

It was the following lunchtime that Jodie stepped off the train to Hastings after four trains and an uncomfortable night at Euston. This was the place she'd sworn she wasn't going to end up, but after everything she finally did have no choice. She dragged herself and her suitcase through the shopping centre and over West Hill to Collier Road, and stopped outside her parents' home. It was a three-storey rambling old townhouse that had always been filled with lodgers and dogs and stray cats and anyone, and anything, else her mother invited in.

The door opened in front of her before Jodie had got close enough to ring the bell. Jodie took a deep breath and looked up into her mother's eyes. 'I thought you might have got stuck at the bottom of the path.'

Jodie shook her head. 'I was just taking a minute.' She looked her mother up and down. She'd always been a bundle of energy, never moved at a stroll when she could stride out or dash from place to place.

'Are you going to come in then?'

'Yeah.'

Her mother glanced down at Jodie's case. 'So not just a flying visit?' Her voice was hopeful.

This was what she'd fought so hard to avoid. It wasn't her parents' anger or disapproval. That wasn't who they were. Sometimes Jodie wished it was. She wished they'd shout at her. She knew how difficult she could be. Having them pretend otherwise only made that worse. 'I need somewhere to stay for a while.'

'Of course.' Her mum's face lit up and then crashed back down into a mask of concern. 'Are you all right?'

There was no point pretending any more. There was no bravado left in her. Jodie shook her head. 'No. I don't think I am.'

Her mum moved carefully down the step, leaning on her cane, and met Jodie on the path, pulling her into a deep hug. 'Then I'm really glad you've come home.' She kissed her daughter on the top of the head. 'Hot-chocolate not all right, or gin-and-tonic not all right?'

Jodie couldn't answer. She was 'need a hug from my mum' not all right.

–

She followed her mum through the house and out to the conservatory, which was really – in her dad's care – more of a glorified house-adjacent greenhouse. Even in December it was full of plants – containers brought in from the garden to overwinter and houseplants lovingly tended all year round. He looked up as they came in.

'Jodie!' He glanced at his wife. 'We weren't expecting you?'

'No. I just thought I'd...' Thought she'd what? 'Drop in,' she finished.

Her dad came and hugged her in welcome, but she could sense him looking past her. 'Just you, is it?'

Of course they'd be expecting Gemma. Another disappointment. 'Erm, yeah.' She pulled back from the hug. 'Gemma and I split up.' She couldn't meet either of her parents' gazes. She knew perfectly well that Gemma had been good for her. She knew that in her head, but somehow she couldn't feel it any more. The face she saw every time she closed her eyes wasn't Gemma any more.

'Oh, I'm sorry, pet.' Her dad frowned. 'In Scotland?'

'No. Before that. Then I… I got a job in Scotland and so I've been up there for, erm, about six, seven weeks.'

Her mum squeezed her shoulder. 'This definitely sounds like a hot-chocolate conversation.'

Two hours later she'd told them everything. Well, not everything. Not about how she'd been fired from Diane's coffee shop. She'd told them most things. Well, not most things. Not precisely how she'd stolen the job in Scotland. She'd told them a lot of things. Well, not a lot of things. Not how she'd snuck away at the crack of dawn after she'd messed up again. She'd told them some things. She hadn't told them about him.

She'd really meant to, but even as the words tumbled out of her, explaining the break-up and the long journey to the Highlands and the castle and the cookery school and the village and the Christmas lights and even how she'd gone undercover at Lowbridge's great rival, every time Pavel hovered on the edge of the story her brain shut down. His name would not pass her lips. Jodie had messed up again and again and again but this one was too awful.

Finally she was done. There was so much more to tell, but she'd given up everything she was able.

Her dad was frowning again. 'It sounds like you were doing well though, pet. Why did you come away?'

She shook her head. He clearly hadn't been listening at all. 'I wasn't doing well. They needed someone who could cook and we lost our band and people kept cancelling.'

'Doesn't sound like any of that was your fault, and they knew about the cooking,' he pointed out.

And that got her stuck at the big thing she hadn't told them at all.

Jodie took a deep breath. 'I lied,' she admitted.

–

'Go to your cookery class.' Pavel's mother was standing, arms crossed, in the entrance to the gym.

Pavel shook his head. 'I'm giving it a miss today.'

'I don't think you are, and you're going to damage your hands if you stay here punching that thing any longer.'

Pavel caught the punch bag that hung from the beam in the garage gym and stabilised it with his hands. 'It makes me feel better.'

'Does it?' Nina perched on the edge of the bench. 'This doesn't look like better to me. You didn't go to work yesterday, and clearly not today either. Mrs Timberley rang last night cos she thought you were walking her dog for her. Young Strachan texted cos he's been at the coach house all morning with no one to tell him what needs finishing off and you're not answering your phone. It's not like you.'

That was true. It wasn't. 'I don't know what I'm like.'

'Yes. You do. You're a good man.'

Pavel shook his head. He'd always thought that. That was who he'd always been. Pavel was a good guy. Reliable guy. Salt of the earth. But that Pavel had been in a trap as well. Always doing what other people needed, being there for everyone, but never wondering what he wanted for himself. And he'd broken out. He'd worked out what he wanted. He wanted her and he'd gone after her despite the risk, despite the fear. He'd chased after the person his heart truly desired. He'd stood in front of her and he'd begged her to stay.

And after all of that, he was supposed to step back into the Pavel-shaped hole in the village and be the person who'd never met Jodie Simpson, who'd never fallen in love, who'd never had his heart ripped out, who'd never tried, really tried for the first time in his life for something he knew was meant to be his, and failed.

'You don't have to be OK.' His mum rubbed her eyes. 'You just have to keep going. One step at a time. Please.'

And now he'd made his mum worry. That wasn't fair. He nodded. 'Just let me grab a shower.'

He was the last to arrive for the cookery session, and he hesitated at the kitchen door. The last time he'd been here he'd walked in thinking the world was at his feet and run out a different man. He took a deep breath and stepped inside. The babble of chatter stopped the minute he walked in.

'Don't mind me,' he muttered.

The two younger Strachans looked to the eldest who looked right at Pavel. 'I'm sorry about your lass.'

The others nodded in agreement. Pavel couldn't respond.

'Right then. Shall we make a start?' Bella clapped her hands together. 'Strach,' she nodded at the youngest Strachan, 'why don't you work with Pavel today?'

And with that Jodie's absence was glossed over and the rest of the world moved on.

'Today we're looking forward to Christmas. We don't have time to do a full turkey but I thought that if we learned the makings of some of the great side dishes then you could make them for your own Christmases, or if you want to, bring them along to join us for Christmas here.'

Pavel looked up. 'Here?'

Bella nodded. She looked even more exhausted than usual. 'Who knows where we'll all be next year? So we thought this Christmas we'd invite everyone who wanted to come along. Christmas here for the whole community.'

It sounded wonderful, but somewhere in his heart Pavel knew it could be Bella's farewell to the village, and if the castle went then all the community groups that had sprung up under its roof would go as well. And then what?

Bella was still talking. 'And for dessert we're going to Poland with a traditional poppyseed cake. This is a makowiec – am I saying that right, Pav?'

'Near enough.'

'And this is eaten at celebrations like Christmas, yes?'

Pavel nodded. 'My granddad's speciality.'

'So I understand.'

And so Pavel understood. This lesson was for him. This was Bella trying to tell him, with food – the only language she knew how to express this in – that these people saw him and cared for him and wanted to find something that would bring him back to himself. So long as he wasn't another thing too broken to fix.

The poppyseed roll, it turned out, was an exercise in patience and understanding that these were ingredients that couldn't be rushed. 'This is a yeasted dough,' Bella explained. 'And the yeast is alive and we need it to bring this dough to life. And like any living thing yeast can be temperamental. You can't rush it or make it move at your pace. You have to give it all the love you can and then let it do its thing, and trust that everything will come together and work out in the end.'

Pavel let himself be talked through the kneading and the rolling and the waiting, and then the dividing and kneading again, before spreading with the rich poppyseed, nut and raisin filling and rolling and waiting again. By the time the roll was baked it felt like part of Pavel – something that linked him back to his grandfather, who must have done all the same things in his kitchen at home and thought of the rest of his family miles away in Poland. It was the same makowiec he'd eaten as a child but it was also brand new today.

He carried the cake home and placed it on the kitchen table in his mother's part of the house. 'Makowiec,' he announced.

'Oh my goodness. I had no idea.'

Pavel raised an eyebrow. 'So Bella thought of this all on her own?'

'No. But I didn't suggest it.'

Pavel shook his head. 'It's fine. I'm glad you did.'

'I really didn't,' his mother insisted.

'I haven't talked to anyone else about...' But of course he had.

'Maybe your young lady isn't quite so bad?'

'A parting gift,' Pavel replied. He wasn't going to get his hopes up again reading anything more into it than that. 'You were right about taking little steps though. I'm going to go back over to the castle later and make sure everything's finished off at the coach house. And they're going to need help getting the ballroom ready as well, with... with Jodie gone.'

His mum passed him a generous slice of the roll. 'But for now, eat your cake, love.'

The coach house was close to being ready for paying guests. All Pavel really needed was to unveil his work, officially, to Adam and Bella. He headed over to the ballroom, to find Adam, Bella and Darcy already in there.

'Hi. I came to see what still needed doing in here.'

Bella spun around, arms extended to encompass the whole room. 'Everything.'

'Not everything.' Adam put his arm around her shoulders. 'For all the mess, Jodie has done a pretty good job of sorting out the junk from the stuff to keep. And this pile is all stuff we can sell, which is great.'

Pavel was pretty sure that was the pile Jodie had been intending to put straight in a skip.

Darcy and Bella looked distinctly less positive. 'Even once it's cleared it needs repainting and everything is filthy,' Darcy pointed out.

'We can do that,' Adam insisted. 'We'll get Flinty in to help. And we can all roll our sleeves up and… we'll make it work.'

'So you're going ahead with Hogmanay?' Pavel hadn't been sure. With Jodie gone everyone would have understood if the laird and his fiancée had decided it was one battle too far.

Adam nodded.

Bella looked at her partner with trusting eyes. 'You're sure?'

'I am. I mean, what choice do we have?'

'None really,' she confirmed. 'We've got too many bookings to cancel now. Although more cancel every day.'

'We don't even have a band,' Darcy pointed out.

'Jodie had an idea for that,' Pavel reminded them.

Adam winced. 'We can't do that though. Can we?'

Bella shrugged. 'They stole them first.' She looked at Pavel. 'You're still in?'

'Sure.'

'But we won't know if it's worked until the day.' Darcy was anxious.

'Then we'll have Hugh on standby with his accordion.' Pavel pulled a face. 'Have you heard Hugh play the accordion?'

Bella's shoulders slumped. 'Yeah.'

'Old Strachan plays bagpipes,' Adam suggested.

'Is he any good?' Bella asked.

'He might drown out Hugh's accordion,' was the most positive response Pavel could come up with.

'Right. Well, I guess we can't worry about what we can't control. We need to focus on the things we can,' Bella announced.

'OK then. I need to check on the horses.' Darcy smiled. 'That's not for Hogmanay. The horses don't know any of this is going on. It's kind of wonderful.'

'And I'm going back to the kitchen to finalise the menu.'

'Before you do that, there's something I need to show you all.' Pavel led all three of them across the courtyard, through the gateway and out to the coach house.

Bella sighed. 'I hope you're not going to rub our noses in another thing we can't afford.'

'Why don't you take a look?'

Bella frowned, but stepped through the coach house door into the hallway. She stopped, dashed down the corridor, opened one door and then another and ran back out to them. 'It's all...' She pointed at the coach house. 'It's all done up!'

'What?' Adam and Darcy made their own way inside, reappearing a few moments later.

'How?' Bella stared at her fiancé. 'Did you...?'

Adam shook his head. 'All Pav, I'm guessing.'

Bella threw her arms around Pavel's middle. 'Thank you!'

Pavel nodded. He was pleased she was happy. That was what he wanted – to make things right and make the people he cared about happy.

'But no.' Bella's face fell. 'We really can't afford to pay you.'

'I don't expect you to. It's a gift. Strach helped and I paid him out of the money I got for working at McKenzie.'

'Yeah, but who paid you?'

Pavel shook his head. 'It's fine. I don't have expensive tastes and it was only a few weeks' work here and there.'

'That's so generous.' Bella rubbed a hand under her eye. 'Thank you so much.' She turned to her fiancé. 'This is great. We can start advertising residential schools or just B & B in the spring and summer. You could do gardening courses, or we could do pony trek weekends and...'

She clapped her hands together as she and Darcy headed back over to the kitchen full of new excitement and plans.

That left Pavel and Adam alone outside the courtyard. His mate looked over at him. 'Thank you.'

'It's nothing.'

'It's not nothing.' Adam took a deep breath in. 'You remember you asked about me leaving?'

That felt like a lifetime ago. Pavel nodded.

'Leaving wasn't brave. You staying here was brave. I was terrified of living up to my dad's legacy. Becoming the laird, all of that, but you've been here doing it the whole time.'

'What do you mean?'

'Picking up where your granddad left off. Being the person Lowbridge needs. It's a lot.'

'I never thought about doing anything else.' That wasn't true any more. 'Until…'

'Jodie?'

'Yeah.'

'Wanna talk about it?'

'No. Thank you.'

Adam nodded. 'Want to get a beer later and not talk about it?'

'Yeah. You can tell me how badly you need this Hogmanay thing to work out.'

Adam pulled his phone from his pocket, opened his email and handed it to Pavel. 'The vultures are still circling.'

Pavel scanned the email on the screen.

> From: John McKenzie
> To: Adam Lowbridge
>
> Hope things are going well with your preparations for the festive season and especially for Hogmanay. I'm sure it'll be lovely for some sections of the community to have the option of a less elevated event to go along to.

'Bastard.'

Adam nodded.

It's so impressive to see you trying to make a go
of one of the smaller estates. Don't forget I'm here
though. Ready to step in when it gets too much.
Best
JM

'When it gets too much?'

'When we run out of money and have no choice,' Adam clarified.

'And when will that happen?'

'If we don't at least break even on Hogmanay then about January second.'

'It's not that bad?'

'Maybe not quite, but there's a lot of cost putting the thing on and every time we have a bump in ticket sales, half of them cancel a few days later.' He gestured to the coach house. 'This will help massively long-term, but if we don't get some money in soon I'm not sure we have a long-term.'

'Seriously?'

'Right now, this baby won't be here soon enough to stop me being the last Lowbridge at Lowbridge Castle.'

Chapter Seventeen

The three weeks Jodie spent living out of her parents' spare room was the longest she'd spent under their roof since she was seventeen. And in many ways it was so easy. She could exist without having to think about who she was, or who she was supposed to be. She could be herself without having to mask or hide.

In other ways, it was harder than being fake Gemma had ever been. She could feel her parents moving around her tentatively, cautiously – scared, she knew, that it was only a matter of time before she pulled a classic Jodie move and screwed something up.

It came to a head on a Saturday morning. Jodie came down from her room to find her mother sat at the kitchen table. 'I've sent your dad out to play golf.'

'Since when did Dad play golf?'

Her mum shrugged. 'He doesn't. But there's a crazy golf on the seafront. He can try that.'

'I think they call it adventure golf.'

Her mum rolled her eyes. 'Well, those people need more adventure in their lives, don't they?' She grabbed two big slices of toast from the toaster, spread them with butter and honey and set them in front of Jodie. 'Anyway, he's not here so we can have a proper talk.'

Jodie knew what was coming. It was going to be a pep talk she'd heard a hundred times before. Jodie needed to pull herself together. She needed to take responsibility. She needed to get a grip and make something of her life.

Her mother sipped her tea across the table. 'What's really wrong, love?'

'Nothing.'

'There's something. You're not like you,' her mum replied. 'You're all flat.'

She supposed she hadn't had much get-up-and-go the last couple of weeks, but she was licking her wounds after Pavel. To be fair, her mum didn't know that. 'I'm fine. Just a rough few weeks.'

Her mother shook her head. 'No. Not just the last couple of weeks.' She took a deep breath in. 'I sent your dad off because I know he wouldn't want me saying this, but I've got to. You've not been yourself for the last few years.'

'What do you mean?'

'Since you got together with Gemma.'

'What are you talking about?' Her mum had gone mad. Gemma had been great for Jodie. She'd been a calming influence, a maturing one and Jodie had messed everything up.

'I didn't say anything to start with because I hoped I was wrong, and then by the time I knew I should say something you'd stopped coming to see us.'

'But that's because we were in Reading and I'm a grown-up. You don't want me coming back here all the time, do you?'

Her mother's mouth gaped open. 'When have we ever given you that impression?' she asked.

'Well...' When? 'You didn't exactly but...'

'But it's what Gemma told you?' her mum suggested.

Of course not. Gemma had tried to help Jodie. She'd tried to help Jodie do better and cause less chaos and make less mistakes – *fewer* mistakes, Jodie corrected herself automatically in her head. *Gemma's* voice corrected her automatically in her head.

'I just wonder if maybe being with her made you feel so bad about yourself that you lost sight of all the good parts of you.'

'That's not right. It's not...' Jodie couldn't finish the denial. All of the pillars in her head that were holding up her understanding of the last few years, the last few weeks, of who she even was, had shaken slightly, and nothing felt certain any more. 'I need to go,' she said.

–

That afternoon Jodie stepped off her train in Newquay, after spending most of the journey googling and trying to remember where Gemma had said she was going when she walked out all those months ago. She remembered Royal and she remembered Sea View and she remembered that it was a mini boutique hotel chain in the south-west. Unfortunately those sorts of words cropped up in hotel names like unwanted Bountys in a Celebrations box.

After a lot of research she'd narrowed it down to one chain that was headquartered in Plymouth, which had already denied any knowledge of a Gemma Bryant, and another whose biggest hotel outside Newquay was near a hamlet called Kestle Mill. And that was where her taxi, which the meter told her was eating through her remaining cash at an alarming rate, was taking her now.

'Don't get so many tourists this time of year,' the taxi driver commented.

'I'm visiting a friend who works down here.'

'Nice. Close friend, is it?'

'Used to be. Actually an ex.' Jodie didn't need to tell him that, did she? But why wouldn't she? No lies. Get it all out. 'It's a sort of apology visit. I messed things up.'

'Trying to win him back?'

Jodie didn't correct the pronoun. There was honesty and then there was self-protection in the company of red-faced men with tattoos on their knuckles. 'No. Just a chance to say sorry.' And prove her mum wrong. 'Closure, you know?'

The driver nodded. 'Closure matters. I had a cleansing ritual done when my ex-wife moved out. Woman from Perranporth came over and waved sage all about the place.'

Jodie reassessed her mental picture of her driver. 'Did it help?'

He tilted his head. 'Maybe. Mostly it made me want a roast. House stank of stuffing for days.'

'Right.'

'Your place is just up here. I'll go down the drive and drop you at the end of the car park, if that's all right?'

'Thank you.'

She hopped out and paid the fare.

'Good luck, my bird. I hope you find what you're looking for.' He handed her a receipt on the back of his card. 'Ring if you need another ride. Yeah?'

The hotel in front of her had ivy around the door, and gardens extending out to the side, quiet in December but ready to burst into spring blooms as soon as the sun returned. Jodie pulled her case behind her and pushed through the revolving door. She wasn't even sure Gemma worked here. Probably she should have asked the taxi to wait. Even if this was the right place, she was probably way too important to be hanging around the lobby.

'Jodie?'

Or maybe not. Gemma Bryant, the real Gemma Bryant, was right in front of her, behind the reception desk. She looked the same as Jodie remembered. But nothing was the same. The pull that Jodie had felt for weeks after Gemma left, the desperate phoning and texting, the need to contact her, was gone. It was Gemma, but she wasn't Jodie's Gemma any more.

'Hi.'

'What are you doing here?'

'I came to see you.'

'How did you...?' Gemma was glancing around, clearly looking for another person to come and intervene. 'How did you find me?'

'You did tell me where you'd got a job.'

'Once. Months ago. Look, I don't know why you're here but you can't just turn up at my work. That is so Jodie.'

Jodie held up a hand. 'I'm not here to try to get you back or anything. I wanted to say sorry.'

Gemma's perfectly made-up face crinkled into a frown. 'You want to say sorry?'

'Yeah.'

'OK. Well, I can take a break in a bit.'

The reality of turning up here and expecting Gemma to change her whole day around was creeping up on Jodie.

'You can wait in the lounge.'

'Thank you.'

While she waited she kept asking herself the same question. She'd told the taxi driver she needed closure. She'd told Gemma she wanted to apologise. She was telling herself she was here to prove that she was right and her mum was wrong. Gemma had been a great girlfriend and Jodie hadn't deserved her. That had to be true. If that wasn't true then how could Jodie be sure that anything she knew, about who she really was, was true?

She kept asking herself the same question, and it was the same question Gemma asked the moment she sat down opposite her in the leather-backed chair in the corner of the hotel bar. 'Why are you here, Jodie?'

And she knew the answer. It wasn't Gemma's face she saw when she closed her eyes any more. It was Pavel's. It was Pavel telling her she had to face up to the damage she caused. Gemma was part of that damage. A big part. Whatever Jodie's mum thought, Gemma was one more person Jodie had broken apart. 'To say sorry. I know I messed us up.'

'Thanks?'

'Is that a question?'

Her ex shrugged. 'I don't really know what else to say.'

'You don't have to say anything. I want you to know that I know that everything that went wrong with us was my fault.' This was her truth. 'I'm too impulsive. I don't think things through and then I do crazy shit. Like when I took over the whole kitchen worktop cos I decided to get into bonsai.'

Gemma laughed. 'That was a bit eccentric.' She nodded indulgently. 'But that's just you. Scatty Jodie.'

Scatty. Jodie felt a prickle of tension. She was scatty. Gemma was poise and calm and competence, and Jodie was scatty.

'I'm sorry.'

'It's good that you're trying to grow.' Gemma smiled. 'I always said you had potential, didn't I?'

She had. Gemma had always encouraged Jodie to be better. She tried so hard to help her see where she was going wrong so she could work on it and be a better version of herself. It wasn't Gemma's fault she'd failed.

'So anyway I wanted to say sorry. I know I drove you away.'

Gemma nodded. 'You understand why I went no contact?'

Of course she did. Gemma had a whole new life. She didn't need Jodie barrelling in and messing things up. And now she'd done exactly that. 'I shouldn't have come here.'

'It's fine. It's good to see you actually.' Gemma glanced down at the empty table in front of them. 'Let me get you a drink.'

'Thank you.'

Gemma came back from the bar with two glasses of wine. 'I can't remember whether you do red or white? Hope a nice Merlot's OK.'

When she'd been with Gemma she hadn't really done either. 'Red's fine.'

Did Gemma frown at that? Jodie put the thought out of her head. Why would she?

'So you're doing OK here?' She looked around. The tone was less homely than Lowbridge, but a touch less in-your-face-corporate than McKenzie. 'It seems like a nice place.'

'Yeah. I mean since I got here I've really turned the place around. They were crying out for someone like me.'

Jodie believed it. 'I've been sort of working in hospitality a bit.' She'd thought about whether to tell Gemma about taking her job offer, but there wasn't any point. Was there? Nothing she'd done was going to come back on to Gemma. Why hurt her even more?

'I don't think Di's coffee shop is quite the same league.'

Jodie shook her head. 'I went away for a bit. After you left. Big estate in the Highlands.'

Gemma narrowed her eyes. 'I applied for a job in the Highlands.'

'Maybe you mentioned it. I don't know what gave me the idea. I wanted to get away, you know?'

Gemma nodded. 'Probably no rhyme or reason at all, was there? Typical Jodie. Just barging in without thinking.' She smiled sympathetically. 'It didn't work out?'

'What makes you say that?'

'Well, you've come back to me. Tail between your legs.'

That was fair. Wasn't it?

'It was a good thing I didn't get that job in the Highlands anyway,' Gemma added.

'Why?'

'Oh, it was a ridiculous little place, and the people who ran it were total amateurs.'

That wasn't right. Bella and Adam were full of enthusiasm and commitment, and they were trying to do what was best.

Gemma continued, 'They kept spouting all this guff about community and preserving the natural environment and goodness knows what else. I sent them this plan for a Hogmanay Gala that wouldn't have worked if you'd had a year to plan it.' She smiled at her own cleverness. 'They didn't have a clue obviously. Thank God I didn't end up having to try to pull that off.'

Jodie's memories of her time with Gemma shook again. None of what she was saying made sense. She was wrong about Lowbridge, but surely Gemma's plan had been good. Not being able to make it work was down to Jodie.

'Anyway, why are you really here?'

Jodie's head was spinning. 'Really to say sorry.'

'Nonsense, Jodes. I can read you like a book, and it's OK. I can see how much you're trying. If you really want to try again then I could think about it.'

Jodie waited for the pull, the need to be back in Gemma's orbit, the need to please her, the need to feel her approval. It wasn't gone entirely, but it wasn't strong. It was a speck of sand in the desert of all the other things she was feeling now. She was confused. And angry. And she didn't feel safe here. She shook her head. 'No. Thank you. I think I have to go.'

The taxi picked her up half an hour later from the tree stump she was perching on at the end of the hotel driveway. 'Did you find your closure?'

Jodie thought she had. It just wasn't the closure she'd been expecting.

Chapter Eighteen

When Jodie came down on Christmas morning her mum was already in the kitchen and her dad was setting the table for eight. 'I thought it was going to be just the three of us?'

Her dad shrugged. 'Up until yesterday morning it was. And then Mrs Ashley next door's cooker blew up doing mince pies so your mum asked her around and she was supposed to be having her daughter and her little one, so that's two more and then…' He paused, counted the place settings, moved one up a bit and started to squeeze in a ninth. 'Then it seemed rude not to ask Colin from the other side, cos his Shirley's a nurse so she's working. And then last thing, your brother rang and him and Livvie were going to be in London but your mum said "Why not pop down?" So they're popping down.' He counted the place settings again. 'Nine.'

Jodie went into the kitchen, where her mother was leaning on her perch stool at the kitchen worktop chopping potatoes. 'I can do that.'

Her mum raised an eyebrow. 'Really?'

'Yeah. I did some cookery classes.'

'In Scotland? At this cookery school?'

'Yeah.' Jodie took up the peeler and set to work. 'I made mash and tattie scones. I'm basically a potato expert now.'

'Excellent. Well, you can start on the sprouts after this.'

Jodie almost giggled as her mother slid the bag of sprouts down the counter towards her. 'You know you don't need to cut crosses in the bottoms of them but loads of people do?'

'I did know that. Yes.'

'And you can fry or roast them with bacon.' She picked up the bag. 'Some people still think they should just end up in the bin though.'

Her mother laughed. 'Like that guy on the internet.' She started up a rough impersonation of Old Strachan. 'Just put 'em in the bin...'

'Where did you see that?'

Her mum shrugged. 'Everywhere lately.'

'I filmed that. In the kitchen at Lowbridge.'

'Really?' Her mother gasped in delight. 'And then it went all viral?'

Jodie nodded. 'It was supposed to be about imaginative things to do with sprouts though. So not really what we were aiming for.'

'I bet it got a lot of people clicking on the cookery school account though? So that's something.'

'Yeah. Maybe it did.'

-

Christmas in Lowbridge this year was going to be a community affair. Pavel was sure his mum had a big hand in this plan, because when had anything happened without her agreement at the very least?

So on Christmas morning he found himself carrying a freshly made makowiec, as well as two carrier bags of wine from the shop and a Tupperware of his mum's honey-glazed parsnips over the Low Bridge, closely followed by

Netty, and her husband Gareth, and Anna and Hugh. 'Flinty and Veronica were staying at the castle last night,' Anna informed them.

'Flinty's probably already in the kitchen telling Bella what she's doing wrong,' Netty joked. 'Is the reverend joining us?' She directed the question at Pavel. 'I mean, not that you'd know.'

'It's fine. And yes. She's got a service in Lochcarron first but she'll be here for lunch.'

Pavel filled the morning fetching and carrying, bringing drinks, carting chairs through into the small hall ready for lunch, which was massive. Everyone had contributed and Bella had catered for twice as many people as attended anyway.

'Smile for the camera, Pav!' Bella's phone moved in front of him. 'It's for Insta.'

He nodded warily and watched her move on, filming the table and the mound of opened gifts and empty glasses. It was the aftermath of the perfect Christmas dinner. He was among friends and family. There was warmth and love and community. He'd opened a pair of ridiculous Christmas socks and eaten more food than he normally would in a month. He was exactly where he'd always belonged. He should be happy.

He really should, but Lowbridge, which had always been his home, felt empty now.

–

Later, after dinner, when the neighbours had gone home and her brother and his partner were dozing in front of the telly, Jodie made her way into the quiet garden at the back of the bungalow. She pulled a blanket around her and leaned back to look up at the stars. There weren't as many here as at Lowbridge. The street lights damped down the view, but there were some, and they were still shining.

Her mum came out to join her. 'Room for another under that blanket?'

'Sure.'

Her mum snuggled in next to her. 'So what's next for you? Back to Scotland?'

Jodie shivered in the night air. Her parents wouldn't want her around forever. Of course they wouldn't. Returning to Lowbridge wasn't an option. The problem now was that she couldn't imagine wanting to be anywhere else. 'I'm not sure. I won't stay much longer though.'

'You can stay as long as you like. You know that.'

'I'll find a job.' Jodie had no idea how. For the first time in her life she'd had a job she actually enjoyed, and that it was possible she wasn't awful at. She didn't think Bella or Adam would be writing her a glowing reference any time soon though.

'I'm sure you will. What's wrong though?'

'Nothing.'

Her mum shook her head. 'I thought it was Gemma but you said that was done with and if anything you've been worse since you got back.'

'I'm just not sure what I'm going to do next.'

'You're sure you can't go back to this place?' Her mother had her phone out again, Instagram open on the Highland Cookery School page. 'It looks like they put on a good spread.'

Jodie watched the reel. Christmas dinner in the small hall, by the looks of things. That must mean they'd finished clearing all the stuff out of the ballroom corridor.

That was good. Everyone was smiling and chatting. Anna, Nina, Darcy, even Veronica was tolerating a paper cracker crown. Jodie felt a pull. She ought to be there. Finally the camera panned round and lingered, just for a moment, over a less smiling face. 'Pavel.' The name was out of her lips before she had the chance to check herself.

'Right. So is that who you're pining over?'

Jodie wanted to protest that she wasn't pining. She knew she'd been nothing but trouble to her parents growing up and she had been determined not to cause them any more worry. At the same time the effort of constantly presenting a happy face to the world – less successfully than she thought she had, it turned out – was exhausting. 'Yes,' she whispered.

'He means something to you?'

'Meant. I messed it up.'

'I'm sure you didn't…' her mother started.

'I did. I really did this time. It wasn't like Gemma.' Jodie hadn't admitted this out loud yet. 'I think you were right about her. Partly at least. I don't think she actually liked me, and I ended up not liking myself either.'

'And that made you think you must be very lucky to have her?'

'Something like that.' Her heart wasn't with Gemma any more. 'Pavel wasn't like that. He's kind and…' Jodie thought back. There were some memories that weren't for her mother's consumption. 'Strong and he made me feel capable somehow.' She shook her head. 'That sounds silly.'

'That sounds lovely,' her mother responded. 'So what happened? Did he break up with you? Do you need me to go round to his house and tell him off? Cos I will, you know.'

Jodie didn't doubt it. What she'd done was too big, too awful, to explain. 'I wasn't honest with him. I was pretending to be something I'm not.'

'What?'

'I don't know. A proper grown-up.'

'Nobody's a proper grown-up. We're all pretending. That doesn't count.'

'Sensible then. Responsible.'

'You're perfectly responsible.'

Recent behaviour would seem to contradict that conclusion. 'I'm not. I'm scatty.' There was Gemma's word again. 'I forget arrangements. I don't think ahead. I'm messy...'

Her mother closed her eyes. 'I mean, you do forget plans sometimes. And you attract mess like nobody I've ever seen, but then other times you can concentrate so deeply and create wonderful things. Like when you're drawing. And really I don't think you can drive someone away by being a bit disorganised.'

Her mum didn't understand. 'Gemma said I was impossible to live with.'

'And this Pavel isn't Gemma.'

'She wasn't as bad as you think.' Jodie's answer hung in the air between them. 'She wanted me to do better. She...' Jodie stopped. She sounded familiar. 'She saw my potential.' It was like she'd heard this speech before. 'She liked things a certain way and... I sound like Fiona.'

'Who?'

'Someone from Scotland. She used to talk about her boss like that. He was a dick.'

Jodie's mum nodded.

'I thought you loved Gemma.'

'What was I going to say? I think your girlfriend is a manipulative cow?'

'Mum!'

'This isn't about her though, is it?' her mum asked.

It wasn't, but all the doubts that Gemma had put there, and all the ones Jodie already had that Gemma had tended and nurtured, were still in her head. Pavel's presence had made them quieter, but now he wasn't here they were screaming at her once again. 'I hurt him, badly.' That was the truth. 'Whatever I do next it won't be with him.'

Her mum wrapped her arms around her and pulled the blanket up to her neck. 'It's getting cold.'

'Do you think it'll snow?'

'Not down here. Lucky you're not still in Scotland.'

Jodie turned to her mum. 'Why?'

'Big storm coming.' Her mother smiled slightly. 'Storm Gemma, I believe.'

Jodie didn't reply. For Lowbridge, at least, Storm Gemma had already hit.

Chapter Nineteen

The wind was starting to get up as Pavel and his mum walked back over the Low Bridge towards the village. He pulled his phone out and checked the weather forecast. The storm warning that had been yellow that morning had been upgraded to amber and they were right on the edge of a red zone. 'Better just check the boat's secure,' he said.

Pavel never slept on stormy nights. He never had. He remembered his granddad always staying up listening to his old radio, and checking the shoreline to make sure all the boats were in. Pavel would sneak downstairs and curl up on the sofa next to him, feeling comforted by his presence.

His granddad would open the curtains in the lounge and they'd sit together listening to the lash of the wind, watching the lightning and counting the gap between the flash and the rumble of thunder as the storm rolled by them. Pavel would never admit to being scared, but big storms still made him feel small. They made him feel out of control. That put him on edge.

When his granddad had been here he'd always seemed like he had everything under control. Right until the end, when he seemed to shrink away, but even then he'd still made Pavel lean in close to him so he could whisper his words of wisdom. With his granddad around everything had felt calmer and like someone was looking out, not just for Pavel, but for everyone. That was the man Pavel had always wanted to be.

He sat up on his sofa, curtains open, and watched the dark clouds roll over the loch. Just after midnight his mum came up, raincoat wrapped around her. 'I couldn't sleep,' she said. 'Wind's too loud.'

He shifted over to let her sit down next to him.

'Your granddad would have been in his element,' she said.

'Yeah. *He* loved storms.'

His mother let out a laugh. 'No, he didn't.'

'What?'

'He hated them. He used to do all that faffing around with the radio and checking in on everyone to keep himself busy.' She rolled her eyes. 'Distracting himself from the big, dark scary thing.'

That couldn't be true. 'Really?' Pavel asked.

His mum nodded.

'But he always seemed so in control.'

'That's what he did wasn't it?' His mum sighed.

'What?'

'Keep calm. Run around after everyone else. Push whatever he was worried about way down.'

'Granddad didn't...' he started, and then stopped. Nearly all of his memories of his granddad were of him in action. Out on the boat, sleeves rolled up in the kitchen, driving the van. He was always doing something. Not quite always. 'He talked a lot about wanting to visit Warsaw again. At the end, when he was ill.'

'I think he missed the family over there more than he said,' his mum replied. 'Especially after his mum and dad passed. I think he felt a bit rootless.'

'He never said that,' Pavel murmured. 'He seemed like he belonged here.'

'That doesn't mean he didn't hanker for somewhere else as well, but, like I said, he pushed it down, kept himself busy didn't he? Running around after everyone else.' His mum gave him one of her more pointed looks. 'Seems to be what the men in this family do.'

He stared at his mum, with her Christmas Lights committee, and her parents and toddler group, and her shifts at the pub. 'Not just the men,' he muttered.

–

Jodie came downstairs on Boxing Day morning to find her dad and brother drinking coffee in front of the breakfast news.

'Strong winds battered the west coast of Scotland last night, reaching gusts of up to one hundred and ten miles per hour, leaving hundreds in communities along the coast without power this morning. Falling trees and debris continue to pose a threat to life.'

Jodie stared. The pictures on the screen changed from the reporter framed neatly by a camera operator to shaky mobile phone footage.

'These pictures, sent in by a member of the public, show the impact on the village of…'

Jodie didn't need to hear the name to know exactly what she was looking at. The roof of Anna and Hugh's garage shop was flapping violently in the winds. A boat, usually beached on the shoreline, was lying on its side in the middle of the road.

The reporter continued. '…where injuries have been reported and villagers are still trying to assess the damage to property.'

'Dad?'

'Yes, love?'

'Can I take the car?'

He turned towards her. 'You don't like to drive.'

'I don't. There's no trains on Boxing Day though and I have to go.'

'Go where?'

She pointed at the screen. 'There.'

Pavel ventured out – when the rain had stopped and wind had dropped to merely inconvenient rather than actually dangerous levels – on Boxing Day afternoon to check on the damage. Some things were easy. Pavel nodded a greeting to a gaggle of Strachans who were carrying a garden trampoline back down the main street to its proper home. Garden benches and fallen gnomes were righted easily enough. Pavel stopped outside the shop.

Hugh was surveying the damage. 'Water's got in, so most of the stock is gone. And the freezers all shorted out so that'll all have to go too. Plus the cost of actually fixing the roof.'

Pavel shook his head straight away. 'No charge for that.'

'Don't be silly. You've got to earn a living too.'

His granddad would never have charged a friend in these circumstances. 'It's fine. The village needs a shop.'

Hugh opened his mouth to object.

'No charge,' he insisted. 'I'll get that tarp properly anchored down right now so you can start cleaning up inside and I'll come over tomorrow to look at it properly.'

'You're a lifesaver, Pav.'

He headed back through the village, promising to come back and fix Mrs Timberley's gate later in the day.

The power was back on, and the shop roof had got the worst of it that he could see so far.

He jogged over the bridge to the castle. From what he could see the coach house still had most of its roof tiles. That was a relief. He headed inside. Bella was in the kitchen. 'What's the damage?'

'Couple of panes in Adam's greenhouse. He's out driving the rest of the estate to check things over.' She paused.

'Not too bad then.'

Her face told a different story. 'And the backup generator failed so we lost all the food for Hogmanay when the power went off.' Her tone was bright but the smile was glassy. 'So yeah. I don't know what we're going to do about that at all.'

Darcy came into the kitchen. 'Did it all magically get better while I was away?'

Pavel could fix this. 'So we need food?'

'And a lot of it.'

'Could you cook the stuff that was frozen right now? Would it keep if you did that?'

Bella rubbed her forehead. 'Some of it maybe. We could cook it to prolong the life and then refreeze it. That won't work for everything.'

'But some stuff?'

She nodded. 'I'll work out what's safe and won't taste like dirt and start on that.'

'Right. They lost the freezer in the shop too. I'll call Hugh and ask what he's got that you might be able to use.'

Bella closed her eyes. 'I don't think we can pay him.'

'I think he'll be chucking it if you don't take it. I'm sure you can work something out.'

'Thank you.'

They set to work on the food. Pavel drove back and forth from the shop bringing over whatever was salvageable. By early evening he was ferrying ingredients back to the village for Flinty and his mum to cook in their ovens or store in their freezers.

The whole community worked like a machine. Chopping, mixing, frying, roasting and repeating under Bella's instruction.

It was close to midnight by the time he slumped onto a stool at the kitchen island, rubbing his eyes. Bella was wiping down the worktops, while Flinty made coffee and Adam, Veronica and Darcy organised the last few dishes into the remaining fridge and freezer space. Finally the group was still.

'What else do we need to do?' Pavel asked.

'Sleep?' Darcy suggested.

'No time,' Bella murmured. 'We still don't have a band, and three more people cancelled this morning.'

Pavel didn't have a clue what to do about that.

The door swinging open behind him made him turn. He was tired enough that he could easily have believed the woman standing behind him was a hallucination, but there she was. Really here. 'Maybe I can help?' Jodie said.

—

Jodie had come straight to the castle when she'd arrived in Lowbridge. It had taken seventeen hours, with a break for a nap in the car and a detour around a closed road near Fort William, but she was here.

She'd known she'd see Pavel at some point. She hadn't thought he'd be the very first person she walked into. He looked up to face her very slowly. 'I'll let you get on.' He

316

walked straight past her without meeting her eye. 'Call me if I can help with anything, Bella.'

'Well, that could have been worse,' Jodie tried to joke. Nobody was laughing. And Pavel had been right there in front of her. The Gemma she'd spent weeks trying to be would have stayed calm and tried to focus on the work that needed doing. She wasn't being Gemma any more. 'I'll be back in a minute.'

Jodie dashed out of the kitchen and into the courtyard, catching Pavel outside the coach house.

'Pavel!'

He stopped and turned. 'You came back.'

'Yeah. I saw the storm. I was worried about...' She nearly said 'everything', but no more lies. 'About you.'

'I'm fine.'

He didn't sound fine.

'They said on the news there'd been injuries.'

He shook his head. 'Netty's Gareth sprained his ankle trying to rescue the green bin.'

'Right. Well, I wanted to say sorry too.'

'Go on then.'

'I'm sorry. I really am.'

Pavel stared at her. 'I don't know what you want me to say.'

She wanted, so desperately, for him to say everything was forgiven and they could turn back the clock to how things were, but she knew she didn't deserve that. 'It's OK. You don't have to say anything. I just wanted you to know that I'm sorry.' There was more than that. 'And that us, you and me, that was real. It wasn't a lie. I promise.'

He nodded quickly. 'Right. Thank you.'

She let him go this time. He'd spoken to her. That was more than she had any right to hope for. Jodie made her way back into the kitchen. The babble of excitable chat hushed the moment she came through the door. Everyone was here – Bella, Adam, Darcy, Flinty and Veronica. Jodie took a deep breath in. 'I am so sorry for everything that happened before, but I saw the storm on the news and I know how important Hogmanay is for you and I really do want to help.'

Adam and Bella exchanged a look.

'You really want to help?' Bella asked.

'I do.'

'You broke that boy's heart.' Darcy wasn't letting her off the hook.

'I know.'

'And you lied to all of us,' Bella added. 'People thought you might be the mole feeding stuff to McKenzie and I said, "No. I trust her." How much of an idiot am I?'

'I didn't tell McKenzie anything. I promise. You trusted me. And I really wanted to be the person you thought I was.' Jodie was determined to stick with her new truth-first policy. 'I'm not Gemma. I never was.' The next part was the hardest to say. She believed it. She really did and the belief itself was new. 'And if you let me help, I really think I can.'

Bella sighed. 'I don't know.'

Veronica cleared her throat. 'It strikes me that we require all the help we can get at the moment.'

'That's true,' Adam conceded.

'And,' Veronica continued, 'whatever her indiscretions, Miss…' She paused. 'Simpson?'

Jodie nodded.

'Miss Simpson was actually very helpful in her time here.'

Bella rubbed her eyes. She looked exhausted. 'Fine. You're in.'

'Really?'

'Yeah. You're on trying to get our customers back. Adam and Darcy are going to sort out the ballroom. I'm going to replan the food to use what we've actually got and then work out how to fill the gaps without spending any money.'

'Yes boss.'

—

By New Year's Eve afternoon they were almost party ready. Now Jodie just had to find them some customers. Her research over the last few days, combined with what she remembered from her time as Fiona's assistant, had been helpful. She talked her bosses through it at the kitchen island. 'So, the McKenzie guests basically break down into two groups. There's the ones they stole from us. So far as I can tell they've paid McKenzie in full already.'

Adam frowned. 'So?'

'So,' Jodie couldn't quite look him in the eye, 'so even if we get them back I'm not sure how we make them pay us as well. If we just say "Hey, why not come to this different party?", they're going to say, "No thanks. We're already here." And if we trick them…'

'Which is your idea,' Bella pointed out.

'Yeah. And we still could, and it fills the room and advertises Lowbridge for the future and all that, but it doesn't make us any cash right now, cos so far as they're concerned they've already paid.'

Both her bosses' faces fell.

'But, then there's the other group.' Jodie had seen when she was working with Fiona that the McKenzie estate was taking bookings through agents and tour operators. She'd mentally logged it as something she should look into for Lowbridge in the new year, but now she realised it could make all the difference to Lowbridge's fortunes today. 'They're all booked through tour operators, and they've paid the operator, but the operator doesn't pay McKenzie until the end of the trip. So...' She let the conclusion dangle.

Adam shook his head. 'So?'

'So if they end up here, then we could totally argue that they had to pay us?'

'And if they say no?'

That was a very real risk. If some of their guests just somehow ended up at the wrong party then it was entirely possible the travel companies would just shrug and claim it wasn't their problem.

'That's why the plan has to work this way,' she explained, trying to keep the wobble out of her voice. Jodie's plan to fill the ballroom had three prongs. Firstly, Bella's council of war had been set to work drumming up as much local interest as possible. Reverend Jill, in particular, had been a star. It seemed like most of her congregations from across the area were now planning to be there. Secondly, Jodie had worked the phones and charmed as many of their previous bookings as possible. As she'd expected, most had politely explained that they now had other plans, but a few had accepted that they'd got the wrong impression about Lowbridge's event being cancelled and reinstated their bookings. The third prong was the biggest, the riskiest, and by far the most legally questionable, and it all had to happen this afternoon and nothing at all could go wrong. In Jodie's experience plans she made did tend to go wrong.

'I want to come with you,' Bella insisted.

Jodie shook her head. 'We can't really stop for puke breaks. And you need to be here. There's deliveries you need to check.'

'I know. What if it doesn't work though?'

Jodie didn't have an answer to that. The headline to her plan was so simple. The McKenzie estate had stolen their customers and their band. Now they were going to steal them back, and just a few extra paying customers besides. The details were a little more intricate. Because of the scale of the McKenzie estate guests were being ferried from their accommodation in the hotel block and the cabin and lodges around the estate in branded minibuses and four-wheel drives.

That was a problem because the local drivers, at least, would know the way, and they couldn't send Lowbridge cars to pick the guests up, because key to Jodie's plan to get paid was that they were able to say the official transport had brought the guests to them and they had simply helpfully offered hospitality to get their rivals out of an embarrassing screw-up. As it turned out, Storm Gemma had helped their plan. Since the storm, Adam's drive over to the enemy side of the hills had confirmed there were trees down across McKenzie's land, so a diversion sign or two wouldn't seem out of place.

Those diversions would send the drivers across the estate to the closest point to the Lowbridge land, and over the border onto a farm track that would bring them down to the castle, where Bella and Adam would greet them in full laird and lady charm-offensive mode and hopefully have everyone into the ballroom and nicely primed with whisky or champagne before too many objections were raised. In short, they were planning to kidnap a Hogmanay party. What could possibly go wrong?

The first thing that could go wrong was that Jodie's lead co-conspirator could very easily refuse to work with her. To take the diversion signs Jodie had carefully created and printed with McKenzie estate logos over to their destination they needed a van, and Lowbridge's favourite man with a van had left every room they'd been in together since she returned.

So now she was standing outside the coach house with a pile of home-made signs at her feet and only Adam's assurance that Pavel had promised he was still in to keep her company. If he did turn up she had three hours, give or take, alone with him and not a clue what she could possibly say. She checked her watch. Five past three. They needed all the signs in place by five thirty. Early enough that people wouldn't already have been picked up. Not so early that anyone had time to notice and wonder if something was awry.

At ten past three Pavel's van pulled up in front of her. He jumped out without a word, opened the side door and lifted her signs in. 'I'm doing this for Adam and Bella.'

'I know. Me too.'

He nodded and climbed back into the van.

Jodie had hand-drawn a map of the McKenzie estate and marked where the van could easily access, without raising suspicion, and which junctions signs needed placing at. She pulled it from her pocket and smoothed it out on the dashboard of the van. 'It's a bit rough.'

Pavel inspected her handiwork. 'You did this from memory?'

'Yeah.'

'It's good.' He tapped one of the tracks she'd marked as accessible to the van. 'We won't get down there though. Not after the amount of rain we've had lately.' He thought for a second. 'If we park up there,' tapping the map again, 'the van'll be hidden by the trees and we can do this part on foot.'

'OK.'

He pulled the van onto the road. 'Do you think this'll work?'

'If it doesn't will Adam really sell to John McKenzie?'

'I don't know if he'll have much choice. Having the accommodation ready helps but that's longer term, isn't it? They need some money now.'

'The coach house looks great,' Jodie offered. It really did. Like everything else he did, Pavel had clearly lavished care and attention on his work. 'You've done a brilliant job.'

He nodded an acknowledgement but didn't reply. Jodie braced herself for the journey to proceed in silence. Silence made her brain itchy. She forced herself to think through the plan to quiet it. *Just concentrate on one thought. Don't let your brain freewheel wherever it wants to go.* A seagull swooped low in front of the van. Jodie remembered being told once that there's no bird called a seagull. There were herring gulls, and black-headed gulls and… she couldn't name any more types of gull. Were terns gulls? Or shags? She giggled at the fact that there was a bird called a shag.

'What's funny?' Pavel asked.

She was supposed to be thinking about the plan. 'Nothing.'

And now she wasn't thinking about the plan or about seagulls. She was thinking about Pavel Stone. About the closeness of him. The kindness of him. The warmth.

The touch. The desperate hole in her heart that he'd left behind. And now her brain was going to all the places she desperately wanted not to be thinking about. The adage that it was better to have loved and lost floated into her mind. Whoever had said that was even more of an idiot than Jodie. Loving someone and losing them was torture.

Dusk fell as they approached the McKenzie estate by the main entrance. They'd decided that was the best option to begin with. Pavel had worked up there recently enough that his van wouldn't arouse too much suspicion around the main car park, and it would give them the chance to scout out how many staff were around. Jodie was hoping that, with the event in the evening and the festive holiday, most of the employees would either be coming in later or fully occupied during the afternoon.

The lights were on in the main visitor centre but the sign outside informed them that the centre closed at four p.m. on New Year's Eve. 'Right. Let's leave the van here. If it's spotted you can say you came to check on something on-site after the storm.'

Pavel nodded.

'We can do the ones in walking distance from here and then drive round to the far side.'

Jodie zipped her black top up to the neck and pulled a dark beanie out of her pocket.

Pavel shook his head.

'What?'

'You worked here less than a month ago. I don't think putting a hat on will stop them recognising you.'

'Dark colours blend into the shadows better. I'm not trying to go unrecognised. I'm trying not to be seen at all.'

'You're not James Bond.'

'When you're in a McKenzie holding cell waiting to be waterboarded and I've got away scot-free don't complain to me.'

'I don't think they have holding cells.'

'You don't doubt the waterboarding though.'

She knew she was watching his face for every reaction and there was, unmistakeably, a tiny hint of a smile there.

'Made you smile,' she teased.

Pavel's face turned back to granite. 'Jodie, don't. Please don't.'

'Don't what?' As if she didn't know.

'Don't act like things are OK.'

She started to protest that she wasn't and stopped herself. She knew things weren't all right. She just couldn't stop hoping that might change.

He pulled the first few signs out of the van and marched off into the forest.

—

They only had one sign left to deploy when they pulled into their final parking spot. She waited while Pavel pulled the van slightly off the track to be better hidden by the trees and checked her map again. 'The junction is up there, and we need people to come this way?' she confirmed. 'Shall I go?'

'I can. I'll be quicker.'

He was right, but the assertion still bristled. 'I can manage.'

'I never said you couldn't. I just said I'd get it done quicker.'

Something prickled at Jodie. 'You're saying I'm not good enough.'

Pavel frowned. 'No.'

'It's fine. I know what you meant.' The same as everyone meant. Jodie wasn't up to it. Jodie wasn't good enough. The tiny flicker of belief that that wasn't true was still small inside Jodie but it was there.

'I was just trying to help.'

'I don't need help.'

'I know. I was just trying to make things easier.'

There it was again. Jodie needed someone to come in and fix things. 'I don't need you to fix me. I'm not a project you can swoop in and make right.' Pavel was Lowbridge's Mr Fix-It. Why wouldn't Jodie be a project to him?

'I don't want to fix you.' His face was pained. 'I never wanted to fix you.'

The red mist was clearing as fast as it had descended. 'Yeah. Right,' she muttered.

'I never wanted to fix you,' he repeated. 'I just wanted to make everything around you as good as it could be. I wanted to make you happy.'

Jodie's heart hurt. 'I'm sorry. Again.' She couldn't look at him. 'That's turning into a theme.'

The silence sat between them for what felt like an eternity. Pavel cleared his throat. 'Do you want to go do the sign then?'

Jodie looked out into the gloom. Pavel was fitter and taller and had been bashing the sign poles into the ground about three times as fast as her. If she tried to think rationally there was nothing to argue about here. 'No. You will be quicker. Do you mind?'

'It's fine. If I'm not back in ten minutes, burn the van and make for the hills.'

Jodie forced herself not to react but that had definitely been a joke. The guard he had up might not be absolute after all. She stared out into the dark and she waited. So much could go wrong with this plan. Any of the drivers could miss the sign, and even if the whole group did make it to Lowbridge there was every chance they'd simply jump back into the minibuses and leave as fast as they arrived. A sensible person would never try this. A sensible person would never even have thought of it.

She checked the time. Eight minutes since Pavel set off. She knew the ten-minute thing had been a joke but, even so, he should have only been heading a hundred metres or so up the track and the ground was soft so setting the sign shouldn't have taken him more than a couple of minutes at most.

Ten minutes. Maybe someone had seen him, but Pavel being around the estate wasn't that odd in itself. He'd done work here before Christmas and whatever McKenzie thought about it the locals still used the footpaths across his land so it wouldn't immediately look like trespassing.

Eleven minutes. So long as nobody in estate management actually saw him hammering the sign in, they ought to be fine.

Twelve minutes. Jodie jumped out of the van and made her way up the track, staying close to the trees, listening for anyone else around her. She heard the voices within seconds, and she knew it was all over.

Pavel was at the junction and Fiona MacCellan was standing right in front of him, her McKenzie estate four-wheeler stopped a few feet away. 'What on earth are you doing?'

'Out for a walk.' That was good.

'With a hammer?' That was less good.

'Oh yeah. I, I found this.' From where she was standing, Jodie caught Pavel moving slightly to the side so the sign he'd been hammering in was hidden behind his legs.

'Where?'

'Where what?' Jodie could picture Pavel's perfect honest face. He really wasn't built for espionage.

'Where did you find the hammer?'

'On the ground.'

Jodie winced.

'Pavel, it's a good job I know you, because a man your size wandering round a forest with a hammer could raise alarm bells.'

'Yeah. Right. Sorry. Like I say, I found it. Someone must have dropped it.'

'Someone else who was wandering about the forest with a hammer?'

'Like a workman or someone.'

Fiona nodded. 'Shall I take it then?'

'Sure.'

He handed it over.

Fiona paused. 'This has your initials engraved on the handle, Pavel.'

'Does it?'

'Yes. Is this your hammer?'

Oh for goodness' sake. Jodie stepped out of the shadows. She had Fiona's attention straight away.

'What are you doing here? You lied…'

'So you heard about that then?'

'I had a very informative chat with Adam Lowbridge. In the end. Nobody was very keen to tell me anything at all.'

'Right.' Jodie searched for the right words. What would Adam have told her? Not the industrial espionage part presumably, so what? That Jodie had tricked them and then moved on to McKenzie?

'I do not have time for this. I've got a ceilidh starting in two hours and the band hasn't turned up.'

Jodie could definitely have explained that if she'd been asked. The band had received a text earlier that morning telling them that due to storm damage to the estate the party venue had been moved.

'So whatever you're doing here, just tell me so I can get on.'

Sod it. Truth first. 'Pavel's here with me. We're putting up signs to redirect your guests to Lowbridge for the Hogmanay party there.'

Fiona's jaw dropped. 'What?'

Pavel stepped aside to reveal the diversion sign behind him.

'What?'

'Yeah. I mean you stole half of them from us anyway. So it seemed fair.'

'I did no such...' Fiona stopped. 'What do you mean "us"?'

So Adam definitely hadn't told her the full story of Jodie's employment at the McKenzie estate then.

'I'm back working at Lowbridge.'

'You never told me you'd worked there before.'

'No. Sorry.' Actually that was true. 'I am sorry. Honestly.' But Jodie's conscience was not the matter at hand. 'You did steal our guests though.'

'Again, we didn't.' She paused. '*I* didn't.'

Jodie's heart jumped a little. Was it possible? 'You didn't know?'

'Of course not. There were some guests that Saira added to the bookings list. She said they were Mr McKenzie's special guests.'

'He didn't say anything to you about them?'

'He's very busy. He doesn't always tell me everything.' There was something different about Fiona, a weariness that hadn't been there before.

'And you stole our band?'

'Saira booked...'

'Mr McKenzie's special request?' Jodie hazarded.

'Yes.'

'Well, isn't Saira bending over backwards to keep Mr McKenzie happy.'

Fiona pursed her lips. 'That's uncalled for. John is...' She didn't finish the sentence.

'Fi?' Pavel's voice was soft.

Tears were glistening in Fiona MacCellan's eyes.

'Fiona, what's wrong?'

'He thinks I'm stupid,' she whispered.

'You're not stupid.' Fiona wasn't stupid. Jodie wasn't useless. They'd both been sold the same lie by people who were supposed to make them feel safe. What did she wish somebody had said to her back when she was trying so hard to please the real Gemma Bryant? 'But maybe you shouldn't be with someone who makes you feel like you are?'

'No.' Fiona shook her head. 'I need to do better. It's my fault. I let him down and so of course he's angry. I push him into things, you know. It's not his fault.'

Jodie felt a wave of nausea crash through her body. She put her hand on Pavel's arm for comfort. He stepped away.

'What things do you push him into, Fi?' Pavel asked quietly. 'Does he hurt you?'

'No. No. Of course not. He's not like that. He helps with things I can't manage on my own. I'd forget my own head. So it's easier if he looks after... where we go and how I present myself and...'

Jodie was aware that time was not on their side. The kind way to do this would be with weeks of therapy. But the unkindest thing would be to let it stand. She stepped towards Fiona. 'I'm really sorry, Fi, but John McKenzie is not a nice man. He's a bully. He bullies you.'

'He's not.'

'He is and he does.'

'He just...'

'What?'

The tears that had been threatening started to fall. Fiona didn't wipe them away. 'He doesn't make me feel good,' she admitted. 'But if I just try a bit harder and...'

'No.' Jodie knew what she needed to say. It might not help Fiona, but it was what she, herself, wished she'd known. 'Someone who loved you would build you up. They'd make you feel like you were enough. Like you were better than you ever imagined yourself to be just the way you are. They wouldn't make you feel like you constantly had to be trying to be different.'

'They'd make you feel braver.' That was Pavel. Jodie couldn't look at him. It was too much. 'They'd make you feel more than, not less than. Always.'

Fiona gave the tiniest little nod.

Jodie hated pushing this, but they were running out of time. 'So you can stay here and make a call and let people know what we're up to. It's fine. You caught us. And then McKenzie wins. Or...'

'Or what?' The fact that she'd even asked felt like a small victory.

'Or you can pretend you never saw us here and come back over to Lowbridge for a proper party.'

Fiona shook her head. 'No. Mr McKenzie wouldn't…' She stopped. 'It was very good of him to take me on.'

'You run this place, Fiona,' Jodie pointed out. 'You're not his right-hand woman. You're the one making everything work.'

'None of this is his achievement.' Pavel's voice was soft. 'It's all you.'

'I just wanted to do a good job.' Jodie could hear the crack in Fiona's voice now. 'It was for my dad to start with. Selling the estate broke his heart.'

'I'm sure he's proud of you,' Jodie suggested.

'Maybe. I haven't seen him so much lately.'

'Not for Christmas?'

Fiona's expression changed. 'I was going to, but then John wanted to spend it together, just the two of us.'

That ought to have sounded romantic. Fiona's tone was anything but.

'And then he didn't show up.' Fiona's fingers were wrapped tightly around the handle of Pavel's hammer. 'I waited all day. I shaved my fucking legs and I put on fake tan because I can be a bit pale, you know. It doesn't look healthy, he says. So I did all that. And he didn't even turn up.' She was waving the hammer as she spat out the words.

'Er… Fi?' Pavel reached for the accidental weapon and lifted it gently, but firmly, from her grip.

Her shoulders slumped. 'I left my dad alone at Christmas for him.'

'I'm sorry, Fiona.' Jodie didn't know what to do.

'We really have to go,' Pavel whispered.

She looked at Fiona. 'Come with us.'

Fiona shook her head.

Damn.

'There's a problem with your plan,' she said.

'There's about a million,' Jodie conceded.

'Probably, but even if you get all our guests, you don't get their money. The ones you say he stole, they've already paid for everything to us.'

They knew that. 'Yeah, but if we could get the tour groups, then we thought maybe we could make them pay us.'

Fiona nodded. 'That might work. But I can't just...'

Jodie snapped. 'Look, I know you're Team John and fine, whatever. Your choice, but we have to go.'

'No. I mean, yes. You do. But I'm not staying to help him out.' There was something different in Fiona's voice. 'I'm so stupid he never thought twice about whether it was dangerous to let me have access to everything.'

'What do you mean?'

'You go back.' Fiona folded her arms. 'I'll make sure all this works out, and then I'll go into the office and I'll transfer an appropriate thank-you fee to Adam for entertaining our guests tonight.'

Jodie couldn't quite believe what she was hearing. 'What?'

Fiona nodded. 'I'm done here. John forced my dad to sell this place. He never wanted to. I don't know what I was thinking.'

'He's a very persuasive person,' Jodie acknowledged.

'I'm not going to help him do the same to Adam though. This stops. Right now.'

Chapter Twenty

The first ever Lowbridge Castle Hogmanay Gala was a roaring success. The band were on fire. The people of Lowbridge and their guests – both accidental and intentional – had scrubbed up well. The room was a riot of tartans and sequins. The dancing was enthusiastic rather than skilled but people did dance. And the food, everyone agreed, was exceptional. Adam, Bella and Darcy charmed their guests and the presence of a genuine laird elevated everything.

Even Veronica's presence was appreciated as she sat, perfectly poised, in a corner. Jodie heard at least one guest ask for a selfie, telling their friends that they'd met a real-life dowager, just like Maggie Smith. The only bigger star of the night was Old Man Strachan, who was constantly surrounded by a gaggle of visitors queueing for selfies and calling out for him to tell them to get in the bin.

Jodie made her way through the crowd, checking everyone was happy and everyone's glass was charged. A dark-haired man in his late thirties stepped out in front of her. 'Are you in charge here?'

'Er, no.' Jodie looked around for Bella but she was busy with another group of guests.

'But you work here?'

'Yeah. Sort of.'

He smiled. 'I'm Kenny. I'm from A2Z Travel.'

The tour company name rang a bell from one of Fiona's endless lists. 'Oh. Great.'

'Yeah. Miss MacCellan told me about the…' He paused for half a beat, the hint of a smile pulling at his lips. 'Mix-up. So good of you to accommodate us.' He handed her a business card from his pocket. 'Do make sure you send the invoice direct to me. My bosses can get weird about changes of plans.'

So Fiona had definitely told him at least part of the story. 'But not you?'

Kenny looked around. 'My visitors are happy so I'm happy.' He smiled more broadly. It was a good smile, open and warm and more than a little bit sexy. If Jodie wasn't so utterly infatuated elsewhere she could have fallen for a smile like that. 'Honestly, I find the whole set-up at the other place a bit clinical. You know what I mean?'

'We're a bit more informal here.'

'It's great.' He turned to head back to his group. 'Oh, actually, odd request – I always used to go to church with my grandma on New Year's Day. She reckoned it was good to start the year on the right front with the guy upstairs, if you know what I mean. She's gone now, but I kind of like to keep up the tradition. I don't suppose you know if there are any services near here tomorrow?'

Jodie didn't, but Jill was sitting at the next table, sipping a glass of red and listening to a selection of Strachans bend her ear about the perils of internet celebrity. Jodie took Kenny from A2Z Travel by the arm. 'Let me introduce you to someone,' she said.

She left Kenny topping up the Reverend Jill's glass, and walked straight into Bella. 'Thank you,' she whispered. 'For coming back. I know how hard that can be.'

'I'm so sorry for everything before.'

335

'I just wish we'd found out who was sharing our information with McKenzie.'

It had slipped out of Jodie's mind with so many other things going on. 'I think I half did. Saira Summers. It was definitely her giving the information to McKenzie, but I don't know how she got it.'

'Saira Summers?' Bella's face opened up in recognition. 'You know her?'

'She applied for your job, for Gemma's job. For… you know what I mean. She was local so we interviewed her here, in the office. Do you think she could have copied down a password or something?'

'Maybe.' Jodie's mind boggled. 'Wow. So I wasn't the worst person you could have hired after all?'

'Technically I didn't hire you.'

'I'm still really sorry.'

Bella shrugged. 'All's well that ends well. And Fiona's conversion to the light side means we live to fight another day.'

'I'm so glad. It has ended well, hasn't it?'

Bella looked across the room to where Pavel Stone was desperately trying to sit out the next dance, despite his mum, Netty and Anna all demanding he get back on the floor. 'Maybe not for everyone.'

'He'll barely talk to me.'

'Can you blame him?'

'Not really. I did try though.'

Bella moved away to rejoin Adam for the next dance. Jodie really had tried over the hours in Pavel's van driving around the rival estate. She'd made jokes to break the ice. She'd let him be quiet. She'd tried to give him space. And she'd hoped he'd come back to her. And she'd failed. She knew now that messing things up wasn't a fundamental character flaw. She wasn't broken. She didn't need to change every fibre of who she was to deserve love. But she also knew that she had hurt Pavel terribly and she might have to live in a world where he never forgave her for that.

On the stage the band leader cleared his throat and leaned in to the microphone. 'So this is the last dance of the year. I always reckon you should never sit out the very last dance. Don't end the year on a regret, and always start the new one living life to the full. Everyone onto the dance floor!'

Not ending the year in regret. That sounded like good advice. Jodie walked right across the dance floor, through the gaggle of women still trying to lure Pavel up for a spin. 'Can we talk?'

'I was going to dance,' he replied.

'No. He wasn't.' Nina put her foot down. 'He's free and he's grumpy. Good luck to you, pet.' She led the others away.

Pavel looked up. 'Outside then.'

They walked away from the castle, past the Dower House and along the side of the walled garden.

'I wanted to say sorry.'

'You've said that already.'

'Not for lying.'

He rolled his eyes.

'I mean I am sorry for lying. But I'm sorry for going.' He wasn't meeting her eye.

'You asked me to stay and I didn't trust myself enough to say yes.'

'It felt like you didn't trust me.'

'No. You're… I thought you were far too good for me.' Truth first. 'You know with Fiona, all the stuff she was saying about John McKenzie?'

'What a shit.'

'It was kind of like that with me and Gemma. The real Gemma. I thought she was perfect and everything bad in our relationship was me. I believed that. I believed that I was so broken that I would break anything good that came near me.'

'So when you went off at me about trying to fix you?'

'It felt like another person who thought I needed to be different somehow.'

'I never thought that.'

'I know…'

He held a hand up to quiet her. 'But then I found out I never really knew you at all, so what does what I think matter anyway?'

'It matters. A lot. To me.' That was what she was trying to tell him. 'You are so good. That's why I ran away. I couldn't face seeing you broken. I couldn't face knowing I would do that to you.'

'But you did anyway.'

'I never thought you'd come after me. When I left you at the Dower House.' Why would he? Jodie was beyond saving. 'I didn't want to drag you down with me.'

'You should have given me that choice.'

'But you always do the right thing.'

'And what is the right thing when you're in love with an identity thief?'

He was in love with her. Jodie's heart grew.

'Just for the record though, asking you to stay wasn't me doing the right thing. I wasn't thinking about being good or honourable or fair. I wanted you to stay. Selfishly. For me.'

'I did want to stay.' There were no words that would make this right. All she had left was the truth. 'I went because I couldn't face the thought of hurting you and I came back because I saw the storm on the news and I couldn't bear the thought that you might be hurt somewhere out here without me.'

'That's why you came back?'

It was. 'And then I saw you and you looked through me and I got scared again. You looked like you hated me.'

For the first time he moved towards her. 'I don't hate you.'

'That's a start. Tell me how to fix this.'

He shook his head.

'I thought you were the man who could fix anything.'

'You don't need fixing. I love you. I think I love you.' Something was holding him back.

'What are you scared of?'

For a moment she thought he wasn't going to answer. She had no right to expect that he would. He took a deep breath in. 'I'm in love with someone I don't even know.'

'You do know me.' Jodie absolutely knew that was true. 'I lied about details, facts and stuff, but I never lied to you about what I'm really like. When we were together, I promise. That was all me.' She stepped closer to him, hoping she might have said enough.

He stepped back. 'And, now every time I look at you I'm terrified you're going to leave again.'

'Only if you come with me.'

'I want to believe you.'

'You can. Home is where you are.' They both knew what that meant. 'So home is here.'

His brow furrowed. 'What do you mean?'

'You're Lowbridge. You belong here.'

'I always have. But not for the last few weeks. I think you did break me.'

Jodie felt like all the air had been knocked out of her. Everything she'd been holding on to was a lie. Gemma was right all along. Jodie broke things and hurt people.

'I mean,' Pavel continued, 'you broke me out of something. It hurts but I think it might be good. I never thought of going anywhere else, or living any other life. But now this life doesn't feel the same when you're not in it. I'm more scared of a life without you in it than of anything else.' Now he reached a hand towards her. 'You promise you won't run without me, my darling?'

His darling. 'I promise. I don't want to run away any more though. I could make this home.'

He was quiet.

'What are you thinking?'

'Just that I've never tried anywhere else.'

Jodie thought about that. Lowbridge was the first place she'd felt like she was capable, the first place where she'd found something she was good at, but now there was one, maybe there were others. 'So the future's unknown?'

Pavel nodded.

'Scary?' she asked.

'A bit, but I think I need to get better at remembering that some things are out of my control.'

'You don't have to fix everything, you mean?'

Finally he smiled. 'Not when it doesn't need fixing.' Down below them the strains of 'Auld Lang Syne' drifted out on the breeze, and Pavel Stone bent his head towards her and found her lips. They stood for a long time, bodies locked together, until finally they moved apart. 'Happy New Year, Jodie.'

'Happy New Year, my darling.'

Epilogue

The breakfast Bella and Flinty rustled up for the guests still standing as dawn broke was a celebration of fat, salt and carbs. Bacon, sausages, black pudding, haggis, tattie scones, mushrooms, eggs, piled up for guests to help themselves.

Jodie pulled up a chair and squeezed in at a big round table next to Pavel. Across the room the Strachans were piling ketchup onto sausage and fried egg sandwiches. Jill was deep in conversation with Kenny the tour guide, and Netty and her husband were half asleep in the corner. Next to Jodie, Darcy was resting her head in her hands. 'How can I be hungover? I haven't been to bed yet.'

Veronica raised an eyebrow. 'I don't think it's the sleep that causes the hangover, dear.'

'How do you look as fresh as a daisy?' Darcy shot back.

'Oh, she grew up here, basically weaned straight on to whisky,' Flinty explained.

Pavel cleared his throat and took Jodie's hand under the table. 'So while everyone's here, we've got something we'd like to tell you.'

Nina smiled. 'You've barely let go of her since midnight. I don't think you need to make a formal announcement.'

'No. Not that. Although, yes, that.' He squeezed Jodie's hand. 'We are back together, but there's something else.

We've been talking and I think we're going to go away for a little while.'

Jill took a gulp of her coffee. 'Pavel Stone going off somewhere? Like Skye or...' She pulled a face in mock horror. 'Oban?'

Pavel stuck his tongue out. 'That's kind of the point. We both feel like...' He looked to Jodie.

'Like we need to work out what we want,' she explained. 'For ourselves. And each other. Like I've literally been living someone else's life.'

'And I have too in a way. Trying to live up to who Granddad was around here. So we're going to go wherever we feel like for a bit and, I guess,' he looked to her for confirmation, 'see where fits?'

'For both of us.'

He squeezed her hand. 'Of course for both of us. I mean I won't leave anyone in the lurch, and it won't be forever and Strach's pretty handy these days with the handyman stuff so I was going to see if he wanted to take my van while I'm not using it and, I mean, I don't want to let anyone down.'

'Pavel,' his mother cut across the monologue. 'You go and live your life. We'll still be here. For both of you whenever you want to come and see us.'

Jodie looked around the table to nothing but nods and good wishes. 'We'll definitely come back.'

Pavel nodded. 'For Christmas at least.'

'Definitely,' Jodie confirmed. 'If not before.'

Only Bella looked bereft. 'I was going to offer you your job back. What are we going to do without you?'

Jodie glanced across the room to where Fiona MacCellan was snoozing gently with her head on a table, next to her father – a late invitee to the party – who was tucking into a bacon sandwich with gusto. 'Actually I did have an idea about that.'

Later when the tables were cleared and the guests waved off, with exhortations to come back for a cookery school or for Hogmanay the following year, Jodie and Pavel were alone in the ballroom where it had nearly started and then faltered so many weeks before.

'Are you sure about this?' she asked. 'We don't even have a plan.'

'I'm sure.'

'So where do you want to go first?'

He paused. 'Where do I want to go?'

'Yeah.'

'I genuinely have no idea.'

She looked him in the eye. 'Really?'

'Truly. I've never even thought about travelling before. I'm excited not to know.'

Jodie saw nothing but honesty in his face. Unlike Pavel though, she was full of ideas. 'Well, I've met your mum so at some point I'd like to take you to meet my parents?'

He pulled a face of mock horror. 'OK.'

'And then I'd love to go places I can draw. You know, the south of France, Italy, Cornwall. Places where the light dances across the landscape.'

He nodded. 'Sounds like a good start.'

She did have one other idea. 'And I wondered about Warsaw?'

'That's where my granddad's family was from.'

She nodded. 'I remember.'

'I've never been there.'

'I know.' Had she misjudged this? 'I mean we don't have to.'

Pavel wrapped his arms around her. 'No. I think I'd like that. I just wish I'd gone with him when I was younger.'

'Can't fix that,' she pointed out.

'You're right.' He smiled. 'To Warsaw, my darling.'

'Your darling?'

'My darling. Always.'

A Letter from Amelia

Hello again,

Thank you for picking up *Cooking Up A Christmas Storm*. I do hope you enjoyed this visit to Lowbridge. I had such a wonderful time revisiting Bella and Adam and all the castle and village 'family' and introducing Jodie felt like a great opportunity to add even more chaos to the mix.

For me Lowbridge provides a little world of joy and fun that I can escape to when I'm writing. Whatever's going on in real-life I always know that, however hard things get, Lowbridge will always have a sense of community and a promise that things will end happily. And I hope it gives that to readers as well.

Jodie and Pavel were particularly wonderful to write about. He's the guy who always does the right thing and she's someone, who despite having the best of intentions, always seems to end up doing the wrong one. Bringing them together and seeing what they can learn from one another was fascinating to write.

If you've enjoyed your visit to Lowbridge I would be so grateful if you could post a review or a rating wherever you bought the book. And I always love to keep in touch with readers. If you'd like to do that too then please go to www.alison-may.co.uk/newsletter, or find me @MsAlisonMay on Instagram, and sign up for my newsletter, and every month you'll get book news, special offers and event updates.

It would be lovely to have you with me on my writing journey,

Amelia x

Acknowledgements

I also need to say a whole heap of thank-yous to everybody involved in getting this book out of my brain and into your hand. This is my twelfth published book and I'm incredibly proud to have made it to this point, but I could not have got here alone.

Thank you first to the fantastic editorial team at Hera. My editor, Jennie, is an actual genius – supremely gifted in finding new polite ways to point out when I've written something that makes no sense at all. This book, like all the others we've worked on together, is immensely improved by your insight.

Thanks as well to Ross, who copy-edited this manuscript so wonderfully and corrected a million tiny errors. Any that remain are, of course, wholly my responsibility. And further thanks to everyone involved with proofreading, cover design, publicity, sales and promotion. It takes a whole team and I hugely appreciate the team Hera have built.

Thanks as well to everyone who put up with how grumpy I was while writing this book, particularly the goddesses of the naughty kitchen, who had the misfortune to be on a writing retreat with me while I was doing my first big edit on this manuscript. I've heard that there are sane and calm authors out there who write wonderfully well-structured first drafts. I am not one of those. For me, most of the work is in the edit – that's when the idea is forced into shape and polished and honed. It's possible that while I'm doing that though I might be slightly less than a complete joy to be around. So thank you to Team NK for putting up with me while that was going on.

And finally, as ever, thank you EngineerBoy. Normally at this point I reference the very marvellous patron of the arts thing you've got going on but this time I have a specific thank-you. Thank you for being willing, and able, to edit xml at 1.30 a.m. to rescue my finished, edited manuscript from apparently terminal IT meltdown. I don't think coding has ever been sexier.